Two brand-new stories in every volume...
twice a month!

Duets Vol. #79

Delightful Lori Wilde delivers a very special Double Duets this month featuring THE BACHELORS OF BEAR CREEK, a miniseries about four fervent bachelors that began in Blaze with #30 *A Touch of Silk*. This author always "brilliantly weaves together lovable characters, charming scenes and a humorous story line," say reviewers at *Romantic Times*.

Duets Vol. #80

Talented mother-and-daughter writing team Jennifer Drew is back with a mouthwatering story about a pastry chef wronged by a reporter, who then sets out to get his "just desserts." Susan Peterson serves up the quirky, delicious *Green Eggs & Sam* about a sheriff named Sam, a sexy redhead and a puzzling case of foul play—or is that fowl play?

Be sure to pick up both Duets volumes today!

Just Desserts

"I can't get you out of my mind, Sara."

Jeff leaned toward her and Sara instinctively did the same.

His breath was minty, and his lips moved over hers, barely touching, but teasing every nerve in her body. She was transported by the pleasure of being in the arms of a man who didn't treat lovemaking like a contact sport.

"I like kissing you," he whispered, his warm breath tickling her ear.

"Me, too."

As a first kiss, it was off the charts. She expected him to kiss her again, envelop her in his arms, maybe even carry her back to his room.

Instead he stepped aside and said, "Let's walk."

Let's walk? He'd lit a fuse, and all he said was "Let's walk"?

No wonder she hated him, despised him—and wanted to have his baby!

For more, turn to page 9

Green Eggs & Sam

"If we're not careful," Sam began.

"This is going to jump quickly past fantasy and directly into reality right here on the front lawn of your house," Haley Jo finished.

He laughed softly and swept her up into his arms. Together they managed the front door and Sam swiftly kicked it shut, then took three strides aross the living room and headed up the stairs.

Haley Jo giggled and laid her head back against his shoulder. "Hope you don't keel over. You don't have to carry me, you know."

"Nah, you're light as a feather." Sam stumbled a bit on the landing. He juggled her weight, teasing her with the possibility of dropping her.

"Giddyap," Haley Jo ordered, reaching behind him to swat his butt.

"Keep that up and I'll let go right here and have my way with you on these stairs."

"Promises, promises," she said, smiling.

For more, turn to page 197

If you purchased this book without a cover you should be aware that this book is stolen property. It was reported as "unsold and destroyed" to the publisher, and neither the author nor the publisher has received any payment for this "stripped book."

HARLEQUIN DUETS

ISBN 0-373-44146-0

Copyright in the collection:
Copyright © 2002 by Harlequin Books S.A.

The publisher acknowledges the copyright holders of the individual works as follows:

JUST DESSERTS
Copyright © 2002 by Pamela Hanson and Barbara Andrews

GREEN EGGS & SAM
Copyright © 2002 by Susan Peterson

All rights reserved. Except for use in any review, the reproduction or utilization of this work in whole or in part in any form by any electronic, mechanical or other means, now known or hereafter invented, including xerography, photocopying and recording, or in any information storage or retrieval system, is forbidden without the written permission of the publisher, Harlequin Enterprises Limited, 225 Duncan Mill Road, Don Mills, Ontario, Canada M3B 3K9.

All characters in this book have no existence outside the imagination of the author and have no relation whatsoever to anyone bearing the same name or names. They are not even distantly inspired by any individual known or unknown to the author, and all incidents are pure invention.

This edition published by arrangement with Harlequin Books S.A.

® and TM are trademarks of the publisher. Trademarks indicated with ® are registered in the United States Patent and Trademark Office, the Canadian Trade Marks Office and in other countries.

Visit us at www.eHarlequin.com

Printed in U.S.A.

Just Desserts
Jennifer Drew

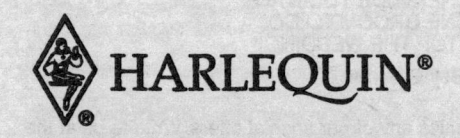

HARLEQUIN®

TORONTO • NEW YORK • LONDON
AMSTERDAM • PARIS • SYDNEY • HAMBURG
STOCKHOLM • ATHENS • TOKYO • MILAN • MADRID
PRAGUE • WARSAW • BUDAPEST • AUCKLAND

Dear Reader,

Chewy chocolate brownies, luscious lemon tarts, tasty trifles, fluffy cakes, exquisite pies...pastry chef Sara Madison knows her way around a kitchen until she stumbles into reporter Jeff Wilcox's arms.

Jeff knocks her culinary karma for a loop, and that's just the beginning of the tempting trouble he gets her into. With him around, she's always in danger of losing her job—not to mention her heart!

With each book we (Jennifer Drew is the pseudonym of mother and daughter Barbara Andrews and Pam Hanson) write, we look for new ways to make you laugh, giggle, guffaw, chortle and grin. With *Just Desserts*, be swept away to the Red Rock country of Sedona, Arizona, along with Sara and Jeff.

But if you see mysterious lights twinkling in the sky, take cover!

Jennifer Drew

P.S. Hearing from readers makes our day! Please write to us at P.O. Box 4084, Morgantown, WV 26504.

Books by Jennifer Drew

HARLEQUIN DUETS
7—TAMING LUKE
18—BABY LESSONS
45—MR. RIGHT UNDER HER NOSE
59—ONE BRIDE TOO MANY*
    ONE GROOM TO GO*
72—STOP THE WEDDING!*

*Bad Boy Grooms

Don't miss any of our special offers. Write to us at the following address for information on our newest releases.

Harlequin Reader Service
U.S.: 3010 Walden Ave., P.O. Box 1325, Buffalo, NY 14269
Canadian: P.O. Box 609, Fort Erie, Ont. L2A 5X3

**To Ralph,
Sweets for the sweet!**

1

THE CACTUS was melting.

Sara Madison patted the ice sculpture with a damp sponge, but it didn't help. The frozen art was beginning to look more like a broken hair pick than a saguaro.

She had to do something. The drip pan would overflow and ruin the whole display she and the other chefs at Dominick's had worked so hard to get ready for the annual Taste of Phoenix food show.

It was less than an hour until all three double doors would be thrown open and the public would swarm into the huge ballroom at the convention center. The high ceiling with modernistic chandeliers and the heavy-duty turquoise-and-navy carpeting weren't enough to muffle the shrieks of panicky chefs and restaurant owners. To her right the owner of Ye Olde Drawbridge English Restaurant was inspecting his unfortunate servers dressed in mock armor that clanked when they moved.

"We'll pass out in these tin cans!" one malcontent yelled. "The frigging air-conditioning isn't working."

Sara sympathized but didn't have time to follow the argument. To her left the head chef of a new Norwegian restaurant was having a hissy fit about his smoked salmon canapés. The wonderful aroma of the spicy southwestern dishes on her table was being masked by a whiff of something alien. The Ukrainians who ran a

Thai restaurant had managed to make their cuisine smell like boiled cabbage.

She looked around desperately for someone to help her remove the impossibly heavy ice sculpture, but the sweating, swearing and shouting food handlers were more into murder and mayhem than good deeds.

Where was her boss when she needed him? Dominick had left ages ago to get another load from his trendy Scottsdale restaurant, but he was supposed to be back by now. She wasn't eager to have him fuss over her already perfect display of desserts, but something had to be done about the rapidly melting ice. It had been his brilliant idea to let his brother-in-law carve the silly thing, or maybe Dominick's wife had pressured him into it. Predictably, the slacker relative had set them up for disaster by letting his creation start to melt even before he delivered it.

"Where are you, Dominick?" she muttered.

He'd be livid if a mere pastry chef like her made the decision to get rid of the drippy centerpiece, but there wouldn't be a chance once the hungry horde of people descended on the table. Typically, Dominick thought the two of them could handle the self-serve display, which meant he was too cheap to pay hourly help.

She raced down one aisle and up another looking for someone who owed her a favor.

"Vic!" She spotted a chef in a hat twice as tall as hers, one of her classmates from culinary school. "Can you do me a tremendous favor? Just help me lift something?"

"Will you look at what they did to my shrimp puffs?" the round, red-faced man bellowed. "They're supposed to be served hot, and some cretin put them on a bowl of ice. I don't know whether to reheat or throw them out."

"Reheat," Sara advised, sure he wouldn't come to her rescue.

No one had time to help her. She started back to her table near the rear of the huge ballroom. Dominick had already had one of his famous fits because his display was at the back. He ignored the fact it was conveniently close to the serving kitchen. Sara had a pretty good idea what he'd say about the melting saguaro. Somehow it would be her fault, never mind that she was only in charge of desserts.

The ego-driven panic in the room was reaching a peak, but it wasn't just about feeding the crowd already milling around in the lobby. It was show-off time, and the only opinion that really mattered was that of Liz Faraday, the *Phoenix Monitor*'s restaurant columnist. Dominick would do somersaults on a hot mesquite grill to get a rave review from the area's top food critic, and he wasn't alone. Everyone with presentations at Taste of Phoenix was keyed up to spot the fifty-something iron lady, and she was easy to recognize. No silly disguises for her, unless you counted her predilection for fancy vintage eyeglasses. Chefs and restaurant owners would go spastic with anxiety when they saw cold blue eyes in pink cat's-eye or rhinestone-studded frames assessing their presentations.

Sara shivered just thinking about the critic, so she understood why Dominick was prone to frenzies and fits over the food festival. Only a few offerings would please the critic, but a good review was better than money in the bank.

Dominick had learned the hard way that the tough-minded columnist couldn't be swayed by fawning or freebies. His pride still smarted from the tongue-lashing Faraday had given him two years ago when he sent a case of the best champagne on his wine list for her daughter's wedding.

This year he was hoping the chalupas with his special sour-cream topping would win acclaim, but Sara thought her pecan rum cake had a better chance. She'd worked past midnight making the two backups in the cooler hidden under the table in case the crowd gobbled up the one on display before Faraday arrived.

A man was already standing by her table helping himself to a lemon chiffon dream bar without bothering to take a plastic plate or fork.

He smiled as she approached, but not at her yummy desserts. She was suddenly aware of how silly she must look wearing a minuscule black skirt—at Dominick's insistence—with her starchy white chef's jacket. She self-consciously brushed aside her wispy bangs, which was all the hair that showed under her puffy chef's hat.

"If you made this, I want to marry you," he said, his dark brown eyes as flirty as his words as he stuffed the last of the delicacy into his mouth.

"When you learn to use a fork, I'll think about it."

Whoa! Why was she being snippy with a stranger who obviously liked one of her specialties? It was Dominick and his alleged ice-sculpting-artist brother-in-law she wanted to strangle.

"Sorry, that was the jitters talking." She apologized with a smile and handed him a napkin with Dominick's logo embossed in gold.

He looked more like a burger-and-fries man than a gourmet, but she couldn't help but be impressed by his rugged but handsome features and dynamite smile.

He stared for a moment, missing nothing from the angle of her hat to the comfortable sandals on her feet.

"Help yourself to anything you like," she said, squirming a bit under his scrutiny.

"We haven't known each other long enough for me to do that, but I'm willing to work on it."

His teasing grin brought out the laugh lines by his eyes. He had the kind of face that drew people, and she liked the deliberately tousled look of his hair, which was several weeks beyond needing a trim. It was hard not to smile at his picture-perfect grin. He had gleaming white teeth and full sexy lips above a strong chin. He was probably about six foot, but standing so close to her five feet two, he seemed taller, more broad-shouldered and more lean-waisted, any girl's blueprint for a hunk.

What the heck was she doing dawdling with an early bird who could be a spy for another restaurant? She walked behind the long rectangular table to put space between them.

"Our beef chimichangas are popular," she said, picking an entrée familiar to any Phoenix resident.

"Did you make them?" He barely glanced at the table, instead scanning the room from one wall to the other.

"No, I'm a pastry chef. All the desserts are mine."

"My favorite part of the meal," he said, looking at her with an intensity that made her uncomfortable. "You don't look like you spend all day with desserts."

Sara had heard that before! Why did people expect a pastry chef to pig out on sweets all day? She was an artist, and she only sampled her work when she was trying something new.

She wanted to give him her standard lecture on food as artistic expression, but there, right in front of her, were bulging biceps only partly covered by a short-sleeved madras plaid shirt.

She badly needed a pair of arms like his to help her remove Dominick's fiasco. If it toppled over, her piña colada cheesecake sprinkled with tiny edible flowers and the beautiful little chocolate cups filled with chocolate mousse and garnished with fresh raspberries would be Dumpster-bound. All her desserts had turned out perfectly, even though it had meant getting up at dawn to arrange them on Dominick's signature glass plates with pedestals. But who would notice anything but the bizarre ice cactus melting over her creations?

Already a few early birds, probably friends of restaurant owners with special passes, were checking out the competition and digging into other displays. They would soon reach her table at the back. She needed help now!

"Our ice cactus is melting," she said, wondering if he might be the hero type who was into rescuing damsels in distress. "I'm afraid one of the arms might break off and ruin everything."

"That would be too bad."

He gave her another sizzling smile, but he obviously wasn't interested in her ice problem. His gaze kept roving around the room.

She coveted the use of those brawny biceps. She had a feeling they'd be firm and smooth and warm against her cheek....

At least they'd certainly be useful!

He was acting a little edgy, or maybe she only thought so because he'd stopped flirting with her. Any girl would enjoy attention from a gorgeous hunk like him, but she wanted that ice monstrosity off her table more than she wanted to banter with a sexy stranger.

When the drippy cactus was gone, she could arrange

the flowers surrounding it into a passable centerpiece, one that wouldn't draw attention from the food. What made Dominick think their splendid presentations needed an attention-getting sculpture? She knew exactly what she'd like to do with the dripping arms of the saguaro when her boss got there.

"Can I help you with something?" she asked, trying to get the man's attention again.

"Do those doors lead to the kitchen?" he asked.

"Yes, it's a serving kitchen for the use of the presenters."

"Do you think anyone would mind if I check it out?"

Sara stopped. Maybe he was into culinary espionage. Or something even darker. She looked him over thoroughly. No way could he conceal any weapon in those close-fitting tan chinos, but she did see a rectangular bulge in his left pocket. He couldn't possibly be that well-endowed. Maybe he carried an overstuffed wallet. She looked away quickly so he wouldn't get the wrong idea—so she wouldn't get any ideas!

"It's out of bounds to patrons, but maybe I could show it to you," she suggested. "I'm going there to get rid of this icy nightmare."

She started to work the wire framework of the flowers away from the drip pan holding the sculpture.

He looked at it skeptically. "You're going to carry that?"

"No, I'll get a cart."

"And heft a hundred pounds of wet ice yourself?"

"Oh, I doubt it weighs that much," she lied, wondering how long it would take him to get gallant.

"You might hurt yourself trying to move that thing." Again with the thousand-watt smile. "I'll give you a hand taking it to the kitchen."

"Well, I guess that would be okay." She tried not to sound eager.

There was no real rule limiting the use of the kitchen, and there was probably nothing he could learn there even if he was spying for another restaurant. The presenters relied on portable coolers for their dishes, which they concealed under well-draped tables rather than risk putting their delicacies in a place they couldn't watch.

"Great! I'll be able to do my good deed for the day. I'll go grab one of those carts." He practically sprinted toward a row of them parked near the kitchen door. That boy really wanted to get into the kitchen.

She wrestled with the tricky problem of removing the wire grid without damaging the flowers. Her conscience was irksome but easily muffled. Her knight in shining armor would only be in the kitchen a few seconds, and there was nothing to see there, anyway. It wasn't as if Maurice of Chez Louis would leave his secret recipe for chicken Normandy lying on the counter.

Darn it, this was an emergency, and she needed any help she could get. Dominick had the most to gain by promoting his restaurant, but she badly wanted her presentations to be a success. This was her chance to enhance her reputation and show off what she could do. She didn't want people laughing at the silly sculpture instead of enjoying her best efforts. And praise from Liz Faraday was better than a raise any day.

"Here you are, Sara Madison," he said, pushing the cart up to the table.

She was startled by his use of her name, but he pointed at the Taste of Phoenix name badge pinned to her jacket.

"I'm gallant and observant," he said in a husky but mellow voice she was beginning to like very much. "If we're going to work together, we should be on a first-name basis."

"We're not exactly working together, Mr...." she said, still struggling to remove the wired flowers without dripping water on the food.

"Wilcox, but call me Jeff."

She didn't intend to call him anything. Her immediate concern was for the cuisine on display. If she spoiled the best Dominick's restaurant had to offer, her boss was likely to serve charbroiled pastry chef on his next menu.

Working cautiously, she moved trays of brown-sugar pralines, dulce con nueces and blue corn quesadillas to make a pathway from the center of the table to the cart. Dominick was going to have a stroke when he saw the sculpture was gone, but he could stuff a chorizo up his nose for all she cared, although it would be a waste of a nice spicy sausage.

Her helper was as strong as he looked. He got the ice onto the cart with minimal help from her—and no grunting.

"Thank you very much. You just saved my pastries from a soggy fate."

"For a smile as pretty as yours, I'd walk over hot potatoes."

He was overdoing it a little on the charm, but he had so much charisma he could rip off his shirt and lay it on the ground for her to walk over without seeming impossibly corny. In fact, she wouldn't at all mind seeing him sans shirt, but for now she had all she could handle, glimpsing the way his trousers tightened over truly magnificent buns when he bent to straighten an edge of the white linen tablecloth caught on the cart.

"I'll take care of this," he said, starting to push the sculpture toward the kitchen.

Why was he so gung-ho to get to the food prep area off the ballroom? It seemed prudent to follow him even though she needed to rearrange the flowers before her boss showed up.

Maybe he was a health inspector. No, not likely. They didn't use subterfuge to see what they wanted to see. Was he an assassin who wanted to conceal himself? A process server?

This was her day for silly theories—she hoped. He was probably just what he seemed, a nice but curious guy.

She held one of the double swinging doors while he pushed the cart and its sloppy load into the kitchen.

"This is mainly a serving room," she said. "Not much preparation is done here."

He lifted the sculpture, pan and all, into the sink, splashing the front of his shirt in the process. The wet cloth hugged a truly spectacular expanse of chest and made one dark nipple and a luxurious sprinkling of hair visible through the thin cotton.

When she could breathe again, Sara had serious reservations about being alone with him, or so she tried to tell herself. Under other circumstances, being one-on-one with the sexy stranger was exactly what she needed, according to her happily married sister, Ellie.

So maybe her social life was pathetic, but she was here to do a job, not make a love connection.

"I can show you the way to the main kitchen if you don't mind hurrying," she went on. "I have to get back to my table."

"No, this is fine."

He stayed by the swinging doors, more interested in the crack between them than in the room.

"I'm not sure you should be here," she warned as

she parked the cart out of the way. "Some of the chefs are paranoid about their specialty dishes. They might think you're a spy."

"I'm not here to pilfer recipes." He softened the denial with a low laugh.

"Well, there's nothing interesting in this room, just the usual counters, stove, coolers. Come to my table, and I'll fix a plate for you."

"Not right now, thanks. Not that anything you dished up wouldn't be delicious."

"You really shouldn't be here."

What was he doing? He was acting like a super spy, but she'd bet her recipe file he wasn't interested in food. Real gourmets always tried to analyze what they sampled and quiz the chef about contents and techniques.

"I have to leave," she said insistently, meaning he had to go, too.

"Wait. Please."

"I have to fix the flowers. My boss will be livid if ours is the only table not ready when the show officially opens."

"Stay just a minute. I'd really appreciate it." His tone was coaxing and seductive.

"No, really, I can't leave a big hole in the middle of the table."

She tried to get past him, but he blocked both doors by standing in front of them. He continued to peer into the main hall.

"If someone tries to come through those doors, you may end up with a broken nose," she warned, annoyed that he wouldn't move aside. "Now, please..."

She tried to elbow him out of the way, but didn't count on hitting a solid wall of muscle. He put his arm around her waist, hugging her against his side.

"Let me go!"

"Please, I need the door shut for another minute or so."

He leaned past her to peer between the swinging doors again. She squirmed and tried to wiggle away, but he didn't react to her struggle.

"If you don't let me go, I'll scream. Really loud!"

It was only a bluff, but he seemed to take it seriously. He spun her around and silenced her by covering her mouth with his.

He was kissing her...until her lips tingled all the way to her toes.

He was good at lip-to-lip. No, sensational! Brilliant stars flashed behind her closed lids, and she almost forgot why he was kissing her.

"Got him!" He released her so suddenly she staggered.

She opened her mouth to scream for real, but all that came out was a startled squeak.

He rushed through the double doors, leaving her to follow in his wake, and sprinted over to a mountain of flesh topped with spiky gray hair and wearing an orange, purple and chartreuse Hawaiian shirt. The very large man popped one of her chocolate mousse cups into his mouth as Jeff reached into the pocket of his trousers.

Sara backed up, realizing how reckless it was to have followed him, not thinking he might be dangerous, but all he whipped out was a small tape recorder. He held it up to the other man's face as she cautiously moved closer to the table to hear what was going on.

"Rossano!" Jeff said loudly. "How are you going to make a living now that your own mother kicked you out of the escort business for taking kickbacks from the girls?"

"Shut up and get out of my face, Wilcox! You and that damn paper have caused me enough trouble."

The huge man scooped up three of her date crescents and stuffed them into his mouth one after another. The delicate confections took hours to make, and he was gobbling them like movie popcorn.

"You caused your own problems by cheating Queen Molly."

"My mother's name is Margaret, Mrs. Rossano to you, scumbag!"

"Touching, you sticking up for her. After your court dates, maybe you can get adjoining cells. But I hear through the grapevine she's still pretty PO'd at you. Wonder if your own mother will put a hit out on you?"

Rossano picked up two slices of cheesecake, flicked off the tiny sugar flowers and sucked the cake into his mouth in two quick slurps. His face was so red Sara worried he'd choke on her masterpiece.

Watching the man's disgusting display, she suddenly realized who the glutton was. Even though she spent most of her time working in the kitchen at the restaurant, she recognized him as a customer called Rosie. He was one of Dominick's regulars, a big eater who ordered three or four entrées at one sitting, then demolished the entire contents of the dessert cart.

She liked this confrontation less and less, and her missing boss was coming toward them with a food tray, looking as though his bald head had been parboiled in the late-afternoon sun.

"Dominick! You Judas!" Rossano shouted. "This chef of yours set me up to be ambushed by a reporter. She hid him behind those doors. I wouldn't have come near your table if I'd known. I came here on your word. Lots of great food, you said. Then I get nailed by a two-bit pencil pusher from the *Monitor*. Like I have anything to say to that rag!"

"Rosie, would I make trouble for my number one customer?"

Dominick was pleading, and that was one scary thing to hear.

"She didn't have anything to do with it," the reporter said. "And the public has a right to know...."

"Does that chef work for you or not, Dominick?" Rossano demanded loudly, pointing an oddly delicate finger at Sara.

"Dominick, I didn't help him. I don't even know him," she protested, angry enough to forget she'd been thoroughly kissed only a few minutes ago, and her lips probably showed it. "That man wouldn't let me leave the kitchen after he helped me get rid of the cactus. I needed his help because you didn't get back. Anyway, it's your fault the ice melted so fast. I wanted a nice, solid cherub that would melt slowly and gracefully, but, no, you..."

"You're fired." Dominick was a screamer, but when he was angry, really angry, he spoke in a hoarse whisper.

"But I didn't do anything wrong!"

"You'll never bake in this town again," he said ominously. "You won't get a job making pies at a greasy truck stop if I can help it—and I can."

Her eyes ached from holding back tears, but she wouldn't give Dominick the satisfaction of seeing her cry. She had hundreds of witnesses who knew she didn't deserve to be fired.

But what had her fellow chefs seen? She'd taken a stranger into the kitchen and hadn't come out until that stranger waylaid one of the food show's patrons.

She'd wanted a reputation, and now she had one—a terrible one!

All she could salvage was her pride. She took off the white chef's hat she wore so proudly, walked to the array of gourmet desserts she'd labored hard to prepare, and crowned the carrot cake with her head covering.

The only thing left to do was retrieve her purse in the second floor lounge and leave.

2

ON THE WAY OUT, Jeff snagged something that looked like a corn chip but burned his tongue like a hot pepper. He raced for the drinking fountain in the lobby and cooled his mouth with gulps of water.

He hadn't eaten since breakfast, but the displays of fancy food were as inviting as a mine field. Hungry or not, he liked to know what he was eating. Unfortunately he couldn't stop to get lunch because he had to get to a computer and finish his story on the continuing investigation of Queen Molly Rossano and her thug son. The pair had beaten one charge of prostitution with the help of some very expensive out-of-town shyster lawyers, but the publisher of the *Monitor* wanted to keep the heat on him. Jeff was more than happy to oblige, even though it meant working all day on a Saturday, which was pretty much business as usual for Jeff.

As he walked to his car in the huge lot, he congratulated himself on running his prey to the ground. What better place to corner a notorious glutton than Taste of Phoenix? Rosie was closemouthed as expected, but Jeff could use that damning phrase, "Mr. Rossano refused to comment."

He didn't feel so great about the little blond chef, though. Who knew that rat Dominick would fire her?

Maybe Liz Faraday could do something for her. The restaurant critic knew every cook in town from spatula space cases to fancy French chefs, and restaurant owners trembled when she burped. She owed Jeff a couple of favors, and contrary to her press image, she was a sweetheart. Her nickname in the press room was Auntie because everyone ran to her with their problems, encouraged, no doubt, by the big plastic container of goodies that always sat by her computer.

Jeff had a good memory for names. He wouldn't forget Sara Madison's, but he wasn't proud of using her to get close to Rossano, never mind that kissing her had been pure pleasure. Her desserts were too rich for his taste, but he wouldn't mind cooking up something else special with her.

Fat chance after the fiasco with Rossano! When had he ever had good luck with women? He always seemed to meet the most desirable ones in the worst possible situations, usually when he was chasing a story. No wonder he lived with his father and could barely remember the last time he'd smiled across a pillow at a lovely lady. He was a perpetual victim of bad timing, or so he liked to believe.

Sara was probably mad enough to slow roast him over a mesquite fire. Sad, because he wouldn't forget those big blue eyes and satiny smooth skin very soon. He could imagine her blond hair streaming down her back—make that naked back. Not even the starchy white jacket could hide the shape of her sensational breasts.

She was feisty, too. He was sure she would have gladly knocked him on his can to get him out of the kitchen. He'd shamelessly tried to charm her, but he'd never planned to kiss her. And what a kiss it was! He could guarantee she'd never concocted a dessert as sweet as her lips.

He got into his old Jeep Cherokee, but before he could start it, he saw a flash of white three rows over. It was her. The least he could do was apologize. Getting out, he walked toward the spot where she'd disappeared, knowing he was crazy trying to find her in the maze of vehicles. It was mid-July and too damn hot to sprint across an asphalt parking lot. Anyway he needed to finish his story so he could go home, shower and slap something edible on the grill, maybe a thick juicy hamburger.

He wanted to check on his father, too. They'd been living together since his parents' divorce nearly four years ago, but lately Dad had been evasive, disappearing without explanation. His old cronies had been puzzled as well, because he hadn't been doing whatever retired old men did.

Damn, Jeff knew he needed to spend more time with his father, but he went from crisis to crisis in his job. He didn't have time to run his own personal life, let alone hang out at bars and go to sporting events to keep his dad entertained.

He cut through several rows of cars, but by the time he'd dodged around several arriving for Taste of Phoenix, he'd lost her.

Walking toward his vehicle, he tried to console himself by imagining the headline for his blistering front-page article on Rossano. He'd nearly reached the Jeep when an idiot in a red compact raced up behind him and stopped within inches of putting bumper prints on his butt.

He turned to chew out the reckless driver and saw the blond chef glaring at him from behind her windshield.

She looked as if she wanted to roll him out like a pie crust, but he walked over to her open window anyway. At least it wasn't a car full of Rossano's goons. In Jeff's line of business, there was always a chance someone would try to rearrange his face.

"Remember me?" she challenged him.

"Sara Madison. You're labeled." He nodded at her name badge.

Her hat was off, and her hair was as long and silky as he'd imagined. The desert wind whipped it around her face and made her cheeks rosy pink. Or maybe her face flamed when she was mad, really mad. She'd roared up to him like an avenging angel, but he figured he deserved the scare.

"I owe you an apology," he said.

He reached through the opening and flicked aside a lock of stray hair caught on her cheek. It wasn't a gesture likely to calm her, but he wanted to touch the spun gold.

"Saying you're sorry won't help! You not only got me fired, I was humiliated in front of every chef in Phoenix. I'll be blackballed for life. When word gets around—and Dominick will see that it does—I won't be able to get a job making clown-face cookies at Billy Bob's Pizza Palace."

"You didn't do anything wrong. I'll talk to your boss." He'd also talk to Auntie, but he couldn't make any promises until the food critic agreed to help.

"Like that will do any good! Dominick fired his own grandmother for not washing the lettuce."

"Maybe I can do something else for you."

"Please, don't! My only consolation is that Rossano will never pig out on my pastries again. I hope he overdoses on soggy-crust pies!"

She put out her hand to raise the window, but he leaned down and captured it, liking the feel of her slender fingers until she snatched them away.

"I'm serious," he said. "Maybe I can help."

"You're not in the restaurant business, and if you have a sister who wants a kid's party catered, forget it! Just because I'm a pastry chef, people assume I'd love to come to their homes and whip up parties for slightly less than they pay their lawn-mower man."

"I didn't mean anything like that. Anyway, my only sister lives in Santa Fe with her family. She's an anti-sugar fanatic, so her kids probably get yogurt and carrots instead of cake."

He was squirming from more than the sizzling pavement under his loafers. It had been a long time since he'd collected any guilt in pursuit of a story, and he didn't like it. The fact that she was petite and gorgeous with pouty lips and silky honey-blond hair made him feel like a bully.

"Goodbye, Mr. Wilcox," she said, gunning the engine.

He was still leaning on the window opening when she accelerated. He stumbled backward, and only good reflexes saved him from a pratfall.

Apology rejected, he thought, his conscience uncharacteristically pricked. It was all in a day's work, annoying people to get a story, but he still wished he hadn't involved her. He couldn't help wondering how it would be to hop into bed with the delectable chef and channel all that anger and frustration into something more fun.

Damn, he needed to get a social life! All work and no play was making Jeff a very deprived boy. However appealing the little chef was, she was too angry about getting fired for what he had in mind.

He hustled to his Jeep, trying to write the story lead in his head as he usually did. Even if sweet Sara were hot for his bod, he didn't have time right now for anything but finishing the assignment. He sighed deeply and blamed his morose mood on the burning sun that made the desert city as hot and airless as the inside of an oven. At least the two-bedroom apartment he shared with his father had central air-conditioning. He'd sweated enough for one day.

MONDAY MORNING Jeff got to work early hoping for an assignment that didn't involve businessmen who smashed kneecaps as employee incentives. Much as he enjoyed nailing a thug like Rosie Rossano on page one, he was hungry for a new challenge, something substantial he could ride to a Pulitzer.

Except for a few bottom-feeding reporters who actually thought vacations were meant to be taken, the whole staff was there for the weekly budget meeting. At the *Monitor*, budget had nothing to do with finances and everything to do with assigning stories and space in the paper.

In the eight years it had taken Jeff to work his way up from a junior reporter at the *Sand Creek Weekly Ga-*

zette to top journalist on a big city daily, he'd never gotten tired of the sight, sound and smell of a newsroom. At the *Monitor* the sea of desks sported grape-colored computer terminals. The constant hum of the hard drives was drowned out by the ringing telephones and the nonstop chatter. The aisles were crowded as the drones of the business speculated about new assignments. A couple slackers were throwing darts at a corkboard plastered with the visage of a colorful governor expelled from office more than a decade ago. Except for the managing editor's solid-walled cubicle, the offices were glass boxes along one long wall. Jeff waved at Joe, a sportswriter who rated one of the coveted private spaces since he'd become a syndicated columnist writing the "His and Hers" advice column with his wife, Amy. The remaining spaces were parceled out to editors, news, sports, lifestyle and the rest.

It was controlled chaos, and Jeff loved all of it from the bitter brew in the coffeepot to the overly eager interns who raced around trying to look busy and worldly. Dad said he was born with printer's ink in his blood, and Len Wilcox should know. He was a retired newspaperman with over forty years on the Saint Paul, Minnesota, *Defender*.

"Hey, Jeff, want to celebrate your birthday at that new foam bar tonight?" Brett Davies yelled over from his computer monitor. "We can watch the ladies get sudsy."

"I'll have to take a rain check," Jeff shouted back, unwilling to commit himself until he got his next assignment, even if it was his thirtieth birthday.

"Right, a rain check. I remember rain. Wet stuff that

falls from the sky. You're a real party animal, Wilcox.''
Brett went back to whipping through e-mail on a computer nearly buried by the debris on his desk.

What the heck! Maybe he should go party hard with Brett. When was the last time he'd kicked back and had some fun? His dad had always managed to get more inches on the front page than any reporter in the Twin Cities and still stop for a few beers after work. Of course, Mom got the short end and finally kicked him out. Now she was living in Santa Fe near his sister, Ginger, and her family, and he had custody of Dad, so to speak. His sister got the better deal.

"Uh-oh," he said aloud, spotting company at his desk near the far end of the newsroom.

Patty from advertising was leaning over, pretending to study the screen of his computer. Dark brown hair cascaded to her waist over a tank top, giving the illusion she was topless. Her short orange skirt rode up so high he'd give odds she wasn't wearing panties. Pretty sure she was still pouting because he'd promised to call her for drinks and hadn't, he bent and pretended to tie the laces on his stubby-toed chukkas. From the waist up, he went along with office protocol and wore a short-sleeved blue dress shirt and a tie with tiny diamonds, but his rugged chinos and boots made him ready for any assignment, however bizarre.

Maybe he *should* call Patty. She had a gorgeous bod, almost as good as the little pastry chef's, and her overbite was sort of cute.

What was he thinking? She was a stalker. Encourage her, and she'd want to exchange keys and collect used napkins as love tokens. He wasn't that desperate for a social life—not yet.

He could avoid Pouty Patty and ease his conscience at the same time. He ducked into the small glassed enclosure the food editor used as an office.

"Morning, Auntie."

Liz Faraday looked up from her computer and stared at him with the icy blue eyes that terrified the town's restaurateurs.

"Happy birthday, Jeffy, have a croissant."

She had a way of reducing her co-workers to the status of needy ten-year-olds with her gravelly voice. The harshness of it had nothing to do with smoking since she was rabidly against it. According to Auntie, tobacco ruined a gourmet's palate. Her face had the leathery tan of women who love the sun, and she wore her iron-gray hair short and straight. Lean for a woman who loved food, she softened her appearance with oddly girlish yellow glasses that had daisies on the bows, and a matching blouse.

"Thanks but no thanks on the croissant. I had oatmeal and toast with Dad."

"How is the old coot?"

Liz had cooked for Len a couple of times when he first moved there, but all they had in common was their divorces. His father avoided her like an outbreak of the plague now.

"I don't see much of him."

"I suppose he hangs out at Fat Ollie's to swap war stories with the old newsboys' club."

Jeff shrugged. Lately, several of the retired newsmen who hung out at Ollie's Bar had been calling looking for his father. This was strange, but his dad was evasive whenever Jeff asked him a question.

"Have you been to your desk?" Liz asked.

"Not yet."

"I made you a cake to take home. Don't let those vultures demolish it."

"You baked me a cake?" Now he did feel like a kid. Served him right for griping to Brett about getting old. One thing a newsroom did well was spread information, useless or otherwise. "Thanks a lot." He was looking forward to digging into it.

Her phone sounded shrill in the enclosed space, and she let it ring half a dozen times.

"Always let 'em think you're busy," she said to Jeff before picking it up.

She listened for a few seconds, and made a sour face. "I'll send him right over." She put down the phone and glared at it.

"His majesty wants to see you." She sniffed. Liz and the managing editor had warred continually since he'd said the lobster Newburg she made for the office Christmas party smelled like stale vomit. "Pronto."

Everything was pronto with Decker Horning. Jeff was curious to hear what he wanted, but first he had a big debt to pay.

"Before I go, I want to tell you I cornered Rossano at Taste of Phoenix," he said.

"I must have missed you there. I like to let them sweat awhile before I show up. How'd it go?"

"As expected, but in order to corner him, I got a pastry chef in trouble."

"Naughty boy. I've always wondered what goes on in the kitchen besides cooking," she teased.

"Actually, I used her to hide until he got there. Turned out he's a big customer of her boss at Dominick's. He fired her because of me."

"That lard head Dominick fired her? Can you believe he tried to bribe me with second-rate champagne? Cretin!"

"That's the guy. Any chance you can help her find another job?"

"Is she the one who made those little cheesecakes on Dominick's table?"

"Yeah."

"They were well done. I approved of them. What's her name?"

"Sara Madison. Can you help her get something?"

"I'll give it some thought."

"Thanks, Liz. I owe you."

"Everyone does. I like it that way."

Jeff retreated, depending on the food columnist's well-concealed soft streak to help right his wrong against Sara. Instead of rushing to his editor's office, he took a detour past his desk to get the cake Auntie had left. He'd chunk off a piece for Deck to make up for the wait. The head honcho of the newsroom expected reporters to materialize in front of his desk a nanosecond after he summoned them. Fortunately, he did have a raging sweet tooth and could be mollified with sugary offerings.

Why did Horning want to see him before the budget meeting, anyway? If he wanted to keep the lid on a new assignment, it meant something potentially big.

Patty had left a present on his desk, too. There, behind

the precarious pile of clutter that always threatened to bury his keyboard, was the ugliest rubber chicken he'd ever seen. She'd plunked the monstrosity right in the middle of Liz's chocolate layer cake. A tag around the chicken's neck delivered her message: "What are you afraid of, Jeff?"

"I'm afraid of psycho chicks from La-la Land," he muttered as he headed toward the editor's office.

Decker Horning ruled the newsroom by intimidation, not easy considering he had to ride herd on a staff of reporters who thought the word no was a synonym for yes. He stood five-five on tiptoes and carried less weight than a mummified cadaver, but the sunken eyes in his leathery face had the intensity of laser beams. He wore navy or black suits no matter how the temperature soared, but Jeff had never seen sweat on the high-domed brow. His striped tie was always straight, and the side part in his thin sandy-gray hair never varied by a thousandth of an inch. He'd been brought here for the job from a sister paper in Vermont. A Yankee to the core, he'd learned more about Arizona politics in three years than any native-born observer.

If Deck had something hush-hush for Jeff, it could be pretty exciting.

"You took your time getting here." From the editor, this was a cordial greeting.

Jeff shrugged, knowing anything he said could be used against him.

"What do you know about SLOT?"

His questions always sounded like hostile interrogations, but Jeff was on top of this one.

"It's Randolph Hill's project, the Search for Life Out

There. They're an underfunded bunch of radio astronomers who listen for signals from space. Their satellite dish is somewhere in West Virginia."

"Hill is no space-alien kook," the editor said. "And what he lacks in government funding, he more than makes up for in private grants and volunteer help."

"Don't tell me he's found little green aliens out there." Jeff knew there had to be a news angle here. He also knew his boss couldn't be rushed.

"I've met Hill several times. He's sensible, well-grounded, a first-rate scientist."

Deck didn't approve of many people, so the guy must walk on water.

"He'll be in Sedona at Las Mariposa resort for a two-week seminar. That's where you come in," the editor said.

"Sounds more like a job for a science writer." Jeff couldn't see himself covering a bunch of dry technical meetings.

"Hill is on a crusade to expose kooks and charlatans, the kind who claim aliens are shopping in the supermarket with Elvis. He's interested in the real possibility of life on other plants, not the hokey stuff people see in sci-fi movies."

Jeff couldn't help but groan. This sounded like tabloid stuff. He was an investigative reporter, not a hungry hack.

"I know what you're thinking," Deck said, his tone softening into what he probably thought was his persuasive voice. No wonder he didn't want the whole staff to know about this assignment. Flying saucers were too weird for the *Monitor*.

"Hear me out," he continued. "While Hill's doing his thing, Arizona's own space guru will be at Las Mariposa at the same time."

"Not Barrett Borden Bent?"

The editor nodded.

Now Jeff knew why he was getting this assignment. B.B. Bent, founder of the First Contact Society, was either a super kook or an unusually wily con man. He claimed to be a scientist who was disillusioned with the attitude of the establishment toward space visitors. Jeff knew that Bent's line was that the government was trying to cover up the existence of aliens and Bent felt the public needed to be told the "truth." If he was what he claimed, Jeff was a superhero posing as an intrepid reporter. He was sure Bent was only in it for the money.

"He's up to something big, and he picked a hell of a time and place to gather his followers," Deck said.

"In the shadow of a legitimate radio astronomy seminar. So the story is B.B., not Hill."

"That's right. Ordinarily I wouldn't waste column inches on a con man like Bent, but we've had a tip from a disgruntled follower. Our source says Bent's collecting huge sums from his First Contact group, supposedly to build an alien landing strip."

"A welcome center for nonexistent little green men? Who would buy that?" Jeff asked.

"Don't underestimate Bent. He's a smooth operator. I ran a background check myself. He's been involved in a desert land scandal, bogus casino bonds and attempts to bribe legislators. He did a couple of years in Kansas for check kiting when he was young, but no one's been able to convict him for anything since then, although they've tried. According to our source, people are mortgaging their homes and cashing in IRAs to throw money at him."

"So you think this is a chance to nail him?"

"Correct. The seminar starts a week from today. I want you in place before the early arrivals check in. Plan on driving up there this Friday. The SLOT seminar officially begins Monday, which will give you a weekend to snoop around."

Jeff grinned his acceptance. Not only would he have a shot at crashing B.B. Bent's racket, whatever it was, but he'd get to stay at the Las Mariposa luxury resort. Hot tubs in the rooms, indoor and outdoor pools...

"Fortunately they're taking on a lot of temporary help for the two big groups coming in the off-season," Deck said.

Jeff's imagination flipped him off a massage table staffed by a gorgeous Swedish amazon and back to reality. He was already planning to rent a tux for evening events.

"Wouldn't I mingle better if I posed as a guest?" he asked hopefully.

Horning's laugh made a donkey's bray seem melodious.

PACKING WAS probably Sara's least favorite job in the world, and having her sister help her did nothing to make the chore a happy one. Just the opposite, because she was really going to miss living with Ellie and her husband, Todd.

"Now I know how it feels to be banished to Siberia!" Sara said, emptying her underwear drawer and throwing the contents into her suitcase. "Thanks to that rotten reporter, I'm blacklisted at every restaurant in town."

"Sedona isn't a frozen wasteland," Ellie said in her usual practical way. "And no one is blacklisted for life at age twenty-six."

Sara's sister folded the pile of undies heaped on top of Sara's shorts and tops.

"At least you'll get your spare bedroom back," Sara said. "I can't tell you how much I've appreciated living with you and Todd these past six months."

"We've loved having you—not that we ever saw much of you. Anyway, you helped with the rent. That meant a lot with Todd working on his master's."

Sara impulsively hugged her sister, then stepped back and wiped an errant tear from the corner of her eye.

Taller and two years older than Sara with short, bouncy blond hair, Ellie had been her mainstay since their parents had moved to Georgia for her father's engineering job. Even though her parents thought Sara's job was too unconventional for a woman, they still had a good relationship. When Sara's roommate had let her boyfriend and his huge Labrador retriever move into their apartment, Sara found life with the trio unbearable. When the dog wolfed down an entire plate of cream puffs she'd just made, then regurgitated them with a vengeance, she'd had it. Ellie and Todd gave her refuge in their apartment in the stucco high-rise near the university, where her sister worked in the admissions office.

It was time to leave this cozy nest anyway, she guessed. Todd would soon get his degree in counseling, and they wanted to start a family. Sara just hadn't planned on moving with only a temporary job to tide her over. She'd gotten the temp position as assistant pastry chef with Liz Faraday's help. Her cheesecake was good, but it still amazed her that the food critic had liked it enough to get her a job at Las Mariposa.

"I'd like to stick Dominick's head in the garbage disposal," Ellie said with unusual vehemence. "I can't believe how he's treated you after nearly four years of slave labor in his food factory."

Ellie stood with feet apart and arms crossed over her chest, looking like a female version of a Viking warrior. She was her only sibling's mainstay, partly because she was even-tempered and practical compared to Sara's more mercurial nature. Even though she'd followed the traditional route of a conventional job and marriage their parents wanted for both their daughters, Ellie was her sister's biggest supporter.

Sara had never seen Ellie so angry on her account, which only proved that Dominick was a putrid piece of chicken fat, a double-dealing creep of the lowest order. He'd blamed her for something that was in no way her fault.

"He called me a jinx," Sara muttered, tossing her toiletries bag into the already bulging suitcase. "He was the one who let his brother-in-law make that ice monstrosity!"

"He's always been too cheap to do things right," Ellie agreed.

"Are you sure you don't mind storing all that stuff for me?" Sara asked, pointing at a stack of corrugated cardboard boxes.

"Of course not. Todd will stack them in the closet for you."

Sara gave the small white-walled room with cheerful sunflower curtains and bedspread one more look and decided she had everything she needed. Who knew how long the temporary job would last? She might have to rely on her sister's hospitality again in a few weeks. She was only guaranteed two weeks' work because a couple of big groups were coming in the off-season. She'd have to work like a galley slave to have a chance at a permanent position.

"If you see Jeff Wilcox's byline in the newspaper, promise me you'll line the birdcage with it," Sara said.

"My canary is pretty fussy," Ellie teased, "but I'll do it. I've got to run. My boss might actually notice I'm gone if I don't get back to work. Call me when you get to Sedona. And watch out for alien abductors!"

"You read the newspaper too much!" Sara said, laughing and giving her sister a hug goodbye.

She was still in the bedroom when Ellie called to her from the front door.

"Sara, you have company. Drive carefully and be sure to call me. I'm off."

Company? Well, her friends did know she was leaving. She'd spent most of last evening on the phone. She hurried out, hoping to see Maryanne or Monica—and froze in disbelief. Jeff Wilcox shut the door behind him and grinned sheepishly.

"What are you doing here?"

"I just came by to…"

"How did you know I was here? This is my sister's apartment!"

"I'm an investigative reporter, remember?"

"Someone at Dominick's told you. Was it the salad

chef? I found a bug in one of his house specials, and he's hated me ever since.''

Wilcox shrugged and tried to look boyishly innocent. She wanted to run an electric beater through his tousled locks, never mind they made him look sexy in a morning-after way.

"I just wanted to tell you how sorry I am."

"You should be! I've been fired by the Mussolini of cuisine. Thanks to you, my career is ruined."

"I'm really sor—"

"No, no, no. I don't want to hear your lame apology. Just go! Go, go, go!" She turned and stalked to the bedroom.

"You have a way with words," he said, following her. "Looks like you're packing."

"Boy, with investigative insight like that, I'm surprised you haven't won a Pulitzer!"

"Guess I deserved that."

He smiled, the most maddening thing he could possibly do, considering she wanted an excuse to vent four years of frustration working for Dominick on his sable-topped head.

"Go away. *A-W-A-Y*. Now."

"I guess that means you don't want to go to lunch with me. I had in mind a nice juicy burger with grease that runs down your chin, crisp salty fries and a milk shake so thick you need a spoon."

"You've ruined my life! Now you want to ruin my arteries?"

"Or maybe a nice salad?" He actually sounded hopeful.

"If you don't leave, I'll call—I'll call..."

She wasn't sure who would rescue her from a handsome hunk who only wanted to buy her lunch.

"No, I'll scream!" As long as she was making threats, she might as well make it a dilly.

"Don't do that. Please. I'll go. I just wanted to see how you're doing. Let you know I'm really sorry—"

"Eek!"

It was more squeak than scream, but she had the satisfaction of seeing his beefcake buns hightail it out of her life forever.

3

A PECKING ORDER existed in every kitchen, and Sara had no difficulty figuring it out at Las Mariposa. She, of course, was at the bottom, discounting only the busboys and dishwashers. At the top was Francisco Cervantes, the executive chef, and no one, not even the resort manager, called him anything but Mr. Cervantes. He was tall and slender with salt-and-pepper hair showing in short sideburns below his chef's cap and a tiny coal-black mustache. His ramrod posture and no-nonsense attitude made him seem more military then culinary. But then, the kitchen had a lot in common with a battleground when there could be up to five hundred guests to feed and coddle, not to mention special catering for meetings, weddings and banquets.

The sous chef, Sonya Sharpe, was his assistant. She divided her time between supervising other chefs and creating the soups that made her a legend among gourmets. Both she and Mr. Cervantes were distantly courteous to Sara, but they obviously didn't consider her to be in their league. Not yet, she thought, determined to be so spectacularly useful they'd beg her to stay permanently.

Her boss was Ken McGrath, the pastry chef. He was Kenny to everyone on the staff and as cheerful as Dominick was dour. If he had one fault, it was enjoying his own creations too much. He could only be described as roly-poly, a smiling, round-faced man only a few inches taller than Sara with a waistline the circumference of a medicine ball. She liked him even if he was a poster boy for coronary artery disease.

All in all, she felt amazingly at home considering she'd been up at five to report for work a half hour before her six-to-two shift. It was hot in spite of the fans and cooling system, no wonder since half a dozen huge ovens had been going for hours. Still, it was an efficient kitchen, large enough so the staff didn't trip over each other. The counters and equipment were all stainless steel and top of the line. White floor tiles were easy on the feet, and everything from the mesquite grill to the huge mixers was conveniently located.

Las Mariposa had all the frills, even handsome waiters in tight black pants and white jackets buttoned at their waists. Sara wore a similar uniform, but her slacks were looser fitting and her starchy white jacket hung to midhip. Her chef's hat was disposable paper, a tangible sign of her low status.

The lunch shift was just starting. She wondered how many employees were quartered in the spartan little rooms in the staff facility. The long, low building was hidden behind a screen of sycamores well east of the main hotel and the lodge, which had the meeting rooms. The regular staff mostly commuted from Oak Creek or Flagstaff. The nearby community of Sedona was too pricey for the resort's workers, but she didn't need to worry about a permanent home until she had a full-time job.

Sara carried a tray of individual cheesecakes adorned with kiwifruit, starfruit and blueberries to one of the large coolers. They weren't her work, unfortunately. She'd spent most of the morning making cheese biscuits and bite-size cookies.

She was about to slide the heavy load onto a shelf when she caught a glimpse of a suspiciously familiar profile on the other side of the kitchen. Before she could check out the guy in a server's uniform, the cooler door bumped her elbow. The cheesecakes started sliding to the end of the tray.

"Oh, no!"

She saved the cheesecakes from disaster with only a tiny bit of crust damaged, but she felt like a klutz. Kenny might not be so cheerful if she ruined his miniature masterpieces. She couldn't get fired again. She wouldn't even be able to get a job at a fast-food restaurant.

"Hey, new girl, is it too hot for you?" Kenny teased. "You look like you just saw a ghost."

"I'm fine," she said, turning on the perkiness for all she was worth.

"Take ten. Get some fresh air."

She wanted to kiss his chubby cheek. The server she'd glimpsed couldn't possibly be a *Phoenix Monitor* reporter let alone *the* reporter who'd started the chain-reaction disaster that had cost her her job. Just to reassure herself, she took off her paper cap and slid unobtrusively through one of the two automatic service doors to the dining room for a better look at the tall server.

Technically speaking, she didn't have any business letting the guests see her, but she just had to be sure the

Wilcox fiend didn't have a twin brother or a clone from outer space.

There he was, back turned to her, serving plates of oysters with salsa on the side to an unsmiling couple sitting alone at a choice table for four covered with a gleaming white cloth. The male diner looked familiar, but only because a larger-than-life poster advertising his seminars was in the lobby. It was the guest of honor, the man inadvertently responsible for her temporary job, Dr. Randolph Hill.

The famous astronomer would look at home at a witchcraft trial, she thought. His casual luncheon wear was a black, long-sleeved shirt buttoned to the neck and worn with a pale gray necktie. He had a dour, pinched face and thin graying hair. He was probably in his late fifties, but the woman with him was a dozen or so years younger.

"Carmela, you're not going to get fat trying a little salsa," he chided.

"Is my husband dictating what I should and should not eat today?" she asked in an annoyed tone that matched his for its lack of warmth.

"Don't be ridiculous."

Sara stayed hidden behind one of the faux columns that added old-world elegance to the dining room. Mrs. Hill was dressed in a long-sleeved black dress with a gleaming white collar, a reincarnated pilgrim except for the professional makeup job that emphasized her violet-hued eyes and pencil-thin black brows. Her hair was raven black, swept into a tight bun.

But it wasn't the famous guests who riveted Sara's attention. Their waiter had dark hair, broad shoulders that left no slack in the tight-fitting white jacket, and long black-clad legs. He leaned over to spoon some salsa for Dr. Hill, and another part of him seemed suspiciously familiar.

Before she could see his face and confirm whether her evil nemesis was really at Las Mariposa, an imposing man in a long white robe strode up to her.

"Miss, would you please be a kind little thing and refill my mineral water?" He handed her a long-stemmed goblet. "My server seems to be otherwise occupied. My table is over there. I, of course, am Barrett Borden Bent."

She stared from the man to the empty goblet and didn't think to tell him she wasn't a server.

He gestured dramatically at his table, his full sleeves embroidered around the edges with odd symbols that were repeated on the hem of the robe. His neon pink and orange running shoes were as eye-catching as his bright green eyes. Surely a color like that had to come from tinted contacts, Sara thought, still too flabbergasted to return his goblet. The man exuded something, whether charisma or too much cologne she wasn't sure. A thick mane of silvery hair was brushed back in waves from his forehead and ears. His face must have been drop-dead gorgeous when he was young, and he was still unusually handsome except for his theatrical expression.

He turned and walked to his table at the same instant the server backed away from the Hills' table.

Sara hurried over and tapped him on the shoulder of his white jacket, intending to satisfy her curiosity and give him the goblet to fill with mineral water.

"It is you!"

She automatically kept her voice low because she was an employee with no business in the dining room, but she couldn't conceal her dismay.

The reporter's deep brown eyes widened in disbelief, but he was too good an actor to let more of his reaction show.

"Can I do something for you?" he asked.

She noticed the discreet staff badge that identified him as Jeffrey and played along with his game.

"The gentleman in the white robe would like more mineral water." She thrust the goblet into his hands. "Perhaps in the future, Jeffrey, you'll pay more attention to all of your tables."

"He's not sitting at one of mine. What the hell are you doing here?" he muttered, keeping a smile on his face.

She wouldn't admit coming to the dining room to check him out, and it was none of his business that she was a temporary assistant to the pastry chef.

"I'm just observing the level of service," she said primly. "If you're going to succeed as a server at Las Mariposa, you really shouldn't take that much time to serve oysters."

"You were clocking me?" He scowled.

"Mr. Bent would like his mineral water now." Fortunately she remembered the guru's name.

"Meet me later," Jeff whispered.

"I don't know about that."

She wanted to believe he'd lost his job at the newspaper and had to hustle as a waiter to pay the bills, but it seemed unlikely. He was probably here under false pretenses, which certainly gave her the advantage in this round of their battle. But she also had to worry whether this rotten reporter would get her fired from another job.

"Meet me at the fountain at midnight," he said.

"Midnight! I'll be in bed. I have to report for work at six a.m."

"I have to work a banquet tonight. I'll be lucky to get away by then."

She caught a glimpse of the robed wonder gesturing impatiently at both of them.

"If you don't water that weirdo, you'll get us both fired," she said angrily.

"Midnight then." He streaked over to placate the irate guest.

"Thanks for considering my schedule," she said under her breath, her enthusiasm for Las Mariposa rapidly waning.

WHEN HER SHIFT ended Sara napped, trying to convince herself she wasn't resting up for her showdown with Wilcox. One of them had to go, and it wasn't going to be her. He owed her something for the fiasco at Taste of Phoenix.

When the time came to meet Jeff, she crept out of her utilitarian little room feeling like a sneak. Employees were allowed to use the outdoor pool after ten when it closed to guests, but generally speaking, they were supposed to be invisible when they weren't on duty.

Meeting by the fountain was a great idea, except she'd counted six of them earlier in the day. Besides the ornate fountain with butterfly sculptures in front of the hotel, there were similar but smaller ones in a garden to the south of the meeting lodge. The paths were illuminated by pinkish lights that gave the grounds a fairy-tale feeling. The large Spanish-style hotel had an old-world quality with pale tan stucco walls and orange roof tiles, but the red rock country surrounding it was uniquely southwestern. Located in the Verde Valley, the hotel was flanked by a spectacular magenta cliff to the west, and the setting attracted visitors from all over the world.

Guests who wanted more privacy were accommodated in one of several small stucco cottages along the creek. Sara had seen the infamous B.B. Bent, flying saucer devotee, going into one of them when she came off work that afternoon. Kenny was walking with her on his way to the employee parking lot and had been more than willing to fill her in on the flamboyant guest. According to the pastry chef, Bent and Dr. Hill loathed each other. Bent had chosen Las Mariposa for a gathering of some of his many followers after learning Hill was holding a seminar there. The summer heat made this the off-season for the resort, so Bent and his disciples had been able to book all of the remaining rooms.

All this gossip wasn't Sara's problem. Keeping her job was, but Mr. Communication hadn't even told her which fountain he had in mind. She guessed it wasn't the large one in front of the hotel, so she wandered through the garden laid out between the lodge and the creek. The help's quarters, screened by trees, was a little past the garden, but after her nap she felt like walking.

Apparently the two space gangs weren't night owls. The grounds were deserted enough to seem eerie. Maybe she was crazy to come out alone to meet her evil nemesis, but it was a lovely place, naturally perfumed by the lush flowers. The splash of fountains and the gurgle of the nearby creek were soothing. She could do much worse than get a permanent job here, but she was superstitious about being anywhere near the *Monitor* reporter. She was afraid she couldn't possibly succeed as long as Jeff Wilcox dogged her steps. She wanted him to go away but had no idea how to make him do so.

Walking around a charming ivy-covered gazebo, she spotted a man pacing beside a small fountain lit by muted blue lights. Several bronze butterflies, the namesake of the resort, seemed to dance in the cascade of water.

Trying hard to be silent, she stepped off the gravel path and approached furtively.

"If you plan to be a sneak thief, don't give up your day job," he quipped when she got closer.

"How did you know it was me? You didn't even look in my direction."

"You're the only girl I asked to meet me by the fountain at midnight."

He was wearing white shorts and a green T-shirt with the logo nearly faded away. His socks were bunched down over white running shoes, and she tried not to stare at his long, muscular legs. Why couldn't she meet someone who looked like him but didn't mess up her life?

"The next girl might like to know which fountain you had in mind."

"You found me."

There was, unfortunately, enough light to see his self-satisfied little smirk. She'd give a week's salary to burst his bubble, to prick his conscience, to crush his maddening self-confidence.

"What are you doing here other than trying to ruin my life—again?"

"I've never seen you out of uniform," he said, ignoring her question.

He stared at her ankles for a few long seconds, then eyeballed her legs, the khaki shorts cuffed just above the knees and the black tank top she was wearing under a white shirt with rolled sleeves and tails tied at her waist.

"Nice, very nice," he said.

His nod of approval only infuriated her.

"This isn't a date! I want to know why you're here. And when you're leaving!"

"You smell nice, too." He stepped close—very close. "I detect a whiff of vanilla with a slight hint of cinnamon. A great aphrodisiac."

"Stop that right now and answer my questions!"

"Questions?"

"I'd like to know if your bosses at the paper found out what a rat fink you are and tossed you out on your butt."

"Yeah, that's what happened. Now I'm waiting tables for a living."

"I don't believe you!" she said. "You're up to something shady, underhanded and despicable, but you're not going to get me fired again. I'll blow the whistle on you. Your job here will be toast."

"So this is the job Liz found for you. Seems like a nice place."

"How did you know Liz helped me?"

"Who do you think asked her?"

"Don't pat yourself on the back too much. It's only a temporary position."

Sara hated that the restaurant columnist's help had been a favor to him. She wanted to succeed on her own, but this lousy reporter had derailed her whole career.

"I'm really sorry about Taste of Phoenix. I get a little carried away by my job."

He sounded genuinely contrite, but she wasn't buying it.

"You're only sorry I'm here because you're working undercover. Admit it. You're no waiter! You were flirting with Mrs. Hill instead of taking care of your tables. That's not how a real server gets big tips."

"You're right, I'm not here for the gratuities," he said. "It's a big resort, Sara. How about we agree to give each other some space? I won't do anything to jeopardize your job if you'll promise not to say a word to anyone about why I'm here."

"I have no clue why you're here."

"You probably don't want to know why. Do we have a deal?"

"You'll pretend you don't know me?"

"If that's what you want."

"And you solemnly swear not to involve me in whatever cockeyed story you're working on?"

"I think I can do that."

"You think? That's not good enough, Wilcox."

"How about if I promise not to jeopardize your job in any way?"

"Okay, promise." She wanted a pound of flesh, but this was probably the best deal she could negotiate.

"I do. On my honor—"

"As a Boy Scout? Oh, save it!"

She started to leave.

"Wait!" he said. "What about your promise?"

"I promise not to get in your way. Is that enough?"

"I don't know. To make our agreement legal and binding, we should seal the deal some way."

"I refuse to cut my wrist and let our blood mingle. And I won't sign anything that can be used against me in a court of law."

"Very sensible. I had something more casual in mind. Like a handshake."

Before she could object, he took her hand in his right one and placed his left above it on her wrist. It was a politician's handshake, intimate because of the double touch, but nothing she could call him on. His fingers were lean and hard, but he knew how to exert pressure without giving her a bone-crushing squeeze.

"We agree not to jeopardize each other's jobs," he said solemnly, moving the pad of his left thumb against the outline of pale blue veins on her inner wrist.

His right thumb was busy, too, stroking her knuckle with a beguiling rhythm.

"That's enough!"

She yanked her hand away, but could still feel how warm his touch was. He'd come to her sister's apartment to ask her to go to lunch with him. Maybe he'd followed her to Las Mariposa to seduce her. He could easily have learned where she was from his friend and her benefactor, Liz Faraday.

And maybe she was getting spacey. Wilcox was obsessed with his job. He'd only used her to get what he needed for a story, and she wasn't going to be his patsy again.

"Ha!" The idea of his following her was so ridiculous she scoffed aloud.

"That's not the reaction I hoped to get," he said.

"Go make googly eyes at the guests and chase down your story, but leave me out of it. You don't know me. Remember that! We've never set eyes on each other."

"Were you jealous when I paid a little professional attention to Carmela Hill?"

"Carmela! See, you even know her name. Professional, my foot. You were drooling on her oysters."

"Okay, you win," he said crossly. "Can I walk someone I don't know back to her room?"

"How do you know I'm staying here?"

"I'm an investigative reporter, remember."

"Well, count to a hundred before you follow me. I don't even want you to know my room number."

"Number nine. I'm in seven."

"Oh, leave me alone!"

She hurried ahead of him, not sure why he agitated her so much. She wasn't exactly angry anymore about his part in getting her fired, only worried he was trouble personified. She was too attracted to him for her own peace of mind—or her own good—especially since the man would probably do anything for a story.

Avoiding him was the best possible defense.

4

SUNDAY used to be her day off. Sara remembered leisurely breakfasts spent reading the newspaper as she sleepily dabbed on lip gloss, not that she needed makeup to make dill rolls and apple crumb coffee cake.

"Up and at 'em," she mumbled to her image in the mirror.

She shook her head, trying to forget the weird dream her alarm clock had interrupted at five. Giant cream puffs turned out to be spaceships, and the aliens who climbed out all looked like Jeff Wilcox with his hair slicked down by gooey filling.

That man was trouble, trouble, trouble! He'd thrown her whole life off course by appearing in it. No wonder she'd thrashed around all night like an octopus doing aerobics.

"Concentrate on the job," she warned herself.

Besides preparing for the dinner service, she had to help Kenny bake for the resort's famous Sunday brunch. It wouldn't hurt to get to work early on a day when the hotel was filled to capacity. The radio-astronomy seminar and the alien convention, or whatever it was, both started tomorrow. The kitchen staff had been warned to prepare for a full house.

She hurriedly made the hide-a-bed and folded it up.

It was a boring little place, but at least the rent was reasonable. A percentage of her pay was deducted for the use of the one-room studio apartment, and she did have a minuscule kitchen nook with an apartment-size fridge and stove. She was already tired of the flat white walls, nondescript orange dresser, gray tweed rug and dark green upholstered couch and chair, but it was cheap living until she knew whether the job would be permanent. Then she'd worry about finding better digs someplace else.

Checking herself out in the mirror on the bathroom door, she passed inspection and stuffed the room key into one of the pockets in the regulation black slacks she'd had to buy. At least Las Mariposa furnished starchy white jackets and paper hats, which she would put on when she arrived for work because they couldn't be taken away from the kitchen complex. All she needed to complete her work uniform was a white shirt. The tank top she was wearing today with the baggy slacks made her look like a gymnast.

Fortunately, it really didn't matter. As hired help, she was virtually invisible as far as the resort's guests were concerned. And the last thing she wanted was attention from anyone on the staff, however hunky—and in one case, dangerous—some of the waiters were.

Darn that reporter! With the whole state of Arizona full of news stories, why did he come here? Why invade her space and disturb her peace of mind by inflicting himself on her? And why was she thinking about him when she should be worrying about hot rolls, not his hot buns?

A sudden soft knock startled her, and she glanced

from her watch to her clock to make sure she wasn't late for work. It would be humiliating to be fetched on her second day. No, she had a half hour before she had to be there, so who was rapping on her door?

She cracked it open, leaving the chain on.

"Wilcox!"

"You can call me Jeff," he said softly.

"You're supposed to keep away from me—far away."

"I have hot coffee." He held up a white fast-food bag. "And bagels with cream cheese."

"I have to go to work."

"Not until six," he said more loudly.

"You'll wake people up."

"Not if you let me in." His voice practically boomed.

If she let him create a ruckus, would it get her fired? She wasn't in a position to take chances. Better to let him in and blister his ears at a discreet noise level.

She slipped off the chain and stood back, waiting until the door closed behind him to vent her frustration.

"You have no right to barge in and—"

"Black or with milk?"

"And try to bribe me with coffee."

He strolled over, set the bag on the kitchenette's fake green-marble counter and pried a plastic lid off one of the disposable cups. The aroma of fresh hot coffee teased her nostrils.

"I'll drink the one you don't want. I'm easy to please. Do you want plain or strawberry cream cheese?" His voice was seductively low.

"You're going to stay no matter what I say, aren't you?"

"Until I have to go to work. I'm on the early shift, too. Have to help set up for the big brunch."

She had just enough time for a quick snack, and the coffee was exactly what she needed to jump-start the day. There was no logical reason not to accept his offering.

"Oh, all right. I'll take black coffee and the plain."

"A pastry chef who doesn't have a sweet tooth. Amazing." He grinned. "No wonder you keep your gorgeous figure."

She wanted to wipe the silly expression off his face. He wouldn't be so cocky if she retaliated by making him all hot and bothered when he was due at work in a few minutes. She was tempted to moisten those spiky black lashes with the tip of her tongue and kiss the laugh lines beside his eyes. How would he like it if she nibbled his earlobes and nipped at his lips? Her lips curled in an evil smile at the thought of leading him on, then dropping him cold.

Was she insane? She'd never, ever been a tease, and she didn't have it in her to be that aggressive, especially not to a man who'd already thrown her orderly world into chaos.

She took the cup he handed her and gulped a big slug of hot dark liquid. It was delicious, which only made her feel more grouchy.

Using a plastic knife, he spread a generous helping of cream cheese on a bagel half and handed it to her on a paper napkin.

"Our first meal together," he teased.

"Hardly, but thank you," she said grudgingly because

good manners were too much a part of her to sacrifice them for this overbearing, pushy, alpha male.

"You're welcome." Again with the grin.

She ground her teeth together, then bit down with the force of a steel trap. With her face partly concealed by the jumbo-size bagel, she checked out his white tank top and black slacks. They were dressed like twins, except his pants fit like a second skin and hers were baggy enough to conceal a ten-pound bag of flour. She didn't like the thought of women guests eyeing him like an especially tempting dessert, which was totally silly on her part. She didn't care if he *was* the sweet course, just as long as he didn't endanger her job. Again.

"How's the job going?" he asked conversationally.

She eyed him warily but didn't answer.

"The cooks seem like a congenial bunch from what I've seen of them," he said.

"Chefs," she automatically corrected him. "The executive chef is fine as long as you remember to salute. The sous chef—"

"The what?"

"Second in command. I have a feeling she'd slap you silly if you added a pinch of salt to one of her soups."

"Sounds grim." He chewed a bite of bagel and looked thoughtful.

"Par for the course. Good chefs are a prickly lot. The great ones are so rare they can get away with anything. At least my supervisor seems pretty even-tempered."

"That's Kenny, the short, pudgy guy?"

"He enjoys every phase of his art," she said stiffly, not willing to hear criticism of one of her own.

"I didn't mean to be derogatory. I'm just trying to

sort people out," he said, licking a dab of cream cheese from his lip and making her wish she'd picked strawberry. "I wonder if the kitchen team pals around. The servers don't get much chance to mingle with the preparers. We have to run our butts off taking care of the customers."

"Guests. And you don't have to be here," she said, implying she did.

"When my editor says to check out a story, I do what has to be done."

"What if there's nothing to write about?" she asked hopefully, washing down her words with the last of the coffee.

"There's a story here, maybe a big one. You won't get rid of me until I've turned over every rock in the place."

"You promised to stay away from me," she warned. "I can't afford to lose another job."

"I won't do anything to jeopardize it," he said so vehemently she almost believed him. Almost. "And I'll pretend I don't even know you in public."

"Good. I have to go to work now."

"You have a couple of minutes. About the kitchen help..."

"They prefer to be called the culinary staff."

She sounded like a snob and didn't care. Wilcox had an ulterior motive for driving into town and bringing her breakfast at the crack of dawn, especially since they could both grab something from the kitchen during their morning break.

"We're all hired help to the guests," he said glumly.

"The chefs don't see much of them, fortunately."

This reporter wanted something from her. She could sense it in his hesitation and didn't like it.

"They must hear things, and you can't tell me they don't gossip. What else is there to do while you're mixing and chopping and stuff?"

"We paint our nails," she said sarcastically. "Are you blind? The kitchen is a madhouse when meals are going out. All you have to do is pick up your orders and amble out to the dining room. We do the real work!"

"You're right. I apologize for minimizing your work. Why is everything between us so confrontational?"

"There's nothing between us! You're my evil nemesis, a jinx, a bad luck charm—"

"At least you admit I have charm."

"I'm going to work!"

"Wait! I apologize for everything I've done and anything I'm likely to do in the future to annoy you. Please listen for two minutes!"

He caught her wrist as she stalked past him toward the door, but dropped it when she glared at him.

"Sorry again, but let me ask you something. If you knew innocent people were being fleeced by a consummate con man, would you want him stopped?"

"Of course, but—"

"And if you could help without being personally involved, without jeopardizing your job in any way, would you be willing to do some small thing to bring him to justice?"

It was the Taste of Phoenix all over again, only this time she knew one small favor could lead to disaster.

"For anyone else, yes, but I've already lost one job, not to mention my reputation, all thanks to you."

"Believe me, all I want you to do is keep your ears open and tell me if you hear anything suspicious."

"Suspicious? How do I know what's suspicious? The salad chef is trying to get cozy with one of the lifeguards, but she's only interested in his spinach salad. Is that what you want to hear?"

"I want to know about Barrett Borden Bent," he blurted, stepping in front of her to block the door.

"Oh, him. The guy in the robe."

"I need to know everything he says or does. Where does he go? What is he planning to do here? Who are his followers? He's so outrageous the staff is sure to gossip about him. How often do they get a guest who thinks aliens are dropping out of the sky?"

Sara was interested in spite of her better judgment.

"He seemed pretty kooky to me," she admitted.

"According to my editor's sources, he's raking in a staggering amount in contributions, telling people he believes aliens are coming. He's bilking his followers for unbelievable sums."

"He's the man you're investigating," she mused thoughtfully. It figured. Randolph Hill was probably too dull and conventional to lure a reporter like Jeff to the resort.

"Yes. I especially want to know why he decided to come here after Randolph Hill announced his seminar. They knew each other as college undergraduates and hate each other. Hill is his severest critic. Calls him a pseudoscientist and a money-grabbing phony. It's a showdown between legitimate science and a cult looking for little green men, according to Hill. You'd think Bent would want to avoid a real scientist like Hill, but instead he's here for reasons of his own."

"I don't have any contact with guests. I don't see how I could help you—assuming I were willing, which I most definitely am not."

"All I'm asking is that you pass along any gossip you hear about Bent. He's flamboyant. He makes a stir wherever he goes. He's also a big blowhard who likes to order people around. He won't be making many friends among the staff. I know the resort has a grapevine, but I haven't tapped into it yet. You're more likely to hear gossip than I am."

"Because the kitchen help stands around doing nothing?"

"No, because you have a trustworthy face. People won't think you're paying attention to their conversations." He was using his soft, seductive voice again.

She was sinking in quicksand. Her first impulse was to pack her bags and make a run for it before it was too late. She didn't want to get involved in Jeff's investigation. The real danger was she'd start caring about him, and the man's job was all-important to him. He'd forget about her as soon as he had his story.

"You promised to leave me alone!"

"I will, absolutely. All I need is an extra pair of ears. You don't even have to acknowledge you know me. In fact, it's better if you don't talk to me directly. Just slip a note under my door if you hear anything at all about Bent, whether it seems pertinent or not. I'll pretend I don't even know you if that will make you happy."

"You bet that would make me happy."

It occurred to her he had as much to lose as she did.

If she blew his cover, his assignment would be history. She was no blackmailer, but he didn't know that. Maybe he would keep his distance if she agreed to pass on information about Bent. It was highly unlikely she'd hear anything of interest anyway.

"I want you to stay away from me, far away. If you do, I'll let you know if I hear anything about Bent," she said.

"Wonderful! I really appreciate it, and I won't bother you in any other way. I won't even walk to work with you. Go first, and I'll wait two minutes before I follow. I'll pull your door shut behind me. We're strangers, never saw each other before yesterday, okay?"

"Okay, and don't forget it!"

"I won't. Promise."

Yeah, she'd heard that before! At least if she pretended to cooperate, he might keep his distance.

She left him behind and hurried to work trying not to think about warm brown eyes and a smile that could light up a room.

JEFF FOLLOWED HER with stealth and cunning, using the flimsy cover of sycamore trees in case she decided to look back. She didn't. He waited a minute after she was out of sight around the corner of the main hotel, then sauntered after her, feeling more like a Peeping Tom than a savvy investigative reporter. He was watching her for the sheer pleasure of it, not because he expected her to come up with much that would help his story. She was so darn cute, right after he made the reluctantly given promise, he decided to break it so he could see her again.

Now that he'd persuaded her to pass on any rumors she heard about Bent, he congratulated himself on his brilliance. He had an excuse to continue talking to her, and a reason to make their meetings clandestine—preferably in her room. Actually, it was a darn good plan. He had to waste so much time on his cover, slinging high-class hash at picky people, that another pair of ears was exactly what he needed.

Decker Horning wouldn't waste his time sending Jeff to investigate a bunch of kooks. There was something big here. All Jeff's instincts told him the robed windbag was hatching something underhanded and illegal.

How, for instance, did Bent know about Hill's seminar far enough ahead to book all the remaining rooms for his spacey followers? Jeff could smell a Pulitzer in the potential for mayhem and grand larceny here, and he wanted to be in the middle of it.

He didn't want Sara involved, though. There was nothing dangerous about secretly feeding him gossip, but that was all he'd allow her to do. She was right about his jinxing her career. He'd blundered badly with a woman he would very much like to know better.

His job as a server was ideal for snooping, but the work sucked. He had a whole new appreciation of anyone who had to wait tables and cater to a lot of demanding people. He hoped the finicky eater who was allergic to thirty-two different foods would sit at someone else's table today.

In spite of how boring it would be to fold half a million napkins and set all his tables exactly right, he was eager to walk through the kitchen to get another glimpse of Sara.

Just shaking hands with her to seal their deal a few minutes ago had gotten to him. He hadn't felt so hot and bothered since Mary Mohocken let him touch her bare breast behind the roller-skating rink. Then his excuse had been the raging testosterone of a high-school sophomore. Why was Sara having this effect on him? And over something as innocent as a handshake?

The Bent story had better break fast before he did something really crazy, like come on to a woman who'd rather cozy up to poison ivy.

With effort Jeff put his mind to work on his job, his real job. One thing worked in his favor. Carmela Hill had staked out one of his tables as the place she and her husband could hold court during meals. Usually the couple was joined by other scientists there for the seminar, but at noon Jeff got a chance to ask a few questions as he served their meals.

He gave them spinach salads and managed to probe for answers at the same time.

"Is your seminar open to the public, Dr. Hill?" He tried to sound as deferential as possible.

"I screen everyone who applies," the man said. "An advanced degree in astronomy or a related science is essential to understand my lectures and workshops."

His tone was cordial, or maybe Jeff had expected him to be remote and unfriendly because he dressed like Dracula's cousin.

"Pretty exciting, the possibility of life in outer space," Jeff said.

"It's almost a certainty, given the size of the universe." His wife started picking at her salad. Hill left his untouched as he warmed to his subject. "But radio astronomy isn't about searching for aliens. Anyone who says extraterrestrials are coming and going like tourists to Vegas is either deranged or a fraud. These individuals do great harm to serious scientific inquiry by feeding lurid tales to the tabloids. If I had my way..."

"Oh, he doesn't want to hear about all that," Carmela said impatiently, laying her hand on Jeff's arm.

"Actually, I think the possibility of real life in space is fascinating." Jeff managed to shake loose her scarlet-tipped fingers without a fuss.

"Tell you what," Dr. Hill said, "if you're off work during any of my meetings, you're welcome to sit in. I'm afraid you'll find it dull without the necessary background, but you're a young fellow. You might hear something that will encourage you to learn more."

"That's very nice of you," Jeff said, deciding not to bring Bent up in this conversation. "Thank you, sir."

He found himself liking Hill a lot more than he expected. The invitation was far more than he'd hoped to get, and it would open the door to asking more questions later. Meanwhile, he had hash to sling and a con man to expose. He had to keep his mind on what he was doing, but it wouldn't be easy with Sara so close—and so desirable.

5

WHERE THE HELL was that man?

Jeff had been trying to get his father on the phone since he arrived at Las Mariposa. Len Wilcox had been acting odd for weeks, and Jeff was frustrated. His father seemed to be avoiding him, and Jeff wasn't sure why someone so talkative and gregarious was being so closemouthed and secretive.

Underlying his annoyance, though, was the very real fear that something had happened to his father. He was ready to shut off his cell phone when a familiar but sleepy voice rumbled. "Hello."

"Dad, I tried to call all day yesterday. Where were you?"

"Here and there," his father said evasively.

"I even tried Fat Ollie's. What did you find to do on a Monday when the temperature hit a hundred and fourteen degrees?"

"I keep busy. When are you coming home?"

"As soon as I wrap up this story."

Jeff winced and belatedly looked around the empty conference room to be sure no one had heard him say that. It wasn't like him to be careless, but he wasn't on top of this assignment the way he usually was. For one thing, his father's peculiar behavior was preying on his mind. And it didn't help to have Sara distracting him. He'd long known women and work didn't mix, especially not in the newspaper game. He needed to be free to work around the clock or be gone long periods of time when necessary.

"Your mother called," Len said.

"What did she have to say?"

Jeff often suspected his father still cared more about his mother than he'd admit. But true love hadn't worked for his parents, and he doubted it ever would for him.

"Don't know. She just left a message on your machine. I picked up your mail. A couple of bills, three credit card offers and a magazine—I forget which one."

Jeff kept a box at the post office. Before his dad moved in with him, it had been easier than putting a hold on mail every time he was away. He'd seen no reason to give it up.

Another oddity. He subscribed mostly to newsmagazines, and his father usually devoured them before Jeff ever saw them. In fact, Len usually regaled him with capsule summaries of the main articles. Once a newsman, always a newsman. Jeff added one more peculiarity to the list. His father was definitely not his usual self lately.

"Dad, I have to go. The SLOT people have finished their main course. Time to clear tables."

"SLOT?"

"You know, Search for Life Out There. I'm at Las Mariposa, near Sedona." This was getting worse and worse. Had his father forgotten what he'd told him about his absence? He lowered his voice and cautiously watched the door of the lodge room that wasn't being used today. "The story on the First Contact Society guru, Barrett Borden Bent."

"I know, you're hot on the trail of little green men. If you meet any, don't get talked into a ride on their spaceship. I hear they're mean little sons of bitches."

His father cackled derisively, implying a real newsman wouldn't get suckered into a tabloid story.

"I'll call you tomorrow. Keep out of trouble," Jeff said, signing off.

To his disappointment, he agreed with his father's assessment of the prospects for a story. The seminar had started yesterday, and the sixty-two participants were the least newsworthy group Jeff had covered in a long time. The only one who attracted his attention was Hill's wife, Carmela. Twenty or so years younger than her husband, she was a trophy wife if he'd ever seen one. In spite of her mostly black wardrobe and severe hairstyle, she had a smoldering sexuality that turned heads. Fortunately he was immune. Unfortunately he was immune because he couldn't get Sara out of his mind.

He sprinted to the luncheon just in time to have John, the headwaiter, chew him out for disappearing.

"Call of nature," Jeff said, rushing to the nearest table to begin clearing the main course.

When groups wanted a private meal at the lodge, the building where most of the meeting rooms were, the food was prepared in the main hotel and shuttled over on a golf cart especially adapted for hauling hot and cold food.

Any other time Jeff would have enjoyed listening to the snatches of information on SLOT's work. He'd seen the enormous radio telescope antennas that looked like satellite dishes in New Mexico, where dedicated scientists listened for anomalies in the radio signals from space. The Eastern Radio Astronomy Lab in Green Hill, West Virginia, was a similar high-tech wonder with a giant antenna in the mountains. There was probably a great science story in the work SLOT did studying distant galaxies, but that wasn't why Jeff was there. Bent was his target.

The guru claimed he had a scientific background, greatly exaggerating his lackluster undergraduate degree in astronomy to his followers. But the more Jeff heard of his schtick, the more phony Bent seemed. From what Jeff had pieced together, Bent's message was aliens had landed, were not warmly welcomed and would come again. He was raising funds and marshaling followers to be sure the extraterrestrials got red-carpet treatment next time.

"Fill the water glasses," John barked at him. "Try not to spill on anyone this time."

Was it Jeff's fault the skinny man with the red beard had knocked his arm just as he leaned over to refill a glass? He would have to be more careful so he wouldn't get fired before he learned what he needed to know.

He'd seen a lot of Hill and his wife, but Bent was harder to track. His meetings were closed-door in the lower level of the main hotel, and his hundred and thirty-five First Contact followers were content to flood the main dining room instead of holding private meals. Jeff had learned the registration numbers of the guests from a cooperative night clerk named Shelly, but at least another hundred or so of Bent's people were drifting in and out of the hotel. They were either camping out in the Sedona desert or staying in nearby motels.

Why was the con man here when he had cause to hate Hill? Bent had been lobbying in Washington to get funds for his organization, but he'd been dismissed as either part of the lunatic fringe or a fraud. Hill, whose work was partly supported by government grants, had been outspoken in debunking the beliefs of First Contact in the media, not that he was alone in thinking Bent's followers were kooks. Was Bent here for revenge on the radio astronomer?

Jeff sloshed ice water in a half-full glass then scooped up a couple of leftover forks and walked to the table used by the servers.

"You're supposed to *leave* the dessert forks, idiot!" the overbearing headwaiter said in a harsh whisper when Jeff tossed them in a plastic tub of dirty dishes. "And what's that lump under your jacket?"

What he had to put up with to get a story.

Jeff opened the starchy jacket to show John the compact cell phone in its waist holder but was careful to conceal the small recorder on the other side. He'd had a shoe repairman attach two holsters to a belt he could wear under clothes when the need arose. It was none of the headwaiter's business, but he had to put up with the jerk or risk blowing his cover.

"My dad's not well. I need the phone with me in case I'm needed in an emergency," he explained, trying not to show his irritation. It would be inconvenient, to say the least, to get canned right now.

"The cream puffs are on the way," John said. "Make sure table two gets some clean forks."

"Yes, sir."

Jeff said it with enough insolence to let the beefy failed linebacker know he wasn't intimidated but not enough to get punched or fired. The kid—he was maybe eight years younger than Jeff—had been dropped from ASU's football squad and lost his athletic scholarship after he flunked most of his freshman classes. He'd worked his way up to headwaiter at Las Mariposa in two years, and this was probably his best career prospect. If the guy wasn't so obnoxious, Jeff would have been sympathetic.

He put new dessert forks back on the table, then looked around the nondescript meeting room with its hardwood floors, round tables, white tablecloths and dark tan room divider that was closed, except for space to let the servers enter from the rear. It made the large room more cozy for the relatively small group of patrons. No story leads here, Jeff thought regretfully, and no way to get out of finishing the luncheon. When the bullnecked, crew-cut headwaiter motioned to him, he made a show of hustling over.

"Go outside and help carry the cream puffs, Wilcox," he ordered with all the charm of a drill sergeant.

How the mighty are fallen, Jeff thought sourly. The kid had gone from padded, helmeted football hopeful to crabby waiter in too-tight pants. The *Phoenix Monitor*'s star reporter had to fetch and carry cream puffs.

He went through the service door and wondered what Decker would say if he gave up on the story now. Probably nothing printable.

SARA FINISHED the last Dutch apple pecan pie and lined it up with the others waiting to go into oven three as soon as the Parmesan rolls for dinner came out. The lunch rush had come early, a virtual stampede of guests when the dining room opened at eleven-thirty. Now it was past one, and the servers were taking care of the few latecomers and setting tables for dinner. There was a pleasant lull in the kitchen activities, and she started to clean her area.

"Sara, we have a tremendous problem," Kenny said, dabbing at his moist forehead with a section of paper toweling.

Kenny's tremendous problems ranged from insignificant, in her opinion, to disastrous, but she was getting used to his dramatic style. At least he was cheerful even when he burned the caramel sauce for the bread pudding.

"The pies are ready," she said, signaling her willingness to obey his slightest whim. She was beginning to like this job and would be very disappointed if she couldn't stay after the two-week trial period.

"Can you drive a golf cart?" her boss asked.

"I suppose so."

How hard could it be? she wondered, thinking of the parade of golfers who putt-putted regularly over a special crossing bridge spanning the highway to get to the resort's nine-hole course.

"Good, I need you to deliver the cream puffs to the lodge. Brad, the kid who's supposed to do it, is so hung over I wouldn't trust him on a tricycle. Drive around the near side of the building. The door on the opposite side of the main entrance leads into a utility area. The servers can handle it from there."

Could someone get fired for getting drunk? She'd be

glad when she felt more secure in her job, because right now, if anyone found out she was helping Jeff spy on guests, she was sure her stay at Las Mariposa would be shorter than two weeks. Until Jeff was far, far away and out of her mind, her job was in jeopardy. Darn, why did she keep thinking about him?

She tossed aside the paper hat, the badge of her temporary status, and hurried to the golf cart. It had been fitted with secure racks to haul food from the kitchen to the meeting rooms in the lodge or to the outdoor lunch bar by the creek, where golfers and swimmers could get a sandwich without changing out of spiked shoes or swimsuits.

"Take it slow and easy," Kenny advised her, following her outside and watching her start the cart. "There's a little dip in the path as you round the corner of the hotel, but otherwise the asphalt is pretty smooth."

"I'll be careful," she promised. "I'll transport your cream puffs like a load of quail eggs."

She had no idea how fragile the little birds' eggs were, but it seemed to reassure Kenny. He went to the kitchen without giving her more warnings.

Driving was fun once she got the hang of it. It wasn't really a golf cart anymore. The front seat could accommodate two, but the back had been converted into cargo racks where trays of pastries rode right behind her head. She made a mental note not to make any sudden stops. The metal trays were heavy enough to stay in place behind the little ridge on the shelf, but she didn't want a cream puff to slide out from under the plastic wrap and end up in her hair.

She rode past the back of the hotel, the tennis courts

and the pool at a speed of maybe three or four miles an hour. Good thing Kenny didn't see her take the corner. The metal trays rattled on the racks, and she looked over her shoulder at the yummy cream puffs. Every little beauty was golden brown and so tempting she almost envied the SLOT people who'd get to enjoy them.

The trip didn't take long at all. The lodge was a one-story stucco building with orange roof tiles, but it didn't have the charm of the older hotel building. Two wide doors in front led to a lobby. Beside the main ballroom that could be divided into two cozier spaces were two hallways on the right with meeting rooms named after native plants—cactus and juniper.

The employees had to make deliveries in the rear, but something was going on. People were milling around on the asphalt path, with the majority in front of the lodge. She had to beep her obnoxious little horn several times, and even then the crowd let her through reluctantly. A couple gave her surly glances that were downright unsettling.

"None of my business," she muttered to herself when she was forced to stop for a pedestrian who refused to give her the right of way. The willowy woman had braids like Medusa's snakes and a long black skirt with zodiac signs embroidered around the hem. She slowly ambled in front of Sara without bothering to look in either direction.

It didn't take the deductive powers of Sherlock Holmes to figure out these were Bent's people, not Hill's scientists, but why were they congregating around the lodge?

"Deliver the cream puffs and run for cover," she told herself.

This was definitely not a crowd of happy campers, and she didn't like the sullen looks they gave her as she tried to weave her way through the stragglers on the path.

If Brad didn't get tossed out for his drunken ways, she was going to yell at him for sticking her with his job. She should get combat pay for threading her way through this mob.

The relief she felt reaching the service door at the back of the lodge evaporated the instant she saw who was waiting for her.

"Hi, I'm Jeff, your cream-puff carrier," he said, mocking the spiel servers were required to give at every table. "What do you think is going on?"

"A save-the-rattlesnake rally?" she suggested.

"Or maybe aliens have landed and are among us?"

"Yeah, right. If you're here to unload cream puffs, get at it."

Theoretically, she was too lowly to give orders to waiters, but she made an exception for Wilcox.

"Something big is happening," he said, ignoring her and the load of pastries.

He was right. People were running, surging toward the front of the lodge.

"Let's see what's happening inside," he said.

He grabbed her hand, practically pulling her off the seat of the yellow-and-white cart, and dragged her through the service door.

The room divider was open a few feet to allow the

servers access to the front area when SLOT'S luncheon was in progress.

Shouting, belligerent people were filling the room, many of them waving posterboard signs. The people attending Hill's seminar remained in their seats, watching with varying degrees of curiosity and annoyance. They were a group of mixed ages, more men than women, most dressed casually in jeans or resort garb. If they had any distinctive characteristic as a group, it was their seriousness. They were polar opposites of the placard-carrying bunch.

"No more cover-ups." Sara read one of the signs aloud.

"They are here. Welcome our alien brothers and sisters," Jeff read.

"Hey, there's Bent." She nodded toward the main door.

The First Contact leader was resplendent in a royal blue robe embellished with shiny gold stars. His wavy silvery hair was so lustrous he'd probably spent the morning in a salon. Even his canvas running shoes were gold, the paint flaking away where his feet creased them.

"Dr. Hill," he shouted in a voice that instantly silenced the howling horde. "It's time for open debate. Our goals are the same as yours, to advance science by confirming we are not alone in this vast universe. We should embrace each other as fellow seekers of truth and share the bounty our government parcels out so meagerly for your benefit only."

"Uh-oh." Jeff pointed across the room where a photographer was recording Bent's impassioned speech.

"He brought his own press. What do you want to bet he's from a tabloid on the kook fringe?"

Jeff was recording the uproar in the room using the handheld recorder he'd taken from the belt holster concealed under his jacket.

"I come prepared," he whispered, gesturing at the compact cell phone on the other side of his lean waist.

Hill left the head table, closely followed by his wife, and walked over to confront Bent.

"I'll have to ask you to leave, *Mister* Bent. This is a scientific seminar for reputable scientists. A doctorate in astronomy, physics or a related field is a requirement to participate. We have nothing to debate with a band of lunatics looking for little green men from Mars."

"You have no right to interrupt my husband's meeting," Carmela said, reminding Sara of a snake spitting venom.

"Carmela, don't waste your breath on this fraud," Hill said, taking her arm since she looked ready to claw Bent.

Bent didn't look quite so unflappable as both Hills turned their backs on him.

"The cream puffs are getting soggy," Sara said, wanting to get out of there before the mob got really ugly. "They'll melt outside in the heat."

The scientists were getting nervous, some trying to sneak out through the crowd. A steely-eyed blond man tried to push through a cluster of Bent's followers, and First Contact struck the first blow. A dark-bearded, wild-eyed believer smashed his sign on the blond scientist's head, and all hell broke loose. The enraged victim shoved his assailant and knocked him against a wall.

Several other members of Bent's group rushed to their comrade's defense. Both Hill and Bent ineffectively shouted for order, but no one paid any attention to them.

"Call the sheriff!" a woman shrieked.

"Dial nine-one-one!"

"Let's get out of here!" Jeff was giving the orders, but Sara was mesmerized by the first mob melee she'd ever seen.

"Come on!" he insisted.

He put his arm around her shoulders and tried to steer her to the service entrance. She started to move as a guy in skimpy purple shorts and a red Love Your Alien T-shirt rolled up a poster and used it like a sword to poke at Dr. Hill. The scientist grabbed it away, and Bent shouted something that sent the First Contact fanatics scurrying toward the exit.

Apparently this wasn't what Bent had planned. She caught a glimpse of his silvery head disappearing through the door to the front lobby.

"There goes Bent," she said.

"Let's go."

She ran hand in hand with him, neither of them looking behind them, although footsteps were thudding on the hardwood floor as others followed them toward the rear door.

"To the golf cart and full speed ahead," Jeff shouted over the racket.

She was laughing so hard it was difficult to catch her breath. Jeff jumped into the cart after her, his hand pushing on her bottom to hurry her along.

Once she was behind the wheel, she circled on the pathway intending to roar—well, putt-putt—to the main hotel and the safety of the kitchen. Nothing here was her fault, but she didn't want to be around when blame was assigned.

"Watch out!" Jeff yelled.

A big blue shape was blocking the path, and she slammed on the brake just in time to avoid a collision.

It was Bent.

"Move over," he ordered her.

When she didn't move, he slammed into her with his big rump and grabbed the wheel. She was knocked against Jeff, saved from tumbling out because he pulled her onto his lap.

"You can't take this cart!" she protested.

She tried to grab the wheel, but Bent was too beefy and too strong. He was wheeling the cart around the back of the lodge while Jeff clung to the edge of the narrow seat with one hand and held on to her with the other.

"This cart is for staff use only!" she said.

She might as well have been talking to a rampaging rhino. Bent put the pedal to the metal, but Sara was determined to thwart his escape even if she demolished the cart. She leaned over, grabbed the wheel and hung on as though her life depended on it.

"Let go," Bent growled.

She saw his plan. He was planning to cut through the pretty gardens, not caring how many plants and flowers he ruined, skirt the sycamore trees, go behind the employees' quarters, reach the creek and follow it to the guest bungalows where he could hide out and pretend nothing was his fault. And she'd be blamed and fired for the destroyed gardens and desserts!

She popped off Jeff's lap, threw herself across the small steering wheel and spun it out of control.

"I said staff use only!"

Bent swiped his big beefy arm at her, but he was too late. The cart careened out of control, tearing up the corner of a cactus garden and heading directly toward one of the small ornate fountains.

There was just enough downhill momentum to send the cart bumping over the edge and into the water.

Water splashed in her face as the cart lurched to a stop. Drenched but in no danger of drowning, Sara clung to Jeff's neck and wiped pastry crumbs off the back of his head. Mentally she updated her résumé. Reason for leaving last job—lost load of cream puffs in a fountain.

"Sara, are you all right?"

Jeff helped her out of the submerged cart while Bent ranted and raved. Her jacket was as soggy as a wet dish towel, and the soaked baggy pants clung to her like plastic wrap.

The crowd must have spotted Bent making his getaway. In no time at all, spectators surrounded the fountain. Worse, Kenny was coming at a run, huffing and puffing.

"I wondered what was taking you so long," he gasped.

"Well, a fight broke out—"

"Oh, no!" Kenny turned stark white, and she feared for his life. "Oh, no!"

He plunged into the fountain, water soaking him to the knees, and splashed to the trademark metal butterfly on the center pedestal.

"My cream puffs!"

They floated around him like bloated fish, some already sinking to the bottom. He reached up and picked one, then another, impaled on the sharp metal wings of the butterfly.

"Fortunately I have some lovely raspberry sorbet for just such an emergency," Kenny said solemnly, staring at the ruined cream puffs in his hand as though tempted to sample them. "What happened?" he moaned, more to himself than to anybody else.

Bent was climbing out of the fountain, trying to sneak away, and Sara was powerless to do anything.

The First Contact crowd was following the example of their leader, moving away to distance themselves from the accident. She was sure her job was history when the executive chef, Mr. Cervantes, and the hotel manager, Larry Winfield, walked to the fountain and stared at the cart with baleful expressions.

"Just a minute, sir," Jeff said loudly. "You're not going to let Sara take the blame."

Bent's robe was trailing on the ground, and Jeff had both feet firmly planted on the hem. Unless the con man wanted to rip it off and beat a retreat in whatever he was wearing under it, he was busted.

"Tell the people how this accident happened," Jeff demanded loudly.

"Just an accident. Perhaps the steering malfunctioned, but I'm not going to sue. You can be assured of that," he said, nodding at the hotel manager.

"You're not going to sue because this whole mess is your fault, isn't it?" Jeff persisted.

"It was a mistake on my part to insist the young lady let me use the cart," he sputtered.

"In fact, you tried to push her off and commandeer it, didn't you?"

"I didn't intend to do her any injury. I merely wanted to borrow it. I am a guest here." Bent glared at Jeff, whom he assumed was only a lowly waiter.

"She told you it was for staff only, didn't she?" Jeff spoke loudly so everyone could hear.

"She may have." Bent was trying to free the hem of his robe, but his captor didn't allow it.

"She did," Jeff said. "I was a witness."

"Yes, I believe she did say something along that line. I was a bit agitated at the moment. I was running to get help, of course."

"At the creek?"

"I was heading toward my bungalow to call for assistance. I'm afraid my followers got a bit carried away. Our intentions were totally innocent. All we wanted was a chance for open, truthful discourse. I don't even know who the bearded man with the sign is. Probably one of the hangers-on. I very much doubt he's even a registered guest. My organization will, of course, share the responsibility with SLOT for any damage." Bent's face was bright red, and he looked ready to pop.

"We had nothing to do with it, you damned faker!" Hill said as he pushed his way through the crowd to confront his nemesis.

"About dessert, Dr. Hill," Kenny said. He was still standing in the fountain clutching a soggy ball of pastry with the cream filling oozing between his fingers. "I can offer a lovely raspberry sorbet in place of the cream puffs."

"Are we all agreed that none of this is Sara's fault?"

Jeff asked, looking at the hotel manager and the executive chef. Both men seemed hypnotized by the exchange between Bent and Jeff. Sara couldn't believe he'd talked to a guest the way he had and not gotten fired.

"Clearly it was not her fault," Mr. Cervantes said, finally snapping out of his trance. "Considering the condition of your uniform, Miss Madison, I believe you may be excused from the rest of your shift."

The executive chef actually remembered her name, and Wilcox had saved her job. Despite the circumstances, she was afraid she was starting to like the reporter. A lot.

6

SARA WASN'T surprised when someone knocked on her door that evening. She was so sure it was Jeff, butterflies fluttered in her stomach.

Common sense told her not to open it, to pretend she wasn't there. But darn it, she wanted to see him. After their misadventure with Bent, she owed him thanks for saving her job. More than that, she was harboring some dangerous romantic fantasies. A dose of the real Wilcox should dispel them.

She opened the door but left the chain on. His face filled the crack, and he flashed her a thousand-watt grin.

"Hi."

"Hi."

"Can I come in?"

Bad idea, but how could she say no?

"I was going to wash my hair."

"It's beautiful the way it is. Too bad you don't wear it down like that all the time."

"Pulled back works better for my job."

"What we don't do for our jobs."

"Yeah." She was having a hard time remembering what her job was.

"I'm not going away. Are you going to let me in?"

Why did he continually issue challenges? Didn't he

see what a bad idea it was for the two of them to be alone together in a small room?

"I guess it's okay for a few minutes."

She tried to sound indifferent, but her heart was thumping and her fingers were clumsy as she released the chain and opened the door. He came in and stood in front of her.

He looked tired. Pale gray half-moons shadowed his usually vibrant eyes, and the tiny wrinkles at the corners seemed deeper.

He also looked so sexy it took her breath away. His hair was damp, as though he'd just stepped out of the shower. Now there was an image that made her tingle! He had a terrific body that not even the loose-fitting gray athletic shorts and baggy white T-shirt could conceal. She got shivers imagining water matting his chest hair and bouncing off round dimpled buns.

She lowered her eyes, hoping he didn't realize she was checking out his legs. The skin was golden brown above the black river sandals he wore without socks, and she speculated how far his tan line went. If he could read minds—or glances—she was going to learn the true meaning of humiliation.

"That was a pretty rocky ride over the edge of the fountain. I wanted to make sure you weren't hurt," he said, dominating the small room just by being there.

"No, I'm fine. You pretty much cushioned the jolt. Are you okay?"

"I've got a big purple bruise on my butt, but I don't sit down much here anyway."

"Oh, I'm sorry."

"Not your fault. Want to see it?"

"Certainly not!" Only more than she wanted her next paycheck.

"I'm glad it happened," he said in a husky voice. "This afternoon was a breakthrough in our relationship."

"We don't have a relationship."

"I thought—"

"You thought I'd be overwhelmed with gratitude because you saved my job."

"Yeah, sort of...no, not exactly."

"Well, thank you for making Bent admit it was his fault." She tried to sound gracious, but Wilcox was the most aggravating man she'd ever met. One minute he was smart and appealing. The next he was outrageously cheeky. Why was he getting to her when she should be running away from him?

"Do you think he accepted the blame too easily?"

"He didn't have any right to jump on the cart."

"No, but he's a con artist, and most of the witnesses were his followers. It's not like his kind to offer to pay for damage. It goes against his nature not to try to wiggle out of it."

She hadn't thought about it that way. But it would have been easy for Bent to lie and say she'd offered him a ride. And she had grabbed the wheel and made the cart swerve. Technically, it *was* her fault.

"Maybe he's nicer than we think?" she asked without much conviction.

"Do you believe that?" He arched one eyebrow, which made him look even cuter.

"No, not really. I guess he didn't want any more commotion."

"That's how I see it. He probably doesn't want to be kicked out of Las Mariposa. He's up to something, and the fiasco at the lodge was only the first step."

"Have you learned anything useful about him?" she asked, her curiosity piqued.

"I was going to ask you the same thing. I'm glad you're interested in the story."

"I'm not. You're the nosy reporter. The only reason I agreed to help is so you'll leave sooner. I'll feel a lot more secure about my job when you're gone."

"Won't life be dull when I go?" His voice was teasing, but his eyes were dark and serious.

"No, I like my work. All I want is a permanent position here."

Who was she kidding? Much as she needed this job, it would be lonely when he left. But her sensible side told her it would be even lonelier if she allowed herself to care about Jeff. He was married to his job. He'd made that perfectly clear. Now was the time to squelch any feelings she had for him. There was more to life than occasional great sex, although she didn't doubt he would make it spectacular.

"What are you thinking?" He asked as if he really wanted to know, and she felt all mushy.

"Nothing."

"Do you want to go for a walk? There's not much else to do until after ten when the hired help can use the pool."

"Walk where?" Their history made her perpetually suspicious. They were still standing by the door because she hadn't invited him to sit down.

"Oh, maybe along the creek. It's cooler now. That's

what I love about Arizona. No matter how hot the days are, the nights are comfortable."

If she said no, she'd have to stay in her room until bedtime, not a great prospect, but she wasn't comfortable with the idea of being alone with him.

"Maybe it's not a good idea," she suggested, knowing her objection was halfhearted and the opposite of what she wanted to do.

"We work together. If anyone notices us, they'll think we're having a summer fling."

"Teenagers have flings," she said, wondering why he made her feel testy so often. "Reporters posing as waiters do not have flings with pastry chefs—assistant pastry chefs."

Her lowly status still rankled.

"Bad word choice," he admitted. "I just want to enjoy your company and pick your brain. Maybe you've learned something and don't realize it."

"What a charming invitation. You'll be wasting your time, though. I haven't heard a thing about Bent."

"Walking with you is anything but a waste of time."

He smiled, melting her resistance. Maybe she was silly to think of refusing. Why not enjoy the company of a devastatingly handsome man instead of vegetating in a dingy room?

Anyway, she was a tiny bit homesick. She missed her sister and Todd and her cozy circle of friends. So far she hadn't had a chance to make new ones.

"Well, okay. I could use some air."

"You look great tonight," he said, letting her walk past him into the hall then shutting her door.

"Thanks."

His compliment forced her to admit to herself she had tried to look good on the off chance he might come by. She was wearing a cotton tank top with scalloped edges in a soft green shade. Her canvas slip-ons were pristine white. The white denim shorts she wore were a whole lot more skimpy than her usual ones. In fact, after she put them on, she checked in the mirror to make sure the creases between her thighs and bottom didn't show.

Outside it was the magical moment between day and night when the western sky was still streaked with orange but the sun had disappeared behind the red rocks of Sedona. Deep shadows under the sycamore trees concealed the employees' living quarters. Jeff stopped under a branch that just cleared his head and took Sara's hand in his.

"There's something I've been wanting to do since Taste of Phoenix," he said solemnly.

"Try my cheesecake?"

"That, too."

He faced her and leaned so close she could smell the fresh bouquet of soap on his skin and see the way a lock of hair rebelliously refused to lie with the rest.

"Sometimes I get obsessive when I cover a story," he said softly. "But I can't get you out of my mind."

"I'm that way about new recipes. I want everyone to share my enthusiasm even though I know they don't."

She knew he hadn't stopped to talk about recipes, but she had that shivery feeling again. Was he going to kiss her? She couldn't stand the suspense.

"I felt like the world's biggest jerk when you got fired."

"Oh." This was not the time to tell him she'd thought that and worse.

"You're so gorgeous it's like looking at the sun. Sara..."

He leaned in, and Sara instinctively did the same.

His breath was minty, and his lips moved over hers, barely touching but teasing every nerve in her body. His hands engulfed her shoulders and slid across her back. It seemed natural to wrap her arms around his waist.

She was transported by the pleasure of being in the arms of a man who didn't treat lovemaking like a contact sport. She pressed so close his anatomy was no mystery, and she freed her mind of everything but the delicious sensation of his lips on hers.

When she opened her eyes, the sky was dark velvet blue. She was seeing stars, but not all of them were in the heavens.

"I like kissing you," he whispered, his warm breath tickling her skin.

"Me, too."

For a kiss, it was off the charts. She knew special when it hit her. She expected him to kiss her again, envelop her in the circle of his arms, maybe even carry her to his room.

Instead he stepped aside and said, "Let's walk."

Let's walk! He'd lit a fuse, and all he said was, "Let's walk"?

No wonder she hated him, despised him, wanted to have his baby!

"Uh-oh, this is not good." She couldn't believe she was thinking of him—of her—of them doing the deed.

"What?" he asked.

She hadn't meant to speak aloud. The last thing she wanted was to let him know his kisses had rocked her world.

"Nothing. A bug." She slapped at an imaginary insect on her thigh and knew this had to be the last time she let Wilcox's face get within six feet of hers.

He took her hand and led her to the path that followed Oak Creek, past the umbrella tables clustered in front of the lunch bar. More sycamores lined the path as they approached the bungalows. The foliage here was dense for the guests' privacy.

To their left the creek gurgled along, the water level low at midsummer. She was tempted to jump onto one of the exposed rocks in the streambed and see how far she could leap from stone to stone without getting her feet wet, but Jeff's arm was around her waist, holding her close against his hip.

A few coach lights on iron poles lit the path as darkness settled over the bungalows. Muffled night sounds murmured around them, and occasionally a burst of laughter from one of the squat little guest houses disturbed the peace. Jeff dropped his arm from her waist and cradled her hand in his, gently rubbing the pad of her thumb.

"So, have you heard any interesting gossip about Bent?" he asked, spoiling the mood.

"No."

"No rumors about his outlandish behavior? No snatches of conversation speculating about why he's here?"

"You don't need to pick my brain, Wilcox. I know whether I've heard any—"

Suddenly he pulled her off the path into a clump of trees.

"What on earth..."

He muffled her words, gently but firmly clamping his hand over her mouth.

She tried to pull his hand away. What made him think he could muzzle her like a dog?

He was craning his head around a tree trunk, straining to see while he blocked her view of whatever was happening.

"Be quiet for just a sec. Please," he whispered.

He pulled his hand away but left her with a very bad feeling about his intentions. Why was it so darn important for them not to be seen or heard? Without their uniforms, they could pass as guests, not that workers weren't allowed to stroll on the grounds of the resort.

He had them wait behind the trees another minute. All she saw were the bungalows, identical stucco boxes with tiled roofs and patios in the back overlooking the creek and the outline of the bluffs beyond. A few of the little dwellings showed lights dimmed by drapes. At the far end of the block, a party, which seemed to be the source of the laughter, moved noisily across the grounds to the main hotel where the lounge had music, dancing and exotic drinks.

"Okay, it's safe," Jeff said.

"What's safe?" She whispered because he did, not because there was any reason.

"All I want you to do is stay here while I do some checking. If anyone comes back, stall them."

"I can't do that!"

"Sure you can. Please, Sara. I really need you to keep watch. I won't take long."

She didn't need to be told it was Bent's bungalow. Wilcox was involving her in a crime. She'd end up making doughnuts in an Arizona prison. She'd look vile in an orange jumpsuit!

"I won't be an accessory to breaking and entering."

"I'm not breaking in. I managed to get a pass card from housekeeping. At worst, it's illegal entry, and I'll get fired, not you."

"You're a double-dealing crook. You lured me here to play Bonnie to your Clyde."

Had he kissed her just to soften her up for his latest escapade? She was surprised how much that hurt.

"You're exaggerating. I'll only take a quick look. A few minutes at most. Please, Sara."

She could imagine him as a little boy, always wheedling an extra cookie or late permission at bedtime in that ingratiating voice.

"If you're afraid, I'll understand," he said in a low, seductive voice.

"Five minutes. Then I'm gone. If Bent comes back and finds you, I hope he sends your sorry butt to Mars on the next alien shuttle."

"You're a doll."

He planted a soft kiss on her forehead and was gone.

Sara closed her eyes until she heard the sound of a door opening and closing. If she didn't see him go inside, she wouldn't have to lie at his trial.

"No, judge, I didn't *see* the defendant enter Barrett Borden Bent's bungalow."

She'd never been so nervous, not even in the eighth

grade when Jimmy Osborn talked her into going down to the school's boiler room at noon break. And that had turned out badly—very badly. He kissed her too energetically, and his braces had hooked on hers and loosened them. Her parents had been summoned for an emergency trip to the orthodontist. She'd deserved to be in trouble, but everyone had been so darned amused.

The luminous numbers on her watch seemed to be stuck. Seconds lasted minutes, and five minutes seemed like an eternity.

"Ohmigosh, ohmigosh, ohmigosh," she said under her breath.

She heard unmistakable footsteps on the path. How could she knock on the door without being seen running out of the trees?

Risking a look, she saw Bent lumbering up the path to his bungalow. He was wearing another of his theatrical robes, this one glowing a sickly yellow when he passed one of the lights.

She was going to be sick. Orange jumpsuits and shackled ankles flashed through her mind, but not for being an accessory to illegal entry. She was going to murder one rotten *Phoenix Monitor* reporter!

For reasons she didn't understand, she couldn't let him get caught red-handed. Summoning her entire reserve of courage, she stepped to the middle of the path to pretend she was returning from an evening stroll.

"Mr. Bent!"

The silver-haired guru squinted in her direction through owl-eyed wire-framed glasses. The great eye color had been contacts. He looked ten years older peering nearsightedly through the gloom with his hair still limp from splashing in the fountain.

"I am so grateful to you, Mr. Bent," she said loudly enough to be heard at the main hotel. "I walked this way hoping to see you, not that I'd intrude on you in the privacy of your bungalow."

"Who are you?" He took off his glasses, blew on the lenses and replaced them.

"Sara, the assistant pastry chef. Remember the fountain—the accident? It was so noble of you to take the blame. Otherwise I would've lost my job for sure."

"I'm a little night-blind, but I'm not deaf, young lady," he said.

"Oh, sorry, sir."

If Jeff hadn't heard her, he was on his own. All she wanted was to hightail it back to her room.

"If you'll excuse me," Bent said.

He tried to step around her, but she was faster than he was.

"I was worried you might be hurt. Have you had a doctor check you out?"

"No, that wasn't necessary. I'm fine. Now, if you'll excuse me—"

"Thank heavens! I know I wouldn't have been able to sleep tonight if I'd caused injury to a famous man like you. I've followed your work in the newspapers, and it's fabulous." She crossed her fingers behind her back as she told one whopper after another.

"Yes, well, thank you. Sara, is it? You can pick up some of the First Contact literature in the saguaro room, lower level of the main hotel. Feel free to help yourself."

"Thank you so much, Professor Bent."

Apparently his lack of a title was a sore spot Dr. Hill had been quick to attack, so she gave him one. He didn't correct her.

"I would be absolutely thrilled to hear one of your lectures, sir. Unfortunately, my job keeps me occupied," she said, trying to give Jeff time to disappear.

She was going to be sick for real. Kissing up to a slime bag like Bent was making her nauseous. At least he seemed to be eating it up. He wasn't trying to get past her anymore.

"Perhaps I can give you the gist of my findings in a private meeting," he said in an oily tone that made her skin crawl. "Of course, we'd have to be discreet. I can't possibly devote as much individual time to my followers as some would like. I wouldn't want to arouse any hard feelings from a First Contact member who wants more attention."

She was going to kill Wilcox! Thanks to him, the old goat was leering at her like a walrus in heat.

"I'd feel guilty having you waste your precious time on me," she said. "But I am so glad you're not hurt. I'll sleep much easier tonight, I can guarantee that."

"If you ever feel a need for some personal illumination on the state of the universe..." Bent gave it another shot but didn't beg.

"Good night, professor. It's been such a pleasure chatting with you."

He mumbled goodbye and headed toward the door of his bungalow, key card in hand.

She ran toward her room hoping she looked like a

jogger, not a panicky felon. If Jeff got caught, Bent would know she'd been helping him.

Every time that reporter came near her, she ended up in trouble. She loathed Wilcox. He'd done it again, involved her in one of his schemes, and she'd been stupid enough to fall for his charm. Was the word *sucker* tattooed on her forehead? Was she wearing a sign on her back that read Kick Me? Why did he think she lived to be his unpaid, unappreciated sidekick? Even Boo-Boo got the leftovers from Yogi's picnic basket heists!

Still, she couldn't help worrying whether he got away all right. She certainly gave him a prolonged warning. But even if she fretted about it all night, she wouldn't go to his room to check.

She opened her door, surprised to find it unlocked. Of course, Wilcox had been the one to close it. It was no trick to keep the door from locking automatically. These rooms didn't have the security of the guest rooms.

Something moved in the darkened room, and she shrieked.

"Don't be afraid. It's only me."

Jeff turned on the light on the nightstand, and she wanted to pummel him.

"What are you doing in my room?"

"I guess you forgot to lock the door."

"No, I didn't. You were the last one out."

"A girl should always be sure her door is secure."

"I'll make doorknob rattling my new hobby. Why are you here?"

She was relieved to see him and tried to convince herself it was only because she didn't want to be implicated in his caper.

"I knew you'd be worried about me."

"My only worry is that someone will catch me helping you with one of your schemes. Did you get out of Bent's room before he saw you?"

"Piece of cake. I went out the back way to the patio. The sliding-glass door locked automatically behind me, so he'll never suspect someone was in his room. Thanks for the warning."

"I merely had a short conversation with a guest," she said stiffly, sitting on the bed and slipping off her shoes.

"Sure you did." He grinned.

"I hate being a spy! I'm constitutionally unfit to be an undercover agent. Why do you get me into messes like that?"

"I like your company. Anyway, I had it under control."

"It's Taste of Phoenix all over again. You don't care what happens to me as long as you get your story. Did you find a Martian under Bent's bed?"

"I didn't find anything, but that doesn't mean there isn't anything to find. I'm just starting this investigation."

"Well, count me out. Pies and cakes are my game, not crime and crooks."

"I really needed you as a lookout. You did a spectacular job. I owe you big time."

"You promised not to involve me."

"I thought I promised not to get you fired. So far, I haven't."

"You won't have any more chances."

"I'm sorry, Sara. The last thing I want is to cause trouble for you. You were perfectly safe tonight."

"You could at least ask before you risk my life, limb and liberty. Not to mention my career."

"If I did, would you go along with me?"

"No way!"

"Well, thanks anyway. Maybe if the baking business doesn't pan out, you can get a job as a lookout for bank robbers. You have a talent for it."

"You are…"

He ducked out the door and shut it just as she scooped up a canvas shoe and hurled it in his direction.

7

SARA WALKED to door number seven in the staff quarters, then hesitated instead of knocking. She squinted at the spy hole, wondering how she looked from Jeff's side. What would he see if he looked through it and saw her standing there bug-eyed with a nose the size of Pike's Peak?

"Chicken," she scolded herself, still not knocking.

She'd hardly seen him for two days. Maybe she should leave well enough alone. He'd roped her into being his lookout and left her to distract that slimeball, Bent. She should be grateful Jeff was staying away from her.

Instead she missed him—well, sort of. For two days she'd snapped to attention every time she caught a glimpse of hair the color of bittersweet chocolate or of round sexy buns in skintight black trousers. Unfortunately, even in the kitchen she hadn't managed to catch sight of him for sure. A small army of servers came and went at every meal, but he eluded her.

He was doing exactly what she'd asked, and she hated it. Worse, she was furious at herself for caring. She couldn't possibly be falling for the rotten reporter who'd made her lose her job at Dominick's. No way!

For one thing, they had nothing in common. He didn't

know a crème brûlée from bubble-gum ice cream and couldn't care less. Her parents didn't understand why she wanted to be a chef instead of something practical like an accountant or a teacher. If they were puzzled by her dedication to pastry art, how could a pragmatist like Jeff understand?

Not that his career made much sense to her. He was like a hound dog sniffing a trail when it came to unearthing a story. He didn't seem to have room in his life for anything else.

She wanted a Mr. Right in her future after her career was well established, but Jeff Wilcox was Mr. Wrong, no doubt about that. The sooner he left Las Mariposa, the more secure her future would be.

Once he got his story, he'd leave. Then she could concentrate on her job instead of fantasizing about the rotten reporter. She rapped sharply on his door. Anything she could do to help would send him back to Phoenix sooner.

She had to knock a second time. He finally opened the door with a cell phone pressed to his ear.

"What do you mean, he's missing?" Jeff motioned her to come into the room but didn't stop talking on the phone. "He has to be someplace."

Unflappable Wilcox sounded rattled. He treated breaking and entering like a walk in the park. What could possibly make him so agitated?

His room was almost identical to hers, but he'd turned it into a combination office and dump. The bed was unmade, the pillows bunched up like punching bags. He was living out of an extra-large dark green duffel bag with clothes spilling onto every available surface. Apparently he didn't believe in using closets or dresser drawers. It looked as if he was visiting, not staying for an indefinite period of time.

"Sit if you like," he said, muffling the phone for a moment.

The only free space was on the bed, so she stood.

"Damn!" he said explosively. "This isn't like him."

His room could pass as temporary housing for a sloppy waiter except for a table overflowing with newspapers, several books and a laptop computer that looked high-tech and expensive, not the kind of equipment summer help brought to play games.

"Sorry about that," he said, after signing off on the phone.

He raked both hands through his hair, turning the sleek, combed look into a tousled mess. Truthfully, she liked it better that way.

He found a spot for the phone on the crowded table and gave her his full attention, seemingly seeing her for the first time since she'd come into the room.

"You look nice."

The way he said it gave her a warm glow but also made her self-conscious. She had changed to come see him, choosing a short white denim skirt and a V-necked sleeveless top in bright raspberry. She wanted him to see her in something besides the starchy jacket and baggy pants she wore to work.

"Thanks," she said. "Is something wrong?"

"Just a family matter."

She knew a little about his family. He had divorced parents and a married sister with kids, but he wasn't forthcoming about whatever had him on edge.

"Oh, I'll leave you to it then," she said, having serious second thoughts about being in his bedroom.

Coming to see him was a bad idea. Worse, he might not want her there. He had been avoiding her, after all.

"No, don't. It's my dad." He stepped between her and the door.

"If you need to talk to him some more..."

"I wish!"

"Has something happened to him?"

She never seen him look so worried, and her heart went out to him against her better judgment. Was she strong enough to comfort this dynamic man without putting her heart at risk?

"I don't know. He's been acting goofy lately, evasive. I haven't been able to reach him the last couple of days, so I called one of his poker buddies. Dad hasn't shown up for their regular games in at least three weeks. The guy I called was kind of ticked at him. Dad cleaned him out about a month ago and hasn't given him a chance to win back any of his money. That's not like my father. I think his friend is worried, too."

"Didn't he let them know he wasn't coming to play?"

"He made some vague excuse the first couple of times, but now even his cronies think his behavior is odd. They're mostly old newsmen like him, and they don't have a clue what he's up to."

"What do you think?"

"I'm worried he may have a health problem, maybe something affecting his short-term memory. I haven't been able to reach him by phone, and none of his friends are any help."

She could hear the frustration in his voice. It had to be terrible not to know where your own father was.

"Have you checked with hospitals?" Dumb question. He made his living running down information. "I mean, with your connections in Phoenix..."

"He hasn't turned up anywhere. I'm going to have to beg for some time off and drive down there. He's been out of contact long enough to file a missing person's report if I can't locate him myself."

"I'm really sorry. You must be worried sick."

"Sara, sweetheart, I know you hate getting involved in my work, but would you please keep an eye out for me? Just so I don't miss anything big while I'm gone."

He looked at her with moist dark eyes that pleaded for help. She felt as mushy as the cream puffs that had fallen into the fountain.

"I can do that," she weakly agreed.

"I'll get back as quickly as possible. I'll find one of my cards for you. It has my home, work and cell phone numbers. Call me any time, day or night, if you see or hear anything suspicious. But don't do anything to make Bent suspect you're spying on him. Promise me you'll stay well away from him."

"That's an easy promise. He wants to give me a private lecture on alien arrivals. I'd rather be knee-deep in leeches."

"You're terrific." He smiled, and the glow on his face was brighter than the sun slowly sinking in the western sky.

"What exactly am I supposed to watch for?" she asked, already dreading the obligation to spy on the flamboyant con man.

"Just keep your eyes and ears open. If you see any shady behavior, pass the info on to me. Don't let him know you're interested in anything he does."

Too late for that, she thought ruefully. Bent already thought she was a cult groupie.

"Thanks, I owe you," Jeff said.

He leaned forward and kissed her cheek so sweetly she was ready to bungee jump into a river full of crocodiles if he asked.

"I'll do what I can." And she hoped she'd soon recover her sanity.

"Here's my number." He rummaged in his duffel, found a business card and tucked it into her hand. "I'll keep in touch."

He squeezed her shoulder and walked her to the door, still assuring her of his eternal thanks.

The guilt hit as soon as he closed the door behind her. He thought she was helping out of the kindness of her heart. Her plan had been to offer help so he'd leave the resort sooner. How could she resist falling in love with him when he was so sweet and grateful? The last thing she needed was the burden of his gratitude.

Her cheek was tingling where he'd kissed her. Her heart was pounding from the light touch of his hand on her shoulder. She was in trouble, big trouble. This love business was like sinking in quicksand with her feet trapped in mixing bowls of hardened concrete.

She hurried to her drab little room and decided it was past time to check in with Ellie. It was a very bad sign that she wasn't missing her sister, her friends or her old life more.

JEFF FOUND exactly what he expected when he got to the Phoenix apartment he shared with his father. Len was nowhere to be found. Half a dozen phone calls confirmed it.

The natural thing to do was contact the police, but his dad would go ballistic if he wasn't actually missing. He'd disappeared several times in the past in pursuit of stories, but he wasn't a working journalist anymore.

Jeff paced the living room, leaving the sliding-glass door to the deck wide open so he could listen for the approach of his father's classic Corvette, long his pride and joy. He didn't hear any traffic noise on the driveway that meandered through the complex of four-unit apartments.

Jeff had a ground-floor place, two bedrooms and two baths. It'd seemed spacious until Dad moved in with a huge brown leather couch, an enormous rolltop desk and a couple of thousand pounds of books, newspaper clippings, files and career memorabilia. Stacks of the stuff jammed closets and filled every available corner in piles that threatened to become paper avalanches. Sharing digs with Dad had reformed Jeff's own casual habits. The place wasn't big enough for two pack rats.

He went to the efficient galley kitchen and made coffee to keep him alert while he paced and fretted. On the counter the blinking red light of the answering machine showed more than a dozen messages were waiting for Len to check them. Jeff didn't run through them. A lot were his calls to his father.

"Damn it, Dad," he said in frustration, looking out the door to the deck with cup in hand. "I have better things to do than worry where you are."

Bent's First Contact group reeked like rotten fish. His instinct told him the confrontation at the SLOT luncheon was only a minor skirmish before the big battle.

But it wasn't just the story that bugged him. He wanted to be with Sara so badly he couldn't concentrate on finding his father or exposing Bent. Next he'd be doing something really goofy, such as writing love poems or begging her to have his babies.

"Dad, where are you?" he muttered.

He gulped the last of the coffee, still too hot for comfort, and was tempted to drive up to the resort. What would she do if he knocked on her door in the middle of the night? He'd love to see her sleepy-eyed in something pink and frilly. A see-through black nightie he could peel off very, very slowly would be even nicer.

Just thinking about her made him hot. He went out on the deck, but it would take more than a desert breeze to cool the inferno igniting below his navel.

There was no future in hankering after the little pastry chef. He had a disappearing dad and a round-the-clock job. He was lousy marriage material, and his track record at relationships was abysmal. It ran in his family. Len had been a pretty good dad when he was around, but a rotten husband. Jeff had never blamed his mom for finally calling it quits. The wonder was she'd put up with her husband's absences and work obsession as long as she had.

He must have missed the sound of Len's car, but he heard the scratching of a key on the door lock and got there before his father could get it open.

"Jeff, I wasn't expecting you back tonight," he said.

"Where have you been?"

"Have I missed something? Now I have a curfew?"

"I left a dozen messages. You never called me back," Jeff said, his anger rising.

"That machine is a damn nuisance. Telemarketers drive me nuts. If you want to investigate a bunch of swindlers, start there."

"Telemarketers don't leave messages," Jeff said dryly.

"Well, the boys have been callin' and leavin' messages beggin' me to play poker. Guess I've won a little too much of their money lately."

"Where have you been?"

"Felt in the mood for a movie. Saw one of those martial arts things. Lousy script. All the jumping around was pretty silly without good motivation."

"You don't like movies. You always pan them."

"Well, I'm retired now. I've got time to give them another chance. Maybe I'll whip up a decent script myself one of these days."

"You haven't been at the movies for two full days. That's how long I've been trying to reach you since our last talk on the phone."

He didn't want to admit how worried he'd been, so he covered it with irritation. The old man would only pooh-pooh his concern.

"What are you doing home? Story finished?"

"Far from it. I thought you were missing."

"Well, I'm not. The day I need a baby-sitter, I'll walk into the desert and keep going until I dry up like one of those weeds that blow all over the place."

Jeff had a lot more he wanted to say, but he'd known the crusty old goat too long to bother. Maybe he was being a mother hen, treating his father like a senile old man. In his place, he'd probably resent being smothered, too. But darn, what was this disappearing act?

"Any mail?" Jeff asked.

"I haven't had time to check."

"Spending a lot of time at Fat Ollie's?"

"None of your damn business if I am. Don't you have a job to do? You didn't get canned, did you?"

"Not yet." Jeff shrugged. If his father wasn't going to tell him anything, he might as well get some sleep before he returned to Las Mariposa. He didn't have to be back until tomorrow's lunch shift, and he was too tired to play road tag with semis at this time of night. Popping in on Sara was a nice fantasy, but she wasn't likely to welcome him with open arms.

"Do me one favor, will you?" he asked his father. "Check your answering machine once in a while."

"Okay, okay. I'm gonna hit the hay. When are you leaving?"

"Fairly early in the morning."

Against his better judgment, he wanted to see Sara before he had to report to John, the bullnecked bully.

8

KENNY WAS trusting her to do more creative baking. This morning he'd let her use her own recipe for zucchini bread, which boded well for future employment.

Thank heavens her professional life held possibilities. So far she'd steered clear of the rivalries and jealousy that characterized many first-class kitchens. She and the sous chef would never be bosom buddies, but Ms. Sharpe had started calling her Sara instead of Madison. No one called the second-in-command Sonya, however, and Sara still snapped to attention when Mr. Cervantes inspected her work. At least no one seemed to blame her for the cream puffs in the fountain.

Her personal life was something else, akin to sitting on a slow-heating grill waiting to be scorched. Besides wanting to see Jeff for his own sweet self, she had news for him. She couldn't wait to share her small triumph.

She took the last beautifully browned zucchini loaves out of the oven and put them on cooling racks. She had to prepare the bread baskets for lunch, lining them with white linen napkins and filling them with freshly baked cloverleaf rolls.

Every time a white-jacketed server reported for the luncheon shift, she was distracted from her job. Las Mariposa liked to hire tall, good-looking males to staff the dining room. The few token women tended to be tall and dressed in the same uniform of tight black trousers and starchy white jackets. Since the job at hand didn't give her a good view of the parade of servers, she was hard-pressed to keep track of arrivals by glancing over her shoulder.

Would Jeff show up for his noon shift? She wanted to be indifferent, but she was acting like a teenager with a monumental crush. Despite all the craziness that had plagued their relationship this far, there was something about him that made her miss him.

She finished the baskets of rolls and walked to another counter to help Kenny brush fresh dairy butter on individual chicken potpies. Fortunately she'd trained herself not to let luscious aromas make her appetite go berserk.

"Kenny, a lady wants to know if there's any garlic in the potpies," a welcome voice said.

Jeff came up behind her and let his knee graze the back of her leg for an electrifying instant. Fortunately the head pastry chef was too absorbed in his work to notice.

"A smidgen," Kenny said. "I only did the crusts, but Sonya can't make oatmeal without using a clove of garlic."

"Thanks, I'll remember that."

Jeff smiled at Kenny, who ignored him since the servers belonged to a lower order of humans, in most chefs' opinions. Sara followed Jeff to the counter where the baskets of rolls were waiting to be delivered.

"I have something to tell you," she said.

"We can't talk here." He picked up two baskets and gave her a secretive little grin.

"How's your father?"

"Not sick or missing. Beyond that, I'm not sure. How about we meet for a late dinner? I have to work a private party, but not for cleanup. I should be able to get away shortly after eight."

Could she wait that long to spill her news? She was so jumpy about this undercover business, even breaking yolks seemed stressful. But unless they wanted to meet in the frozen food locker and risk becoming human Popsicles, she didn't have a choice.

"Okay," she said with reservations.

At least she knew what Jeff liked to eat—fast food with lots of fries. It wasn't as if she'd agreed to a romantic dinner for two with candlelight and a violinist.

"Good. I'll come to your room as soon as possible. Wear something nice."

Wear something nice? Before she could ask what he meant by that, he dashed to the dining room to take care of his tables.

She obsessed over his wardrobe suggestion until her shift ended at two, then went to her room and took a much-needed siesta.

Her first thought when she awoke in the cold, stale air-conditioned atmosphere of her temporary digs was, *Wear something nice.*

She did own something besides work clothes. Her social life in Phoenix had its ups and downs, but she couldn't complain about a lack of men—only the absence of one special one.

The decision of what to wear was still hard. What if she dressed like it were a real date, and he showed up in grungy clothes perfect for a place where toys came with the food? She decided to chance it and put on something that would knock the wind out of his sails.

Jeff knocked on her door just as the big red numbers on her alarm clock by the bed turned to eight-seventeen.

She slipped into dainty black heels that added two inches to her height, smoothed the skirt of her black mini dress over her hips and adjusted the thin straps that left most of her shoulders bare. She'd arranged her hair so curly tendrils fell down the sides of her cheeks, and she didn't need makeup to appear flushed.

If he was wearing baggy shorts and a raggedy T-shirt, she was going to feel like an idiot for listening to him. She took a deep breath and opened the door.

"Hi," he said.

Who was this gorgeous man? He was wearing a black blazer with brass buttons, lightweight gray slacks and a shirt so white it dazzled. He even had on a tie, a genuine necktie in muted shades of dusty blue and gray, not one of the bolo things so popular in Arizona. His hair was damp but parted on the side and combed into a wave across his forehead. As always, his deep brown eyes dominated his face.

He smiled, and she let out a low whistle.

"Do I know you?" she teased.

"I'm the tall, dark and handsome stranger who thinks you're beautiful."

"Th-thanks."

He's only an ordinary biped, she warned herself, *certainly not someone to stammer over.*

"I did some research," he said, standing in the doorway. "The best Mexican restaurant in Sedona is El Supremo. Thought it'd be a good idea to make a reservation. I can cancel if you'd like to go somewhere else."

"No, El Supremo sounds wonderful. They'd have to be good to use a name like that without opening themselves to ridicule, wouldn't they?"

"That's what I thought." He grinned sheepishly and stepped aside to let her walk into the hallway. "I'm a neophyte in the world of gourmet dining. There's a lot you can teach me."

The way he said it made her think he could teach her a few things, too.

They walked up a garden path to the employee parking lot, which was the farthest from the main hotel. She expected him to drive something utilitarian, all-terrain or four-wheel drive to help track down stories. Instead he led her over to a low-slung silver-blue sports car.

He opened the door for her and helped her slide into a luxurious interior upholstered in worn silvery leather.

"Nice wheels," she said, trying not to sound too impressed.

"That's why I borrowed them from my dad. Told him I had a date with a gorgeous woman and didn't want to make her ride in old Betsy."

"Betsy?"

"I like to name my vehicles alphabetically. My first one was Angie, short for Angelica. Drove her until she blew a gasket with a hundred and seventy-two thousand miles on the odometer. I haven't trusted Betsy since I had to put in a new transmission three years ago."

"How old is this car?" she asked when he'd settled down behind the wheel and put on his seat belt.

"Over twenty-five years. Dad got it when I was five,

and he's treated it better than he ever did Mom. He's been behaving so erratically, I didn't want him taking any long trips in it. My car is good enough for him to use around town. Not that you don't deserve a classic car for our first date."

"It's not a date. I only agreed to go so I could tell you what I learned."

"Would you mind if we eat first? I had a sausage-and-egg biscuit about twelve hours ago and nothing since."

"You're allowed to eat lunch when the dining room closes."

"Didn't have time. Remember, I'm working two jobs."

"Then I'm wasting your time."

"No, darlin', you certainly are not."

He started the car and eased his way out of the parking area.

She had to admit their conversation sounded like first-date small talk. They covered places they'd lived and people they knew in a general way as they wound their way toward town.

"Why did you decide to be a pastry chef?" he asked finally.

"I love doing creative things, and my desserts make people happy."

"And maybe a little fat?" he teased.

"An occasional sweet treat is good for morale and mental health," she said. "People who appreciate fine food aren't necessarily overweight. They eat selectively. What about your line of work? What do newspapers do for people?"

"I deserved that question."

"Well?"

"Well, here we are," he said, pulling up to a pink stucco restaurant with a green-striped awning and red-jacketed parking valet.

He was a lot better at asking questions than answering them, but it didn't matter. She was caught up in first-date excitement, something she hadn't experienced in ages. There was nothing quite like being with a handsome, charming man who was doing everything but handstands trying to please.

For a fast-food man, he certainly knew how to arrange a dinner date. El Supremo was everything a south-of-the-border experience should be. The decor included a lush tropical garden with plants and trees in huge earthenware pots and broad skylights. The colors were warm and bright, from the smooth ruddy brick floor to the red, yellow and green pattern of the seat covers on wrought-iron chairs.

They were seated against a far wall at a table for two made intimate by a cove of greenery. Before she could begin to absorb all the ambience, a server in a bright burgundy jacket and black trousers had delivered the best margarita she'd ever tasted.

"May I order for you?" Jeff asked over the sound of a mariachi band wafting to their table from the lounge area.

She was too surprised by his offer to object.

"That would be nice, thank you," she said.

He didn't disappoint. Their salads had fresh, crisp greens trimmed with avocados, fruit and cheese. Her entrée was a chimichanga with shredded beef and green chili with tortilla boats on the side filled with sour cream and guacamole. He had a mushroom, chicken and cheese enchilada with warm crispy taco chips. They sampled each other's dinners, sipped sangria and talked about everything and nothing as if they'd known each other for ages. The dining style at El Supremo was leisurely, and the waiters gave excellent service without hovering.

"Would you like dessert or an after-dinner drink?" Jeff asked, his eyes sparkling even more than usual as the candle in a glass globe between them burned low.

"No, I couldn't possibly. This was wonderful, Jeff."

"I'm glad you enjoyed it." He positively glowed with satisfaction. "How about coffee?"

He liked it the same way she did, strong and hot. She accepted a refill, not because she especially wanted it but because she didn't want the evening to end. She wished their relationship had started this way instead of...

Whoa, girl! she thought, startled by the way she was thinking about Jeff. What relationship? He was still trouble with a capital T, and she'd better not forget it.

"I think it's time to get back to business," she said.

He blinked like a man who'd been caught catnapping.

"You're right," he quickly agreed. "I don't mix work and play as a rule, but I wanted to do something to thank you for helping me."

Was there a worse way to spoil a romantic dinner than by writing it off as gratitude? She was angrier at herself than at him. The man lived for his work. Everything else was secondary, and she'd better not forget it.

"Do you want to tell me what you learned?" he asked after an awkward moment of silence.

"One of the room service waiters was bragging that he delivered a bottle of the best champagne on the wine list to Bent's cottage."

"So your news is that Bent has good taste? Or expensive habits?"

"No, I didn't read dozens and dozens of Nancy Drew mysteries for nothing," she said triumphantly. "He ordered the champagne with two goblets."

He nodded, trying to look interested, but he obviously didn't get it.

"Two glasses with a bottle of Las Mariposa's best, which is very good indeed."

He wasn't impressed with her big lead. She felt let down but wasn't willing to concede defeat.

"Obviously he's up to something more than work," she said, trying not to sound exasperated by Jeff's denseness.

"You do have a point, I guess. Good work."

"Don't be condescending. Bent is obviously having an affair with someone."

"He isn't married. Been divorced twice, so he probably is—"

"That's not the point! He hit on me, but he didn't dangle high-priced champagne as bait. He must have ordered it for someone he really wanted to impress."

"Maybe you are on to something."

He smiled and reached across the table to push a tendril away from her cheek. Suddenly it was very hot in the restaurant.

"You know, that's not a bad idea," he said.

"Bent having an affair?"

"No, ordering champagne. For us. To celebrate."

"No, thank you. We don't have anything to celebrate."

"That's it! You're a genius! I should kick myself for being obtuse."

Jeff's sudden enthusiasm startled Sara and made her forget how warm she was.

"What are you talking about?"

"What was Bent celebrating? His confrontation with Hill was a major flop. Didn't even get him a few inches in the papers. The *Monitor* keeps tabs on people who have story potential, and he didn't get a whisper of publicity from it. So maybe Bent's secret agenda is coming together the way he planned. Let's get back to Las Mariposa."

"Thank you for the dinner," she said stiffly when they were outside waiting for the valet to bring the classic Corvette after Jeff had hurriedly paid the tab.

Jeff took her hand, squeezed it and softly murmured, "I lied."

"About what?"

"I wanted to be with you tonight. The dinner had nothing to do with gratitude."

She couldn't believe how good his words made her feel.

They said little as they started back, but Sara felt as though they'd passed beyond the need to fill their time together with words. When they stopped at a light before reaching the highway, Jeff rested his hand on her knee then slowly pushed her skirt higher. She put her hand on top of his to press it hard against her nylon-clad leg.

A horn sounded impatiently behind them.

"I guess a green light means go," he said, his voice too soft and husky to be talking about a traffic signal.

"It means go," she confirmed.

She took a deep breath, totally aware of the heat and scent of his body in the confined space. His body chemistry gave his aftershave the sweetness of vanilla cookies baking in an oven, and she wished she could snuggle against him.

The road to Las Mariposa twisted and turned to a higher elevation. The dark silhouettes of the cliffs seemed even more impressive because the Corvette rode close to the road, taking the curves like the engineering marvel it was. Jeff drove expertly, neither speeding to show off nor poking along like an insecure mountain driver.

When they reached a straighter, less demanding stretch, he reached over, took her hand and laid it on his thigh.

"I don't want to distract you," she said.

His muscle was firm under the slippery cloth of his trousers. She drummed her fingers for a moment, then worried he'd think she was nervous.

She was. Where was this evening leading her, and did she want to go there? Her heart said a resounding yes, but the longer she knew Jeff, the more complicated her life became.

"Want to play a mind game?" he asked, his voice soft and sexy.

Oh, yeah, there was an idea. She'd love to let him know what she was thinking, especially her curiosity about how it would feel to...

"I'll start," he said. "Would you rather run barefoot

through a hundred cherry pies or kiss a hot bachelor on his funny bone?"

She laughed with relief. The choice was silly enough to put her at ease.

"It's a lot of work to make that many pies. I guess it depends on where the funny bone is."

"You have to answer the question as asked. It's the rule."

"Your rule! I guess I'd have to take pity on the person who made the pies and kiss the funny bone."

"Good answer. Now it's your turn."

She wanted to know everything there was to know about this man, especially how important his job really was to him.

"Would you rather wait tables for the rest of your career or be celibate for the rest of your life?"

"You're a wicked woman."

She held her breath, wondering if he'd choose his job or his love life. The silly game was taking on more significance than she would let herself admit.

"You made me answer, so you have to," she said when he hesitated.

"I don't know if I'm capable of doing either."

"Not an answer."

"Ask me something easier, like whether I'd rather walk on hot coals or live on sushi."

"Which of those would you choose?"

"No contest, hot coals. Now it's my turn."

"You didn't answer my question."

"You asked me whether I'd choose hot coals or sushi. That counts."

"You cheated!"

She pulled her hand away and bunched it with the other on her lap, resolving not to say another word to him.

He chuckled softly but didn't try to defend himself.

Minutes later they reached the resort and drove into a rear entrance to the employee lot.

"It was a lovely dinner. Thank you," she said, deciding a dumb game was no reason to be cranky.

"My pleasure."

He got out and hurried around the front to open the passenger door for her. Somehow the hand that helped her out ended up around her waist, and their bodies came together. She looked at him in the soft light from a lamppost just as his mouth descended.

She could feel his kiss all the way to her toes, and her lips parted with a will of their own. He wrapped his arms around her, holding her so close they were breathing in unison. His tongue slid between her lips and teeth, then against her tongue. She closed her eyes and saw stars brighter than those in the brilliant canopy of the sky.

"Not here." He released her and stepped back.

"Not here," she repeated, meaning somewhere else.

He locked the car and took her hand, leading her down the dimly lit path. Sounds of a pool party wafted through the grounds, occasional shrieks of pleasure carrying in the still night air. Down by the creek a man and a woman seemed to be arguing, their words indistinct even if Sara had cared to listen.

The squat building where temporary employees stayed showed several squares of light, but less than half of the dozen utility apartments were occupied. Those staying there were mostly young men hired on a temporary basis. Sara rarely saw them.

Inside, the corridor was deserted. Jeff released her hand when they stopped in front of her door.

"This is where I ask your place or mine?" he said softly. "Give you a chance to tell me to get lost."

He gave her a small, self-deprecating smile, the tiny frown lines by his eyes deepening. He never seemed unsure of himself, which only made his hesitation more appealing.

She took the key out of her little black leather shoulder pouch to give herself time to think. Trouble was, her brain was the only part of her not in overdrive.

"I'm not prepared." She was talking emotional readiness but realized she'd phrased it badly.

He took the practical tack.

"I am."

"You planned—"

"No—yes, sort of."

"Which?"

"I hoped."

He took her in his arms and kissed her slowly, then trailed his lips to the sensitive hollow below her ear. She shivered—strange, because the hall wasn't air-conditioned—and pressed against him to share his warmth.

It was all the invitation he needed to take the key from her, open the door and kick it shut behind them.

This wasn't real. It couldn't be happening. Wilcox was her evil nemesis, the cocky reporter who'd nearly scuttled her career. Nothing good could come of this. All he cared about was his career.

It was the last cry of a drowning woman. She ran through all the reasons to avoid him and fell into his arms in the dark room.

His hands wandered down her back and cupped her bottom, making her squirm even closer. He suckled the fullness of her lower lip, hot-wiring places she'd never suspected were erotic.

"Do you mind if I turn on a light?" he whispered.

"No."

He moved to the bed, and the yellow glow of the lamp on the nightstand made the situation seem more real. She was about to do something really unwise with someone really wrong, and she wanted him so much she was ready to rip off her clothes at this very instant.

Amazingly, Jeff had the cooler head and greater patience. He slipped out of his blazer and beckoned her with his eyes.

She'd never made the bed after her afternoon siesta, but he didn't seem to notice. He sat on the edge and gazed at her with bedroom eyes that melted her last tiny bit of resistance.

"Sit on my lap," he said.

He patted his thighs, and she remembered touching his leg in the car. He had wonderful legs, muscular and strong. No way she could refuse his invitation.

Somehow the lap thing didn't quite work. Her miniskirt rode up, and her panty hose were slippery. She slid between his legs when they started kissing. He helped her up, but her bottom tumbled to the side, leaving her knees across his lap.

"Lie back," he said, kicking off his dressy loafers and lying down on his side.

She lay facing him, exchanging fun kisses that neither demanded nor committed them to anything. But my, he was a good kisser. Who knew necking was still so much fun? Gradually they lost bits of clothing. He slid her dress over her head because it was twisted around her breasts and decidedly uncomfortable. She loosened his belt when the buckle threatened to leave an impression on her hip. He squirmed out of his shirt and took her hand, guiding it to the zipper on his trousers.

It was decision time. She was no tease, and nothing had ever felt as good as being beside him, letting his hand rove over all her private little pleasure places. She reached out and lowered his zipper one little nub at a time until he sighed with anticipation.

Did she have enough nerve? He was hard and huge under the stretchy cotton of his skimpy black briefs. She quickly withdrew her hand, suddenly timid of so much masculinity.

"When you're ready," he murmured, sounding a bit stressed but wrapping her in his arms.

She loved his bare chest, reveling in the whorls of soft dark hair on the muscular contours. She rested her cheek in the curve of his arm, tickled one chocolate-dark nipple with her tongue and longed to stretch out naked against him.

He fondled the black satin cups of her bra until her nipples ached pleasurably, then hovered over her and stripped off the garment.

"You're more beautiful than I imagined," he said, kissing her breasts and rolling his tongue across the hard, dusky pink nipples.

They kissed, greedy for the taste and touch of their

lips locked together. His breath was hot on her cheek and eyelids. She tickled his ear and throat with hers. She was feverish and eager but doubtful anything could be better than the touch of his hands and lips.

When he parted her thighs, still encased in nylon, she pushed his hand against her and felt teary-eyed with anticipation.

"Let me."

His voice was hoarse as he went on his knees on the floor and slowly rolled the panty hose over the swell of her hips and down her legs until they fell off the tips of her toes. His lips roamed up one leg, then the other, finally focusing where she wanted—needed—him the most.

When she thought she'd explode, he stood and pushed impatiently at his loosened trousers and briefs, lowering them into a tangle around his ankles and none too smoothly freeing himself. He was a bit awkward, but her heart pounded even more because of it.

"Oh, my, oh, my, oh, my." She unintentionally gasped, not shocked but wowed by the huge ruddy pinkness of his erection and the sheer cuteness of his adorable behind.

He stumbled toward his discarded jacket, took a foil packet from an inside pocket and returned to straddle her parted thighs.

"You wined and dined me with that in your breast pocket? What if it had fallen out at El Supremo?"

"I am El Supremo," he teased, typically avoiding her question, not that she really cared when he bent forward and brushed his lips against her tender, well-kissed mouth.

"Here." He handed her the packet.

She fumbled with the package and made a slow job of opening it, but he didn't seem to care, not in the least.

Now that the moment was here, she tensed, worried she might not be all he expected, afraid she'd never find release for her aching heaviness.

He stroked her thighs and groin, made lazy circles on her belly and kissed her torso, all the while beguiling her with gentle little nudges between her legs. His finger surprised her, and she heard her breath pounding in her ears.

Then he slowly, carefully joined his body to hers.

She wrapped her legs around his torso, clutching at his sleek, slippery bottom, making him plunge deeper and deeper as her nails dug into his muscular buttocks.

Their connection was electrifying. Someone was moaning, and she only vaguely knew it was her. Women sometimes faked the screaming, didn't they? She clamped her mouth shut so he wouldn't think she was acting, but sounds kept welling up in her throat.

Then he went rigid, she went ballistic, and fireworks exploded everywhere.

"Wow!" she said when the power of speech returned.

"I'll take that as a compliment."

He sounded a little smug and very, very happy. She couldn't fault a man who pulled her to the pillows and cradled her like a fragile china doll, at the same time helping her ride the most incredible roller coaster of sensation.

"Where do we go from here?" she murmured sleepily as a deep peace enveloped her.

"Give me a few minutes," he said, brushing moist curls of hair from her forehead, "and we'll see."

9

SOMETIME in the night one of them had had the foresight to set her alarm. Jeff thrashed around and slapped at the nightstand a few times, trying to find and silence the earsplitting annoyance.

"Oh, baby," he said, rolling toward her and burying his face in the golden hair fanned out on the pillow. "It can't be morning already."

Enough daylight seeped into the room through closed drapes for him to admire the smooth curve of her hip and the flawless skin on her back.

He moved closer and discovered a minor ache that confirmed they really had made love three times last night. It had to be his record, and he still wanted her fiercely and urgently. Nothing like this had ever happened to him.

He stretched lazily and realized he'd thought of it as making love. Amazingly, that's what it had been for him. He'd never met anyone like Sara, never before had sex like a man possessed and certainly never wanted a woman the way he wanted her.

He glanced over his shoulder and forced his eyes to focus on the bedside clock. Just enough time for a shower before he rushed to work. He'd better go to his room. If he tried to shower with Sara, he'd never make it to the dining room before noon. He wasn't ready to get fired, not when his intuition told him things between Bent and Hill would soon come to a head. Today was the last day of the First Contact gathering, so if anything was going to happen, this was the day.

So far he had suspicions but no proof, an idea but no story. His brain must be clogged with lint. When he was with Sara, he could barely remember why he was at Las Mariposa.

One thing he did recall with startling clarity. If he got Sara fired from another job, she'd hate him for life.

"Time to get up, sweetheart," he whispered close to her ear, unable to resist lightly kissing the lobe.

"Too sleepy," she mumbled, curling into a fetal position and tempting him to stroke her cute little behind.

"You have to go to work," he urged.

"Work?" She was still groggy, but the fog was lifting.

"You bake, me serve. Come on, sweetheart. I don't want to leave until you're on your feet. Don't want you getting fired."

He'd said the magic word and was rewarded by seeing her leap from bed stark naked. Even with unruly hair and bleary eyes, she was the most delectable female he'd ever known. If he didn't get out of her room, he might topple her back on the bed.

"What time is it?" she asked with a note of panic.

"Don't worry, you have half an hour, time for a shower."

"The yeast rolls have to rise. I should've gone in early."

"Yeah, right."

She looked at him and burst out laughing.

"Well, maybe not."

"You okay?" he asked, trying to sound like a gentleman even though she looked sleek and satiated in the best possible way.

Darn, he'd like to kiss her eyes awake and slip inside for a quickie. More than that, he'd like to spend all day with her, in or out of bed.

He got up and gave her a chaste little kiss on her rosy pink lips, all he dared in the circumstances. She watched as he bent to gather his clothes, most of them scattered on the floor.

"You have cute buns," she said as she watched, making no move to cover herself.

"Thanks. I thought they were just regulation issue, but then, I never see them."

He was pleased in an embarrassed sort of way, but he couldn't get his trousers on fast enough. He'd better make that a cold shower.

"Bent's party is tonight," he reminded her. "A garden party, no less. That will be a mess to serve."

"I absolutely refuse to deliver food unless they provide amphibians," she said, still watching him intently without moving.

He loved it that she was comfortable without rushing for a robe or something. It was all he could do not to take her in his arms.

They were both stalling, reluctant to go their separate ways. He wanted to tell her how fantastic last night had been but didn't know how to begin. He was a professional writer, but words failed him. If he said she was the best lay of his life, it would demean their lovemaking. If he said nothing, she might think it didn't mean anything special to him.

"About last night..."

He made the mistake of looking directly at her again. He completely lost his thought as he remembered how it felt to have her smooth, shapely legs wrapped around him.

Each breast was a perfect handful, firm and beautiful. Her tummy was taut and flat with a tight little navel that seemed to wink at him, and her beguiling triangle was a mass of ringlets. Still, he loved looking at her face the most. She had beauty that went beyond a perfectly symmetrical face, lively blue eyes, a pert nose and full, sensual lips. He could spend the whole day analyzing the way her shapely brows arched when she showed emotion. Her habit of pursing her lips when she was thoughtful made him feel mushy and vulnerable. He squirmed knowing how much power she had over him, but meeting her had been wonderful beyond belief.

He realized he was dangling his briefs in one hand and rumpled dark socks in the other. He threw on his pants and stomped barefoot into his cordovan loafers. Bundling his underwear with his blazer, shirt and belt, he grinned sheepishly at Sara.

"Nothing like dirty laundry to trash the romantic mood," he said.

"You looked great last night—all dressed up, I mean."

Her compliment took his breath away.

"You look great now."

"Oh!" She seemed startled to realize she was standing there casually naked. "Oh!"

She threw one arm across her breasts and dropped the other to cover herself farther down.

"It's okay. I'm leaving," he said, increasingly reluctant to do so.

She bent and grabbed her dress from the floor, giving him an awesome view of her beautiful behind. One more minute of voyeurism, and neither of them would surface before the sun went down again.

"Have to get ready for work. I have a split shift, breakfast and dinner. I'll see you later," he promised as he forced himself to walk to the door and open it.

"Goodbye," she said.

Now he had to worry whether she meant goodbye forever or goodbye for now. Life was so damn complicated when a woman got to you, but he couldn't pretend he regretted a single moment with Sara.

He showered slowly, not much caring if his boss, John, got on his case. One way or another, this job was winding down. Trouble was, he had squat for a story.

Bent was a phony, no doubt about that. Maybe the champagne with two glasses was significant, but nothing about the old goat's sex life would be printable. The *Monitor* wanted to expose him as a fraud, not go into competition with the tabloids. So far he'd been too cagey to tip his hand. He was undoubtedly milking his followers for astronomical sums, but he was too clever to give away his game.

Jeff stepped out of the shower and started dressing, thoroughly disgusted with himself and with Decker Horning. His editor should've set him up as a guest so he could mingle more easily. He spent far too much time working his butt off slinging high-class hash. He needed to interview more of Bent's followers. There were sure to be a few who were disillusioned enough to give Jeff some hints. He needed a more comprehensive background check on both Bent and Hill, and Deck was going to have to get him some extra help for that. He was going at this story like a rookie, and there was no point blaming his father or Sara for distracting him. He was a pro, but he'd been acting like a reporter on a high-school paper.

What if the tip the *Monitor* had received about Bent had been based on a grudge? What if the alien chaser was on the level, a genuine kook instead of a con man? Management would quickly forget Jeff's work in bringing down Rossano if he blew the Bent story. Or if he'd wasted all this time when there was no story. He might have chucked it earlier if he hadn't wanted to be close to Sara. Politics, mobsters and corruption were more up his alley than little green men.

Damn, he was tired. He needed a solid eight hours to clear the cobwebs from his head, but he didn't regret a single second of sleep lost with Sara.

SARA HURRIED through a shower, dressed in her most utilitarian cotton panties and bra and pulled her wet hair into a ponytail.

"I don't want to go to work," she said to the steamy mirror over the bathroom sink.

She surprised herself by admitting it. What she really wanted was to crawl into bed and sleep around the clock, or better still, sleep in Jeff's arms, cuddling against his broad, silky-haired chest, their legs entwined.

Even leaving Jeff out of the picture—which was practically impossible—she didn't much want to report to the kitchen. Getting to make zucchini bread aside, working here wasn't like Dominick's where she could make whatever she liked as long as it pleased his customers and made a profit. Mr. Cervantes ran his staff as if they were at boot camp, even managing to suppress the whining and temperamental outbursts typical in most kitchens. Where was the fun if you didn't dare vent once in a while?

Kenny was a nice boss, but he was a pressure cooker waiting to explode. A misplaced swirl of frosting was enough to ruin his day, and he was still obsessing over the soggy cream puffs lost in the fountain.

Maybe she wasn't ready for big-time baking. She'd liked working in Dominick's slapdash kitchen because he paid little attention to her work most of the time. Meat was his passion, big red chunks swimming in a sea of sauce.

Or maybe she was so darn tired she was goofy.

"Goofy over Jeff Wilcox," she told her mirror.

She hurried, but not because she was eager to start preparing fancy desserts. She hoped to steal a minute or two with Jeff if there was a lull in the breakfast rush. The man was habit-forming. She was addicted to having him around.

Luck was with her. She didn't have to wait to see him. They both left their rooms at the same moment and linked fingers.

"Haven't I seen you somewhere before?" he asked.

His attempt at humor fell short, mainly because his sour expression gave him away. He looked as if he'd just gargled with vinegar.

"Walk with me," she said, seeing no reason to avoid being seen with him now that she wasn't worried about the job. "We have to hurry."

Compared to being with Jeff, work held all the appeal of a cruise on a garbage scow. But she had to remember he'd soon be leaving the resort and going back to Phoenix, back to a job that was everything to him. How much would she see him then?

Unfortunately she still had to keep this job. Her résumé would read like a rap sheet if she was fired two times in one month.

"Yeah, we'd better get to work," he said, releasing her hand and opening the door to the outside.

"You sound a little crusty," she said as she sprinted to keep up with him.

"Trouble in the desert city. Our source has disappeared."

"Your source?"

"Bent's disgruntled ex-follower, the one who put us onto the story. She isn't answering her e-mail or phone. Another reporter went to her home, and she's bolted. Either she concocted the stuff about Bent being crooked or she's running scared."

"Which do you think it is?"

He stopped abruptly, giving her a chance to catch her breath.

"He's a phony, no doubt about it. He rakes in huge sums from the believers, but there's no story unless we can prove fraud or misappropriation of funds."

"Can you do that?" She was more interested in his story than she wanted to admit. In fact, there was nothing about Jeff that didn't intrigue her.

"Deck, my boss, has half the newsroom backing me up, but so far zilch. If there's a story, I have to find it here. It's not going to pop out of a computer. We haven't been able to find where he banks all his loot. Who knows, it could be in a vault at the bottom of the Grand Canyon or even a Swiss account, where we'll never find it."

"What are you going to do?"

She fervently wanted him to stay longer at Las Mariposa even if it meant she would be taking big risks to help him.

"Serve breakfast." He smiled and continued to walk. "The rest of the day I'll try to cut a few of Bent's followers out of the herd, if that's possible. There have to be a few malcontents in First Contact. Maybe a spouse who was roped into coming or someone Bent has pissed off."

"I'll think of you while I make lemon tarts with a splash of Cointreau."

"Do that."

He took her hand again and led her around the back corner of the hotel to a spot obscured from sight.

The pool was closed, and she could hear the pool cleaners working behind the privacy fence. Seize the moment, she thought, putting her hands on Jeff's shoulders and tilting her head.

He didn't disappoint. His kiss was as sweet as the first one last evening. It did nothing to make her eager to start working.

"What else are you baking today?" he asked huskily.

He didn't care, and she knew he didn't care, but she was willing to recite every recipe in her file to keep him close. He kissed her lowered lids and tickled her forehead with warm whispers of breath. Stolen kisses were tremendously exciting, she decided, trying to focus her mind on the work list for the day.

"I'm supposed to make pistachio tarts with almond flavoring and a generous dollop of amaretto."

"You're trying to get the guests drunk on dessert?" he asked.

"Beats me. Rum-soaked plum bars are on the schedule, too." She stepped away reluctantly. "I've never made them before, but Kenny said they're easy. That's what he usually gives me, the easy stuff."

By the time she did all her regular baking and made seven-layer chocolate tortes with candied walnuts, she'd have to put in a twelve-hour day. She would be paid overtime, but money couldn't compensate for time away from Jeff.

"Is all that fancy stuff for Bent's outdoor party tonight?" he asked.

"Yes, I'm pretty sure it is. If they eat enough of my desserts, they'll be seeing little green men from Mars behind every cactus."

He rolled his eyes. "Yeah, they're seeing things stone-cold sober, so it's hard guessing what a booze-soaked dinner will do to their imaginations."

"Seeing what things?" She looked toward the kitchen entrance where a couple of servers were going in to work. They were still half-asleep and didn't look in her direction.

"All I know is what I've overheard in the dining room. Some of the alien chasers loosen up after a few after-dinner—or after-lunch—drinks. I heard a couple of women obsessing about mysterious lights in the sky earlier in the week. They clammed up when one of them spotted me clearing a table nearby. Everyone I've talked to is secretive. The First Contacters like to give the impression they know something no one else does. The true believers are definitely charged up about something, but so far no one's talking, not even to their friendly waiter."

"Maybe Bent sent them e-mail from Mars," she said dryly.

The more she saw of his followers, the more skeptical she became. Even the ones who looked perfectly normal acted sneaky, as if they were up to no good. Of course, that was only her interpretation. She'd be sorry if real aliens landed and took her to their ship, but it wasn't on her list of worries. Losing Jeff and her job were.

"Yeah, right, or they cracked the secret military files about flying saucers." He sighed. "Get to work, wench, before all this talk of the paranormal makes me hopelessly horny. Right now I'd like to rack up a score on the tennis court that would give the resort something real to buzz about."

"If you're going to talk delightfully dirty, I had better report to work. All I need is to be fired for lascivious behavior. A nice final touch on my résumé."

Maybe she was still giddy from last night, but her whole life was beginning to seem like one big joke.

"Go," he ordered, turning her by the shoulders and giving her a tap on the bottom. "I'm sworn to protect your job, remember?"

"Oh, pooh."

She rubbed the offended cheek, which in fact tingled

but didn't smart, and tried to give him an evil look. It was hard to do when she was giggling.

"I'll see you later," he said.

"Aren't you going to work?"

"Yes, but I mean that I'll see you for real, not a passing glimpse."

"I'll have to work most of the afternoon, I'm afraid," she said.

"That's okay. I have a lot of people to run down, including some of Hill's group. It's time this superhero reveals his true identity, selectively of course. But I'll catch up with you. You're on my radar."

"Do you want me to help you?"

She was going bonkers. She'd go anywhere and do anything to be Jeff's sidekick.

"You're volunteering?"

"Maybe."

"It's hazardous work with no pay," he said, falling into step beside her as she slowly moved toward the door to the kitchen.

"No rewards at all?"

"Many rewards, but not monetary," he promised. "If you're a good girl."

"A good girl!"

She quickly looked in all directions, saw no one and swatted his bottom.

"Payback," she said.

"Ouch!"

"You're faking. It was a love tap."

"Yeah, I knew that."

He leaned down and kissed her, a quick one that took off the last of her lip gloss.

"You need your mouth wiped," she warned.

"Not a chance. I want big John to drool with envy."

"Doesn't matter to me. Kenny wouldn't notice if I wore blue lipstick and purple eye shadow. Now if I don't put enough raisins in the cinnamon coffee cake, he'll pick up on that immediately."

They'd stalled too long already. She was a woman with a career, such as it was. She had to go into the kitchen and start doing what she'd been hired to do. She pulled open the heavy door and held it for Jeff so she'd feel in control and dedicated to duty.

"Thank you, ma'am." He leaned toward her and whispered into her ear, making her shiver with pleasure. "I want to kiss you from the tip of your nose to your big toes."

She giggled and walked into the kitchen.

10

IT WAS a tailgate party without the gate. Jeff and a harried crew of servers were providing the tail, and he'd been running his off since John roped him into setting up for the outdoor banquet at five o'clock. Now it was late evening with the sun sinking in the western sky, great for scenery but lousy for serving a huge boozy banquet.

"Why the hell can't they eat inside?" Brad, the kitchen gopher, groused as Jeff helped him unload trays of fancy little cracker things from the converted golf cart.

"Good question," Jeff said.

He'd been wondering the same thing as he set up serving tables on a paved area behind the lodge. The First Contact crowd had swelled to double or triple the number of those registered as hotel guests, and they were still coming. The traffic jam kept the security staff hopping, and Bent had ordered enough food to feed a stadium of football fans.

The meal would be a buffet, and already people were spreading blankets on the ground for picnic-style dining, rightly suspecting there wouldn't be enough portable tables and chairs for everyone. The gardens with the resort's famous cacti collection were in danger of being trampled, and two servers had been assigned to keep people away from them. A few people had started using the fountains as garbage cans. Bent must have laid out a tremendous sum to bankroll a party like this. The question was why?

"Need any help, big boy?"

Sara came up behind Jeff and put her hand on his shoulder as he was easing a tray of salmon hors d'oeuvres on to the table. He laughed at himself because she'd startled him.

"I tried to find you earlier," he said, grinning like a chimp and not caring.

"You can't believe how much we had to bake for this party. It's an orgy."

"Oh, I believe," he said, steering her to a spot behind the tables where they were less apt to be overheard. "I've lifted a couple of tons of it."

"I meant what I said. How can I help with your real job?"

"Bent is laying out a fortune for this party. If he's the con man we think he is, he expects a big payoff from it. Something's going to happen. I can feel it in my bones."

"And they're such nice bones."

"Are you flirting with me, Sara Madison?"

"Outrageously, unabashedly, you bet."

"Good, I'd hate to think I was only a sex toy to you. Did I tell you I've been propositioned fourteen times since I got here?"

"No! You're making that up," she said, her mouth agape.

"I wish!"

"Wilcox, go help with the cash bar," John yelled at him.

"I'm not a bartender," Jeff yelled back. He was getting damn sick of taking orders from the overbearing pain in the butt.

"Doesn't matter. They're swamped at the bar." John gave Jeff a look that said, "Do it or find yourself another job."

"Bent's people are everywhere," Jeff grumbled.

"I'll walk you down to the creek," Sara said. "You can tell me what to do."

"I don't want you taking any chances," he said emphatically.

"I can keep my eyes open while you're stuck making drinks."

"You could watch for Bent, but don't go anywhere near him. I don't trust the guy."

"I can handle Bent."

"Sara, don't be brave. Be cowardly. Keep out of his sight. Don't even think of approaching him."

"But I could—"

"No."

They were passing the thicket of sycamore trees that partially concealed the drab building where employees lived. He took her hand and pulled her off the path, not stopping until they were behind a concealing clump of foliage.

"You must have some use for me," she said.

"Lots of uses."

He pulled her close and kissed her soundly. It took all his willpower to release her.

"Be serious, Jeff. I can be a second pair of eyes and

ears. I'm going to do it anyway, so you might as well give me some clue what to watch for."

He growled close to her ear, making her giggle and back away.

"Stop that!"

"I take that as an invitation."

He kissed her again, longer and harder, ready to chuck the job and the story to tumble Sara between the sheets. Just to be with her. He liked sparring with her verbally as much as he liked seeing and feeling her.

"I've heard John is one mean dude. You'd better get to work," she said.

"He won't get me fired tonight. This party is more than the staff can handle. I'm surprised you haven't been drafted to help."

"Mr. Cervantes wouldn't hear of it. He thinks chefs are an elite group."

"Mr. Cervantes is a snob."

"Well, yes, but he runs a tight ship."

"You like that?"

"Sometimes, but you'd better get to work. You'll be mad at yourself if you get fired before you get your story."

He sighed. "You're right, but I'm worried about you. Don't do anything reckless. Promise."

"All right. I'll just watch Bent's cottage. If I see anything suspicious, I'll tell you."

"Okay."

He had a bad feeling about involving Sara. They'd been lucky when he searched Bent's bungalow, even though she had handled herself well. Bent was investing a lot in this party, so he must be gearing up for something big. Jeff wanted Sara well away from it.

"And, sweetheart," he said in what he hoped was a seductive tone, "we'll talk when this shindig winds down."

"Yes, I'd like to...talk."

She walked away, her bottom wiggling provocatively in navy shorts. If she'd dressed to take his mind off his work, she'd succeeded. Her halter top was made of some stretchy pink material with skinny straps on her sleek golden shoulders. A hint of flesh showed between her shorts' waistband and her top, and his fingers itched to touch her.

"Be careful," he warned again, but she was too far away to hear his husky words over the thunderous rumble of the large crowd eager for food, drink and excitement, not necessarily in that order.

STANDING in a clump of trees watching an unlit bungalow was just plain boring, but Sara decided to stay a little longer. She couldn't see Jeff at the sandwich bar serving as a drink stand, but the crowd pressing around it was high-spirited—make that loaded with spirits—and noisy. He'd probably be stuck there for a long time, and there was nothing she wanted to do but be with him.

The sky was dark, and the lights on the grounds didn't penetrate her little thicket. It was a bad place to be found by an amorous drunk but a good place to see any activity near the bungalows. She suspected she was wasting her time, since everyone she needed to spy on was at the party, but everything she did without Jeff seemed dull and pointless. Was this true love? If it was, why was it so complicated? She had the awful feeling he was only hers as long as his assignment lasted. He was married to his job, and she wasn't up to being a part-time mistress.

She was getting drowsy, bored with watching and definitely short of sleep, when someone opened the door of Bent's bungalow.

It wasn't Bent. His nighttime visitor was considerably more slender and, from what Sara could make out in the dim light from the path, definitely female. She was wearing a black running suit and a baseball cap pulled low over her forehead.

Unless Sara's imagination was playing tricks, Dr. Hill's wife, Carmela, was sneaking out of Bent's cottage carrying something in what could be a duffel bag.

What should she do? Jeff had warned her not to do anything risky, but Carmela was hurrying away from the noise and activity of the party. She'd soon be out of sight, so there wasn't time to get Jeff.

Was Carmela connected to the investigation of Bent? Did Sara want Jeff to get his story and leave the resort? Absolutely not! But she cared too much about him to let this opportunity slip away.

What was Carmela doing in the cottage of a man her husband hated? All the scientist's wife needed was a ski mask to be a chic burglar. Where the heck was she going? Was it possible Hill was the real bad guy, using his wife to break into other guests' rooms?

Nah, not likely, but Carmela had Sara's attention. To satisfy her curiosity, Sara had to know where the creepy lady in black was going.

Following her past the darkened cottages was easy,

but Carmela was sure to spot her on the well-lit entrance road. Sara needn't have worried. Mrs. Hill kept to the shadows and avoided the lights of the resort. She crept out to the bridge over the highway that golfers used to reach the course. It was just wide enough for a golf cart and designed for daylight use. Only widely spaced, recessed lights, which were kept low to avoid creating a glare for motorists passing underneath, illuminated the span.

Sara waited until Carmela was all the way across so she couldn't hear her footsteps, then made a dash for it. The ramp down the bridge had a gritty, paved surface that allowed her to run without slipping, but tailing the woman got harder when Carmela went beyond the lights of the clubhouse and disappeared somewhere beyond it.

The nine-hole course had lush grass fairways. Maintaining them was an extravagant waste of water in a dry state, Sara thought, although it was probably essential to attract the hotel's clientele. At least she could run in relative silence except for her rapid breathing, brought on more by nervousness than exertion.

She lost Carmela.

Wait. A faint light was bouncing around on the ground, probably the beam of a small flashlight. Sara moved forward silently.

Carmela was standing on a rocky outcropping in what was probably the golf course rough. Her flashlight was lying on the ground, shining on the bag she'd carried from Bent's cottage.

Sara watched wide-eyed with curiosity as Carmela took out a boxy object and put it on the grass next to her.

Sara didn't like the spy game. She didn't like being on the golf course in the dark where snakes and scorpions could be slithering all around her.

Suddenly the risk seemed worth it. Carmela was holding something that looked like a large Christmas wreath. Picking up the box she'd removed, Carmela began doing something and the round-shaped object rose above her.

Sara's mouth dropped open in astonishment. Carmela Hill had just launched a flying saucer.

The lights on it dipped and fell, scurried in different directions, then Carmela sent the object across the highway in the direction of the resort gardens.

Sara didn't dare move, didn't dare confront Carmela or race back to tell Jeff. All she could do was watch helplessly while Carmela's UFO darted across the resort and did a show for the true believers who were probably so full of food and drink they were already having their own visions.

Sara was having a close encounter, and it was totally bogus.

After a few minutes, the halo of lights swooped back to Carmela, but it seemed like ages to Sara. She had to get to Jeff, but not before Carmela finished her act. Sara crept as close as possible without being detected.

The stunt was brilliant in its simplicity. She saw Carmela pack a remote-controlled model plane, the kind men and kids loved to play with. Lights had been rigged in a wire circle on top to give the appearance of a UFO when Carmela sent it soaring over the First Contact party.

Sara wanted to pounce on the deceitful woman, but Carmela was bigger and possibly armed. She belatedly heeded Jeff's advice and decided not to risk confronting her. She didn't have to wait long for Carmela to hurry away with the evidence of her fraud, and Sara was quick to follow.

FOR THE FIRST TIME that evening, the party guests deserted the bar. So did the two bartenders, who took advantage of the excitement to slack off. Jeff found himself alone, staring at lights that zipped across the resort grounds and disappeared on the other side of the highway.

Pandemonium reigned by the lodge, where the party had turned into a mob scene. The excitement was unreal as First Contacters began hugging one another, some of them crying with joy. Jeff was torn between finding Sara and watching Bent manipulate his followers. Earlier the con man had brought out a huge box painted with stars, which had been guarded by a couple of thugs. All evening he'd been working the crowd for contributions to welcome their alien brothers and sisters, assuming, of course, that space visitors came in two genders. The nonbelievers, resort staff and SLOT skeptics who observed his performance, scoffed at his idea of a landing pad and hospitality center for space visitors, but Bent successfully milked the crowd. They'd probably turn their pockets inside out and empty their bank accounts now that proof of an alien ship had supposedly arrived. And Jeff had no evidence to prove what the darn lights really were.

Decker was going to hate this story, and Jeff was going to hate writing it even more. But right now, all he wanted was to find Sara.

She wasn't watching Bent's cottage anymore, but then, it had been a boring job. He'd only agreed to have her wait there because it was a safe distance from the night's activities.

He circulated from the line of sycamores to the fountains and garden, then back to the lodge through clusters of naive believers. He hated the hysteric reaction of the First Contact people and at the same time felt sorry for them for being so gullible. If that had been a ship from outer space, he'd eat his laptop computer.

Sara was nowhere to be found. He tried to ignore the knot of anxiety that cramped his stomach as he questioned staff people who might have noticed her. He thought of checking her room. The window was dark. She wouldn't go to bed when so much was happening.

Much to his relief, she found him when he went to the temporary bar intending to search along the creek behind it.

"You won't believe what I saw!" she said.

She was breathless and flushed, and he took her in his arms automatically, feeling the rapid beat of her heart as he held her close.

"I know, a flying saucer."

"No, I saw Carmela Hill flying a remote-control model plane with lights. She came out of Bent's cottage, and I followed her to the golf course. She made it fly over the resort. *That* was the UFO."

"Carmela and Bent in cahoots?" He whistled through his teeth. "She helped him set up his followers for a big score? I knew he never believed in little green men!"

"She's been a big phony all along, pretending to hate Bent. Remember how she snarled at him when his followers invaded the SLOT luncheon? It was all an act. She's no dutiful scientist's wife. Now you can expose both of them."

"I can't."

"What do you mean, you can't?" She pulled away from him.

"I need hard evidence to write about it."

"I'm a witness. I saw her come out of Bent's place and fly that model plane. I don't make up stories like that."

"I believe you, but we need concrete evidence to go public in the *Monitor*. Carmela can probably round up witnesses to swear she loathes Bent and never went near the golf course. It would be your word against hers."

"What about the champagne for two?"

"I checked it out with the room service waiter. He didn't see a woman when he delivered it."

"So basically my stakeout was a bust," she said morosely.

The crowd had deserted the area by the bar, but Jeff and Sara could still hear the excited buzz of the believers. Bent was likely having no problem bilking them out of their life savings to build a fantasy landing strip for aliens. None of his followers would believe Dr. Hill's wife had been behind the sighting.

"You did great," Jeff said, "but no more sleuthing on your own, okay? I don't want you getting hurt."

"We can't let them get away with this."

"They won't, I promise." He brushed a soft kiss on her forehead. "I need something from my room. Stay here and watch the path to the bungalows. I'll be right back."

She stayed behind the bar and found herself pressed into bartender duty when a very drunk but exuberant couple came up demanding vodka on the rocks. What ice remained was floating in a tub of water, and the inebriated party guests settled for plastic cups filled to the brim with the clear liquid. She couldn't find the cash box. The bartenders must have taken it away, so she couldn't give them change for a twenty.

"Keep the change, little lady. This is an historic occasion. The world will take notice now," the burly, bearded man said.

"You tell 'em, honey," his companion said, running her fingers through her upswept hairdo, which was dyed brilliant orange. Her tongue snaked out to lap at the vodka.

When they moved away, Sara didn't know whether to abandon the bar or keep covering for Jeff. Fortunately, he didn't make her wait long.

"What's that?" she asked, looking at a small, black, rectangular object in his hand.

"Camera."

"You're going to take a picture of Bent and Carmela together?"

"I wish! She'll probably avoid him until they're both well away from here. Wonder where her husband thinks she is."

"He's not here. I just heard one of the SLOT members say someone else took his meetings today. He had to see someone in Phoenix, I guess."

He looked at her with admiration and smiled his approval. "You're a wonder. Now you'd better go to your room and keep out of sight."

A loud cheer went up from the direction of the lodge.

"No way. I'm sticking with you."

"Sara, much as I love your company—"

"Sticking like glue."

"I may be committing a felony."

"You're going to break into Bent's cottage?"

"Alone," he insisted.

"No, I'm coming with you."

"Okay," he said, "but we have to hurry. When Bent wrings the last dime out of his followers, he may check out and disappear."

"What do you think we'll find in his room?"

"Not we, me. You stand watch."

"No way! Look what happened last time. I'd rather take my chances on breaking and entering than have Bent catch me alone outside again."

With a sigh of resignation, he took her hand and propelled her down the path that followed the creek to the guest bungalows.

"How will we get in?" she asked when they reached the concealment of the trees opposite Bent's door.

"Wait here."

"Stop that!" she protested, following him when he darted to the door.

He took a strip of metal out of his trouser pocket. Before he could start poking around to pick the lock, the handle turned under his hand, and the door crept inward.

"Carmela must have left it open in case she needed to get inside," Sara said.

Jeff led the way into the living room and eased the door shut behind them, taking care to set the lock.

"Here's our UFO," Jeff said with satisfaction, seeing

the remote-control model peaking out of its duffel, which was sitting on the desk. "Pretty clever, really. A lot smoother than tossing pie pans or using a kite."

He snapped several shots of the plane and the controls beside it before covering it up again.

"Now we have the evidence. Let's go before Bent comes," Sara urged.

"We have a picture of a toy plane. It's not evidence until I can link it to Bent and prove he used it to defraud his followers. We need a paper trail, like a sales receipt for the plane, but that still isn't enough for a *Monitor* story."

"I don't like this."

The soft scrape of footsteps outside the door made them both jump.

"Someone's coming!" she whispered frantically.

Jeff grabbed her hand, and they raced toward the bedroom to the sound of the lock being released. The only way out was through the sliding-glass door to the patio overlooking the creek, but there wasn't time to open it.

"In here," Jeff whispered, pulling her to the room's one closet. He slid the door shut just as they heard the front door opening.

Bent was speaking in a muffled voice, and it took a minute to realize he was talking on a cell phone.

"He's alone," Jeff said. "Now how the hell are we going to get out of here?"

Crowded behind Jeff, Sara was enveloped in yards of clinging material. She'd backed into Bent's lineup of robes. The one flapping in her face smelled of stale sweat, and she ducked away from it, grabbing Jeff's waist to keep her balance.

"What are we going to do?" she whispered.

She was pressed against Jeff's backside with nowhere to go except into the forest of smelly robes.

"If he doesn't go out again, we'll have to wait until he's asleep and sneak out."

"What if he decides to pack his robes and leave?"

"Then we have a problem, Houston."

"Why do I let you get me into these messes?" she asked.

"Me? I told you to go to your room."

"What if he puts the plane in this closet?"

"If he opens the door, we're busted, but he may not be eager to have us blab about his remote-control UFO."

"Ouch!"

"What's the matter?" he whispered urgently.

"You backed onto my toe."

"Sorry. Here, wiggle up beside me." He moved over an inch.

"There's no room."

"I've been in tighter spots," he said, close to her ear.

"With other women?"

"Do you really want to know?"

She did, of course, but didn't say so.

He made room by putting his arms around her and holding her so close she could hardly breathe. Even hot and bothered, he smelled much, much nicer than Bent's theatrical robes.

"Oh!"

"Sorry, I didn't know where else to put my knee," he said so quietly she strained to hear.

She was facing him, sitting on his knee as she used to sit on her father's when he gave her horsey rides. But she wasn't a squealing little kid anymore. Jeff's hard kneecap was making her crazy. She wiggled to ease the pressure and found out he had a big problem, a very big problem.

"I didn't mean—not here— Sorry." She wasn't sure why she was apologizing.

"It's not a convenient place, but you do have that effect on me."

He managed to find her mouth—actually she made it easy—and kissed her long and hard, cupping her bottom and pushing her against him. She moaned with pleasure, a little too loudly in the circumstances.

"Quiet!" he ordered.

"You made me—"

He clasped one hand over her mouth, but the other was so delightfully busy she couldn't resent it.

"Bent's here in the bedroom," he whispered.

"Uh-oh."

"I think he went into the bathroom." He stopped to listen. "Yeah, he's in there. I hear water running."

"Can we get past him?"

"No, it's not the shower, so there's no chance."

"I'm never going to do anything like this again," she vowed. "It's too scary."

"Hold on. If he does catch us..."

"Have you considered the possibility that he's dangerous?" she asked. "You know, guns and ozzies and stuff like that."

"I don't think there's a weapon called an ozzie."

"Well, you know, a machine gun."

"Be cool—and quiet."

"Is the water still running?"

"Yes, but it doesn't help us. He'll see us if we try to get to the patio door."

"Leave this to me."

She yanked at her shorts, sliding them as low on her hips as possible without losing them, and exposed her tummy and navel. She had to give the old goat a distraction.

"Get out the back as soon as you can," she ordered, opening the door just enough so she could slip out before he could stop her.

Once in the bedroom, she planted her bottom against the door and used her legs as leverage so Jeff couldn't get out without knocking her over. Then she fluffed her hair, making it fall over her shoulders.

Licking her lips nervously, she planted one hand on her hip, partly to hold up her shorts, and tried to look as seductive as possible, considering she was scared to death and keeping Jeff in the closet with butt power. Behind her she could feel him trying to push the door open, but she stayed firm.

Bent came out of the bathroom and tossed a robe on the bed. He wasn't quite as frightening in yellow shorts and an orange T-shirt that said Aliens Are Among Us.

When he caught a glimpse of her in the light spilling from the bathroom, he jumped as if he'd sat on a cactus. He hit a light switch.

You would think he just saw a pointy-headed green alien, Sara thought with some satisfaction, less afraid.

"What the devil are you doing here?" he asked, with none of his professional con man congeniality.

"I've been thinking about your offer." She purred as

seductively as possible to a man who had fat legs covered with gray goat hair. No wonder he wore robes!

"What are you talking about?"

He sounded angry but his eyes told her he hadn't missed her short shorts and bare belly.

"I was so excited when I saw the UFO. I mean, I just had to see you. I'm dying to know where you think it came from. You're the wisest man I've ever met."

"This isn't a good time."

His protest was pretty weak, so she strolled toward the door to the living room, deliberately throwing her hips from side to side.

"I know how valuable your time is, but I'd do anything…"

She let her voice trail off, partly from distaste at what she was doing but mostly because Jeff was listening on the other side of the closet door.

"Well, I do need to unwind," Bent said, following her. "Come sit by me on the couch."

"Oh, I was so hoping we could be together under the stars. Maybe the alien ship will come back just because they know you're here."

She'd reached the front door. He was wavering. She was slightly nauseous, but desperate situations called for desperate measures.

As soon as Bent got within reach, she took his arm and let her fingers graze the inside of his elbow.

Yikes, he did have a body odor problem. No wonder his robes stank. She gritted her teeth and slinked outside with him in tow.

She sighed deeply, counting to herself to gauge how long it would take Jeff to get through the patio door.

"Oh, look, there's a bright light over there, over the golf course," she said, trying to sound breathless and enthralled.

"Merely a bright star in the heavens, my dear."

The old windbag put his arm around her waist and spread his fingers on her bare midriff. She counted faster. Had it been a full minute? Jeff should be gone by now, but what if the investigative reporter couldn't resist a little snooping in the cottage? How long could she stand Bent's disgusting attentions?

"Sara, I've been looking everywhere for you," Jeff's voice boomed from behind her. "You have a phone call."

"Jeff!"

She broke free of the moist, pudgy fingers slipping under her waistband and ran to her rescuer.

"The young lady and I..." Bent began, sputtering as his easy victim got away.

They didn't wait for him to finish, instead hurrying away as fast as possible without sprinting.

"You came for me," she said happily when they were well away from Bent.

"Did you think I'd leave you to hang out to dry?"

"I thought you might need time in the cottage. I'm grateful, but, of course, I can take care of myself."

"Can you now?"

He pulled her behind a sycamore tree and ended the argument before it began.

11

THE NEXT MORNING Sara was put on duty at one of the portable cook-to-order stations in the dining room, making big Belgian waffles for the Sunday brunch crowd. Jeff was serving beverages to his tables, and she couldn't help watching him whenever she had a chance. She was looking forward to having Monday and Tuesday off, but would she be spending them with him?

She was putting a pecan waffle on a plate when Randolph Hill rushed into the dining room.

"Ladies and gentlemen, may I have your attention, please," he said in a loud voice. "I returned from Phoenix an hour ago, and my wife is missing. The hotel management hasn't been able to shed any light on where she may be. Her luggage and an empty purse are still in our room. Unless someone here has seen her this morning, I'll have to notify the police she's missing."

Sara's first thought was that Carmela had run off with her coconspirator, taking the loot from last night's fundraising, but she spotted Bent at the far side of the room. He was demolishing a skillet of ham, eggs and fried potatoes with a stack of pancakes on the side, calmly wolfing his meal at a table with three of his followers.

She glanced at Jeff, and he raised his brows in puzzlement.

"I saw her in the lobby early this morning when I went out for a run," said a thin, studious-looking man with rimless eyeglasses who was attending Hill's seminars. "It was around five."

"Thanks, Jim." Hill looked genuinely worried in spite of his stern exterior.

"She's been abducted. I'm sure of it!" A woman with graying braids stood up. "The UFO must have come back and taken her. Tell him, Mr. Bent."

Bent put his fork down and looked uncomfortable. "We mustn't be hasty, Lucretia, dear."

"What the hell is she blathering about?" Hill demanded.

A babble of voices assailed him, everyone trying to give his or her version of the mysterious lights the night before.

"This is nonsense," Hill said when he could finally make himself heard over the excited noise. "My wife is an avid runner. Most likely she went out early this morning and has had an accident. I'm going to call the authorities if hotel security can't find her soon. If anyone sees her, please notify the front desk immediately."

Bent, Sara noticed, was stuffing food into his mouth like a man expecting a famine.

"I know where she is," the braided true believer insisted. "She's been taken. I'm a sensitive. I know things."

Hill ignored her and left the room. Bent pushed aside the skillet and attacked the pancakes with knife and fork.

The all-you-can-eat buffet table was suddenly deserted. The guests in the dining room forgot about getting extra helpings and buzzed like a swarm of agitated bees.

Jeff was going to jump ship. Sara could see him arguing with John at the back of the room. When he stalked away, she followed him out the main entrance to the hotel lobby.

Before she could catch up, he ran to one of the hotel's two elevators and got on. The door closed, and all she could do was watch the indicator until the car stopped on the third floor

She pushed the up button and seethed with impatience until the second car returned to the lobby.

The elevators were in the center of the hotel, so when hers stopped on the third floor she had a choice between the right and left corridors. She went right, then swerved to the left and nearly collided with Jeff.

"What are you doing?"

For once he didn't tell her to go away because it was dangerous.

"This is Hill's room. I knew it would come in handy sooner or later to know his number. Look at this goopy green stuff I found on the carpet. Looks like somebody wiped the rest off the door. My guess would be Hill."

He caught a smear of it on his finger, sniffed knowingly, then held it under her nose. It definitely wasn't edible. She sniffed, then touched a glob on the door.

"Feels like the slime stuff kids play with," she said, remembering a ten-year-old boy in her sister's apartment building who loved the icky concoction.

"Just what I thought."

"Weird."

She watched Jeff wipe his finger on his white jacket,

which didn't indicate an intention to return to his job at the hotel.

"Someone wants Hill to think his wife has been abducted by aliens. He's too smart to fall for a green-slime trick, but imagine the hysteria if First Contact believers get wind of it," he said.

"They'll go bonkers."

"If Carmela really has disappeared, she isn't with little green men from Mars," Jeff said.

"If she's gone, why is Bent still here? Why didn't they both sneak away?"

"I was pretty busy last night." He grinned sheepishly. "But I seem to remember the First Contact party went on until dawn on the resort grounds."

"Your point is?"

"Bent couldn't let his followers see him leave with the loot. He has to play it cool. Most likely, he's going to skip the country after he has a chance to cash the checks tomorrow. If he's booked on a flight from Phoenix, he won't leave the resort until he can go directly to the airport and get on a plane."

"We're the only ones who know Carmela is his accomplice. No one will connect her disappearance with him, but he can use the uproar to quietly sneak away," she added.

"Bent probably rented an extra car for her. What better time to leave than while her husband's away overnight?"

Jeff stripped off his server's jacket and tried to conceal his holstered cell phone and tape recorder under the T-shirt he was wearing.

Much as she loved seeing his muscles ripple under the

white cotton knit, at the moment she was more interested in Bent's scheme.

"What are you doing?" she asked.

"Wiping off the slime before one of Bent's followers comes down the corridor and sees it."

"I take it you're not going back to the dining room," she said.

"Not an option, since I told John he has the brain of a sheep and the people skills of a rabid dog."

"And he didn't rearrange your face?"

"He wanted to, but I saved him the trouble by quitting and getting the hell out of there. Did I get it all?" He gestured at the door.

"There's a little smear under the door handle."

He wiped away the last trace of slime with the sleeve.

"What now?" she asked, watching him wad up the jacket and drop it on a housekeeping cart down the hallway.

"I'm going to follow Bent if he tries to sneak away. I'm betting he'll head for his car first chance he gets."

"Of course, he's depending on his followers to provide a diversion. I can see the headlines in the *Monitor*. Aliens Abduct Scientist's Wife and Leave Slime Trail."

"My editor would assign me the Martian beat if I came in with a story like that."

He walked rapidly to the fire stairs at the end of the corridor and swung open the door so forcefully it banged against the wall. She had to run to keep up with him.

"I'm going with you."

"No way. This isn't a game."

"You're not leaving without me."

He was going down the concrete stairs two at a time.

She had to yell to be heard, and her voice echoed in the stairwell.

"Wilcox, wait for me."

He stopped on the lobby level before opening the door.

"What about your job? Aren't you supposed to work until two?" he asked.

"I'll worry about that."

Surprisingly, she wasn't at all concerned. Maybe tomorrow she would be, but she wasn't letting Jeff out of her sight today. She deserved to see this through to the finish.

"Come on, then."

Jeff grabbed her hand and went out to the main floor, which was crowded with Bent's followers still chattering about Carmela's disappearance. The con man wasn't among them.

They raced out the main entrance, and she was surprised to see Jeff's father's Corvette parked only a few yards away in a spot reserved for arriving guests.

"You're lucky they didn't tow your car," she said.

"It looks like it belongs here," he said, running to the driver's side.

"I don't see Bent."

"You will. He's parked just beyond the curve in the entry road. I bribed Brad to keep tabs on the car for me. One more thing I have to do. Stay here, and I'll be right back." He sprinted to the hotel.

She waited impatiently for five, ten, nearly fifteen minutes. Was this Jeff's way of keeping her out of it? She was ready to look for him when he came running toward the car from the main entrance.

"Where have you been?" she asked.

"Just taking care of a few details."

They got into the 'Vette, and he eased the powerful sports car down the driveway until he saw Bent's rented vehicle, a white compact.

At least Jeff hadn't ditched her. She was too excited about catching Bent to fume about the long wait.

"Now the tricky part," he said.

Instead of waiting behind Bent's car, he pulled onto the two-lane highway and turned left.

"What if he goes right?" she asked.

"He won't. Our boy will head toward Phoenix. He's sly, so he'll have a plan to cash all the checks from contributors before he disappears."

"He might drive instead of fly."

"If he does, we'll be right behind him. Remember, he doesn't know anyone is on to him."

"And he still thinks his followers will go berserk when they find green slime on Hill's door," she said with satisfaction.

Jeff was good at this business. Not much got past him.

He found a level spot along the road and pulled off.

"Now we wait?" she asked. "Won't he see us?"

"He'll see a Corvette with a couple necking. With everything he has on his mind, he won't give it a second thought."

"What was that part about necking?"

He leaned over and nuzzled her ear, but that was all. She wished the seats were more conducive to cuddling.

"I've got to stay alert." He patted her knee and glanced into the rearview mirror.

"Wouldn't want you falling asleep," she teased, giving him a little squeeze that made him yelp.

"Bad girl."

He said it affectionately, then bent his head, giving every indication he planned to kiss her. Before he could, a white car streaked past them on the highway, throwing up a stone that pinged against Jeff's door.

"Damn." He pulled out so fast the tires squealed.

Sara knew how to get to the main highway and drive to Phoenix, but Bent wasn't headed that way. After a few miles he turned onto a dirt road that went through picturesque red bluffs, then followed a switchback that made it difficult for Jeff to tail him without being seen. He dropped back and slowed so much Sara was afraid they would lose Bent. Fortunately there were no turnoffs.

"Got him!" Jeff said after a few tense minutes.

Bent's car was parked on a broad shoulder. A dark four-door sedan was waiting farther up the road. It was a perfect place to stop for a scenic view, but the con man wasn't there to admire the scenery.

Jeff pulled up so close he practically touched Bent's rear bumper. He jumped out of the car and handed Sara his cell phone and a scrap of paper from his pocket.

"Time to call in reinforcements," he said. "Dial this number and say we caught up with them on a dirt road about seven miles from the resort entrance. I made sure we had backup when I went to the hotel."

As she punched in the number, Jeff raced toward Bent's car and ambushed him with the tape recorder.

The person on the other end of the phone answered immediately with a curt, "Yes."

Sara gave the message, pretty sure she recognized Hill's voice.

She also recognized the person hunched low in the seat of the second vehicle. It would take more than a baseball cap to disguise the woman she'd followed across a dark golf course.

Walking toward Jeff, Sara could see Bent's face was flushed with annoyance as he tried to beat a retreat toward the dark sedan, carrying a large maroon suitcase and a matching duffel.

"You've always appreciated publicity, Mr. Bent," Jeff said, cutting him off and holding the recorder close enough to catch anything Bent mumbled. "Where do you plan to build the alien landing strip?"

"I'm not at liberty to discuss real-estate holdings at this time," he said pompously. Apparently he still didn't realize he'd been busted, and he seemed to enjoy the attention too much not to spout off at Jeff. The man wanted to be in the limelight, good situation or bad.

"When do you plan to start construction? Have you selected a contractor? What's the anticipated cost?"

Jeff moved closer, an overeager reporter trying to pin down a reluctant interviewee. He seemed unusually pushy even for him.

"I recognize you," Bent said, his eyes widening. "You're the waiter at the resort, the one who can't remember to keep water glasses full."

"You weren't at one of my tables."

"What the hell are you trying to pull?"

"I work for the *Phoenix Monitor*."

"So you were working undercover. You're some kind of hotshot celebrity chaser."

"Not exactly. Now about last night's alleged sighting of a UFO..."

"Barrett, let's go!" Carmela urged in a piercing voice.

"I'm coming." He tried to sidestep around Jeff, but he was too flat-footed and slow.

"My editor doesn't take no for an answer. If I can't talk to you here, sir, I'll have to follow wherever you—and Mrs. Hill—are going."

Bent glanced at the sleek Corvette, no doubt convinced the sports car could follow anywhere he went in the sedate rental. Sara could tell he was trying to figure out the best solution, but none was coming. She watched as Bent squirmed, but she was more interested in Carmela than him.

She edged her way close to the dark car. She didn't know how they could stop the two swindlers from escaping. Her question was answered when a parade of four cars roared up the dirt road, two state troopers in the lead.

Two troopers got out of the front car and hurried toward Bent. A single officer in the second vehicle got out and walked more slowly toward the dark rental. Behind the police, Hill was getting out of a black two-door and Brad jumped out of a vintage VW, his complexion florid with excitement.

Sara was the only one close by when Carmela started to take off, throwing dirt and stones with her rear tires. Sara yanked open the passenger door and jumped in beside her.

"Are you going somewhere, Mrs. Hill?"

Carmela hesitated an instant, as though she expected

her to be Bent. Sara had just enough time to reach over and snatch the key, killing the motor then throwing the key out the open door on her side. When she turned to Carmela, Randolph Hill was standing next to the driver side window, staring at his wife with a look of chilling contempt.

Sara got out in a hurry.

Bent was cuffed, and he seemed to shrink beside the burly trooper who was reading him his rights. In wrinkled gray slacks, Bent had legs like an elephant, but no self-respecting pachyderm would stick its toes into neon pink running shoes like his. He was pathetic, and oddly enough, Sara didn't feel the least bit triumphant. She was glad to be done with the whole sordid business, but Jeff was taking in every word for his story.

"Cool," Brad said, coming up beside her. "Way cool."

The lanky young kitchen gofer had been on her list since she'd ended up on a golf cart in the fountain because she'd had to do his job, but he was the only one not in confrontational mode. She was glad to see his bleached-out spiked hair and freckled face.

"Wilcox is one awesome dude," he said.

Hearing it from Brad, she wanted to argue the point. She wasn't sure how she felt about the job that owned Jeff.

"Can you be arrested for faking a UFO sighting?" she asked, realizing she might have to do the whole witness-for-the-prosecution bit if Carmela was charged with a crime.

"That's the least of Bent's troubles," Brad said with

knowing smugness. "Jeff told me he has an outstanding warrant for arrest on fraud charges in Nebraska."

It was the longest sentence she'd ever heard from Brad. Maybe he was a semi-intelligent life form after all.

As if reading her mind, he added, "I'm going to law school when I get my undergrad loan paid off. I like the big words lawyers use. Warrant, probable cause, habeas corpus."

"Just what the world needs," she said. "Another ambulance chaser."

He grinned. "Bet you thought I was just a pretty face, but Wilcox brought me in on the case because he saw through my jovial kitchen-boy disguise."

"Yeah, right. How did he find out about the Nebraska warrant?"

"Big editor dude got lucky. Bent pulled a scam years ago in Omaha. Called himself Colonel Wesley Wilbur Waxford, USAF retired. Don't know what it is with him and alliteration."

Sara was surprised Brad knew what alliteration was, but his humanoid skills weren't the big shocker. Why didn't Jeff tell her about the warrant? *She* was supposed to be his sidekick.

The sun was blazing hot, and the bluffs around them were as desolate as Mars, but the mess finally sorted itself out. Carmela and Barrett Borden Bent, alias Colonel W.W. Waxford, were packed into the caged back seat of a patrol car. Bent kept stuttering about wrongful arrest suits.

Jeff asked Brad to drive Sara back to Las Mariposa.

"I have to go in to the office," he explained. "I'm under deadline on the first story of the series."

"Don't you have to pack your bags or something?" Sara asked.

"Brad has my stuff in his Bug. I had him pack for me."

She looked over, and Brad was hustling Jeff's stuff into the Corvette faster than he ever worked in the kitchen.

"Brad played Watson to your Sherlock Holmes?" she asked.

"No, he only helped the last couple of days when the situation got really sticky."

"How long have you known Bent was a wanted man?"

"Not long." The famous Wilcox evasiveness. "I couldn't have done it without you. Thank you, Sara."

He leaned over and kissed her forehead. Her forehead! Was he dumping her? She opened her mouth, but no words came out.

"Hope you don't mind riding back with Brad. I really have to get to work."

One of the troopers called him, and he jogged over without a backward glance.

ON MONDAY she'd planned to go to Phoenix to spend two days at her sister's. She wanted to cry on her shoulder, then have a long weepy conversation with her friends Monica and Sheryl.

She spent a long, miserable night after Jeff left. Monday she didn't have enough energy for the short trip home. Jeff had said they'd talk, but they never had. She still expected him to call, so she stuck close to her cell phone all day.

They had had a relationship, however brief. She needed some kind of closure. No, she needed Jeff, but she hated herself for being right about him. His job did come first, and she'd always known it. He didn't even say goodbye!

By Tuesday she was angry enough to caramelize him for a flan.

By Wednesday she was so despondent she didn't even care that her double-chocolate layer cake turned out lopsided. She built up the sunken side with whipped cream icing and wondered how long the feeling of having her heart ripped out would last.

12

HE WAS as rotten as Bent, Rossano and all the other scumbags he'd helped bring down. He picked up the phone a dozen times a day, wanting to call Sara, but words completely failed him. What could he say to the woman he loved to distraction but was determined not to marry?

Jeff stared at the desert vista from the patio of his apartment. Dad had asked him to be home by eight that evening because he had a big surprise for him. Jeff didn't have a clue what the old man was cooking up, but there was nothing he really wanted to do. The five days since he'd left Sara had seemed like five months. He'd missed her every minute of every waking hour, and thoughts of her kept him awake at night.

He was ashamed of the way he'd left her hanging, but there was nothing he could say without hurting her more. He was afraid of his feelings. If he saw her, he'd beg her to marry him. That was the sure way to ruin her life. He wasn't marriage material any more than his father had been. They were both newsmen, and the story always came first. He couldn't ask Sara to share the kind of life he lived.

Wandering into the living room, he speculated whether his father's big surprise was a night on the town.

Jeff hadn't said anything to Len about Sara, but Len was too perceptive not to pick up on his brooding. That is, he would've if he'd ever been around. He seemed to be gone more than Jeff was.

"We're here." The door behind Jeff swung open.

We? Jeff hadn't expected anyone else, but his father was gregarious. It wasn't surprising he brought a buddy home.

"Sophie, this is my son, Jeff. Jeff, say hello to Sophie Ferris."

"Nice to meet you, Sophie," Jeff said, taking the woman's hand with automatic courtesy and a whole lot of curiosity.

His dad had a girlfriend?

She had fluffy white hair framing a round face that wore wrinkles like beauty lines. When she smiled, she was prettier than most women half her age. Maybe her waist had thickened, but she still had some eye-catching attributes on display in a peach crepe jumpsuit with long, billowing sleeves.

"Come on, everybody, sit down. I want you two to get acquainted," his father said.

"Len has told me a lot about you, Jeff. He's really proud of the work you do at the *Monitor*," Sophie said.

Good ol' Dad had told him zilch about her, which definitely put him at a disadvantage for small talk.

"Eh...do you live in Phoenix, Sophie?"

What a lame conversation starter.

"Yes, I'm a transported Midwesterner from Detroit. My husband and I retired here, but he passed away the second year we were out here. By then, though, I loved it too much so I stayed."

"Lucky for me she did." His father was grinning like a schoolboy with a crush.

"Where did you two meet?" He really wanted to ask when.

"At Kelly's Fitness Center," she said, beaming at Len. "I thought he had the cutest butt in the place."

Wonder of wonders, his father blushed.

"We've been keeping company for a couple of months now," Len said.

"Why didn't you tell me?"

"Guess I wanted to be sure I could make the relationship work. Sophie knows what a lousy husband I was the first time around. She's willing to take a chance on me."

"Dad, that's great, but you didn't need to keep it a secret. I was worried every time you were gone."

"Yeah, well, I'm sorry about that. No offense, son, but I wanted to work it out on my own. Didn't want any advice."

Jeff could read between the lines. His father didn't want any advice from a son who didn't have a successful love life.

"Len has been working— I can tell him, can't I?" Sophie asked.

"Sure, honey."

"Len has been working part-time on the Scottsdale paper. He put a down payment on a house in Sun City for us."

"Pension or no pension, I was sick of sitting around like an old man."

"Well, I'm happy for both of you," Jeff said. He also felt like a loser, a total failure in the love sweepstakes.

"Bottom line is, we plan to get married in the fall. All I need is a best man. That's you."

"I'd be honored," he said, meaning it.

SARA'S second week as a temporary employee at Las Mariposa passed, and she was still on the work schedule. No one said anything to her about staying or not staying. Kenny had had a quiet hissy fit because she left her post at the brunch last week, but he didn't hold a grudge. Fortunately she'd disguised the lopsided cake before he noticed her goof.

Another whole week went by, and Jeff never called. Her life became a routine of work, then jogging and swimming every evening. When she tried to read, tears blurred her vision. When she turned on the small TV in her room, the images seemed remote and unconnected to reality.

Behind the huge overwhelming pain of missing Jeff, a second sense of loss was building. She was homesick. She had acquaintances at Las Mariposa, but no real friends. She missed Ellie and Todd's good-natured bickering and her sister's warm support. She wanted to go home even if meant taking a job at some fast-food joint.

"I love working with you," she told Kenny ten days after Jeff left, "but I miss being in Phoenix. I've given Mr. Cervantes two weeks' notice, but he said it's okay to leave at the end of this week because business is slow in August."

"I thought you'd be leaving. Jeffrey wasn't much of a server, but I can see where that wouldn't matter to you."

A smile split his round face, and she couldn't resist

giving him a big hug. As bosses went, he was one of the best.

She returned to Phoenix on a stifling day in early August, moving in with Ellie and Todd until she could get a job.

For a couple of weeks she put in applications and waited. The pain didn't go away, but at least she had family and friends to distract her. Once she made the big mistake of driving past the *Phoenix Monitor* building. The pain hit her immediately. She vowed never to go near the place again.

Finally she got a break. Dominick sold his restaurant to a couple who owned several in Tucson and wanted to expand to Phoenix. She applied, told the truth about being fired by Dominick and got the job three days after her interview. She could hardly wait until Ellie got home from work to tell her.

"I'm going back to work at Dominick's without Dominick," she proudly announced the minute her sister got home.

"Sara, that's wonderful! What happened to Dominick?"

"Sold out. The new owners think he bought a fast-food franchise in Vegas."

"Great! When do you start?"

"That's the downside. They're renovating, completely gutting the kitchen and generally sprucing up the rest of the place. They're not scheduled to open until December first."

"Well, don't worry. You're welcome to stay here as long as you like. I really missed you."

"You're the best sister in the world, but I won't be a

complete parasite. I'm going to do some temp work for a caterer I know, Marge Reed."

"You hate catering."

"This will be mostly weddings, reunions, big parties. No kids' birthday parties or bridge luncheons. I love making wedding cakes."

"Someday you'll have one of your own."

"If you tell me to call that *Monitor* reporter again, I'll scream."

The catering business wasn't all wedding cakes and chocolate mousse, but Sara didn't mind the frantic rush to provide food for the special occasions in other people's lives. She could make shrimp puffs in her sleep.

Usually she worked behind the scenes in the large, professionally equipped kitchen Marge had added on to the back of her brick ranch-style home. When two or more events were booked at the same time, Sara sometimes had to help serve.

The last weekend in September was a logistical nightmare. She didn't know how Marge, slender, silver-haired and smiling no matter what the crisis, could balance so many client demands without becoming unbalanced herself.

"I know this is last minute, but Russ broke his ankle doing some darn fool stunt," her boss said as Sara finished baking on Saturday morning. "That's what happens when I rely on college kids for part-time help. Can you help out at a wedding reception this afternoon?"

"Sure, I'll be glad to." The more she worked, the less time she had to brood about Jeff.

"It's in the back room of a bar called Fat Ollie's. I've never catered anything there, but the menu is pretty simple. Sandwich makings with deli meats and assorted cheeses. The usual chips and condiments. The bride had the cake made at a bakery, so all you have to do is set up and clean up afterward. Mary will go with you."

Mary was Marge's daughter, not nearly as hardworking as her mother, but she was a sweet-faced teenager and good company, even if she did make Sara feel old at the age of twenty-six.

When she and Mary got there with the food in one of Marge's vans, they found Fat Ollie's was a neighborhood tavern without anything to distinguish it from hundreds of others in the city. The bar was dark polished wood with a brass rail and a big mirror behind the shelves of liquor bottles. It was semidark with recessed neon lights along the ceiling. The tables had black Formica tops, and the chrome chairs had cracked red-leather seats and backs, but it probably hadn't been decorated for a 1950s look. More likely no one had bothered to redecorate since then.

The newest thing in the place was dark green heavyduty carpeting, which extended into a large back room with plenty of long tables, folding wooden chairs and sports memorabilia on the walls. The small kitchen was off this room and was obviously incidental to the tavern's business.

Whoever picked this place for a wedding reception had to be sentimental about Fat Ollie's or desperate for a place to hold it.

She and Mary set up the relatively simple meal, due to be served around five o'clock, and had time to kill before anyone came. The bar wasn't without diversions, at least for her teenage helper. Mary, dressed in a black miniskirt and baby blue tights that matched the short-sleeved cotton jacket her mother provided to all employees, made a friend. Jack was a college student working as a part-time bartender, and Mary was smitten. Ordinarily she would have worked in the small, not particularly well-equipped kitchen, and Sara would have watched the tables and seen to the guests' needs.

"Please, please, please let me take care of the tables," Mary begged.

Sara didn't mind. The longer she went without wedding plans of her own, the more her enthusiasm for other people's receptions waned. She'd be delighted when her real job started in December, but meanwhile, Marge paid reasonably well, and catering filled Sara's empty hours.

"No problem," Sara said. "I'll work the kitchen. Your mother will like you taking responsibility for the guests' happiness. You will be responsible, won't you?"

Sara knew Marge would not like the bartender at all. But it was a big city, and he was too good-looking in a muscle-bound way to do more than flirt with a high-school girl. She hoped.

When the wedding party arrived en masse with lots of talk and laughter, she was glad enough to let Mary take the bowl of corn relish out of the fridge and work the party. Sara pulled the tab on a can of iced tea she'd brought for herself and perched on a stool by the kitchen counter until she was needed.

At first the voices were just noise, and she paid little attention. Then she heard a fragmentary string of words in a voice that was achingly familiar.

No, it couldn't be. She was hearing things.

Mary came into the kitchen with a nearly empty bowl of barbecue-flavored potato chips.

"Need a refill here," she said, keeping an eye on the doorway where she could see the dark-haired Romeo handing out drinks.

"Whose wedding is this?" Sara asked.

She couldn't believe she'd never asked. Marge had said Fat Ollie's, and in the rush of getting ready at the last minute, it had never occurred to her.

"Ferris and something. I think it started with a W. Mom said they'd paid in advance."

"Think, Mary. Could it have been Wilcox?"

"Yeah, I think that's it. I need the chips."

Sara dumped a bag into one of Marge's big plastic bowls and heard the distinctive low-pitched voice again.

There was no outside door in the kitchen. That had to be a code violation, or maybe not if Fat Ollie's didn't serve food. Either way, she couldn't get out without walking through the reception room to the main door.

Jeff was marrying someone else! She felt light-headed from shock. She desperately wanted to leave before he saw her. She crept to the kitchen door and peeked around the jamb, making sure she wasn't seen. There he was, resplendent in a black tux with satin lapels and a dark green cummerbund and bow tie. He was grinning broadly, and the pleated white front of his shirt made him look gorgeous.

But she hated him! The least he could have done was tell her.

Had he been engaged when he involved her in the alien chase at Las Mariposa? Had he shared her bed knowing someone was waiting for him in Phoenix? Or was this a spur-of-the-minute thing?

He was despicable. She wanted to hurl the uninspired sugary mound that passed as a wedding cake at his stupid grin.

Even more, she wanted to get away and never lay eyes on him again. What could possibly be more humiliating than catering a wedding reception for the man she loved—had thought she'd loved. She hated him to pieces!

His back was turned, those wide shoulders slightly hunched as he talked to one of the guests, a short, elderly woman who looked entranced by his dubious charms.

This was her chance. She couldn't abandon Mary, but she could hide in the catering van until the party broke up, even if it went on all night. Mary was too busy making goo-goo eyes at the bartender to care. All Sara had to do was sneak out while Jeff's back was turned.

She made it halfway to the door when she heard her name.

"Sara!"

She kept going and reached the alley, but he was right behind her.

"Sara, stop, please!"

She sidestepped a Dumpster and reached the blue van parked in an area beside the concrete building reserved for deliveries during the week.

"You don't need me to congratulate you on your wedding," she said.

"Congratulate me?"

He did a terrible thing. He laughed.

"I'm not the groom."

"Not the groom?" She felt like an idiot.

"My dad is. I'm only the best man."

"Oh."

Part of her was weak with relief, but she was too angry to think straight.

"Come inside and meet him."

"No! I mean, I'm only here as the caterer."

"I thought you were working at Las Mariposa. I thought you had a great job there."

"A lot of things—and people—aren't as great as they seem at first."

"I don't blame you for being mad at me." He looked so sorrowful she almost felt sorry for him—almost. "I'm sorry, deeply sorry for the way I left. I was planning to drive up there after the wedding. Really."

"That makes everything all right?" It was no time for sarcasm, but she couldn't help it.

"No, it doesn't. We need to talk, Sara."

"I've heard that before."

"But not here." He glanced around the unsavory alley. "All Dad's old newspaper buddies are here, so the party will go on until Ollie closes up. But I can sneak away in a couple of hours. Let me take you home."

"I'm here with my boss's teenage daughter. I have to drive her home in the van. Anyway, we have nothing to say to each other."

"I have a lot to say to you."

"I'm still at my sister's. You could have called me any time."

"I didn't know. Plus, I was afraid."

"Oh, sure, you'll take on mobsters and aliens, but I'm too scary."

"Give me half an hour, your place or mine. Please." He ran a hand through his hair, giving it that tousled, sexy look she loved.

"Ellie and Todd are doing steaks on the grill for friends."

"I'll follow you to the caterer's. You can leave the van and follow me home in your car if you have it there."

"Maybe." She knew she would do it and hated herself for giving in so easily. Maybe she needed to yell at him before she could get over him.

THE HAPPY COUPLE was finally off for their honeymoon in Vegas, and Sara was really there, sitting in Jeff's living room while he made stupid apologies for the clutter his dad had yet to remove. Jeff wanted to take her in his arms and never let her go, but it would be safer to cuddle up to a saguaro cactus. His adorable little pastry chef was seething with anger, and he didn't know if he could ever make things right between them. But he was damn well going to try his best.

"I was an idiot," he said, pacing because he didn't dare sit beside her on the couch.

"We both agree on that," she said dryly.

"I always thought the Wilcox men were unfit for marriage. My dad sure was. He made my mother's life miserable until she finally dumped him. But he wasn't an ogre, just obsessed with his job."

"Like you are."

"Was."

"Like I believe that."

She was rearranging a couple of his dad's ratty throw

pillows as though she were into home improvement. At least she was a little bit nervous. He was petrified he'd blow his last chance with her.

"When I met Sophie, I started to see my dad in a new way. He and Mom were never suited for each other. It was a personality clash from day one, and he used his job to avoid coming to grips with their problems. Just the way I've been using mine to avoid repeating his mistakes."

Sara didn't say anything, just stood and walked to the patio door. She sort of hunched her shoulders while she stared at the starry sky over the desert community.

He didn't know what her reaction meant.

"The bottom line is, I love you, Sara. There's nothing I want more than to marry you."

She looked at him, but he couldn't read her face in the dim light from one floor lamp.

"I have a real job starting in December."

"That's nice." Not what he expected or wanted to hear, though, after proposing to her.

"At Dominick's."

"You're going back to work for that jerk?"

"No, he sold the place, but my job will be the same. I'll still have to go in at the crack of dawn and bake."

What was she saying? He wanted to take her in his arms, but her arms were locked across her breasts. It was a defensive posture if he'd ever seen one.

"If you won't marry me, at least forgive me," he said, unable to hide his misery. "I should have called and been up-front with you. Instead I buried myself in my job and tried to pretend things were back to normal. I missed you, Sara, and I'll quit my job if it will make you happy.''

She stepped close. The sly little grin on her face was more confusing than encouraging.

"You aren't very good marriage material, Wilcox. Can you cook?"

"I haven't starved yet."

"I want to see your refrigerator."

"Okay. Are you hungry? Or is this some kind of test?"

She headed for the kitchen and didn't answer.

He clicked on the kitchen light while she opened the fridge. It was stuffed with odds and ends his father had left. Once he brought Sophie out of the closet, so to speak, he loved cooking for her. Go figure.

"Needs cleaning," she said.

"I'll have to ask Dad what he wants. It's mostly his stuff. They moved into their new house a few days ago, but he still has a lot here."

"Blue cheese, malt vinegar—that doesn't need to be refrigerated—buttermilk, smoked salmon. Your father has good taste."

She picked up an aerosol can of whipped cream and sprayed a little dab on her finger. He felt dizzy with anticipation when she licked it with the tip of her tongue.

"Still sweet," she said.

"I love you, Sara."

"It won't be easy to deal with our crazy hours, but I guess we both have to work for a living."

"But we don't have to live to work," he said adamantly. "Are you torturing me because I never called?"

"Of course I am. I wanted to flambé you. Trouble is, I love you."

"You love me?"

"Madly."

"You'll marry me?"

"Oh, yes, you better believe it."

She took aim with the can and dotted his chin and both cheeks with fluffy dabs of whipped cream. Then she pulled his head close and slowly licked it away, holding his arms at his sides while she did.

"I love whipped cream," she said in a husky whisper he hadn't heard in much too long.

"I love you."

It was the best kiss of his life, and maybe the longest.

"Now I feel forgiven," he said at last. "And I love you, love you, love you."

"Me, too."

"You love you?"

"You're not going to copyedit everything I say, are you?"

"Not if you won't make me eat food I don't recognize."

"Wilcox, this is going to be one crazy assignment."

"Our marriage?"

"That, too." She grinned.

"If you're going to live here, maybe you'd like to see the bedroom."

"Just promise me our story will never end."

She kissed him so hard he nearly lost his balance.

He took her hand, but she pulled back and grabbed the whipped cream she'd left on the counter.

"I hate to let a good ingredient go to waste," she said.

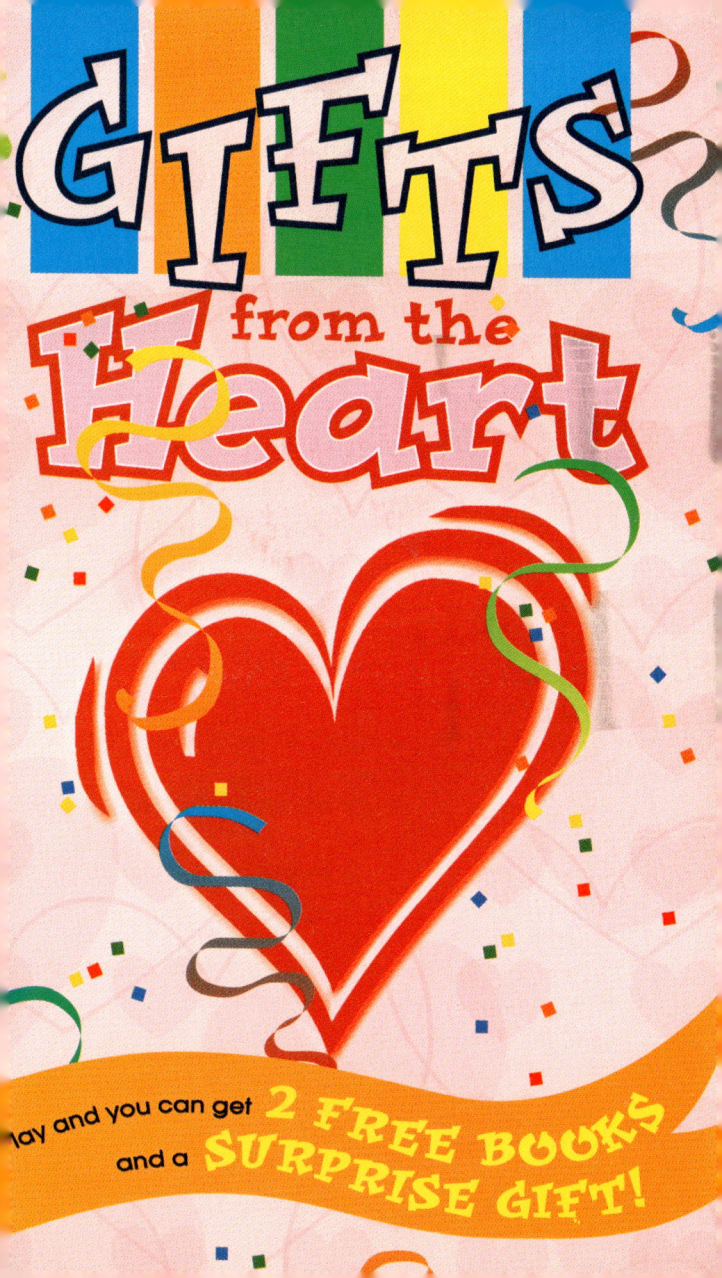

GIFTS
from the
Heart

...ay and you can get **2 FREE BOOKS** and a **SURPRISE GIFT!**

GIFTS from the Heart

Play Gifts from the Heart and get 2 FREE Books and a FREE Gift!

HOW TO PLAY:

1. With a coin, carefully scratch off the gold area at the right. Then check the claim chart to see what we have for you — **2 FREE BOOKS** and a **FREE Gift** — **ALL YOURS FREE!**

2. Send back the card and you'll receive two brand-new Harlequin Duets™ novels. These books have a cover price of $5.99 each in the U.S. and $6.99 each in Canada, but they are yours to keep absolutely free.

3. There's no catch. You're under no obligation to buy anything. We charge nothing —**ZERO** — for your first shipment. And you don't have to make any minimum number of purchases — not even one!

4. The fact is, thousands of readers enjoy receiving books by mail from the Harlequin Reader Service®. They enjoy the convenience of home delivery... they like getting the best new novels at discount prices, **BEFORE** they're available in stores...and they love their *Heart to Heart* subscriber newsletter featuring author news, horoscopes, recipes, book reviews and much more!

5. We hope that after receiving your free books you'll want to remain a subscriber. But the choice is yours — to continue or cancel, any time at all! So why not take us up on our invitation, with no risk of any kind. You'll be glad you did!

A surprise gift

FREE!

We can't tell you what it is... but we're sure you'll like it! A

FREE GIFT!

just for playing **GIFTS FROM THE HEART!**

Visit us online at
www.eHarlequin.com

NO COST! NO OBLIGATION TO BUY! NO PURCHASE NECESSARY!

PLAY GIFTS from the Heart

Scratch off the gold area with a coin.
Then check below to see the gifts you get!

YES! I have scratched off the gold area. Please send me the 2 Free books and gift for which I qualify. I understand I am under no obligation to purchase any books as explained on the back and on the opposite page.

311 HDL DNR9   111 HDL DNLU

FIRST NAME

LAST NAME

ADDRESS

APT.#

CITY

STATE/PROV.

ZIP/POSTAL CODE

♥♥♥♥ 2 free books plus a surprise gift
♥♥♥ 2 free books   ♥♥ 1 free book

Offer limited to one per household and not valid to current Harlequin Duets™ subscribers. All orders subject to approval.

(H-D-07/02)

DETACH AND MAIL CARD TODAY!

trademarks owned by Harlequin Enterprises Ltd.

The Harlequin Reader Service® — Here's how it works:

Accepting your 2 free books and gift places you under no obligation to buy anything. You may keep the books and gift and return the shipping statement marked "cancel." If you do not cancel, about a month later we'll send you 2 additional books and bill you just $5.14 each in the U.S., or $6.14 each in Canada, plus 50¢ shipping & handling per book and applicable taxes if any.* That's the complete price and — compared to cover prices of $5.99 each in the U.S. and $6.99 each in Canada — it's quite a bargain! You may cancel at any time, but if you choose to continue, every month we'll send you 2 more books, which you may either purchase at the discount price or return to us and cancel your subscription.

*Terms and prices subject to change without notice. Sales tax applicable in N.Y. Canadian residents will be charged applicable provincial taxes and GST.

If offer card is missing write to: Harlequin Reader Service, 3010 Walden Ave., P.O. Box 1867, Buffalo NY 14240-1867

BUSINESS REPLY MAIL
FIRST-CLASS MAIL   PERMIT NO. 717-003   BUFFALO, NY

POSTAGE WILL BE PAID BY ADDRESSEE

HARLEQUIN READER SERVICE
3010 WALDEN AVE
PO BOX 1867
BUFFALO NY 14240-9952

NO POSTAGE
NECESSARY
IF MAILED
IN THE
UNITED STATES

Green Eggs & Sam

Susan Peterson

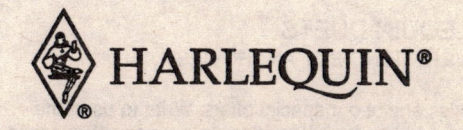

HARLEQUIN®

TORONTO • NEW YORK • LONDON
AMSTERDAM • PARIS • SYDNEY • HAMBURG
STOCKHOLM • ATHENS • TOKYO • MILAN • MADRID
PRAGUE • WARSAW • BUDAPEST • AUCKLAND

Dear Reader,

I love the Adirondack Mountains and small towns. Wait a minute! Let me rephrase that: I love the Adirondack Mountains and small towns as long as it's summertime. Winter is another story. So when I decided to write Haley Jo and Sam's story, I knew it had to take place during the beautiful summer months.

I don't think there's a more delightful experience than living in a small town and finding yourself surrounded by the camaraderie and suport of those around you. Of course, as Haley Jo finds out, that means that everyone knows your business. But even Haley Jo recognizes that her new neighbors' insistence on sticking their noses into her business is all about caring. I've always felt supported and encouraged by the people around me. It makes me want to share it with my readers! I hope you come to love Reflection Lake as much as Haley Jo does.

Enjoy!

Susan Peterson

Books by Susan Peterson

HARLEQUIN DUETS
49—EVERYTHING BUT ANCHOVIES

Don't miss any of our special offers. Write to us at the following address for information on our newest releases.

Harlequin Reader Service
U.S.: 3010 Walden Ave., P.O. Box 1325, Buffalo, NY 14269
Canadian: P.O. Box 609, Fort Erie, Ont. L2A 5X3

With love to Kevin.
You taught me how to be a real mom.

Special thanks to my Sisters of the Lake.
I love you guys.
You are my heart and my soul.

1

HALEY JO SIMPSON took one look at her boss, Dr. Benjamin Rocca and decided that overweight, fifty-year-old men should never wear leopard-patterned thongs, while lying spread-eagled on a vibrating bed. Especially when the controls were switched to high.

It wasn't that Haley Jo was a prude. Far from it. She wasn't much different than any other single, red-blooded, twenty-four-year old. She had needs, and one of those needs was sex. She just didn't want that particular need fulfilled by her much older, quickly balding, very married boss.

Unfortunately, Dr. Rocca didn't seem capable of grasping that concept. A regular horndog, he'd made the last three months of Haley Jo's life miserable. Mainly because the man didn't seem capable of understanding the word *no*.

Sighing, Haley Jo slung her black lace bra over one shoulder and pulled the belt of her shower robe tighter. She figured she was left with one of two options. She could act indignant and scream, leading to the very real possibility that he'd fire her on the spot. Or she could muster up an air of sweet innocence and treat her boss's intrusion into her hotel room as a silly mistake.

Either way, the task ahead of her was a delicate one. She needed to get him to leave, but she couldn't afford to lose her job as his receptionist. Not with her rent due in exactly three days, and Mrs. Preston, her landlady, already poised to throw her out.

Haley Jo pulled off her shower cap and flung it behind her into the steamy bathroom. No doubt about it, Dr.

Rocca's invitation to be his guest at the Sixteenth Annual New York State Dental Hygienist Conference had a few more strings attached than they'd originally discussed. Not that she shouldn't have known better.

In any case, her best friend, Melanie, had a lot to answer for. Haley Jo had agreed to step in and take her place at the conference when Melanie's boyfriend put his foot down about her going. Unfortunately, Mel hadn't made it clear on what Dr. Rocca expected in way of payment for the trip.

Haley Jo jammed her hands on her hips and effected a small scowl. Best to use a no-nonsense approach. "Uh, Dr. Rocca, I'm trying to get settled in. Do you think you could conduct this fashion show down by the pool or something?"

He didn't budge. Or at least he didn't voluntarily budge. Instead, he undulated up and down, looking a bit like her Grandma Stella's favorite dessert of green Jell-O.

Haley Jo stepped closer to the bed. She couldn't see too well as the steam from the bathroom was drifting into the room. But if she wasn't mistaken, it looked as though a collection of tiny brown wrappers lay scattered across Rocca's chest.

She frowned. What the heck?

She glanced at the bedside table. Sure enough, the good doctor had helped himself to the entire box of gold-foiled chocolate-covered cherries the management had delivered to her room earlier. For pity's sake, the guy didn't even have the decency to leave her some of her own candy.

Irritated, she poked a finger into his flabby upper arm. "Come on, get up! Playtime is over."

Nothing.

She poked harder. "Dr. Rocca? Come on, you have to get up."

He didn't move. Haley Jo giggled. It sounded nervous and high-pitched even to her own ears. Maybe the guy was in sugar shock. "Come on, Dr. Rocca. This isn't funny."

No reaction. Not even a flutter of an eyelash or a whisper of air between his chocolate-covered lips.

Haley Jo grimaced and grabbed a hairy shoulder between her fingers and shook. He simply moved up and down on the bed. The color of blue caught her eye.

Startled, she leaned closer. One of her scarves, the sheer blue silk one that went so perfectly with her cream-colored Versace knockoff, was wrapped around his thick neck and pulled so tight his skin pinched up around it.

A touch of panic shot through her, and Haley Jo reached out to press her fingertips against his neck, searching for a pulse. His skin felt warm, but there was no reassuring flutter of life. She snatched her hand back and straightened up.

She might not have M.D. after her name like her older brother, Trevor, but Haley Jo was smart enough to know that Dr. Rocca wouldn't ever have another opportunity to parade around in his fancy thong again.

Turning on her heels, she raced to the door and yanked it open. Cool air from the hall rushed up beneath the hem of her short robe and goose bumps pebbled her flesh.

At the other end of the hall, the elevator opened and a bellhop, pushing an overloaded luggage cart, stepped off. He smiled in Haley Jo's direction. "Did you need something, miss?"

"Could—could you maybe call the police?" Haley Jo stammered.

The bellhop's smile faded. "Are you okay, miss? Is something wrong?"

Haley Jo fidgeted, suddenly conscious that her wet skin had plastered her silk robe to her body. "It seems that my boss, Dr. Rocca, is dead."

The guy's warm brown eyes widened, and his gaze traveled down to gape openly at her chest. "Dr. Rocca is dead, ma'am? Like as in heart attack dead?"

Haley Jo cringed. It wasn't too hard to figure out what the bellhop thought the two of them had been doing to cause the suspected *heart attack*. One famous, overweight boss hanging out in his young employee's room in the middle of the day—whatever could they have been doing?

Haley Jo shifted her feet. Well maybe it *was* a heart

attack. After all, Dr. Rocca had scarfed down at least two complete layers of the expensive chocolate. Chocolate so rich it could send a person into a chocolate-induced ecstasy. An ecstasy so steep and sweet that it had bumped poor Dr. Rocca's cholesterol-challenged heart into a fatal arrhythmia.

She shook herself. Fat chance anyone would buy that explanation. There was no denying the scarf tied around his neck. And something told Haley Jo that Dr. Rocca hadn't been playing dress-up with her accessories. "I—I think someone murdered him."

That got the bellhop's attention up off her chest region. In fact, his mouth dropped open and he gaped at her. Then something seemed to kick in and he snapped to attention, whirled around and stepped back into the elevator.

He stabbed one of the buttons on the panel. "I saw the sheriff down in the lobby talking to the manager. Don't touch nothing, lady. I'll get him!" By the time the doors started to close, the guy's attention was focused back on her breasts.

Haley Jo glanced down at her robe. It was pulled taut over her breasts, her nipples poking out like two missiles waiting for launch. Nothing like a murder to make things a bit more prominent than was appropriate.

Haley Jo jerked the top closed, trying unsuccessfully to cover the very breasts that every man she'd ever known since age thirteen had ogled like they were two cones of cotton candy sitting just out of their reach.

Haley Jo glanced around, trying to figure out what to do next. No chance she'd go back into the room, not even for some clothes. But standing out in the hall was bound to become embarrassing. Anyone could come by and spot her huddling in the hall in her bathrobe.

"You gonna scream, lady?" a small voice asked. "You sure look like you're gonna let one rip."

Startled, Haley Jo whirled around, saw no one, then looked down. A scrawny little girl of about eight or nine, in stubby brown pigtails, with a pale face and a wad of gum the size of a golf ball shoved up in one corner of her wisecracking mouth, stared her up and down.

"Where'd you come from?" Haley Jo asked.

"You mean what part of my mom's anatomy did I come from or were you talking about something else?"

Haley Jo frowned. "Pretty smart-mouthed for such a shrimp."

"My dad says I'm pigcocious." She tilted her head to one side and crinkled up her pug nose. "Is that a good thing or a bad thing?"

"Definitely bad. No woman wants to be called anything with the word *pig* in it."

A wide smile splashed across the girl's face. "Pigs are really smart. My daddy says they're smarter than dogs even."

"That may be true—you being a country girl and all, and me being a city girl. But believe me when I say that you *do not* want to be compared to meat that sizzles and squirts oil while frying in a pan."

Speaking of pigs, Haley Jo glanced toward the open door of her room. The thought of the little girl getting an eyeful of Benjamin Rocca's very dead body was not something she considered kid-approved viewing.

"What's your name?" As she spoke, Haley Jo stepped away from the open door and guided the kid with her. It was important to keep the girl occupied until whoever was coming to take care of things finally came.

The name question seemed to stump the girl for a moment. She paused and her brown eyes narrowed as if she were considering something important. Then she said, "Tiffany. My name is Tiffany."

"Pleased to meet you, Tiffany. I'm Haley Jo."

"Is that guy in your room really dead?"

"How'd you know there was a dead guy in my room?"

"Because you told Tommy. I was riding up and down on the elevator with him." She lifted up her shirt and scratched her belly. "Tommy doesn't have a girlfriend. I figured that maybe he'd be interested in a younger woman." She flashed what she probably thought was an alluring smile, but it came off looking sweetly innocent, tugging at a place somewhere deep inside Haley Jo that she hadn't even known existed.

When Tiffany didn't get the response she expected, she went on to other subjects. "I've never seen a dead body. You think maybe I could get a look at this one? I won't touch nothing. I know about not touching stuff at a crime scene."

"You're a regular Dick Tracy, aren't you?"

Tiffany pulled herself up to her full height. "My dad is the chief of police so I know all about that kind of stuff."

A sick feeling hit the pit of Haley Jo's stomach. She figured that her luck had just gone from bad to seriously bleak. One minute she'd been happily showering, minding her own business, and the next she was discussing dead bodies with a child genius who just happened to be the daughter of the local chief of police. Imprisonment could only be right around the corner.

Haley Jo wondered if prisoners still got one free phone call. She could call her brother Nate. As a big-city cop and the oldest, he was the logical choice. But Haley Jo knew better. Nate had been pretty clear last time he got her out of a pickle that he wasn't interested in getting another call. And her other brother, Trevor, was just starting his residency in emergency medicine in Los Angeles. He didn't have the money or the time to fly back east to get his little sister out of another one of her silly jams.

She gnawed absently on her thumbnail. It wasn't as if she could call upon her ex-boyfriend, David. He'd thrown her over for someone else after calling Haley Jo too *high maintenance*.

She clenched her fists. Ha! Too high maintenance. What a joke. All Haley Jo had asked of David was an occasional phone call to let her know they were still actually a couple.

She'd never made any real demands on David.... Okay, so she'd pressured him more than a few times for a date. But that's because she believed that a girl deserved a dinner and a movie out once in a while. A pizza, a six-pack of beer, two WWF wrestling videos, and a clumsy grope or two on her apartment sofa did *not* qualify as an actual date in Haley Jo's book.

Of course, all her girlfriends rallied around and told her to forget David—that he wasn't worth the two pounds she usually gained by bingeing on a mountain of Peanut M&M's. But then, all her girlfriends had steady, well-paying jobs and boyfriends who actually believed in taking them out on real dates.

Haley Jo figured her life was quickly going from moderately pitiful to seriously disastrous. Especially with her very married boss dressed in a thong stretched out dead on her bed.

SHERIFF SAM MATTHEWS didn't usually take crap from anyone, but he was pretty sure that the pompous little manager of the Climbing Bear Resort was giving him a load of hooey.

The manager had called him earlier in the day to ask if he'd stop out at the resort to discuss a series of troublesome pickpocket incidents involving several of the resort's more prominent guests. Thefts that had occurred while the guests had ventured into town. Sam's town.

Sam considered himself a peaceable kind of guy. He didn't mind giving a brief rundown on a case to any citizen who asked for one. Particularly when it's a case like a pickpocket who lifted the cash from the victims' wallets, but left their credit cards and dropped the wallet or purse into a convenient trash can. Although the case could have a big effect on the tourist business, the thief seemed to be a bit of a gentleman. But gentleman or not, if there was one thing Sam worried about it was tourism. If someone ripped off the local tourists, it meant the loss of revenue for the town. And for a small Adirondack resort town like Reflection Lake, New York that could mean big trouble.

But instead of being grateful, the manager seemed bent on getting into an argument. From the pinched expression on his face, Sam figured that the guy was reconsidering his invitation. He probably realized that a police presence in the main lobby was attracting more attention than he liked.

Sam was sure the manager was sweating bullets, concerned that having Sam stand in the middle of his marble inlaid lobby in a police uniform and a gun would result in a few of the guests checking out early.

Sure enough, the manager nudged Sam's elbow and tried to guide him toward a suite of offices located behind the massive mahogany check-in desk. "Perhaps we could continue this discussion in my office."

"I really don't have the time." Sam glanced toward the front doors. "My daughter is outside waiting for me in my truck." Actually, Sam had his fingers crossed that Prudence was outside waiting as instructed.

The manager's lips formed a meaningless smile. "Perhaps you should invite the little darlin' in. I'll have one of my assistants bring her a nice ice-cream soda while she waits."

Impatient, Sam shook his head. The manager wasn't a local. Not when he referred to Prudie as *little darlin'*. Locals knew better. They had firsthand knowledge of Prudie's tendency to change her name as often as she changed her clothes, and her pure delight in running wild through the town.

"Prudie's fine where she is," Sam said. "Let's finish up and I'll push off. The sooner I get back to the office, the sooner you'll have some kind of answer about these robberies."

The hotel manager cringed at the word *robberies*. He glanced around nervously. "Perhaps we could keep our voices down. No need to upset the guests."

The words were barely out of the man's mouth when Sam glanced across the lobby. The elevator doors opened and a young man in a purple uniform stepped off. Sam suppressed a grin. Tommy O'Reilly, one of the local kids. He'd forgotten Tommy was old enough to go out and get a summer job.

Sam frowned. Tommy's expression told him something was wrong. He looked downright stunned.

Brushing past the startled hotel manager, Sam made his way over to Tommy.

As he approached, Tommy blinked and his face transformed from dazed to relieved. "Chief! Boy, am I glad you're still here. You gotta come up to the fifth floor. The lady in 522 says there's a dead guy in her room."

A shocked silence settled over the crowded lobby. Several guests turned to stare. So much for keeping the guests *unaware* of what was going on.

He looked at the manager. "Call 911. Then call my office and tell them to send over a squad car."

The manager snapped off a string of commands to his assistant and then turned back to Sam. "I'll come with you. You might need my key."

Sam nodded and motioned Tommy to get back on the elevator.

Tommy stepped inside and then stopped, a panicked look darting across his face. He glanced around the enclosed space as if trying to find something. "Damn!"

"What's wrong?" Sam asked, as he and the manager joined Tommy.

The boy jumped and his gaze slid sideways. "Well, uh— I was giving Prudie rides up and down on the elevator, and well, she must have gotten off when I stopped at the fifth floor." He shoved his hands in his pockets. "I'm sorry, Chief."

Sam punched the fifth-floor button. "You mean to tell me you left my ten-year-old daughter on the same floor as some crazy woman yelling that there was a dead man in her room?" He clenched his teeth and hit the close door button twice. The doors slid shut. "And while we're at it, how the hell did she manage to get from my truck to inside the elevator?"

Tommy shrugged helplessly.

"I left Prudie in the truck with strict instructions not to twitch so much as an eyelash." The elevator started up.

Tommy bobbed his head up and down like some kind of demented chicken, looking about ready to cry. "You know Prudie, Chief. She don't listen to nobody. You included."

Sam resisted the immediate urge to take Tommy down a peg or two. Mainly because everything the boy said was right—Prudence Patricia Barnard Matthews rarely listened to anyone, including her father.

He folded his arms, and stared at the numbers overhead, determined not to lose his cool. Prudie was notorious for trying his patience. But Sam loved her more than he could ever explain to another human being, and he could only hope that she was unharmed. However, knowing Prudie, she was probably up on the fifth floor dusting for fingerprints and interrogating possible suspects.

2

THE SHAKES had set in, and Haley Jo figured it had a lot to do with finding her deceased boss gyrating on her bed, a chocolate-covered cherry stuck between his teeth. Things like that tended to put a real damper on a person's day.

For Tiffany's sake, she tried to hide the tremors, folding her arms tight across her chest and leaning up against the wall. But her knees still felt as soft as the inside of a perfectly roasted marshmallow, and she wished whoever was coming would get there already. If she had to wait much longer she'd have a full-blown case of the screaming meemies.

At that same moment, the elevator doors slid open and *he* stepped off. The kind of guy a woman dreamed of finding alone on the up elevator, when she got on for a trip to the top. And if the elevator just happened to get stuck between floors, no sane woman would ever consider leaning on the alarm button.

Unfortunately, the guy was also wearing a shiny, very official-looking badge pinned to a khaki shirt. Haley Jo sighed. Just her luck. She looked like something fished out of the local swamp and they'd sent up a cute-looking cop.

She looked more closely. Damn, but they grew their cops tall here in the north. She pushed herself off the wall and straightened up. Not a good idea to look like riffraff around the police.

Her interrogator stood at least six foot one with a cap of thick hair so black it was almost blue. His eyes were hidden behind a pair of mirrored glasses, but Haley Jo had a feeling they'd be blue. As blue and clear as the sky touching the top of White Face Mountain on the morning she'd driven up into the Adirondacks.

The reflective lenses were fixed squarely on her, and from the way his nicely chiseled lips were clamped together into a thin line, Haley Jo figured that she came up embarrassingly short in whatever assessment he had already made of her.

The lenses never wavered, and Haley Jo felt the hot rush of heat start at her neck and flood her cheeks. Something told her that the cop was taking his time, examining every inch of her scantily clad body.

Uncharacteristically nervous, she glanced down and noticed the widening gap at the top of her robe, revealing the full swell of her breasts. The fact that her bra was also slung over one shoulder didn't help things.

She yanked the lapels back together and stuffed the bra into her side pocket. Sometimes it paid to flash the local police, but now wasn't one of those times.

"Get back down to the truck, Prudie," the cop said, his tone crisp and curt. "And I strongly suggest you buckle up and freeze your fanny to the seat. We'll talk later."

Haley Jo looked around. Who the heck was he talking to?

Tiffany stuck her head out from behind her. "I didn't do nothing, Daddy. I was just talking to my new friend, Haley Jo. She was telling me all about the dead body in her room."

Haley Jo cringed. Oh joy, the kid was going to dig her into an even deeper hole than she was already in. She stepped away and shot a look of betrayal in the girl's direction. "I thought you told me your name was Tiffany."

Tiffany-Prudie shrugged and shot her a grin that said, *you can't fault a girl for trying*. "I hate the name Prudence. It sucks. Tiffany sounds so much better." She twirled the end of one of her pigtails. "It was meeting you, Haley Jo, that made me decide to change it. You were my inspiration."

Haley Jo rubbed the tiny ache which had sprung up between her eyes. Wonderful! Not only was the cop going to think her guilty of showing Prudie a dead body, but now he probably thought she'd convinced his little princess to change her name.

She glanced at the cop from beneath lowered lashes, trying to gauge his reaction to this new development. His expression didn't look too reassuring. In fact, he looked as if he'd just bit down on a mouthful of rusty nails.

Haley Jo put on her best groveling expression. "I swear to you, sir, I didn't let your daughter anywhere near the room or the body."

The mirror lenses of his sunglasses still didn't move; instead, they stayed focused squarely on her. "Get down to the truck, Prudie." His voice was low and rough, like distant thunder on a hot summer's day. It promised trouble to come.

A tiny bubble of fear bounced along the edge of Haley Jo's nerves. She pushed it aside. She could handle the situation. She could handle this cop. She was good with people; people liked her. Or so her mother always said.

Beside her, Prudie's shoulders slumped. She glanced at Haley Jo and smiled a hesitant smile—a smile asking for forgiveness. Haley Jo wanted to flash her an answering smile, but she didn't dare. Not with Dirty Harry watching her every move.

Prudie sighed and walked over to the elevator. Once onboard, she poked her head back out. "I want a bra just like the one Haley Jo has, Daddy. See it sticking out of her pocket? Black lace! Can we stop at Ames on the way home so I can get one?"

"Get down to the truck, Prudie," he said.

Haley Jo wasn't positive, but she thought she heard a touch of weariness in his voice this time. She shoved the scrap of black lace deeper in her pocket and smiled apologetically.

His stonelike expression never wavered. Apparently lingerie shopping wasn't on his list of approved father-daughter outings.

Prudie waved to her as the doors slid shut, and Haley Jo tried to wiggle her fingers without attracting the attention of the cop. But from the slight tightening around the corners of his mouth, she knew he hadn't missed it. She was pretty sure this guy didn't miss much.

He crooked a finger at her. "You. Come with me." He glanced at the hotel manager. "You, stay here. Send the troopers in when they arrive."

The manager nodded, looking noticeably relieved.

Haley Jo edged closer to the manager. "Uh...if you don't mind, I'll wait here, too. I'm not real keen on going back in there."

The cop clamped an iron hand on her upper arm and tugged her toward the door. "I'm really not interested in what you'd rather do or not do, lady. At the moment, I'm the only cop on the scene, and I don't plan on letting you out of my sight."

He nudged her again, creating an unexpected little zing to zip up the center of her spine. She stumbled, and then righted herself by grabbing on to his forearm. His skin felt warm and supple beneath the tips of her fingers. Surprised at her reaction, Haley Jo snatched her hand back and stuck it in her pocket as if to protect it.

Seemingly oblivious to her reaction to his touch, the cop pushed the door open. "The body is in here?"

Haley nodded numbly, oddly aware that her toes barely skimmed the surface of the carpet as he hauled her through the doorway.

"What's your name, miss?"

"Simpson. Haley Jo Simpson." She swallowed hard and glanced up at him, feeling the same way she did when she gaped up at a skyscraper. Overwhelmed. Slightly in awe. It was hard to remember he was simply a policeman. A policeman who was questioning her about a dead man in her room.

She studied his face, determined to get over the feeling of intimidation swimming around in the pit of her stomach. Tiny lines around the outside of his sunglasses stood out white against the tan of his skin, telling her that he was a man who spent a lot of time outdoors. A small-town cop in the middle of the wilderness. Not a person to be afraid of, she told herself.

"You're the chief of police, right?" she said.

"That's right. I'm Sam Matthews." He reached up and removed his glasses, clipping one stem over the lip of his chest pocket. She'd been right. The eyes were brilliant blue.

Although he was speaking to her, his attention was on the room. "Are you here in Reflection Lake on business or pleasure, Ms. Simpson?"

Haley Jo searched for any sign of sarcasm with the *pleasure* comment, but she couldn't detect any. "I—I came for the Annual Dental Hygienist Conference. I've never been before but Dr. Rocca—my boss—said it would be a good experience for me. I'm scheduled to start a dental hygienist training program in two weeks."

Matthews walked over to the bed and pressed two fingers to Rocca's neck. "And the gentleman in the bed would be who?"

Haley Jo swallowed hard. "My boss—Dr. Rocca."

"And the two of you came to the conference together?"

She nodded.

"And then checked into this room?"

Haley Jo shook her head. "N-no. You've got it all wrong. We flew up to Albany, rented a car and drove up here together. But this is my room. Dr. Rocca has his own room down the hall." She made a motion as if to grab her purse. "I think I marked down his room number in my day planner."

"Never mind. I'd rather you didn't touch anything for the moment." His tone told her he wasn't convinced. "When I check with the desk downstairs, I'm going to learn that you paid for your own room, right?"

Haley Jo shifted, digging her bare toes into the thick, warm pile of the carpet. Thankfully she found some warmth, because the stare Matthews was shooting in her direction had the potential to freeze her solid in two seconds flat.

She sucked in a covert breath of air and tried to think. She needed to slow down. It was important not to rush to explain things. No matter how hard she tried to explain the financial arrangement surrounding this conference, Haley Jo was pretty sure Chief Matthews was going to jump to all the wrong conclusions. Heck, anyone would.

"Dr. Rocca paid for both rooms. He put it on the card he uses for business. He said that attending the conference would make me a better employee. That it would pay off for him in the long run."

"No doubt," Matthews said dryly.

Haley Jo gritted her teeth. "You're twisting this all around and making it into something it isn't. I came here to attend the conference, and Dr. Rocca came because he was asked to lecture."

"Somehow the good doctor's outfit doesn't jibe with what the well-dressed lecturer is wearing these days. A bit on the sleazy side, I'd say."

Haley Jo didn't bother answering. What could she say? Deny that Dr. Rocca had a weekend of hanky-panky planned? She'd only agreed to come because she thought she'd be able to keep him at a distance, mostly by staying two steps ahead of him and his wild libido the entire weekend. She never figured on him making his move two minutes after they had checked in.

"Do you have any thoughts on how he ended up like this?" Matthews asked.

"You mean how did he get dressed like that?"

The chief sighed. Obviously they weren't communicating too well. "No, I was referring to the fact that he's dead."

Haley Jo shook her head. "I'm not sure. I went in to take a shower, and when I came out, he was lying on my bed with all those candy wrappers scattered around him, and chocolate smeared on his face."

"So you're suggesting he OD'd on chocolate?" As he

spoke, Matthews leaned forward to flick the end of her scarf—the one tied around Dr. Rocca's pudgy neck.

"No, I wasn't saying that," Haley Jo said. "I'm not an idiot. But I also can't explain the scarf. Last time I saw it, it was neatly folded in my suitcase. I laid it on top because I didn't want the silk to crease when I closed the zipper. Silk doesn't wrinkle—I know that—but it can get creased or caught in the zipper if you're not careful. I—"

"Ms. Simpson, I'm not interested in hearing your thoughts on how to pack silk properly."

Haley Jo bit her bottom lip, trying to get a grip on her runaway tongue.

"Do me a favor, will you? Try to focus here."

She clenched her fists. "I'm doing the best I can. This is very scary for me. It's not every day that I get interrogated by some guy with a gun."

"I'm a cop, Ms. Simpson, and cops wear guns. Get over it." Matthews lifted Rocca's left wrist and glanced pointedly at the thick gold band on Rocca's ring finger. "Did he happen to mention any personal problems before changing into this lovely outfit? Like the fact that he was married?"

"What exactly are you implying?"

"Implying? Hell, I was outright asking if you knew he was married before you decided to shack up with him," he said.

Haley Jo exhaled hard. "You know, it isn't very nice of you to assume something like that. I never planned on coming up here for a wild weekend of sex with my boss." A wild weekend of sex with someone else maybe, but that was another subject entirely. And not one she planned on discussing with Chief Matt Dillon Wanna-be Matthews. He didn't need to know that lately Haley Jo had been feeling like some kind of sexual camel—wandering the barren wastelands of singlehood without so much as a nibble of interest.

She pulled herself up straighter, trying to ignore the fact that the hem of her robe slid up her leg another inch. If she wasn't mistaken, a touch of amusement seemed to tug at the corner of the chief's mouth. "Whether you believe it or not, I happen to be a very good receptionist. And I have potential. Plans to better myself." He wasn't laughing so she continued, "And even though Dr. Rocca assumed that I was interested in sleeping with him, I wasn't." She tugged on her belt again. "I happen to be a very moral person."

Haley Jo crossed her fingers. Hopefully lightning didn't strike people inside hotel rooms. "Okay, maybe saying I have high moral standards is stretching the truth a bit. I'm not saying that I've never had sex or anything. I—"

Matthews held up his hand. "Whoa, lady. *Way* too much information. I'm not interested in getting a rundown on every aspect of your personal sex life. I simply asked if you were aware of Dr. Rocca having any personal problems."

Haley Jo bit the corner of her cheek. She was babbling. It never failed—put her in a tight situation and she babbled like a fool. At least that was what her brothers always accused her of doing.

"I wasn't aware of Dr. Rocca having any problems," she said. "I know his wife really well. She's a great person...okay, maybe she's a teeny bit bitchy at times. But it probably isn't easy being married to Dr. Rocca."

"So you knew he was married, yet you accompanied him to the conference alone?"

Haley Jo jammed both fists on her hips and stuck out her chin. This cowboy was starting to get on her nerves, bigtime. "It wasn't like I came as his date or anything like that. We work together. We drove up to the conference together. We both checked into our *own* rooms. End of story."

Matthews smiled, but Haley Jo couldn't help feeling as though it was the same kind of smile a shark gave right before it chomped on some poor, defenseless, little reef guppy.

Her knees were a little weak and she started to sit down in the chair next to the dresser.

"Don't sit," Sam snapped and then forced himself to take a deep breath.

The woman seemed to have no grasp of the trouble she was in. Instead, she smiled sweetly and folded her arms, apparently unaware that between the deep breath and the folded arms, she had just pulled up the hem of her skimpy outfit another tantalizing inch. Sweet Caroline, but she had nice legs.

A loud knock tore his attention away from her, and Sam had to admit that he welcomed the interruption.

"Come in," he said, feeling irritated but not exactly sure why.

He was almost relieved to see a pair of burly state troopers push open the door and step inside. Too much longer in the company of Ms. Haley Jo Simpson and Sam figured he'd be ready for a trip to the bat house. The woman was a total flake. An undeniably tasty-looking little flake, but a flake nonetheless. It was almost a relief to know he could hand her over to the troopers and excuse himself from the whole scene.

He recognized both troopers. New recruits who had arrived at the local barracks only two or three months ago. Raw. Right out of the police academy and still in awe of their own self-importance.

With interest, he watched as the two took in the sight of Dr. Rocca in all his glory. Their response was minimal. Even with only two months under their belts, the two obviously knew how to school their expressions. But their reaction to Ms. Simpson almost made Sam smile. Mainly because Ms. Simpson was a genuine showstopper, and the two men's expressions definitely confirmed that fact.

Of course, Sam understood. Hell, he had struggled himself earlier not to react to her appeal. A man would have to be totally devoid of testosterone not to feel anything when they got a look at Ms. Haley Jo Simpson in her minute scrap of raw silk, barefooted and more than a tad rattled.

Of course, the copper-colored curls cascading down over

her small shoulders and onto a truly magnificent chest didn't hurt matters any.

Disgusted with himself, Sam raked a restless hand through his hair. Hell, he sounded like some kind of sexist pig. But then, there was no getting around the fact that the little lady had what guys in high school used to call a *really nice rack*.

Too bad the package included a grating downstate accent and an excessive urge to tell anyone within arm's length her entire life's history in a single stream of consciousness. Not to mention her inability to focus longer than a New York minute.

The taller of the two troopers cleared his throat and managed to croak, "Afternoon, Chief."

Sam nodded curtly. "Are the forensics unit and coroner on the way?"

Their attention didn't budge from Ms. Simpson, but they both nodded in unison.

"Gentlemen, would you mind tearing your eyes off Ms. Simpson for a moment."

Both snapped around, the smaller of the two blushing a bit. "Sorry, sir. Both are on their way. And Lieutenant Grant should be on the scene at any moment."

The taller one's gaze was already drifting back in the direction of Ms. Haley Jo. Sam figured it would be prudent to see that she was clothed a bit more modestly before the rest of the law enforcement contingent arrived. Otherwise, no one was going to get anything done.

He noticed the manager hovering around the doorway. "Have you got anything she can put on? An extra uniform or something?"

"Why can't I just get something out of my suitcase?" she asked, her hand dropping away from the lapels of her robe. Bad move. The material immediately parted, revealing the creamy upper curve of both her breasts. Someone— Sam wasn't sure who, but hoped it wasn't him—sucked in a quick breath of air through his teeth.

From the expressions on the two troopers' faces, Sam

figured one or both of them was going to swallow his tongue at any moment. "Nothing can be removed from the room, Ms. Simpson, this is the scene of a murder."

Her green eyes widened a bit at the word *murder,* and Sam found himself marveling at the clear, almost iridescent shine to them. He glanced away, telling himself he needed to concentrate on the case.

"Oh, right. I should have realized that," she said. "I— I watch *Law and Order* all the time." She shot a hesitant smile up at the trooper closest to her, her lips parting in the most alluring way. "Personally, I liked Benjamin Bratt the best. Although, Jimmy Smits was pretty good, too—cutest little tush on that guy." She laughed and Sam shook his head. Hell and damnation, the woman giggled and the two troopers smiled like they were at a cocktail party.

He opened his mouth to interrupt, but she kept right on rolling, "My best friend, Melanie, she liked the other guy—the one who starred in the show for the first few seasons. You know the one. He ended up leaving the show because he wanted to make it big in motion pictures. It was really sad. He was all famous, and then suddenly he simply—"

"Ms. Simpson," Sam said wearily.

She didn't even pause for a breath. "And then I heard on one of those tell-all shows that he'd gotten into some kind of trouble. But there was no telling Melanie that. She had a bird every time I even mentioned it. But I—"

"Ms. Simpson," he said from between clenched teeth.

She stopped in mid-sentence and glanced up at him with a look of innocent surprise.

"We really don't need a blow-by-blow description of your TV watching habits. This is a murder investigation, not the *Oprah* show."

Her face crumpled a bit. "Oh, yeah. Sorry. I just forgot what I—" Tears welled up in her eyes, and her fingers tore at the fringe on the end of her belt. "You'll have to excuse me. I think I'm a little more frazzled than I thought."

Both troopers glared at Sam, letting him know that he

was in the running for a Bully of the Year award. The taller one awkwardly patted her shoulder and murmured something soft.

Impatient, Sam stepped forward and brushed the two policemen aside. Another minute and one of them would probably be calling room service to order her tea and toast.

He touched the small of her back to guide her toward the door. He tried to ignore the blast of heat that shot up through the tips of his fingers. The woman was a damn furnace.

He dropped his hand. "Would you mind joining me outside the room, Ms. Simpson? I think these two gentlemen have some work to do."

She nodded, the threat of tears apparently over.

As they stepped out into the hall, the manager hustled up to meet them. He shoved a blue cotton dress into Haley Jo's hands. "I asked housekeeping to send this up. It's an extra uniform." He glanced around, and then used his key to open the room across the hall. "You can change in here, miss. It's an empty room."

Haley Jo reappeared a few minutes later.

Sam realized that he'd been wrong to hope that the dress would cause less of a problem than the robe.

She'd donned the dress as asked, one of those snap-up-the-front uniforms. It was a simple garment, produced to serve a purpose. Unfortunately, it was also made for a woman with a lot less chest.

Haley Jo had managed to get the upper half secured, with the exception of the very top snap. But it was the two snaps below that caused Sam some concern. Both seemed overly stressed, giving anyone who was paying attention a tantalizing glimpse of black lace.

He pulled his gaze up off her chest and met her clear green gaze. She shrugged, and he had to struggle to keep from glancing down to see if the motion caused the two maxed-out fasteners to pop.

Luckily, he was saved from further comment when Andy

Grant, the state trooper who was to assume charge of the investigation stepped off the elevator.

"How's it going, Chief? Heard you had some excitement brewing over here." Andy strolled down the hall with his usual rolling gait. Andy was a full six and half inches shorter than he, and Sam knew his good friend just squeaked past the state trooper height requirements. But the guy more than made up for it in the area of brains, which was the main reason he was the investigator in charge of the crime scene.

"It's all yours, Andy." Sam motioned toward Haley Jo, again taking pleasure in watching another man's expression as he got a load of her.

To give Andy credit, he didn't lose it. He blinked once and then assumed his usual bland expression. "Ma'am," he said, nodding his head.

"Ms. Simpson is registered as the only occupant of the room," Sam said. "It's her boss, a dentist, who will be needing the coroner's service. And just so you know, the good doctor won't be using his drill again—if you get my drift."

"I get your drift and it's not appreciated," Haley Jo said. "And while we're on the subject, I'm a little tired of your innuendoes." She turned a tentative smile on Andy. "Is there somewhere I can wait? I don't appreciate having to stand around in the hall. And I really would like to be wearing my own clothes."

"We'll be dealing with that all real soon, ma'am." He glanced over at Sam again. "You going to assist on this one?"

Sam shook his head. "No thanks. Just keep me posted. I have to get Prudie over to the ball field. And I've got to admit that I'm real content handing this one over to you."

He shot a meaningful look in the direction of Haley Jo and Andy's smile got even wider. "Well, if you're sure…"

Sam fished his sunglasses out of his chest pocket and slipped them on. "Oh, I'm real sure. No doubt at all." He moved down the hall and called over one shoulder, "Afternoon, Ms. Simpson. Best of luck to you."

She didn't respond. Not that Sam expected any reply. The animosity between the two of them was pretty thick there at the end. But nonetheless, he could feel the heat of her stare against the back of his neck.

It was no small relief to step back into the elevator and punch the down button. He watched as the door slid shut, trying without much success to ignore the pair of frightened green eyes that stared at him just before he left. They seemed to accuse him of desertion. As the elevator started moving, Sam Matthews told himself he was one lucky guy since he would never have to stare into those eyes again.

3

LATER THAT EVENING, Sam threw a damp dish towel over his shoulder and rinsed out the sink. Wearily, he glanced around, glad that he'd gotten things cleaned up in a relatively short period of time. There was nothing worse than getting up in the morning and facing a sink full of dirty dishes.

The thought made him smile. Who'd have thought that he'd reach a point where he'd actually take pride in the tidy appearance of the oversize kitchen? If his mother was still alive, she'd get a kick out of this unexpected touch of domesticity in her rough-and-tumble son.

Not that he was bucking for the title of Martha Stewart of the North Country, Sam thought ruefully. When he and Prudie had first moved into the place, he'd felt a bit overwhelmed. Hell, truth be known, he'd been in way over his head. Five bedrooms, a country kitchen, three fireplaces, and he with an infant daughter and no wife.

But the house had come with the job—one of the few perks the chief of police in the tiny town of Reflection Lake enjoyed. So over the years Sam and Prudie had settled into the old, rambling Victorian house on Main Street, making it home, and it wasn't long before Prudie dubbed it their rattle-trap shack, but Sam knew she loved every nook and cranny of the old place. If he ever quit the job as chief of police, he knew she'd be heartbroken.

But Sam had no plans to quit. He liked the job and he liked the fact that his office was attached right to the house. A few steps down an enclosed walkway and he was at work, no need to get wet in a rainstorm or cold in the winter. When Prudie had been a baby it meant never being far from her. And now that she was older, it meant never having her far from his supervision, which, considering Prudie's disposition, was a necessity.

Snapping a lid on a plastic container, Sam stuck the leftover meat loaf in the refrigerator. It would make a nice sandwich for tomorrow's lunch. Especially with so much left, what with Prudie deciding during dinner that she was now a vegetarian and couldn't eat meat loaf or any other kind of meat ever again. Sam wondered what she'd say at breakfast when she found out that bacon was meat.

He grinned and draped the towel over a nearby rack, careful to make sure that the hem matched the hem of the other towel on the rack. As he exited the kitchen he grabbed a bag of pretzels, flicked off the lights and walked to the bottom of the stairs. He listened.

Silence.

Relief washed over him. Apparently, Prudie had decided that she'd challenged him enough for one day. He'd already climbed the stairs five times to make sure she was tucked in and the TV was indeed off. He didn't doubt she'd simply gone undercover, hiding beneath the sheets with a flashlight and her new Harry Potter book. But as long as she was quiet and the TV was off, Sam was satisfied.

Plopping on the couch, Sam kicked off his moccasins and grabbed the remote. As he flipped aimlessly through the stations, he munched on a handful of pretzels and glanced at the clock on the mantel—9:45 p.m.

In all probability, he could manage another hour before falling asleep. Just enough time to catch a documentary he wanted to watch on the History Channel. But he'd call it a night after that because there was no chance he'd make it through the late news without nodding off, and at thirty-three, his back wasn't in any mood to withstand another night on the lumpy couch.

He hooked a foot under the hassock and pulled it closer. But as he settled his feet on top, someone rapped on the front door. His Great Dane, Razor Beak, charged headlong down the main staircase, a deep-throated growl emanating from his giant muzzle.

Sam knew from experience that the dog had been asleep on Prudie's bed. The great beast considered it his assigned duty to spend his nights stretched out next to her. But let anyone try to invade their domain, and that was the signal for Razor Beak to come down the stairs like a rolling rock of granite.

Groaning, Sam pulled himself up and slipped his shoes back on. The single worst disadvantage of small-town policing was that Sam knew he was *it* when it came to dealing with any and all problems of the village's population. And that included problems that tended to develop in the middle of the night.

He opened the front door.

Standing on his front steps stood Little Ms. Deadly Receptionist and Future Dental Hygienist, Haley Jo Simpson, conveniently flanked on either side by the same two troopers who had shown up earlier at the resort.

Haley Jo smiled up at him; one of her cheerful, *hi there, I'm back in your life* type smiles Sam had a feeling she was famous for. The smile disappeared as fast as it appeared when Razor Beak stuck his head out the door and rumbled a nasty greeting to one and all.

Haley Jo tried to step back, but the two men on either side of her didn't budge, effectively hemming her in. She reached out and tentatively patted Razor Beak's massive head, her brilliant green-painted fingernails glittering merrily beneath the dim porch light. Sam wondered when she'd had time to do her nails—probably during her interrogation. His assessment of Andy's skills as a tough cop slipped a notch.

"Nice doggie," she said. "Please don't take a chunk out of me, dog."

Apparently deeming her harmless, Razor Beak nudged her in the stomach, and Haley Jo stumbled back against the two cops. Both grabbed her and propped her back up. She managed to squeak out her thanks.

Sam reached down and shoved the beast out the door. Razor loped off into the darkness, bent on finding some real criminal types to feast upon.

Straightening up, he leaned a shoulder against the door frame. "Why do I have the feeling that this isn't a courtesy call before shipping little Ms. Haley Jo Sunshine off to a downstate slammer?"

Both troopers laughed. The taller one pulled off his hat and gave him an apologetic grin. "Sorry, Chief," he said. "We thought Lieutenant Grant might have gotten ahold of you by now. He sent us over. He's—" the trooper shifted nervously, glanced at his partner and then shrugged "—well, he's got a big favor to ask."

Sam stepped back and motioned the three inside. "I know I'm going to regret this. What kind of favor?"

Haley Jo brushed past him, her arm touching his, and Sam braced himself for the expected zing. Sure enough, a tiny electric shock ran up the length of his arm, and tickled something low in his belly.

Damn. How did she manage to do that? It was enough to send a man careening off the edge of control.

Sam was pretty sure he didn't want to feel anything, especially attraction when around this woman. It was embarrassing. But then, from the light blush that crept up along the side of Haley Jo's neck and into her cheeks, Sam figured she'd felt something, too.

She looked tired, her ringlets of burnished curls seeming to sag a bit. Her heavy-lidded eyes, the ones his mom would have called Hollywood bedroom eyes, seemed almost swollen, the dark lashes brushing her cheeks as she blinked in the bright light of the living room.

The major change was in her clothing. Gone was the blue uniform. Apparently, the troopers had allowed her to get some of her own things. Unfortunately, it didn't mean she was any better covered than when she was at the hotel. The nicest thing he could say was that her taste in clothing bordered on the flashy side.

She'd changed into something that could only be described as a slip. A slinky, slippery-looking little number which, believe it or not, looked like rattlesnake skin. Who wore a dress that looked like rattlesnake skin?

The straps on the dress were so narrow Sam figured he could have plucked one off and used it as dental floss. As a possible concession to an Adirondack evening's chill, she had pulled on some type of gauzy cover-up, knotting it directly below her breasts. She plunked herself down on the arm of his couch, watching them all expectantly.

"Lieutenant Grant wanted you to know that he's cleared Ms. Simpson of any direct involvement in Dr. Rocca's murder," the taller trooper said. "But he's concerned that she might actually be a target of the killer. It seems there's a little more to this Dr. Rocca than we'd all originally thought."

"Not a big surprise." Sam gave Haley Jo a nod, not sure where all of this was going. "But I'm thinking that there wasn't a big need for you to stop by to tell me this in person. A simple phone call would have worked just fine."

Both troopers glanced at each other, the smaller one shrugging as if to signal that he thought his partner should just go ahead and say whatever they were holding back.

"Well...Lieutenant Grant thought you might be agreeable to helping out with the investigation a bit."

Sam shrugged. "Andy knows I'm always willing to lend a hand."

The two troopers smiled, and a touch of suspicion tickled the back of Sam's neck. Perhaps he shouldn't have spoken so quickly. "Anyone interested in coffee? I'm getting the feeling that I'm going to need the caffeine."

The shorter of the two managed an apologetic look. "No thanks, Chief. We really need to push off. We have a ton of paperwork to get through."

Both troopers edged out the door, but Haley Jo kept her seat on the arm of his couch. Her dress, if the damn thing could be called that, slid halfway up her slender thighs, and her open-toe, three-inch heels swung back and forth on the tips of her painted toes. Sam couldn't help noticing that her legs were bare beneath a sweet tan.

He forced himself to glance away. He seriously needed to get a grip. "I don't have any difficulty with you gentlemen leaving. But it would appear that you've left someone behind."

The smaller trooper had already disappeared down the walkway but the taller one hastened to say, "Uh...sorry, Chief. That's the uh...favor Lieutenant Grant is going to call you about. He would really appreciate it if you'd keep Ms. Simpson here in protective custody." He was talking fast as he jammed his hat back on his head. "I'm sure he'll be calling any minute now to explain things. Night, Ms. Simpson." He was out the door and into the already rolling police cruiser before Sam had a chance to open his mouth.

Sam started to shut the door, but it was knocked back open by Razor making a reappearance. Apparently there was a shortage of prey, and he wanted back in.

Sam locked the door after the mutt sashayed through and then turned to regard his uninvited guest. "It would appear that they've taken off without you."

Haley Jo laughed. "I think what you meant to say was that they dumped me on you."

He shook his head, but he knew he didn't look very convincing. In any case, Andy Grant had a lot to answer for when he finally got around to calling and explaining why Haley Jo Simpson was sitting in his living room as if she owned it.

She hopped down off the arm of the couch and walked around the room, trailing her fingers lightly along the surface of things as if memorizing them by touch. "They're afraid of you, you know? All the way over here the two of them argued back and forth about who was going to actually tell you that you were stuck with me." She stopped, turned around and cocked her head. "Do you have a bad temper or something?"

Sam snorted and bent down to scoop up a rawhide chewy

the size of a small country Razor Beak had deposited in the middle of the floor earlier in the evening.

Razor growled deep in his throat, registering his protest that anyone dared to move one of his belongings. But Sam ignored him and tossed the slobbery thing into the mutt's junk box near the fireplace.

If Haley Jo tripped over the damn thing, she'd end up in the hospital with a dislocated hip. The house wasn't geared to accommodate women in heels. Sam and Prudie usually clomped around in L.L. Bean boots or sneakers. "No, I've never done a thing to either of those two. And no, I don't have a bad temper."

She gave him a hard look, lifting one perfectly plucked brow in disbelief.

He shrugged. "Okay, I admit to letting off steam once in a while. I don't tolerate incompetence well, and I'm not opposed to letting a person know that."

She pursed her lips and nodded knowingly. It irritated him. How the hell had he gotten into this position of standing in his living room being judged by some dippy redhead who didn't know when to shut her mouth? An absolutely delicious-looking mouth with a fascinating little indentation in the middle of its full bottom lip... Sam wondered what it would feel like to run his tongue across the center of that little indentation. Would she squirm and sigh softly? Sam gritted his back teeth. He needed caffeine. Quick.

She surveyed him with those disturbingly brilliant green eyes and smiled. "I have a feeling that you make people uncomfortable."

He frowned. "What do you mean? I'm very good with people."

She shrugged and started moving around, investigating the room again. "You just strike me as the kind of guy who smolders a bit too much. That kind of stuff makes people nervous. And those two troopers were twitchy as all get-out knowing they had to come here and talk to you."

"Probably because they were feeling guilty about dropping you off on my doorstep and felt sorry for me."

"No need to get insulting."

He glanced over, surprised to see her leaning around the corner, poking her head into his kitchen. It gave him a rather startling look at her nicely rounded tush, and the ache he'd experienced earlier when she'd accidentally touched him at the hotel leaped back into existence. For pity's sake, didn't the woman realize that when she wore her dresses that short she needed to remain in a stand-up position at all times? If she bent over much farther, Sam figured he'd know her as intimately as her gynecologist.

She turned back around and blushed. "Sorry. I get a little nosy sometimes."

Sam quickly averted his eyes. He didn't want to get caught trying to cop an indecent peek.

She walked back and plopped down on top of her suitcase—which, Sam suddenly realized, was sitting right inside the door. Not only had the two state goons deposited her on his doorstep without any real explanation, they'd dropped off all her belongings, too.

"Sorry for the late hour." She glanced toward the stairway. "I guess your wife and Prudie are asleep upstairs, huh?"

"Prudie's asleep. And there's no wife."

Her eyes widened a bit. "No wife, huh? Divorced or widowed?"

"Divorced." He tried to make his tone cold enough that she'd get the idea that it was a closed subject. "Prudie and I live here alone."

"Sorry. I didn't mean to bring up a painful subject."

"Not painful. We divorced a long time ago and any pain I might have felt is long gone."

"Buried you mean."

"Excuse me?"

"The pain—it isn't gone, it's just buried," she said matter-of-factly. "You can't ever really get rid of emotional pain. It just goes underground and pops when we least expect it."

Sam opened his mouth to say something and then closed

it again. When had their conversation taken this philosophical turn? And how the hell had they gotten on to the topic of his divorce? If he knew what was good for him, Sam would get Ms. Haley Jo out of his house and over to his office. Distance from this woman was the only game plan that was going to keep them both sane and alive over the next few days. If he was lucky, he'd be able to assign the bulk of the guard duty to his deputy, Chester Smart.

"I can see that you don't believe me. You're probably a stuffer," she said, nodding in what he was sure she thought was a wise manner.

"Excuse me? A stuffer?"

"You know—stuffers are the kind of people who never accept any of their negative feelings. They just stuff them down. Stuff them down." She threw up her hands. "Until finally they simply explode."

"Rest assured, Ms. Simpson, I'm not about to explode."

She smiled knowingly. "Sure. That's what they all say—right before becoming a trembling, quivering mass of emotional pain."

"Ms. Simpson—"

"Call me Haley Jo. Everybody does."

She yawned and stretched, and the gauzy thingamajig covering her upper chest pulled across her breasts. Sam swallowed against the sudden dryness in his throat and made a mental note to get out more often. The crazy feeling skittering around in his head could only mean that he needed to spend a few more Friday nights down at Kellum's, drinking a few beers, talking to some of the unattached local ladies and taking one or two of them for a quick turn or two around the dance floor—

Haley Jo broke into his thoughts. "Would you mind terribly if I took you up on that offer of coffee? I've been up since the crack of dawn, and if I don't get some caffeine in me, I think I'll be doing a face plant in the middle of your living room."

Sam welcomed the request. If he stayed in here watching her, he was afraid he'd do or say something to make her believe he wanted her to continue the analysis of him. Better to be doing something. "No problem. Coffee coming right up."

He headed for the kitchen.

"You mind if I sit on the couch?" She stood up, looking to all the world like a lost waif.

"Make yourself at home," Sam said, and then as soon as he said it, he wanted to take it back. He didn't want her making herself at home. He wanted her out of his house and most certainly out of his life. But before he could correct any misconceptions she might have gotten from his comment, the phone rang.

Sam picked it up and growled into the receiver, "This had better be your best song and dance ever, Andy."

His good friend's warm laugh rippled over the wires. "Guess she's already there, huh?"

"You know she is. Your two goons left her about ten minutes ago. They snuck off like two thieves in the night. That was after telling me that you'd be calling to explain. So explain."

"I did some quick checking on her boss, Dr. Benjamin Rocca."

"And?"

"The man couldn't keep his hands off the ladies—we kind of figured that. But he also couldn't stay off the phone to his bookie. He was in debt so high that his practice was about to fold under the pressure."

Sam glanced over at Haley Jo. She had wedged herself into the corner of his oversize couch, her shapely legs tucked up beneath her. Her high heels lay discarded in the middle of the rug. Razor had moved around to sit in front of her, laying his massive head in her lap. The damn dog never had it so good. She gently stroked his sleek ears with one hand while flipping through the channels with her other.

"So, the lovely Ms. Haley Jo was just one of many?"

"Actually, it seems like she was telling the truth. According to a few of the women working for Dr. Rocca, he'd been trying to get friendly with her for the past three months. They say she was polite but firm—telling him she wasn't interested."

"Then why make the trip up here with him?"

"Apparently he had another little lovely scheduled, but she ended up canceling on him at the last minute."

Sam could hear the creak of Andy's chair as he leaned back. He leaned a hip against the counter, positioning himself so he could see into the living room. "So how'd Ms. Simpson end up the lucky one?"

Grant sighed. "I got it from two different sources that he threatened to fire her if she didn't go with him."

"That would make our Dr. Rocca a real prince of a guy."

"You ain't kidding," Grant said. "The more I learn about the guy, the more I hate him."

From the living room came the sound of the eleven o'clock news starting. Haley Jo had started throwing pretzels into the air for Razor. Sam figured that if the beast came down on one of her perfectly painted toes she'd go straight through the ceiling. "So that brings us back to why Ms. Simpson is sitting on my couch in my living room."

"I need you to keep her with you in protective custody for a short time."

The kettle on the stove took that moment to send out a shrill whistle. Sam clicked off the burner, measured instant coffee into two heavy ceramic mugs and poured boiling water over it. "And the reason I'm going to do this is...?"

Andy laughed. "Because you owe me." And then his voice took on a more serious note. "And we don't know if he told her something on the trip up to the resort. The candy found in her room was laced with a strong sedative. It was delivered to her. I want to make sure she wasn't a target, too."

"It seems unlikely," Sam said, slowly stirring the coffee. "Especially since you've already determined that she really isn't mixed up with this guy."

"True. But I'm not willing to take any chances. Are you?"

Sam glanced back into the living room. Haley Jo was talking softly to Razor, rubbing her cheek up against his jowly muzzle. Lucky dog.

"No, I wouldn't like to take any chances."

"Great! I knew I could depend on you. I'll keep you up-to-date on my progress. Make sure she keeps a low profile."

"Yeah, sure. That's like asking some pop diva to dress conservatively for the MTV Video Awards."

"Chief, I didn't know you were so hip. Only proves I made the right choice in tagging you for this job." Andy clicked off before Sam could demonstrate just how hip he was.

Sam set the cups and spoons on a small tray, added the cream and sugar and then paused to take a deep breath. Andy had made it clear that he was stuck with her. But he figured he'd make the best of it. Above everything else, Sam considered himself a professional. A coolheaded professional who knew how to keep his personal life separate from his job. With any luck, Haley Jo would hit the road again in a few days and his house could get back to normal. Until then, he'd get her settled—in his holding cell, *not* here in his house.

4

HALEY JO GLANCED UP from her spot on the couch when Sam Matthews reentered the room. He carried a tray with two mugs, a small ceramic creamer and bowl of what was probably sugar.

He smiled, and she couldn't help noticing that it was one of those extra-polite smiles a man gave a woman who was driving him totally bonkers. Not bonkers in a wildly, delicious sexual way. Bonkers in a way that said Matthews was trying hard to think of a way to wiggle out of this whole situation.

But in spite of the forced quality of his smile, there was no denying that it was a killer of a smile. Devastating, actually. Dazzling white teeth, sexy dimple in one cheek and a touch of devilishness in his baby blues. Haley Jo decided that Sam Matthews must set more than a few women's hearts aflutering when he pulled them over for a traffic infraction. In fact, it was cute enough to make her want to go outside, get in a car and race down the middle of Main Street in hopes of getting him to chase after her with his siren wailing and lights flashing.

Too bad he was so uptight and...and correct. It made her want to reach up and slide her fingers through his hair. Rough him up a bit. Mess the thick black strands around until they tumbled down over his forehead into his eyes.

Whoa. Wait a minute.

Her little daydream had just gone over the top. She was definitely more exhausted than she'd originally thought. She glanced at the clock sitting on the mantel.

After eleven.

Well, that explained it. She was overtired. Time to regroup and get a good, firm grip on her raging hormones. If she didn't, Haley Jo was sure she'd end up jumping the local chief of police. And considering her current predicament and the level of wariness in the chief's face, Haley Jo figured such an action was a crime punishable by imprisonment or death here in Nowheresville, NY.

Matthews set the tray on the coffee table and leaned across to hand her a cup of the steaming brew. Haley Jo nodded her thanks and dropped the TV remote on the cushion beside her. Without a word, he bent down and scooped it up, depositing it in a small pouch attached to the side of the TV.

"Sorry," Haley Jo said, taking a small sip of coffee. "I'm not the organized type."

He glanced at the remote and then back at her, shrugging. "It just has a tendency to get lost pretty easily around here. Prudie and I have a system to make sure that doesn't happen."

Haley Jo laughed. "Half the fun at my place is the routine reconnaissance mission to find the TV remote or the cell phone. Both have the tendency to walk off at the most inconvenient times."

She set her mug on the end table, careful to see that it sat squarely on the cork coaster. She was pretty sure that if she'd slipped and put it directly on the polished wood of the table, Mr. Neatnik would cringe and reach over to put it on the coaster.

"Last time I looked for my cell phone I found it stuffed in my mailbox in the downstairs front hall," she said.

Matthews took a slow sip of his coffee, regarding her with unsmiling eyes. "That must have been a bit inconvenient." The sarcastic edge to his voice wasn't lost on Haley Jo. He glanced at his watch. "Look, it's getting late and I'm sure you're tired. Why don't I show you where you're going to be staying."

Haley Jo scrambled to her feet, skittering her toes across

the rug in an effort to get them back into her heels. "Sure thing. I didn't mean to hold you up."

"Not a problem."

But something told Haley Jo it was most definitely a problem; in fact, she was the problem. A problem he couldn't wait to get rid of.

He set his cup down and picked up her cosmetic case, tucking it under one arm. With his other hand, he grabbed her suitcase. "You can bring your coffee and finish it over there."

Haley Jo nodded and balanced herself on one leg, reaching down to pull on the straps of her sling back heels. "Sure thing. Lead the way."

"We'll go out the side door. My office is across the breezeway."

His office? Haley Jo was sure her mouth dropped open. What did he mean his office? Hadn't he just got through saying it was late and he was going to show her to her room? She trailed after him. Did he mean that she wasn't staying here at the house? Where did he expect her to sleep? In a jail cell?

Sure enough, that's exactly what he expected. They went outside and down a short covered walkway to a small brick building. He used a heavy key ring to unlock the side door and then stepped back to allow her to step inside.

The office was brightly lit, but there was nothing bright or cheerful about the place. With a sinking heart, Haley Jo surveyed her new home.

Calling the office drab was a gross understatement. The place was all gray walls and gunmetal-colored furniture.

A long counter at the front of the room partitioned the entrance from the general work area. Several beat-up desks squatted in a loose-knit cluster in the middle of the room. Behind one of them sprawled a giant of a man, his feet propped up on the edge of his desk, watching a small ten-inch TV.

As they entered, he almost fell over backward in his haste to get to his feet. "Evenin', Chief. I thought you'd have hit the hay by now." He reached over and turned off the sound of the TV.

"I got sidetracked." Sam motioned toward Haley Jo. "This is Ms. Simpson. She's going to be staying with us for a while. This is Chester Smart, one of my deputies."

Chester turned a pair of dark brown, very suspicious-looking eyes on her. "Ma'am." His voice and posture held all the warmth of a challenged junkyard dog.

"Pleased to meet you, Deputy Smart," Haley Jo said, sticking out a hand.

Chester started to hold out a hand and then pulled it back at the last minute, stuffing it into his pocket. Haley Jo found herself standing there with her hand awkwardly sticking out. She smiled wanly.

"Shake the lady's hand, Chester," Matthews said wearily.

Chester reddened, grabbed her hand and engulfed it in his giant paw, pumping it up and down. "Sorry, miss."

Haley Jo felt as though her hand slid across his. He dropped her hand and then rubbed his own along the side of his khaki pants, his dark-brown eyes apologetic. "I was working on my truck this afternoon, and my hands are kinda greasy."

Matthews sighed and reached over to pull a tissue out of a box, handing it to Haley Jo. "You might have mentioned that before taking off poor Ms. Simpson's hand."

Chester shrugged and grinned sheepishly.

"No problem," Haley Jo said cheerfully. "It's wiping right off." She scrubbed at her palm with the tissue.

"Chester takes the night shift—we have 911 out of Elizabethtown so all calls go through there first."

"I'm the night person," Deputy Smart said. "I like working nights."

Matthews laughed. "You prefer nights because you don't have to deal with people."

"I like people well enough, Chief. It's just more peaceful at night."

"No argument there. We do get plenty of peace and quiet around here. Too much, according to the youngsters."

"How's that?" Haley Jo asked.

"We get the family crowd in the summer—people bringing the kids up camping and such. Ski season is a little busier. We get the overflow crowd from Lake Placid. But even then the most we have to deal with is a couple of rowdy skiers down at Doug's Ski Bunny Hut."

Haley Jo grinned. "The Ski Bunny Hut? Is that anything like the Play Bunny Mansion?"

Chester snorted. "Unfortunately not." He reached up and scratched his head, and for the first time, Haley Jo noted that he had long hair, thick and brown, pulled back in a ponytail. Pretty liberal town that allows the cops to wear nonregulation hair. She wouldn't have expected Mr. Law-and-Order Matthews to tolerate a break with regulation like that.

"Come on. I'll show you where you're going to sleep." Matthews touched her arm and motioned toward the back.

Haley Jo jumped and rubbed her upper arm. Man, it was like the guy stored electricity in his hands. Warmth tingled along the surface of her arm, and the tiny hairs stood on end. "Back there?" She craned her neck to peer down the dark hall.

Chester frowned. "You're gonna make her sleep back there, Chief?"

Chester's tone told Haley Jo that even he thought the chief might have gone off the deep end.

Matthews nodded. "She'll be safer there than if we put her up in one of the local hotels."

Chester dropped back down in his chair. "If you say so, Chief." His voice said otherwise. "Might be safer, but it sure isn't a place for a nice lady... Some of those skanky broads down at Doug's maybe, but not a lady like Ms. Simpson."

Matthews sighed. "How many times do I have to tell you not to call the women down at Doug's skanky?"

Chester blew out a disgusted breath. "Hell, Chief, that

ain't an insult. Those broads live to be called skanky. Their reputation depends on it."

"Just do me a favor and can the trash talk. Okay?"

"Sure thing, Chief."

Haley Jo smiled sweetly at Chester, trying to let him know that she wasn't mad at him. Heck, he hadn't called her skanky. A lady no less. That was worth a gold star at least. It certainly showed he had better manners than his uptight boss.

Seemingly unruffled by his deputy's skepticism, Matthews motioned for her to follow. At the end of the hall, he flicked on a light and stepped aside to allow her to enter the back room first.

A flood of harsh light illuminated Haley Jo's new living quarters, and she immediately wished the chief would flick the switch back off again.

It was worse than she had anticipated. Much worse.

This wasn't just a room at the back of the local police station. It was a jail cell—two jail cells to be exact.

The ugliness was almost blinding. Bland beige linoleum floors, gray cinder block walls and thick metal bars enclosing two small cells. Her new home.

Each cell contained a cot with a thin mattress, flat, almost nonexistent pillows and a tightly tucked gray wool blanket—with hospital corners no less. Apparently the chief believed in neatness here, too.

Both cell doors yawned open, but that didn't make them any more welcoming.

"Which one?" Matthews asked.

"Which one what?"

"Which one do you want to sleep in? Your choice."

Haley Jo clutched her heart. "Be still my heart. I don't think I can handle this level of generosity."

"No need to be dramatic. Just pick."

She shook her head. "Sorry. It's impossible." She waved a hand. "The opulence. The dazzling display of grandeur. It's a bit overwhelming."

Matthews shrugged, his expression unamused. "Fine. I'll pick for you."

He brushed past her and entered the cell block on the left. With one hand, he heaved her suitcase up on the bed and set her cosmetic case next to it. "It gets damp in here sometimes—even in the summer. I hope you've brought something warm to sleep in."

Haley Jo thought about her skimpy tank top and tap shorts packed away in her bag and decided the chief was going to get a big surprise when he found her in the morning lying on the cot frozen solid like a raspberry Popsicle.

Matthews didn't wait for her response but instead, motioned toward the cell door. "Come on, I'll show you the bathroom."

Haley Jo tagged after him, feeling the sting of tears smarting at the back of her eyes. How the hell had she managed to get herself into this mess?

She'd really thought going to the conference with Dr. Rocca would have gotten him off her back...without him getting on hers. It didn't take a genius to know that if she hadn't gone with Rocca, he would have fired her. Booted her tush right out of the office onto the street. And if that had happened, nothing would have saved her from living on the streets until she'd found another job. Haley Jo had already decided she wasn't going to ask her mom or brothers to ever bail her out again. Twenty-four was old enough to handle life's little curveballs on her own.

But in spite of her initial strategy to feign cooperating with Dr. Rocca's slimy plan of seduction, Haley Jo now realized that nothing had prepared her for the tubby little dentist's murder. Or her subsequent arrest.

Of course, the fact that she'd been pretty much cleared of the murder charges was seriously overshadowed by the state police's belief that she might actually be a target, too. Little ole Haley Jo a potential murder victim? Who'd have thought? Certainly not her.

And now, to top everything off, she was expected to sleep in a smelly, damp jail cell guarded by Chief I-Don't-

Have-A-Sense-Of-Humor Sam Matthews. Unfortunately, no one but Haley Jo seemed to see this as a problem.

She glanced up. Matthews was already halfway down the hall, heading for the front again. Great! The bathroom was off the main office. Obviously, privacy *was not* going to be a high priority in this hotel.

She took off after him, the smooth soles of her heels skidding on the shiny linoleum. She saw him stop, and she really thought she'd have time to stop, too, but she hit him from behind, slamming up against his broad back like a Mack truck going downhill without any brakes. It was like hitting a wall. A very hard, unmovable brick wall.

She stumbled backward, teetering on the outer edges of her heels. For a brief moment, she thought she was going over. But Matthews reached out and grabbed her, his fingers like cool steel on tender flesh. He steadied her and kept her from making a graceless flop to the floor.

He stared down at her, his gaze seeming to cut through her like a sharp knife through new bread. The air around them had suddenly changed—becoming hot and thick.

"Slow down," he said.

She nodded and swallowed hard. "I—I'm just nervous. I've never slept in a jail before."

"It's a bed like any other bed. You get in it, close your eyes and go to sleep."

She nodded again. "I think I can handle that. The getting in and closing my eyes, anyway. It's the sleeping part that might be problematic."

He shifted, and she felt his thigh brush against her hip. Oh, no doubt about it, sleep was going to be a major difficulty.

He looked about to say something, but instead, he clamped his mouth shut and stared down at her, his body looming over her. Haley Jo wet her lips. Man, the hall had gotten warm. A tiny trickle of sweat slid down between her breasts.

"You're going to end up killing yourself running around with shoes that high," he said.

"Well, that shouldn't bother you, right? At least it would get me off your hands."

"You always this much of a smart aleck?"

She shrugged, trying not to get a crick in her neck from staring up at him. "My mother always said, 'Haley Jo, your mouth is like the local landfill—all trash.'"

He laughed. Something low, deep and totally sexy. She stared at those magnificent lips and sucked hot air.

Oh jeez, how come she had to be stuck with the sexy-looking policeman who seemed to think she was a complete airhead? Why couldn't he think she was a witty, sophisticated city girl instead of a total nut job?

He stopped laughing and the hall suddenly seemed small, intimate and very private. From the front of the building, she could hear the TV droning on. But here in the hall, the sound seemed miles away.

The subtle light in the hall cast a pale glow, highlighting the dark hair that had fallen down across his forehead, and she noticed for the first time the slightest hint of stubble covering his jawline. Somehow he didn't look so polished and correct now. Of course, that made the attraction building in the pit of her belly kick up another notch.

"Well, if you're going to be hang out here for a few days, you're going to need to wear something lower."

"Were you referring to my shoes or my blouse?" Had she really said that or had she just thought it?

He grinned, and his gaze drifted down off her face to her breasts. Oh yeah, she'd actually said it. She held her breath.

"I like what you have on right now. But if you want, I can hack a few inches off those heels."

Haley Jo took in a shaky breath. Was he actually flirting with her? Because she sure as heck was flirting with him.

His gaze shifted back up to her face. Her mouth to be exact.

"In fact, if you like, I'll take the hacksaw to them myself."

"Are—are you kidding? Do you know how much a pair of decent heels cost?" It was difficult to get the words out from between her lips. They seemed stiff and unnatural—as if him staring at them changed them. Made her more conscious of them.

He shook his head and leaned in closer, his hands on either side of her, trapping her between them. "No, I can't say that I've bought a pair of heels lately." He lifted one hand and traced the edge of her jaw. Fire started to burn where his fingers touched.

She gulped and opened her mouth, but nothing came out.

"I'm more of the hiking boots type myself," he said.

Her heart beat hard against her chest. "Well, if you ask me, high heels have gotten much too expensive." Her voice broke and she turned her head, leaning in to the stroke of his hand. "I just bought a pair of Angiolinis. Of course, they cost me more than a single paycheck, but I just had to have them. I figured I could eat noodles and crackers for a month to pay for them. But Melanie told me that—"

"Do you ever know when to shut up?" he whispered, his face somehow and inexplicably buried deep in her hair.

"Knowing when to shut up is definitely not one of my strong points," she mumbled, lifting her head to give him free access to her neck. Oh gosh, his lips were right below her ear, laying down a series of kisses so hot and erotic that Haley Jo thought she might burst into flames right then.

"My mom used to say that I—"

He took her chin in the palm of his hand and turned her toward him, settling his lips over hers. She sighed, but he trapped the sigh in her mouth.

Something warm and wonderful tickled the tips of Haley Jo's toes and then shot up the length of her legs to settle deep in the pit of her belly. Goodness, but the man knew how to kiss.

She was done for. Totally toasted—as crispy as a McDonald's french fry. She leaned in closer, moving her mouth under his and standing on tiptoe so she could slip her hands up around his neck and tunnel her fingers into the soft hair at the back of his head.

All feeling seemed to melt out the bottom of her feet and

she wrapped one leg around his, trying to keep herself from doing a face plant in the middle of the hallway. But suddenly she felt his hands clamp around her upper arms again and peel her off him as if she were a piece of clinging seaweed.

"I'm sorry. My mistake." He stepped back.

"But I—"

Haley Jo reached out and touched his arm, but Sam shook it off and turned away. He raked a shaky hand through his hair and tried to gather his scattered thoughts. What the hell had gotten into him? Had he lost his mind? The woman had been placed in his custody for protection and here he was mauling her in the back hall.

"That shouldn't have happened. I apologize."

"You don't have anything to be sorry for. I liked it. In fact, we should try it again."

Sam stiffened and turned back, ready to blast her with the hot breath of anger that rose up into the back of his throat. But he stopped, staring down at her wide-eyed gaze. It wasn't her fault. He'd been the idiot to step over the line. She had just gone along for the ride.

She seemed to sense the anger tightening his shoulders and she dropped back to lean against the wall. She reached up and touched her fingers to her bottom lip, the one with the tiny indentation he'd forgotten to investigate in the heat of the kiss.

She traced the line of her lip as if testing it for bruises. He wondered when she'd scream and charge him with attempted assault and can his butt. She had every right to do something like that.

Instead, she seemed to be struggling to catch her breath. Her dress seemed a size too small as her nipples pressed hard against the flimsy material. Sam swallowed against the dryness that had invaded his mouth, and closed his eyes for a moment, trying to will away the ache in his groin that made it almost impossible to stand.

"That should never have happened," he said again.

"What do you mean it shouldn't have happened?" Her

voice was punctuated with short pants, as if she'd run a great distance and now continued to lean against the wall trying to catch her breath. "In case you were visiting another planet while we were standing here kissing, I was most definitely grooving on what we were doing. Can you honestly say you didn't enjoy it?"

Sam clenched his back teeth. How was he supposed to answer that? Sure he'd been *grooving* on it. Truth be known, he was so hard he could hammer nails with a certain body part and never blink an eye.

But that didn't make what he'd done right. And if there was anything Sam Matthews believed in, it was acting ethically. Kissing a guest in his jail definitely came under violating those ethics.

He glanced down the hall toward the front office. The TV crowd was screaming and the grunts from people hitting the mats drifted down the corridor. He could hear Chester mumbling under his breath, no doubt trying to tell his favorite wrestler how to take the other guy down.

He glanced back at Haley Jo. She hadn't moved, still watching him with those giant, green-glass-colored eyes. He heaved a sigh. "Look, I'm telling you I'm sorry. I was totally out of line, and I have no idea why it happened."

She blew out a small puff of air. "Well, hell, I know what happened. The two of us got a little horny and acted on it."

"Well, I shouldn't have acted on it. This is a police station, not the local submarine races."

Her hand flew to her mouth and she giggled. "Oh, gosh! Did you used to hang out at the races, too? My mom would always send my brothers to the local beach to haul my fanny home." She shook her head. "But since they usually went up there with their dates, they'd always ended up staying."

She frowned. "Of course, in the process they'd scare off the guy I'd managed to convince to ask me out—"

She glanced up at him, a slight twist to one corner of her adorably kissable mouth. "—I say *convince* because no one wanted to date me because of my brothers. They were mean, ugly and six foot three. They'd scare the guy off and then make me sit in the front of their van until they were ready to leave."

Sam shook his head. He needed to get this conversation back on track pronto. He did not need to be flirting with Haley Jo while standing in the back hall of his office. He needed to be over in his house, in bed...alone.

"You need to get some sleep and I need to go back over to my house." He nodded his head toward the front office. "Chester is here all night, so you're safe. If you need anything just let him know."

Her smile disappeared and her eyes pleaded up at him. "I really have to stay here? Sleep in that—that jail cell?"

"Sorry, that's the extent of our hospitality here in Reflection Lake. You'll be fine."

"Sleeping behind bars—locked in—I'll have nightmares."

"So leave the door open. No one said I was going to lock you in."

"Then anyone who wants can walk in."

He schooled his expression to hide his exasperation. It wasn't her fault that he had no patience for this. Not when she was looking so forlorn. So lost. It nudged to life feelings he thought he had stowed away somewhere long ago. "No one is going to walk in on you, Ms. Simpson. The office is perfectly secure, and Chester is here all night."

"But what if he gets a call and has to go out?"

"Jake is out in the patrol car all night. And if Jake needs backup for some unforeseen reason, Chester calls me and I go out."

Her shoulders slumped as she seemed to understand that no amount of complaining was going to get him to change his mind.

"Fine."

But he could tell from her expression that it wasn't *fine*. He stood waiting. For what, he had no idea. He had already told her that this was how things were going to be. No wide-eyed innocent look was going to change anything. Even when it was accompanied by a heavy sigh that did interesting things to the spaghetti strap hanging halfway down the middle of her upper arm.

He shifted to his other leg. Damn but he needed a cold shower and a good night's sleep to get the picture of her out of his uncharacteristically addled brain.

"All right then, I'll be off. Sleep well," he said.

She nodded but didn't speak.

He turned and walked down the hall, turning around once to see that she still stood there watching him go.

"I'll see you in the morning," he said.

She didn't answer, but the look in her eyes told him all he needed to know about her feelings on his outright desertion. A very similar look to the one she'd given him earlier in the day. How had the woman managed to get under his thick skin so quickly and with such ease? He'd thought only Prudie had that kind of power over him.

5

HALEY JO PADDED back down the hall and stood in the doorway of the cell, surveying her new home. *Prison* might be a more accurate description.

Unfortunately, nothing had changed in the few minutes she'd taken to shamelessly grope the local law enforcement officer. The place was still a dark, little hidey-hole. Not that it was dirty or anything. No chance of that happening with Chief Matthews on the job. The place smelled of Lysol and pine. But for some reason, Haley Jo couldn't get past the idea that she was expected to sleep in an actual jail cell.

She gritted her teeth. No way was she giving up and going to pieces. Somehow, she'd make the best of a lousy situation. Mainly because that was what she was good at—making the best of things.

She marched into the cell, reached down and unzipped her suitcase. Grabbing her pajamas and robe off the top, she clutched them to her chest and headed back down the hall to the bathroom.

Chester barely glanced up from his TV when she reentered the outer office. The forward hunch of his shoulders told Haley Jo that he probably wasn't in the least bit inclined to chat.

She sighed and let herself into the tiny bathroom. So much for using the big deputy for dealing with any sudden attack of the lonelies. She stared at the tiny shower stall with the stark white plastic curtain, the overhead chain commode and the old-fashioned pedestal sink with the cracked bowl and chunky faucets and bit back tears. This was worse than her first apartment, the one she'd rented when she'd moved out on her own.

Reaching behind her, she fumbled for the lock. There was nothing there. No lock. No bolt. She sighed. At least the bathroom in her first apartment had a lousy lock on it.

She pinched the bridge of her nose and forced the tears back. No way was she going to cry. Things could be worse. A lot worse. She could be facing a stainless steel toilet and sink located right in the cell.

A few minutes later, she emerged from the bathroom, her face and teeth scrubbed clean, clothes over one shoulder and her robe wrapped securely around her. Of course, Chester was still mesmerized by the TV.

"Night," she called, standing at the head of the hall, half hoping he'd ask her to stick around for a cup of hot chocolate and a bit of conversation.

He waved, but didn't look up.

She shrugged and continued back down the corridor to her cell. Sitting on the edge of her cot, she leaned down and pulled her purse into her lap. From the front office, she could hear the roar of the crowd and Chester's muted laughter.

Her mind drifted back to twenty minutes ago and the kiss. What had happened to the two of them? It was like someone had stuffed her head with firecrackers and set them off by remote control.

She rubbed the tip of her finger across her bottom lip, touching the very spot Chief Matthews had kissed so thoroughly. Who'd have thought a cop—an uptight, by-the-book fanatic—could kiss so deliciously?

She grinned and pulled her knees closer to her chest. It had felt so nice. Better than nice. It had felt downright sinful. She straightened out her legs, her toes curling in memory. This was too delicious to keep to herself. She needed to tell someone.

Anyone.

Most assuredly Melanie.

She dug around in the bottom of her purse. She really

did need to clean the thing out. She grinned and pulled out her cell phone. Lucky for her she hadn't left it locked up in her mailbox at home.

She paused, her finger hovering over the buttons. Sam—she figured she could call him Sam now that he had kissed her so thoroughly—would not approve. She shrugged. Heck, he'd been the one to play Cinderfella, disappearing when things had started to get interesting. She hit speed dial.

The phone rang once and someone snatched it up. "Hello?"

"Mel, it's me—Haley Jo."

"Jo-Jo!" Melanie squealed. There was a slight pause and then she came back on with a whisper, "Where are you, girl? I've been worried sick about you."

"Relax, sweetie. I'm okay. Hang on a sec." Haley Jo cocked her head and listened. The wild grunts and bone-chilling slams of bodies hitting a wrestling mat drifted down the hall. Obviously Deputy Smart wasn't going to overhear anything he wasn't supposed to.

Haley Jo rested her elbow on one knee and pushed the receiver closer to her mouth. "Okay—I can talk. What did you hear?"

"I *heard* that Dr. Rocca was murdered, and that the police had put you in protective custody." Melanie's voice dipped even lower as if she, too, were struggling not to be overheard.

"Well, what you heard is what happened."

There was a moment of silence. Haley Jo figured that any discussion including confirmation that Dr. Rocca was dead was more than a little shocking for poor Melanie. The man might have been an annoying lech, but that didn't warrant being marked for murder.

"Oh, my gosh, Jo-Jo! I was the one who was supposed to go to the conference with him. It could have been me!"

"Don't think that didn't cross my mind when the cops came and hauled my fanny off to jail."

"They really put you in jail?"

"I'm talking to you right this minute from a jail cell."

"Get out of here!"

"Can't—I'm in jail. Remember?"

Haley Jo slumped sideways and rested her elbow on the pitiful excuse for a pillow. Okay, so she wasn't actually *locked in,* but she was lonely and needed a little sympathy. It had only taken her a few minutes to realize she wouldn't be getting any from Mr. Tall, Dark and Totally Uptight, Chief Matthews. And if there was anything Haley Jo knew, it was that a lady needed to get her sympathy from whomever and whenever it was offered.

"This is just too weird for words. How come they put you in jail?" Her voice lowered to a hush. "They don't think you killed Dr. Ben, do they?"

"No. Or at least they aren't *saying* they think I'm the killer." Haley Jo shifted the phone to her other ear. "They said that I needed to stay here until they cleared things up—for my own safety. They think the killer might have been trying to knock me off, too."

Melanie didn't answer, but her shocked silence shot out over the phone wires loud and clear. Haley Jo pushed herself back up to a sitting position. "You still there, Mel?"

"I'm here. But hang on a sec."

Haley Jo heard her girlfriend set down the phone, and then, a few seconds later, she heard a click and the sound of another line opening.

"There. I'm on the portable," Melanie said. Haley Jo heard her walk back and hang up the other phone. "I'm going to go out and sit on the fire escape. Cy is in the living room, and you know how he gets when I'm yakking on the phone."

Oh, yes indeedy, though Haley Jo had never met Cy, she knew full well. Mainly because Melanie's so-called lover didn't hesitate to make his views known on the subject. He'd yell and shout whenever Melanie tried to talk on the phone. And to make matters worse, the miserable thug refused to have anything to do with any of Melanie's *empty-headed bimbo* friends.

She waited as Melanie opened the window and climbed over the sill onto the fire escape. Before Cy had moved in, Haley Jo and Melanie spent many an evening sitting out on the fire escape, drinking wine coolers, discussing men's finer points—of which there were too few they decided—and calling out to the cute guys walking by. Of course, since Cy had moved in, they hadn't had the chance to indulge in this favored pastime.

"Okay, I'm settled in," Melanie said. "Jeez, I'd forgotten how high it is up here. Did we really used to sit up here and drink?"

"Most assuredly. And you had the habit of sitting on the rail with your legs dangling over the side while yelling, 'Look at me, I can fly.'"

"Criminey! I must have been drunker than a skunk."

"Just slightly crazy."

Melanie giggled. "All right, enough silliness. What's this about you being in jail? Do I need to come up there and bail you out?"

"Chief Matthews says it's only for my own safety."

"I'm coming up anyway."

"Yeah, right. Like Cy would let you. Get real, Mel. You and I both know that he won't let you go down to the local grocery without a tracking device strapped to your ankle."

A heavy sigh crackled over the wires. "Well, that's a bit extreme. But I have to agree that he is the jealous type."

"Don't worry. I'll call every day and I'll let you know as soon as things are straightened out. Will you—"

"Oh, shoot! Cy's calling me. He'll be ticked if he finds me out here gabbing on the phone. Call me tomorrow!"

"Don't tell—" the phone clicked in her ear "—anyone where I am," she finished.

Blinking back her disappointment, Haley Jo shut off her cell phone and stuffed it back into the bottom of her purse. So much for a comforting chat from her best friend.

She tugged aside the covers and slipped her legs under the stiff, starched sheet. Lordy, but they were so stiff it was like sliding between two pieces of cardboard. She couldn't help but wonder if the good chief ironed the dang things with spray starch.

She snuggled down into the thin pillow and tried to drown out the sounds of the TV. Chester appeared to have moved on to some type of cop show. The guns going off and the sirens wailing in the background were good clues.

As she closed her eyes and drifted off, Haley Jo wondered if Chief Matthews slept in the raw.

SAM OPENED the refrigerator and surveyed the contents. Pretty slim pickings. Either he needed to get over to Saranac Lake to shop in the near future or he and Prudie would be reduced to consuming noodles and crackers. Not that Prudie would mind.

He reached for a soda and then at the last minute grabbed the lone beer sitting on the bottom shelf. He needed a little extra sustenance tonight. Something to calm his uncharacteristically jangled nerves.

Straightening up, he used his knee to nudge the door shut. A comfortable darkness settled over the kitchen. Through the open window over the sink, the sound of crickets drifted in with the smell of lilac and freshly mowed grass.

He leaned back against the edge of the counter and rolled the side of the ice-cold bottle across his hot forehead. Scant relief.

What he really needed to do was stuff the bottle down the front of his pants and cool off the part of his anatomy that still held a very affectionate hard-on for his newly installed guest.

He groaned as an image of Haley Jo flashed across his brain. Her petite frame backed up against the wall, and her copper-colored curls shimmering in the dimly lit hallway. Damn. Maybe a cold shower was in order.

What was wrong with him? It wasn't as if he hadn't dated any women since Peggy left. He might not be the Don Juan of Reflection Lake, but some thought he was quite the catch.

Quite the catch. Who was he kidding? That term went out with black-and-white TV. In fact, he was pretty sure it was a term his mother had used when he was a pimply-faced teen and agonizing over whether or not any girl was ever going to accept his invitation to the movies. His mom had ruffled his hair and told him that someday a nice girl was going to recognize him as *quite the catch.* There was no getting around it now—he was seriously out of touch.

Laughing, Sam twisted the top off his beer. Foam spilled over the rim and slid down over his fingers. The sharp smell of yeast filled his senses as he took a quick sip.

Perfect. Ice and the sharp tang of the beer washed over his tongue, cooling the very spot that still burned from touching Haley Jo's sweet lips. Tearing off a paper towel, he wiped off the bottle and then headed for the living room. Razor Beak lifted his head, and with a short grunt pulled himself to his feet. Without a backward glance, the dog leaped up the stairs. He was eager to return to Prudie's bed now that Sam had returned to the house and he wasn't responsible for guarding the downstairs.

Sam checked the front door, shut off the lights and then headed up the stairs himself. He paused in the doorway of Prudie's room and leaned against the frame as he took another short swallow of beer.

This used to be his favorite pastime—watching Prudie sleep. When she'd been a baby, he'd stand over the bed for hours on end, staring down at her, awed by her miniature perfection.

Prudie always seemed to approach sleep with grim determination, her tiny mouth pursed as if in deep concentration with a small frown etched between her eyebrows. Sam used to think it was because she was having a bad dream. But after a while, he realized that her frown came because she hated to let the day end. To Prudie, sleep was surrender, and she was one person who hated to surrender to anything.

When she was younger, Sam would lie in bed with her and read her favorite stories. He'd stretch out in her little bed, his feet hanging off the side, and cradle her up against him, holding the book on his belly. Prudie would stare up at him with solemn brown eyes, her favorite blanket wrapped around her thumb as she slowly stroked her cheek.

For years, the book she begged him to read each night was Dr. Seuss's *Green Eggs and Ham*. She never seemed to tire of it, and in his heart, Sam knew why. *Green Eggs and Ham* was Prudie's connection to her mother.

It had been a gift from Peggy on the occasion of her first visit, four years after she had left town, abandoning them both. An impressionable five-year-old, Prudie had been enchanted with her mommy's flamboyant beauty and carefree laughter. She hadn't wanted Peggy to leave again. In fact, she had cried and hung on to Peggy's leg, promising that she'd be good.

But Peggy left anyway, somewhat confused and pleased by her daughter's show of affection but as usual, in a rush to get somewhere. Since that visit, Peggy's letters, postcards and phone calls had dribbled in, decreasing in number with each passing year.

Prudie refused to talk about the visit, and after a few years, she didn't ask for the book to be read anymore. But Sam knew that the book was never far from his daughter's side.

He bent down and smoothed back a strand of soft brown hair. Prudie lay on her stomach, her legs tangled in the sheets. Sam smiled at the familiar frown hanging beneath her wispy bangs. He reached down and untangled the sheets, pulling them over her thin legs.

She moved restlessly, and a book slipped out from beneath the covers and fell, thumping softly on the carpeted floor. Sam bent down and picked it up. He sighed and traced his index finger over the title of the familiar Dr. Seuss story. He set it on the small oak stand.

Nothing like the thought of his ex-wife to put things in their proper perspective. But in a way, he was glad the thoughts were here to remind him that his behavior with Haley Jo had been way out of line. He was a dad. A dad who needed to focus on his daughter, not his libido. As cute and sexy as Ms. Haley Jo Simpson was, Sam knew that she didn't fit into his current plans of parenthood.

He was almost out the door when a tiny voice stopped him.

"Daddy?"

He stopped and turned back around. "Go back to sleep, baby girl. It's late."

Prudie sat up, blinking sleepily. "I heard voices. Did you have to go out?"

"I just went over to the office for a few minutes to talk to Chester."

"I thought I heard Haley Jo's voice—you know, the lady we met at the hotel."

"Go to sleep, Prudie. Tomorrow's another day."

"Will you read to me, Daddy?" Her voice had taken on that familiar wheedling tone that all children use when overtired.

"Not tonight, baby girl. It's time to go to sleep." He walked back to the bed and nudged her beneath the sheet. She didn't protest, slipping beneath the warm covers and snuggling down into her pillow.

"I was sure I heard Haley Jo's voice." Her own voice was muffled in her pillow. "I really liked her, Daddy. She was nice...and pretty." Her eyes popped open and she stared up at him. "Don't you think she was pretty, Daddy?"

Sam tucked the sheets around her and pressed a soft kiss to his daughter's forehead. "Yes, Prudie, she was a nice person."

"That's not what I asked. I asked if you thought she was pretty."

Sam sighed. Obviously he wasn't getting out of here unless he answered the question. "Yes, she was very pretty."

Prudie giggled and turned over onto her back. "She probably thought you were a nerd, Daddy. How come you're such a nerd? Why can't you be like Candace Wright's daddy? He's got spiked hair and plays the drums."

"I'm too old to be hip, gremlin."

"Hip? Nobody says hip anymore, Daddy." Her eyes were closing despite her valiant attempts to keep them open.

"I do, sweetie. Nightie night."

"Nigh—" her voice drifted off.

Sam walked down the hall to his lonely bedroom. Funny, he'd never considered his comfortable room as lonely before tonight. But now, somehow the thought of getting undressed and climbing into the big four-poster bed wasn't as appealing as it usually was.

Shrugging the feeling off, he shucked his uniform and stuffed it in the hamper next to the closet. He shut off the light and climbed into bed. As he rolled over onto his side, he wondered if Ms. Haley Jo Simpson was feeling as lonely as he was right at that very moment, and whether she slept in the raw.

6

HALEY JO HUNCHED her shoulder and tried to burrow deeper into the mattress. Partially comatose, she was at a loss to figure out why her bed had grown so lumpy. It felt as though someone had shoved a crate of boccie balls under the mattress pad. Her whole side and shoulder felt bruised and battered.

"You look like some kind of weirded-out Lone Ranger in that thing," a tiny voice said.

Startled, Haley Jo rolled up onto one elbow and pushed the sleep mask up off her face. Light flooded her eyes, and she stared groggily in the general direction of the voice. A slightly blurry Prudie Matthews peered at her from a perch on the end of the cot, a large book open in her lap.

Haley Jo glanced around feeling more than a little disorientated. Oh jeez, it hadn't been a dream, she really was sleeping in a jail cell. Soft light filtered down through the bars of a tiny window overhead. Apparently she'd made it through the night.

She groaned and flopped back down, pulling the pillow over her head.

"What time is it?" she asked.

"About six."

Haley Jo lifted the pillow just a tad. "Six o'clock? As in *six o'clock* in the morning?"

Prudie nodded, and Haley Jo pulled the pillow tighter against her face.

"You aren't going back to sleep are you? It's really difficult to read with all that atrocious snoring going on."

Haley Jo flipped the pillow off her head again and glared

in Prudie's general direction. "I do not snore!" She raised herself back up on one elbow. "And where does a ten-year-old get off using words like atrocious?"

"I'm smart."

"Yes, I remember you informing me of that fact over at the hotel." She nodded at the book. "What are you reading—the Theory of Relativity?"

"No, silly. I was rereading my favorite book." She closed the cover and shoved the book down alongside her. "And you do snore."

"I don't."

Prudie reached into her pocket and extracted a bottle of bright-red nail polish. She bent a leg and wiggled her toes. "There's no sense in arguing about it. I'll get you on tape if you like. You've got this very gross little snort at the end of every snore. It's very unattractive if you ask me."

"Thanks so much for letting me know that I not only snore, but I sound gross doing it." She yawned and stretched.

Prudie shrugged and slid the brush out of the bottle, careful to wipe the tip on the lip of the jar. "I was just being honest. You wouldn't want me to be dishonest, would you?"

Haley Jo opened her mouth, and then closed it again. How did one respond to a comment like that from a ten-year-old? Thank God, she'd never had kids. She sat up, her sleeping mask slipping down around her neck.

"Isn't that my nail polish?"

Prudie laughed and swiped a wet sheen of glossy red over her big toe before looking up. "Of course, it's yours. You don't think my father would buy me something labeled Sinfully Red, do you?" She went back to coating her toenails.

Haley noticed the child was wearing *her* silk paisley bathrobe, the hand sewn one with the tasseled belt. She had knotted the belt loosely around her skinny, almost nonexistent waist.

She had also conveniently borrowed one of Haley Jo's

sequined scrunchies and swooped her hair on top of her head. The ends stuck out in every direction, giving her the look of a startled bird.

Apparently moving into one of Chief Matthews's jail cells meant having your belongings mauled by his daughter. Haley Jo scrubbed her face and swung her feet over the edge of the cot.

Something hard jabbed her in the back of her thigh, and she jumped. A quick look told it her it was just another lump. The mattress was riddled with them.

It was a wonder anyone was able to sleep on the thing. Not that it hadn't escaped Haley Jo's attention that anyone staying in this joint probably wasn't thinking much about their sleeping accommodations. More than likely the vast majority of the occupants spent their time trying to sober up.

Thank God she hadn't called Nate. He'd have had a bird seeing her sitting here in a jail cell—even if it was an *unlocked* jail cell. Haley Jo knew she'd pulled some boners in her lifetime, but this particular predicament took the prize.

Prudie shoved her foot across the expanse between them, laying it on Haley Jo's bare thigh. "Will you do my little toe? I always mess that one up."

Sighing, Haley Jo held out her hand and accepted the nail polish. She bent her head and carefully lacquered on a slick layer of brilliant red nail polish.

Prudie straightened out her leg and studied the full effect. "Perfect! Shannon is gonna go green with envy when she sees this." She lifted her other leg and set it on Haley Jo's lap. "Here. Do the other one, too. You do it without it getting all smeary along the sides."

A vague trickle of dread slid down Haley Jo's spine as she dipped the brush back into the nail polish. No doubt Chief Matthews would take a pretty dim view of his daughter's newly painted toes. But Haley Jo also knew that she was no match for Prudie without her first cup of caffeine.

Prudie shifted her skinny butt on the mattress and grimaced. "How'd you ever sleep on this thing? It's like lying on a bag of rocks."

Haley Jo lifted her head and rubbed her tender left hip. "Tell me about it. I can feel every bone in my body this morning."

Prudie scooted closer, her movement pulling open the silk robe. For the first time, Haley Jo noticed what she was wearing underneath—a worn T-shirt and a pair of faded denim shorts.

But it was what Prudie had pulled on *over* her shorts that almost cut off Haley Jo's oxygen supply.

Holy cow! The kid was going to get her killed. She'd donned a pair of Haley Jo's black, totally lace, totally decadent, I-haven't-had-sex-in-six-months-and-need-it-now killer bikini undies. They were pulled up around her waist, the bulky material of Prudie's jeans bunching up and poking out around the skimpy lace.

Haley Jo swallowed hard. If Prudie's father saw this, Haley Jo knew she'd be sitting on a rail out in the middle of Main Street, covered in black tar and surrounded by townspeople wielding bags of duck feathers.

"Please tell me you aren't wearing my underwear," she croaked.

Prudie cocked her head to one side, the topknot bobbing wildly on top of her head. She gave Haley Jo one of her mischievous grins. "They're so rad, Haley Jo. I hadda try them on. Shannon is going to turn purple after green. She's going to want a pair, too."

From the outer office, Haley Jo heard the side door click open and heavy footsteps hit the floor. She glanced at Prudie in alarm.

"Prudie! Sarah's here to pick you up," Chief Matthews called from the front.

Prudie jumped up. "Oh, no! I forgot. I've got piano lessons." She started for the open cell door, walking on her heels, her toes pointed north in an attempt to keep her polish from smearing. "See you later, Haley Jo."

Haley Jo reached out and barely managed to grab the belt of her bathrobe. "Oh, no you don't!"

She yanked and Prudie squealed with laughter, reeling backward to land in Haley Jo's lap. "Hey, let me go. I have to leave."

Haley Jo pressed a finger to her lips and shook her head. She glanced frantically in the direction of the front office. Heavy footsteps hit the linoleum floor of the short hall, coming in their direction.

Haley Jo quickly wrapped the robe tighter around Prudie's skinny body and knotted the belt. "Let me handle this. Whatever you do, *do not* open your mouth or the robe."

The words were barely out of her mouth before Chief Matthews stepped into the room. He carried a tray, and a frown line shot up between his dark brows.

Haley Jo smiled and draped a casual arm around Prudie's shoulders. "Morning, Chief. I was just about to send Prudie on her way."

His no-nonsense gaze took in the makeup and clothes spewed across the cot and wedged in between sections of the bars. "I didn't expect to find my jail cell converted into a rummage sale."

Prudie opened her mouth as if to say something, but Haley Jo quickly pulled her head in against her side and patted the little imp's cheek, stifling any comments.

Prudie giggled.

"No rummage sale here, Chief. I just misplaced a silk scarf and Prudie was helping me look for it." She dragged Prudie along with her as she stood up and pretended to search through her suitcase.

"Which one?" he asked.

Haley Jo turned around. It took her only a minute to realize that someone—no doubt, Prudie—had tied her entire collection of scarves around the bars of the cell. She flashed a weak grin in the chief's direction and then started to unknot them, stuffing them into her bag. "Never know where those little suckers are going to get to."

Prudie laughed and jumped up on the cot. "I did it! I figured Haley Jo needed some cheering up. This place is too blah." She paused, a sparkle entering her eyes, the kind of sparkle that made Haley Jo extremely nervous. "Hey, Daddy, we could use some of your ties and put them around the bars to decorate Haley Jo's room."

The chief sighed audibly. "This isn't Ms. Simpson's home, Prudie. She's just staying for a few days until her case is straightened out. We won't be doing any interior decorating."

Prudie shrugged and glanced over at Haley Jo. She looked heavenward and her expression said it all— *See what I have to put up with?*

Of course, Haley Jo barely noticed. Her only thought was on the fact that if Prudie continued to jump up and down like a demented jumping bean it was only a matter of time before the darn bathrobe slid open and revealed what she was wearing.

She darted a glance in the chief's direction and caught him staring at Prudie's feet. His frown deepened. Great. He'd noticed the nail polish. This guy didn't miss a thing.

"Go change into sneakers, Prudie. Miss Beverly will have a cow if she sees those wild toes swinging off the edge of her piano bench while you practice your scales."

Prudie's face crumpled. "It might make playing my scales a little more interesting. Besides, my toes look rad. Right, Haley Jo?"

Haley Jo closed her eyes for a second and made a silent plea heavenward. *Please don't let her drag me into this,* she said silently to herself.

"Right, Haley Jo?" Prudie persisted.

"Best that you do what your dad says, Prudie," Haley Jo said, trying to ignore the look of disappointment on Prudie's face as her smile disappeared and her shoulders sagged.

"No one ever goes along with me," she mumbled as she hopped down off the cot. Obviously she knew when she was beaten. "I'll do what you say, but I'm putting my sandals back on as soon as I get back from piano lessons." She walked out of the cell and headed down the hall, the hem of the robe dragging on the floor.

"Prudie, you're forgetting Ms. Simpson's robe," Sam said.

Haley Jo's fingers tightened around the rail at the end of the cot.

Prudie turned around. "But she told me I could wear it while she was here, Daddy." She shot Haley Jo a sweet smile. "Didn't you, Haley Jo?"

"Yes, I surely did. She can wear it as long as she likes." Just as long as she doesn't reveal what she was wearing underneath, Haley Jo thought.

Matthews glanced back and forth between the two of them. Haley Jo could see the tiny frown between those dark brows knitting even deeper. Obviously, he suspected that something was up, but he didn't question them any further. He simply nodded. "Okay, get going. Sarah doesn't need to sit all day in our driveway waiting for you to show up."

Prudie nodded and skipped off down the hall.

"And don't forget to change into sneakers," he called after her.

Prudie giggled and disappeared around the corner. "Sure thing, Daddy."

Chief Matthews shook his head and turned back toward Haley Jo. He lifted the tray in his hands. "I made you some breakfast. I wasn't sure how you liked your eggs so I just scrambled them."

"It smells delicious." Haley Jo crossed her legs, tugged at the hem of her pajama top, and subtly tried to shrug the strap to her top back into place. It teetered on the edge of her shoulder for a moment and then slid back down the side of her arm. Oh hell, so much for modesty.

To make matters worse, her tap shorts had hiked up her thighs, baring most of her legs. She grabbed the blanket and pulled it across her lap. Maybe he wouldn't notice. She sighed inwardly. Who was she kidding? Sure enough, when she looked up, she saw that his gaze had drifted downward, lingering for just a moment on the tops of her thighs.

Haley Jo reached across and grabbed a pair of Indian silk pants. "Would you mind turning around for just a sec?"

"Sure. No problem."

As he turned away, Haley Jo stepped into her pants, but as she stood to pull them on, her gaze drifted over to study the long lean line of his back. Smiling, she contemplated the width of his shoulders and the smooth glide of his muscles beneath the freshly ironed cloth of his tan shirt. Her gaze slid down to his slim waist, and then lingered for a minute on the suggestive tautness of his butt beneath the crispness of his khakis. Holy Hannah but the man was nicely packaged.

She bit her upper lip. What was she thinking? He was the chief of police for pity's sake. She forced her attention back on her pants, her fingers fumbling with the tiny buttons. She swore softly as the tip of one nail snapped off.

"You okay?" he asked.

"Fine. Just a minute." She stuck the finger in her mouth and sucked. The darn thing stung. She finished buttoning with one hand.

Time to regroup. Sam Matthews might be mildly attracted to her, but he had made it perfectly clear last night that he wasn't going to pursue that interest any further than the wild kiss they'd shared during a weak moment. Silly fantasies about getting locked up by some sexy hunk of a lawman would have to be tucked away for another time.

Impatient, he half turned around. "You done yet?"

She whipped a sheer white shirt out of her suitcase, pulled it on and then sat back down. "Okay, it's safe to turn around."

His light eyes flicked over her before he leaned down to put the tray on the tiny table next to the cot. She noticed that the ends of his dark hair were damp.

The clean, sharp scent of soap floated up and filled her nostrils. He'd come right from his shower, and she had a sudden startling image of him showering—a strangely erotic and deliciously wicked vision of hard muscle and tanned flesh covered with soap and cascading water.

It took all her strength not to groan aloud. This was worse than she'd originally thought. She was only around the man for two seconds and she was already lusting after him. Obviously she'd been without a man much too long.

She accepted the plate he handed her and was surprised when he pulled an empty chair over and straddled it. His eyes locked on hers. "You mentioned last night that your family doesn't live here in New York."

"I guess this means you're back to interrogating, huh?"

She shoved a forkful of the eggs into her mouth. They were delicious. A spicy taste with a tinge of lemon flavoring. Apparently Chief Matthews was no slouch in the kitchen. Under different circumstances a discovery like that would get him labeled as potential boyfriend material.

"This isn't an interrogation. Just polite breakfast conversation."

"Well then, you won't mind my asking a few questions too—seeing as this is just polite breakfast conversation and all."

She studied him carefully, trying unsuccessfully to convince herself that he wasn't as sexy as he looked—that the long legs straddling the chair and the unruly lock of hair eroding his straight part didn't make her stomach do funny flips. Maybe what she was feeling had to do with the eggs. They were probably too spicy.

"Go ahead. What's on your mind?"

You, Haley Jo thought. But instead, she asked, "I was wondering how long you've been the chief of police?"

"I've been chief for about five years. Before that I was one of the deputies."

"Have you lived here all your life?"

He shook his head. "Not so fast. It's my turn."

"I didn't realize we were taking turns."

He smiled and a little dimple peeped out then fled. "It's only fair. Have you always lived in the city?"

Haley Jo nodded and swallowed another mouthful of

eggs. Heavenly. She needed to find out how he made these things. She could easily live on them. "Well, almost all my life. I moved there when I was fifteen."

"Family?"

"I've got two older brothers—both living out west. My dad died when I was twenty—heart attack. But my mom's alive. She's got a little place out in California, close to my brothers." She scooped up another forkful of eggs. "Which is a good thing because even though we love each other dearly, we tend to rub each other the wrong way." She paused with her fork poised halfway to her mouth. "Hey! No fair. You asked two questions. It's my turn now."

He propped an elbow on the back of the chair and rested his chin on the heel of his hand. His expression could only be described as amused.

"How come your wife divorced you when you're such an unbelievably good kisser?"

His blue eyes widened ever so slightly. Apparently, she'd taken him by surprise, and he was definitely the kind of guy who wasn't used to being surprised. Or maybe he just hadn't expected her to get personal so quickly.

"I would guess she just wasn't as into kissing as much as you are."

She grinned. "Definitely her loss. How long did—"

He held up a hand. "Not so fast. It's my turn again."

"But I was supposed to get two questions."

"Not according to my count. What made you decide to become a dental hygienist?"

"Easy. I went to work for Dr. Rocca and soon learned how much more the hygienists were making than the receptionists." He raised an eyebrow and waited, making it clear he expected her to elaborate.

"My friend Melanie and I work the desk. We do the phones, deal with the patients and handle all the filing. One of the girls who is a hygienist in the office started showing me what she did. I found it fascinating."

She checked to make sure he hadn't fallen asleep, but he

still seemed attentive. No obvious signs of drool or boredom.

"Dr. Rocca took notice of my interest and encouraged me to enroll in a local program. He was going to make sure my work schedule didn't interfere with my classes."

"What about Melanie? She wasn't interested in going?"

"She can't stand tongues...well, tongues inside mouths that she's not kissing anyway. Oh, and she's pretty particular about pain, too. She doesn't like people weeping or moaning...moaning in pain anyway. Moaning for other reasons she can handle."

He raised an eyebrow, and Haley Jo knew she was babbling again. She sighed. Dang. The guy just didn't realize how his nearness made a girl think about things she shouldn't be thinking about. It was criminal.

"Anyway, Melanie likes her job. I'm the one who is looking for a change."

"But wasn't your friend Melanie the person who was originally supposed to go on the trip with Dr. Rocca?"

Haley Jo nodded.

"So, if she wasn't interested in becoming a hygienist, why was she planning on going to the conference?"

"Look—Melanie's a bit of a scatterbrain when it comes to relationships. She and Dr. Rocca had a thing going up until she met her new boyfriend. I agreed to bail her out by going on the trip so she didn't have to deal with Dr. Rocca."

"Were you having an affair with Dr. Rocca, too?"

Haley Jo glared at him until he held up his hand in surrender. "Okay. Okay. You already told me no."

"So glad you remembered."

"Was Dr. Rocca aware that—"

"Hey, hang on. You've asked more than your allotted questions. It's my turn again."

"But I have a follow-up question."

"Too bad. You're cheating." Haley Jo couldn't help marveling at how easily he had maneuvered them off the subject of his former marriage. "You said you're divorced, but you didn't mention whether or not you're involved."

"Involved in what?"

"Don't get cute. Are you involved in another relationship?"

He reached over and grabbed the coffee mug sitting on her tray and took a sip. "No—no other relationships."

She took the cup from his hands and took a sip, too, watching him over the rim. "Interesting."

"But then, I'm not looking for one, either."

Ouch. That was direct. Haley Jo struggled to keep the disappointment off her face. "I'm sorry to hear that."

"No offense, but I'm just too busy raising Prudie to get involved with anyone."

He took the cup back, and his long, tanned fingers brushed hers. But before she could respond, someone cleared his throat.

"Well, isn't this a cozy scene."

Sam glanced up to see Andy Grant standing framed in the doorway of the cell. His thumbs were stuck in the front of his belt and an amused smile toyed with the corners of his mouth.

"Morning, Andy." Sam settled back in his chair, suddenly conscious that he'd been leaning forward watching Haley Jo a bit too intently, his fingertips burning where they'd brushed her hand. "Haley Jo was just telling me about her decision to become a dental hygienist." *And like a guy on a first date, you got caught up in talking about your own life,* he thought.

Haley Jo smiled and waved a fork. "Hi, Lieutenant Grant. Good to see you again."

"Got any more of that coffee?" Andy asked, dragging a chair from outside the cell so he could sit down with them.

Sam started to get up. "I'll get you a cup. I think Chester started a fresh pot before he left this morning."

Andy held up a hand. "No, don't bother. I've had enough already. Gail is trying to decaffeinate me."

"A decaffeinated cop?" Sam shook his head. "I didn't think such a creature existed in this day and age."

Andy laughed. "Gail says I'm miserable to live with all wound up on caffeine." He shrugged. "Personally, I think my disposition has more to do with the fact that when I get home and find that no one has mowed the lawn or put out the garbage, it gets me little cranky."

"So what's the word on the Rocca case? Anything new?" Sam asked.

Andy leaned forward and snagged a slice of toast off the tray. He gnawed on the crust as he considered Sam's question. "I got a few faxes from the city this morning. The NYPD is cooperating fully with us." He smiled at Haley Jo. "You'll be pleased to know that you have a squeaky clean record, Ms. Simpson."

Sam didn't miss the triumphant glance she shot in his direction.

"Of course I do," she said. "In spite of what *some* people around here seem to think, I'm a good, law-abiding citizen."

"No one said you weren't, Haley Jo. I'm simply being cautious," Sam said. "You can't expect me to forget the fact that you were found half-naked in a room with an equally naked dead man."

"You aren't alone with that memory," Andy said dryly. "From the reports I got, there weren't too many people at the scene who will ever be able to forget Ms. Simpson's condition of undress."

A tinge of pink crept up Haley Jo's cheeks and touched the tips of her ears. Sam struggled to keep the corners of his mouth neutral.

Andy continued, "But now we're more interested in finding out anything further about what happened before you actually discovered Dr. Rocca's body."

"You mean like when I was in the room?" Haley Jo asked.

Andy nodded. "That, and what you remember after the two of you checked in. Don't hold anything back. You might think it's an insignificant little detail, but Sam and I might see it in an entirely different light."

Haley Jo leaned forward and set her plate with her half-eaten eggs back on the tray. Sam could tell from her expression that she recognized that their conversation had taken a sudden turn for the serious.

"We signed in. Dr. Rocca paid with his card. A bellboy took our bags up. I was dropped off at my room first." She paused. "Dr. Rocca made a point of telling me that he was right across the hall, but I figured to be out of my room and downstairs exploring before he even had a chance to unpack." She glanced at Sam and then away again.

Andy leaned forward. "Anything else? Don't hold back on us—even if you think it's not important."

She shook her head. "I swear I'm not holding back." She jerked a hand through her riot of red hair. "I'm sorry. There's nothing."

Sam shifted in his chair. He didn't miss the increased level of distress in her voice. She was feeling guilty about not being able to help, and it was winding her up tighter than a drum.

She braced herself against the cement wall and drew her legs up to her chest. It was if she had set up a barrier between herself and the two of them.

Sam knew he needed to get her to relax, to remember they were the good guys and they weren't going to whip out the rubber hoses and harsh lights any time soon.

He leaned forward and placed a hand on her bare foot. She shivered slightly, and her clear gaze shifted to him. He smiled reassuringly. "It's okay, Haley Jo. You're doing just fine."

She swallowed hard and nodded, but her shoulders remained tense. He reached up and unlaced her hands, taking one into his own. It was cool and dry. Almost too cool. He held it between both of his, allowing his own warmth to seep through to her.

"Do me a favor," he said. She nodded almost too rapidly. Too eagerly. He grinned again and squeezed her hand gently. "I want you to just listen to my voice. Take a deep breath, let it out and then close your eyes."

She sucked in a monstrous breath and shut her eyes so tight the end of her nose pinched in. She seemed to forget to let the breath out and started to turn red.

"Breathe, Haley Jo," he ordered.

She let it out in a giant whoosh.

"Okay, now—gentle breaths. Nice and easy. Slow and smooth. In and out," he said.

She nodded again and started breathing at a gentler pace. She opened one eye and peeked at him. He stroked the top of her hand. "Keep your eyes closed."

He gave her a few minutes to get into the rhythm. "Okay, now I want you to think back to riding the elevator up to the fifth floor. Nod your head when you've got that picture fixed in your brain."

A few seconds later, she nodded, a slight smile touching her luscious lips. Damn. He needed to keep his mind on the job and not on her lips.

"All right, the elevator doors open."

She nodded again.

"—and you're glancing down the hallway." Her breathing was soft and even. "You can see your room and you step off the elevator. Who's in the hallway, Haley Jo?"

"Dr. Rocca is beside me and the bellboy is right behind me," she said. Her fingers tightened in his. "There's someone standing next to the fire extinguisher."

Her eyelids started to squeeze tighter and he gently stroked her hand with his. "Relax. Let it come on its own."

She nodded.

"Is the person a man or a woman?"

"I—I can't really tell...it looks like a man. He's wearing a baseball cap and dark-brown clothes—deliveryman's clothes."

Sam exchanged glances with Andy. Now they were getting somewhere. "Walk toward the man, Haley Jo. Does he say anything? Do you say anything to him?"

"I nodded to him. Dr. Rocca just walked right past him."

She leaned her head back against the wall, exposing the slender column of her neck. Sam swallowed hard, trying to keep his gaze up off the smooth slide of her white skin leading down to her chest. The woman needed to wear more clothes. Her top was just too skimpy for an interrogation session.

Sam jumped when Andy poked him. The state trooper was grinning knowingly and jerked his head in the direction of Sam's hand. He noticed for the first time that he was gripping her hand so tight that her tiny hand had totally disappeared in his.

"Let's keep our attention focused on the right subject," Andy whispered.

Sam scowled but loosened his fingers. "What did the man look like, Haley Jo? Describe him to me."

"He was a little taller than me, but not that much taller. He was bulky—like he worked out. I could see the muscles in his shoulders."

"Was he wearing long sleeves?"

She shook her head. "No. Short sleeves. He—" She stopped short, and there was a frown between her eyes.

"What?"

"He had something on the back of his hand—between his thumb and index finger."

"Focus on his hand, Haley." Sam forced himself to keep his voice soft and calm. "What is it?"

Her white upper teeth gnawed at her lower lip and her voice trembled slightly. "I can't remember."

"You're trying too hard, Haley Jo," Sam soothed. "Relax."

She reached up and knocked a fist against her forehead. "Think, dammit. Think."

Sam reached out and gently pulled her hand back down, his hand wrapping around her tiny fist with ease. "Take a deep breath and let it come on its own."

She nodded and sucked in a breath, reclosing her eyes.

The little frown sprang up between her eyes again. "It was something small...and round." She dropped her head forward, her cheek resting on her knees. Suddenly she looked up, a triumphant gleam in her eyes. "It was a tiny cyclone—all black and twisty like. It was narrow and got wider at the top."

"Good," Sam said, unable to control the grin of approval that broke out across his face. "Interesting tattoo but not so rare that we'll never be able to trace it." He glanced at Andy. "Any way to narrow it down, Andy?"

Andy twirled the brim of his Stetson between his fingers and nodded. "I'll put it out on the computer right away." He got to his feet. "I'm going to send a police artist over, Ms. Simpson. I'd like you to try to put a composite sketch together with his help. Until then, if you think of anything else, be sure you talk to the chief."

Sam stood. "I'll walk you out, Andy. I have a few questions."

7

ANDY LEANED DOWN, pulled open the door of his cruiser and slid behind the wheel. "Now that's one smart lady."

When his friend glanced up at him, Sam couldn't miss the wide grin. A grin that was obviously for his benefit. Sam wondered how long it would take before Andy started giving him the business about how rough it must be to provide protection for such a fine-looking woman.

"Quite a looker, too," Andy said.

"Oh, really? Can't say that I've noticed," Sam lied.

"Yeah, right. And pigs are flying over Reflection Lake right this minute."

"Sorry I missed that," Sam said absently, focusing his attention on a loose-knit group of teens clustered around a bike rack across the street in front of the Silas Reed Public Library. All were dressed in colorful swim trunks with towels slung over their shoulders. Sam wondered what they might be up to.

The boy in the middle, Billy Flannigan, whipped his towel off his shoulder and snapped it in the air. One of the boys, the nerdier looking one of the group, made a grab for it. But Billy was too quick for him. He whirled around and snapped the towel against the boy's upper thigh. The boy let out an angry howl and the group laughed. When he charged his aggressor, Billy jumped backward into a mock fighting stance. The young lions were obviously establishing order.

"Are you ignoring me?" Andy asked.

Sam glanced back at his friend. "Not at all. I heard everything you said."

"Yeah, right. You're lying when you say you didn't notice how delectable Ms. Simpson is. When I walked in I thought I was going to have to get you a bib, you were drooling so bad."

"All right. All right. I admit it, she's attractive. But that doesn't change the fact that she's crazier than a loon and flakier than one of Sally O'Neil's breakfast biscuits."

Andy smacked the heel of his hand against the wheel. "I knew it. You're smitten with her."

"Smitten? Do people even use that word anymore?"

"Don't try to change the subject. Admit it—you're so rattled by her that you can barely see straight."

Sam sighed. "So what if I am? What are you going to do—pass her a note in study hall and see if she wants to go to the prom with me?"

Andy laughed. "I don't have to. I already know how she feels about you."

As much as he fought it, Sam couldn't resist asking, "So what exactly does she think of me—according to you, anyway?" He frowned. "And how the hell would you know in the first place? Are you psychic?"

Andy's grin got wider. "You're such an innocent when it comes to women, Sam. What would you do without my help to guide you through this minefield?"

"Probably get a lot more work done. So how do you know how she feels?"

"What you *really* want to know is how she feels about you."

"So quit stalling and cough it up."

Andy laughed. "She couldn't keep her eyes off you. Every time you moved, talked or breathed those exquisite green eyes were on you."

Sam waved a hand, dismissing Andy's interpretation. "That's ridiculous. She's just nervous about being locked up here while you and your merry band of nitwits try to figure out if she's in any danger."

"Locked up? You kinky devil you."

Sam rolled his eyes. His hope of getting anything useful

out of his friend went bust. Andy had a well-known reputation for being relentless when he thought he had something worthwhile to rag a friend about.

"Come on, admit it," Andy urged. "You actually like the woman."

"I like the fact that she's easy to talk to."

"I wasn't interested in whether or not you think she's a great conversationalist."

"Fine. She's easy on the eyes, too. Satisfied?" He glanced at the boys again, but they had moved off farther down the street.

"Actually, no. For personal reasons I need to know whether or not you're going to ask her out."

"Have you forgotten that you're already married?"

"Very true. But my brother-in-law has been moping around the house since his girlfriend dumped him, and I've been trying to think of a replacement. Haley Jo might be just the right thing to get him off my couch."

"Forget it. No one is asking her out while she's in my custody."

Andy laughed. "Now that sounds a bit possessive."

"Not at all. I'm simply doing my job."

Andy shook his head. "You're sad, Matthews."

"Oh brother, here we go. Dr. Andy's in-depth analysis. Do me a favor and spare me."

"In case you haven't noticed, every woman you meet you compare to Peggy. Peggy's gone, buddy." Andy reached down and turned the key in the ignition. The cruiser rumbled to life. "You know I'm right."

"I know nothing of the sort. And I don't compare every woman I meet to Peggy."

"Then why haven't you had one single serious relationship in the entire nine years since she left?"

"Because I haven't felt the need for a serious relationship."

"Casual dating gets old."

"Not true. It's very freeing."

Andy protested, "Whether you're willing to admit it or not, men have intimacy needs, too."

Sam had to laugh aloud at that one. "Do me favor, Andy, and don't embarrass yourself by getting into a discussion about intimacy and commitment. If I remember correctly, Gail had to drag your lazy, commitment phobic butt behind her cruiser for several miles before you agreed to get married."

"That's only because I enjoy the chase."

Sam snorted. "Gail did all the chasing, but you live in that dream world of yours." He glanced once toward his office and then away again. He didn't need to look as though he were trying to make eye contact with Haley Jo in order to weasel out of a conversation with Andy. Obviously, the guy was reading too much into their relationship as it was.

"In any case, just for the record—I don't have any intimacy needs. Especially ones that include some flaky gal who plans on hightailing it back to the city as fast as her little high heels will carry her once this situation with Rocca is settled."

"So, if you knew that she'd stick around would you reconsider?"

"Reconsider what?"

"Dating her."

"Oh, for Pete's sake. I'm guarding the woman, not interviewing her for the position of girlfriend."

"You could do a heck of a lot worse."

"Let's just concentrate on Dr. Rocca's killer for right now. Okay?"

Sam didn't bother telling his friend how off base he was on the entire Haley Jo Simpson issue. It would take too much time and effort, and at the moment, Sam didn't think he was up to the challenge. Especially since a part of him, a place deep inside, was daring to whisper the very same thing.

HALEY JO STEPPED OUT of the bathroom and glanced around the office. Not a soul around. Apparently Chester got off duty as soon as the chief arrived in the morning. She wondered who watched over things once the night shift went home and the chief was out patrolling his little kingdom.

Through the plate glass window, she could see Sam and Andy Grant still talking. Sam stood with one hip resting against the driver's side of Andy's cruiser, his muscular forearm draped casually along the side of the roof. The morning sun hit his face full on, and he squinted slightly. Haley Jo tried to ignore the tiny catch in her breath at the sight of him.

His expression, however, wasn't as casual as his stance. In fact, he appeared more than a little irritated with whatever it was the two of them were discussing. It was a relief to know that someone other than she had the ability to set the good chief's teeth on edge.

Haley Jo whipped the towel off her head and vigorously rubbed the last bit of water out of her curls. She thought about getting the hair dryer out of her suitcase and trying to do something to tame the mess occupying the top of her head, but then decided it wasn't worth the effort. Who was going to see her? The chief? He'd already made it perfectly clear that even though she got his motor running, he wasn't about to indulge.

She glanced up and almost jumped out of her skin when she found that he had straightened up and was staring in the window straight at her. The blue of his eyes seemed ready to cut a hole in the glass.

For a minute, she wondered if he had somehow tapped into her thoughts. Ridiculous. He wasn't a mind reader—no man was. She'd learned that from experience. Smiling sweetly, she waved three fingers in his direction. Sam nodded curtly and then shifted his attention back to Andy.

Maybe he was distressed that she was standing in the middle of his office with wet hair and a bathrobe. Haley Jo shrugged. Too bad. It hadn't been her decision to room here at Chief Matthews's local Bide Awhile Hotel and Jailhouse.

"You must be the girl mixed up in that murder over at the Climbing Bear Resort," a voice said.

Haley Jo turned around to see an ancient woman with iron-gray hair holding open the side door. "Uh...Hi," Haley Jo said, whipping the towel up to self-consciously cover the opening at the top of her robe.

"Fine time to get modest, girlie. You've been standing in front of the window for the past five minutes. The whole town has had a look at you by now." She set one end of a three-legged metal cane on the doorstep, grabbed the side of the door frame with a tiny gnarled hand and pulled herself up with a soft grunt.

"I ought to tan Sammy's hide. I keep telling him to put in an extra step there to make it easier for me to get in and out, but does he do it?" She glared at Haley Jo with a pair of sharp blue eyes, magnified by a pair of thick lenses. "Of course not. Inconsiderate little cuss."

Haley Jo swallowed hard. How was she supposed to respond to that? Especially since she couldn't quite picture anyone calling the six-foot-two chief of police *little*. Instead, she did the safe thing. She nodded and smiled politely.

Leaning heavily on the cane, the woman stomped over to the desk closest to the front counter and plopped down in the seat with the huge cushion in it. "I'm Eleanor Seals."

"Haley Jo Simpson, ma'am." Haley Jo scooted across the space separating them and offered up a hand.

Mrs. Seals waved her off. "I never shake, girl. I've got arthritis and until the meds kick in I don't touch anything. And nothing touches me." She nodded her head toward the desktop. "Including that infernal computer keyboard. Which in case you're wondering, annoys the chief to no end."

The woman laughed, a stiff crackling sound, like paper crumpling. She readjusted her hips in the chair, wincing a little as she moved. "I imagine the man's going to be mighty glad when I finally retire. He fancies that he'll be able to hire himself a *real* secretary. One who knows how to use all these newfangled machines."

Haley Jo nodded again but glanced around in confusion. Newfangled machines? She didn't see anything that qualified as new or fangled. In fact, the only up-to-date piece of equipment in the place was the Gateway computer, a fax machine and the worn-out-looking copier squatting in the corner. But the scowl on Mrs. Seals's face told Haley Jo she didn't want to hear any disagreement.

"Well, are you going to stand there all day half-naked or do you have plans to put on some clothes in the near future?"

Haley Jo jumped. "Oh, sorry, ma'am. I was just on my way to change."

She glanced once more in Sam's direction, but Andy's car was pulling away from the curb, and Sam was striding across the street toward the library.

Apparently, he had no qualms about leaving her in the care of the dragon lady. No surprise there. In fact, she should have expected it. After all, this was the same guy who took off last night after getting her all hot and bothered.

Sighing, Haley Jo did the only thing she knew how to do in this situation. She retreated to her cell.

TWENTY MINUTES LATER, Haley Jo paused in the middle of rearranging her new home. The steady thump of something hitting the hallway floor told her that Eleanor Seals and her sturdy cane were headed her way for a visit.

Already dressed, Haley Jo wasn't worried about getting scolded or whacked with the cane for her appearance, but she did harbor a bit of concern that Mrs. Seals might not be too pleased to find her making unauthorized changes.

She pushed the cot to the other side of the cell, gritting her teeth when the metal legs squealed in protest.

"Mercy me, you're a noisy one. What are you up to?" Mrs. Seals said.

"Oh, nothing much." Haley Jo stood up and brushed

her hands off. She hoped Mrs. Seals didn't make a habit of coming to the back of the building too often. Maybe she wouldn't notice anything out of order.

"Sure sounds like something to me." The elderly woman surveyed the tiny cell. Her quick gaze took in everything—the fringed shawl Haley Jo had carefully tacked over the barred window and the batik sarong draped over the cot like a bedspread.

"Why, this looks lovely." An unexpected smile broke out across her wrinkled face.

"Really? You like it?"

"Well, as much as one can like a hole in the wall like this."

Haley Jo laughed. "I guess you're right. I'm kind of limited in what I can do." She bent down and pushed her suitcase under the bed. "But if I'm stuck here, I thought I'd give it a few personal touches." She straightened up. "You don't think the chief will mind, do you?"

"Honey, that man has trouble if someone so much as moves a paper clip. But don't you worry. I won't let him yell too loud."

Haley Jo was somewhat reassured by that comment. Something told her that Eleanor Seals could hold her own against the self-assured chief of police.

"It looks perfectly lovely," Mrs. Seals said. "In fact, if I'm not mistaken, things seem more roomy. Spacious even. How'd you do that?"

Haley Jo grinned. "Feng shui."

"Fungie what?"

"Feng shui. It's the art of living harmoniously." Haley Jo perched on the edge of the cot. "It's a belief that a person can harness the power of everything around her. I've been reading about it."

"Sounds pretty hocus-pocus to me."

"No, it's a science. Really." She grabbed her purse and dug around for her compass and handy how-to book. She pulled them out. "I'm not an expert by any means, but it's interesting."

"Well whatever it is we could use a little of it around here. But before we start sprucing things up, I came to tell you that the police artist is here." She glanced toward the front as if to make sure whoever was out there wasn't listening, and then said, "Just so you know—Ollie LaTour is a little on the strange side. But he lives in Reflection Lake so we all kind of put up with him."

Haley Jo raised an eyebrow, not sure she was ready for any more surprises. But Eleanor didn't bother to explain. Instead, she thumped her way back down the hall. With an odd sense of trepidation, Haley Jo followed, bracing herself for just about anything.

WHEN HALEY JO REACHED the outer office, she figured that the police artist, Ollie LaTour, had gotten tired of waiting and left. In his place stood a bald giant. A huge, burly mountain of a man in a studded leather jacket and black leather, fringed pants and cowboy boots with elaborate silver caps on both pointy toes.

But it was the studded dog collar around the guy's thick neck and the plethora of ear piercings up and down the inside edge of both the guy's ears that made him seem a bit over the top for your typical small-town citizen.

Of course, being a city girl, Haley Jo couldn't say the dog collar or the piercings shocked her all that much. She'd seen plenty in her own neighborhood. But somehow the outfit didn't seem like something one would wear while visiting the local police station, let alone a getup a person would wear while actually *working* for the police.

"Ollie, this is Haley Jo Simpson. Haley Jo—Ollie." Eleanor moved over to her desk and eased herself into her chair. She waved a hand at the two of them. "You two kids go draw pictures over at the chief's desk, but do me a favor and keep the noise to a dull roar. I've got some letters to get out." She shuffled through some papers, mumbling to herself about the chief dreaming up things to keep her busy.

Ollie nodded and his bald pate caught a shine off the

overhead lights—a shine so bright it almost blinded Haley Jo. She blinked, wondering if he buffed his dome to get such a high gloss. The silver earrings caught their own shine.

"After you, Ms. Simpson," he said. His voice was high and sweet, like a young choirboy's. Haley Jo had to watch his lips to be sure it was really he who had spoken.

She moved over to sit in one of the chairs next to the chief's desk, and Ollie took the chief's tall seat. He reached into a leather satchel hanging over one massive shoulder and pulled out an artist's drawing pad. The tablet of paper looked almost ridiculously small in his huge hand. But when he fished around inside and retrieved a pencil, pulling it out and clutching it in his meaty fingers, Haley Jo had to really work to suppress a smile. The thing looked no bigger than a toothpick in his hand.

"Ready to start?" he asked.

Haley Jo nodded, watching as he crossed one beefy leg over the other and balanced the drawing pad on top of one massive kneecap.

"Nowadays, most artists use a computer or templates, but I prefer to do it the old-fashioned way." He flipped open the pad. "I kinda view each piece as its own individual masterpiece."

Haley Jo managed a nod.

"I take a lot of pride in my work," he said.

"That's very commendable." Haley Jo bit down on her lower lip to keep from smiling. Obviously Ollie considered each assignment a direct order to recreate the *Mona Lisa*. Maybe he wasn't aware that they were really supposed to piece together the likeness of a possible murderer.

He pulled out a container of artist's markers. "I even like to give my pieces a little color."

Haley Jo frowned. "Don't you just put it through a copy machine and it turns it into black and white?"

He bestowed a tolerant smile on her. "Sometimes they let me make a few copies in color. But even the black-and-white ones come out showing my attention to detail." He opened the container and set it up for easy access. "First off, why don't you tell me the shape of his face."

"I think it was long—with kind of a square chin. I couldn't see it too well. He had a hat on."

"What kind of hat?"

"A baseball type hat."

Ollie's hamlike fist flew across the paper. Haley Jo leaned forward, cutting a quick glance in Eleanor's direction to make sure she wasn't listening. "That's quite a lovely collar you're wearing."

"Why thank you. I have several. This one's my favorite." Ollie paused. "What kind of mouth did he have?"

"Kind of long and thin lipped." Haley Jo watched him whip off a mouth. "A little thinner than that."

He used his eraser and fixed the lines.

She nodded. "That's better." She glanced at Eleanor again. She seemed engrossed in her typing. "You wouldn't be offended, would you, if I said that you don't look like a typical resident of Reflection Lake?"

He laughed, something high and sweet and long. It sounded like a young girl on a date for the first time. "Heck no, I wouldn't be offended. People say that all the time."

"May I ask how you ended up here?"

"He married Tina Sykes," Eleanor piped up from across the room. "And since she's mayor of our town and still has two years left on her term, she was obligated to return from her wild and wanton Las Vegas vacation last year."

Haley Jo raised an eyebrow in Ollie's direction.

He grinned and nodded. "She's right. Tina came to Vegas with her bowling team—for a big championship tournament—and she and I met while playing craps."

"Played more than craps if you ask me—seeing as she came back here pregnant." Eleanor sniffed. "But then, Tina always did have a taste for the different—if not outright bizarre."

"You calling me bizarre, Eleanor?" Ollie asked, a sweet smile still curling the ends of his tiny rosebud mouth.

"If the shoe—or in this case boot—fits, wear it."

"You have a child?" Haley Jo asked, hoping to avert an argument.

Ollie nodded. "Little Ozzie. He's two months old." He fumbled in his back pocket, pulled out his wallet and flipped it open to a picture.

It was a photo of a chubby little guy in a Harley-Davidson leather jacket and chaps. Haley Jo hadn't realized they made leather duds that small. A leather cap was perched on what was obviously a very bald baby head. Like father, like son. In this case, the apple had definitely not fallen far from the tree. Ozzie was the spitting image of his daddy.

"He's adorable."

"Thanks." Ollie fairly beamed as he snapped the wallet shut and stuffed it back in his pocket. "You'll probably get a chance to meet him in person at the end of the week if you come to the hockey game."

Haley Jo perked up. Hockey game? Action. Excitement. People. Something that might actually keep her from going totally stir-crazy.

Eleanor glanced up and frowned. "She's in protective custody, Ollie. She won't be going to any hockey game."

"Oh, sorry." Ollie shot Haley Jo an apologetic look. "So what else do you remember of this guy? What kind of hair did he have? Were his ears showing or covered?"

Haley Jo stored the hockey game information for future exploration. "His hair was brown and he wore it short. I don't remember much about his ears. They must have been pretty close to his head."

Ollie's pencil scratched across the paper with lightning speed. He reached over and grabbed a marker and shaded in the guy's hair. "What color were his eyes?"

Haley Jo shrugged. "Something dark—probably brown, too. I couldn't see them too well because he had the hat pulled down low."

Ollie whipped off a hat brim and shaded the guy's eyes. "How about his nose?"

Haley Jo closed her eyes, straining to see the guy in the hallway. "It was short. Kind of puglike."

Ollie fiddled with the nose a bit until Haley Jo told him he had it right. Then they went on to the guy's neck and shoulders.

"So, when is this hockey game being played, and why is it so important?"

"Friday night. It's the first time the chief's team gets to play the Blue Panthers."

"And the Blue Panthers would be..."

"Only the best team in the men's summer league. The chief has been champing at the bit to get his team up to par so they could get an invite to play them."

"And they're going to get their collective behinds royally kicked," Eleanor said sourly from her desk.

"Better not let the chief hear you say that, Eleanor," Ollie warned.

Eleanor snorted. "He knows exactly how I feel about such foolishness. Grown men playing hockey like a bunch of teenagers. And the whole town sitting in the stands watching them like they've got nothing better to do."

"You're not going then?" Ollie asked.

"Are you kidding?" Eleanor's expression was incredulous. "I wouldn't miss it for the world. I even got in on the pool Chester's got going—plan on winning too. Now the two of you need to hurry up and finish. Haley Jo has some redecorating to do around here and we'll never get to it if you two don't get that silly picture done."

"You were the one eavesdropping," Ollie reminded her gently.

Haley Jo held her breath, but Eleanor just nodded and went back to her keyboard. When the keys started clicking again, Haley Jo leaned forward. "She scares me a little."

"You're not the only one," Ollie whispered back. "Everyone in town is scared spitless of her. When she walks down the street, the crowds part to allow her to pass." He grinned and sat back. "So, what kind of shoulders did this guy have?"

Haley Jo shifted gears and tried to concentrate on the task at hand. But in the back of her brain, she continued to mull over their conversation about the hockey game. Every piece of information she was able to glean about the chief intrigued her more and more, and for some unknown reason, Haley Jo found herself wanting to learn everything she could about Sam Matthews.

A FEW HOURS LATER, Sam flung open the front door of his office and stepped in from the bright sunlight. He used the back of his hand to wipe a line of sweat off his forehead. He hadn't expected things to heat up quite so quickly. After chasing the boys off the dam, he had been sorely tempted to jump in to cool himself off.

"Eleanor—" He stopped short and stared.

Haley Jo and Prudie stood frozen in the center of his office. Hal, the proprietor of Adirondack Mountain Hardware next door, stood in front of the counter, a chain saw buzzing in his bearlike hands. A gaping hole had been cut out of the middle of the front counter.

Hal shut off the saw and all four of them pushed their safety glasses up on top of their heads. They smiled sheepishly in unison. Eleanor recovered first. "We didn't expect you back so soon. I thought you'd gone on your rounds."

"That's obvious," Sam said dryly. "May I ask what's going on—seeing as this is my office and all?"

Eleanor frowned. "Don't get your shorts in a knot. We're just Funky Shoeing this office."

Prudie giggled. "That's feng shui, Mrs. Seals."

Eleanor's frown deepened and Prudie quickly wiped the grin off her face. Even Prudie was smart enough to know that when Mrs. Seals got in a snit, no one was spared.

"Nobody likes a smarty pants, Miss Prudence," Eleanor said. "Fung Shoe. Feng shui. Who cares what it's called. All I know is that this office has been the same since the last chief of police took office thirty years ago. I say it's time for a change. And Haley Jo is just the person to help us do it."

Prudie grinned. "I agree. So what comes next, Haley Jo?"

Sam held up a hand. "Uh...I happen to like it fine just the way it is...or rather, was."

Eleanor waved him off. "You'd have a fit if someone changed toilet paper brands on you. Leave us be. We're creating."

"Nothing wrong with being a loyal customer," Sam said, defending himself. "And what's wrong with liking things in a certain way?"

No one answered.

"You aren't big into change, are you, Hal?"

Hal shrugged, looking guiltier. "Sorry, Chief. I thought they'd consulted you about making these changes. I can try to put the piece back in if you want."

"No, that's okay. Finish up." He turned and looked at Haley Jo. "Why the need to put a hole in my counter?"

She grinned, apparently thinking that he was genuinely curious. That he'd happily accept her whacked-out explanation. "You were blocking your positive *qi*."

"My what?"

"Your positive *qi*. The office's life's breath. The nourishing force that is the underlying essence of all things."

"Heaven forbid. We certainly wouldn't want that to happen," he said with a frown. "How did you determine that I was so gauche as to have done something like that?"

She looked puzzled, not yet sure if he was being sarcastic or not. "Well, we did a personal trigram for you."

"A what?"

"A trigram, Daddy," Prudie piped in. She grabbed a piece of paper off the desk and waved it at him. "It's based on your birthday and the fact that you're a man." She showed him a mathematical equation. "It tells Haley Jo which—" She looked at Haley Jo. "Eight, right?"

Haley Jo smiled and nodded.

"Which eight directions are good for you and which ones are bad for you. That's how she knows where we should put everything. Cool, huh?"

He glanced over at Haley Jo, and she smiled proudly. He hated to burst her bubble, and Prudie's too, but this had gotten way out of hand.

"Look, everyone, as much as I appreciate the thought, I need to get back to work. Redecorating is not on the agenda for today."

Prudie's face fell. "But, Dad, I—"

"Help Hal clean up, gremlin."

Her lips tightened into a straight line and Sam knew she wasn't happy. She marched over, grabbed the broom and started sweeping up the sawdust.

"I'm sorry, Chief Matthews. I should have waited until you came back before jumping in and making any changes." Haley Jo bent down and held the dust pan for Prudie. She smiled up at his daughter and softly whispered, "It's okay. Don't get upset."

Her good-natured acceptance of his dictate only served to make the chief feel even more guilty. "No harm done. We'll just leave things as they are for now."

Sam walked over to his desk and pretended to sort through his mail as they finished cleaning up. When they were done, Prudie grabbed Haley Jo's hand and headed for the back of the office. He watched them leave, concerned about how quickly Prudie had become attached to his temporary guest.

AN HOUR LATER, a steady rain started. Rain lashed the front window and a stiff wind blew the excess water along the sidewalks and into the gutters. One minute it was sunny and cloudless, and the next thunderclouds rolled in and took over. In short order, the day became a dreary, overcast mess.

Sam stood at the front of the office and watched the storm sweep down Main Street. After a few minutes, he glanced over his shoulder in Eleanor's direction. She was still typing away at the computer, her mouth pinched with disapproval.

If things went according to the norm, Sam figured that

she wouldn't talk to him again for a few hours or possibly a few days. Of course, it always seemed to irritate Eleanor when her sulks didn't have the desired effect of putting him in his place. Instead, Sam tended to look at her deep freezes as a chance to actually get more done around the office.

But this time that didn't seem to be the case. Although Eleanor seemed industrious enough, typing up a storm and slapping completed forms into file folders and stomping over to shove them into the file cabinet, Sam found himself struggling to concentrate.

He glanced toward the ceiling. Somehow he'd managed to upset all three of his women in one fell swoop. He figured it was some kind of personal record. He froze. Had he actually said *all three of his women?* This was not a good sign.

He turned away from the window and surveyed the office. He hadn't bothered to change anything back once he'd put a halt to Haley Jo's redecorating scheme. Primarily because if he hadn't been so bullheaded, he would have realized that the place did look better. Even he could see that there was a greater feeling of space. Of light.

He shoved his hands into his pockets. He couldn't do much about it now. He had managed to make a fool of himself. But then, even a fool could do the right thing and apologize. He walked through the new opening in the counter and headed for the hall.

"Make sure you apologize real nice," Eleanor said, tapping the print key with a flourish and giving him a triumphant glance over her reading glasses.

"What makes you think I'm going to apologize?"

"Because even you know when you've been an ass. You do know you were an ass, don't you?"

"Type the monthly report, Eleanor."

Sam walked down the hall. Trying to deal with Eleanor on a daily basis was like trying to walk bare naked and blindfolded through a poison ivy patch. It would be best to cut his losses and go eat crow.

He found Haley Jo curled up at one end of the cot, a

blanket over her feet and a book open in her lap. An unfinished game of Monopoly sat on the opposite end of the cot. No doubt Prudie had conned her into a game before she'd left for dance lessons.

The cards and game pieces were scattered haphazardly across the brightly colored gauzy cover-up she was using as a bedspread. For a moment, Sam was tempted to go over and carefully put all the pieces back in the box and tidy up. But then he remembered why he was there. An action like that would most likely not endear him to her.

He leaned a shoulder against the cool metal of the door and waited. She didn't look up right away, but he knew she was aware of him from the slight tightening of her narrow shoulders. When she finally glanced up, her expression was wary, but there was no sign of anger or distress. Sam figured she had taken a moment to carefully school her face because something told him he had hurt her feelings earlier.

"I came to apologize," he said.

She closed the book with a snap and pushed back several tight spirals of curls. "There's no need for you to apologize. It's your office. I was totally out of line thinking it was okay to rearrange things without checking with you first."

"I overreacted."

"No, you just like things to be organized. Eleanor told me that. I should have listened." She smiled, something slow and easy, like the sun peeping out from behind a cloud. It was a strangely comforting smile when he considered how miserable he'd been feeling a few minutes ago.

"Usually things like that don't get to me."

"Are you *sure* about that?"

He laughed. "Okay, you caught me. I don't handle change well at all."

"See, don't you feel better now that you've admitted that? Confession really is good for the soul." She nodded toward the chair he had sat in earlier when they had been getting along so famously. "Want to sit down for a few minutes?"

He nodded and moved to sit down across from her. "I figured I better get things straightened out or else Eleanor won't talk to me for days."

"Why do I get the feeling you aren't all that bothered by that?"

He laughed. "You must be psychic. Sometimes it's the only peace I get." He nodded toward the game spread across the end of the cot. "I appreciate your playing with Prudie. She loves board games."

"She's fun if a bit ruthless in her approach."

"She does have a bit of a competitive streak."

"Bit? The child wouldn't loan me twenty dollars to help pay her rent when I landed on Park Place."

"She always cleans my clock, too." He smiled and leaned forward, clasping his hands together in front of him. He didn't want to make her angry again, but he needed to talk about her budding relationship with his impressionable daughter. "Prudie is a lovable kid. She likes you but—"

"But you don't want me to disappoint her by getting too close and then leaving."

He raised an eyebrow. "How did you know I was concerned about that?"

She grinned and shrugged. "Hey, you're the one who said I was psychic."

"Well, in any case, I'd appreciate it if you went easy on the best pal stuff. I don't want her too hurt when it comes time for you to leave."

"I can't say I'm going to ignore her overtures of friendship, but I'll be careful of her feelings."

"That's all I ask. That and your promise to keep a low profile around here."

"I'm guessing that redecorating the entire office doesn't meet your definition of a low profile."

"That would be a good guess."

She let loose a low, sexy laugh. "Wow, sure are a lot of regulations around here. I'm going to need a rule book."

He didn't comment but simply waited.

Finally, she sighed and nodded her agreement. "Okay, unobtrusive, unassuming and quiet as a mouse. That's me."

"Thanks." Sam stood up. "I appreciate your cooperation."

"Just one point of clarification."

He paused at the door to the cell and turned around. She had moved to sit at the edge of the cot, her legs dangling over the side and her head tilted. Her hair cascaded over her shoulders, curling and twisting in a chorus of reds against her pale skin.

"You're not telling me that I have to cower back here the entire week, are you?"

"No—no need to cower. Just low-key."

She grinned, her smile radiant. "Okay, I can handle that."

Sam had a sinking feeling the woman had never *handled* anything in her life in a *low-key* kind of way—including the moment she had come into the world. She was a grandstander if he'd ever seen one. Personally, he was pretty sure he was in for some major trouble keeping Haley Jo quiet.

But he simply nodded and headed back to his desk, determined to wait for the other shoe to fall...or in Haley Jo's case, the other three-inch heel.

8

HALEY JO FIGURED that if the state police didn't hurry up and find the murderer soon she'd either die of an anxiety attack—caused by Eleanor's car backfiring every morning when she arrived and each evening when she left—or she'd keel over from boredom. A person could only play so many games of Monopoly or Connect Four before tipping over the edge and losing it permanently.

Two fairly tense days passed at the Reflection Lake police department. But things around the office were kept interesting by the lively sparks going off between Sam and herself. Sexual sparks. Haley Jo figured that at this rate, one of them, probably she, was going to burst into flames at any moment.

She knew that Sam hadn't meant to scare her the other day with all his talk about keeping a low profile. And in her heart, she knew that he had a good reason to say what he did. But the thought of someone actually looking for her with the express purpose of closing her mouth permanently gave Haley Jo a clear-cut case of the heebie-jeebies. But even that wasn't enough to kill the interesting chemistry boiling up between the two of them.

Sighing heavily, she pulled open one of the office file cabinets. The drawer was a mess. Sam Matthews might be a good chief of police, but he definitely didn't have a flair for an organized filing system.

On second thought, Haley Jo decided that the culprit had to be Eleanor. Sam probably didn't even have a clue as to the pathetic condition of his file drawers. And if he did know, he'd probably have nightmares every night.

She pulled the drawer out farther. Different color files were jammed into every available slot, and nothing appeared to be alphabetized by any system she had ever come across.

This was going to be a tougher job than she'd originally thought, but since there was nothing else to do—what with the chief putting the nix on any future decorating plans—Haley Jo figured the job would keep her from going quietly insane.

"Is the chief around?"

Haley Jo glanced up to see Prudie's sitter Sarah standing in the doorway, with a distracted look on her face.

Eleanor, who had been idly chatting with Haley Jo and trying to keep her from going stir-crazy, set her mug of hot tea down on the desk. "He's out on a call, Sarah. What can we do for you?"

Haley Jo studied the young girl's face, aware that Sarah's expression seemed slightly distressed. She closed the file drawer, immediately concerned that something might be wrong with Prudie. "Is everything okay, Sarah?"

"It's my boyfriend, Karl. He's locked his keys in his car out at the marina." Sarah checked her watch. "He has a job interview at four, and if he doesn't get the keys, he'll miss the appointment." She wrinkled her nose in annoyance. "He needs this job. At the rate he's going, he'll never be able to pop the big question, and I'll be a dried-up old maid at age twenty."

Haley Jo wondered what that made her at twenty-four and no ring in close proximity. No man, either. Well, maybe that was an exaggeration. In actuality, there was a man in sight, but the chief wasn't looking too interested in cooperating.

Sarah glanced at Haley Jo. "Oh, sorry. I didn't mean to say that a person is an old maid simply because—"

Haley Jo waved a hand. "Don't worry, Sarah. I knew what you meant."

Sarah smiled apologetically. "It's just that Karl keeps promising he'll have the money to pop the question soon.

But it isn't going to happen if he keeps missing these job interviews. He's such an airhead sometimes."

Always sympathetic toward a fellow airhead, Haley Joy stood up. "You go ahead and get on over there with the keys. The chief should be back any minute. I'll keep an eye on Prudie until he gets back."

"You don't think he'd mind, do you? I mean you're here, and I'm due to go home in half an hour anyway."

"Sam won't mind," Haley Jo said. Not much he wouldn't. But she wasn't a potential ax murderer or anything. So maybe he wouldn't get too upset.

"You go give Karl the keys, and we'll see you in the morning."

Sarah smiled gratefully. "Thanks, Haley Jo. Prudie's in the living room watching cartoons." She gave a quick wave and scooted out the door.

Haley Jo glanced over at Eleanor. "He *won't* mind, will he?"

"Relax. You did the right thing. You go sit with Prudie and I'll finish up here."

Haley Jo took the breezeway to the main house. She found Prudie stretched out on the floor in front of the TV, her head resting on Razor Beak's sprawled body. A can of pop and a bowl of chips sat within easy reach.

"Hey, lazybones," she called out.

Prudie lifted her head and grinned. "Haley Jo!" She patted the floor next to her. "Come watch cartoons with me."

Haley Jo crossed the room and plopped down next to the girl.

"Wanna sip?" Prudie asked, holding up her soda. She dropped back down, propping herself up against the dog. Razor Beak grunted softly.

"No thanks, sweetie. I'm fine."

"Come on, lean back. Razor won't mind."

Haley Jo gingerly leaned back and the dog's bristly hair rubbed the back of her neck. Razor lifted his head for a minute and sniffed her, but then lay back down, apparently content with the two of them resting on him. It was kind of comfortable. Soft and warm. She scrunched her shoulders in a bit, feeling the dog's heartbeat against the back of her head.

Prudie reached over and handed her a chip, her eyes staying glued to the cartoon characters rampaging across the screen. Haley Jo nodded her thanks and nibbled the edge of the chip. Too many of these things and she'd swell up so fast she wouldn't be able to get into any of her clothes. She turned her head and fed the chip to Razor. She paused and sniffed.

A strange odor seemed to rise up around her.

Prudie, oblivious to the scent, continued to munch on chips and slurp her soda. Haley Jo turned and buried her nose in the dog's neck.

Holy crow! She snapped to a sitting position.

It smelled like rotting garbage and cow manure all rolled into one lovely fragrant package. Haley Jo scooted away from the beast.

Prudie popped another chip in her mouth and raised an eyebrow. "What's wrong?"

"Razor's been frolicking in something decidedly unpleasant."

Prudie frowned, turned her head and inhaled. She jumped up, laughing. "Eeeuwww! I wondered what that was. I bet he's been rolling in cow pies again."

"Again? Your dog routinely rolls in cow manure, and you continue to allow him inside the house?"

Prudie leaned down and planted a potato-chip-crumbed kiss on Razor's muzzle. "Hey, he doesn't know any better. It's like doggie perfume to him."

"Well, we need to clean him up or we'll all end up smelling like him. Where do you hose this beast down?"

Prudie sat back on her heels and grinned. "Oh, goody. A bath. Razor Beak loves getting a bath."

"Couldn't we just take him out back and use the garden hose on him?" Haley Jo asked hopefully.

"No way. Daddy always bathes Razor in the bathtub.

That way he can use the back scrubber to really get him clean."

Haley Jo tried to wrap her brain around the thought that the chief of police used his personal back scrubber on his cow-manure-rolling dog. She suppressed a shudder. Definitely not a pretty thought. Best not to even go there.

Instead, she studied the mutt's huge shape. How the hell did one actually get a beast this size in a bathtub in the first place?

Prudie seemed to read her mind. "Daddy uses ham slices to get him to climb into the tub. That way he doesn't have to lift Razor in."

First reasonable suggestion she'd heard so far. Haley Jo clapped her hands. "Okay, you get the ham. I'll get the shampoo—I've got something that will mask any odor that beast can throw at us."

Laughing with delight, Prudie ran for the kitchen, and Haley Jo headed back to the office and her cosmetic bag.

LESS THAN a half hour later, Sam opened the back door and let himself into the kitchen.

"I'm home, Prudie!" He snagged a chip out of the bowl sitting on the counter and picked up the mail lying in a stack on the table. He leafed through the letters, setting aside the ones that needed immediate attention.

He paused and glanced out the back window in the direction of his office. An overwhelming urge washed over him to go check up on Haley Jo. It might not be a bad idea to catch her up on the latest developments of the case. She'd probably appreciate an update, and the thought of an appreciative smile breaking out across her face was enough to make him yank open the door and run down the breezeway.

But instead, he went back to perusing the stack of bills. If he went over there he might end up inviting her to dinner. And after dinner he might just invite her to sit on the couch. And once she was on the couch, his arm might find its way up along the back of the couch to touch the soft, copper curls at the nape of her slender neck. And then it would be downhill from there.

Tossing the mail on the table, he headed for the living room and safety.

"Prudie!" He poked his head into the back study. No one. "Sarah? Prudence? Anyone home?"

He walked to the end of the stairs and paused. Muffled laughter and a wild rock beat filtered down the stairwell. Puzzled, he took the stairs two at a time.

The bathroom door was partially open and the radio was going full blast. He knocked lightly and then pushed the door open with his palm.

Chaos greeted him.

Razor Beak stood in the middle of the tub, his girth taking up every inch of the shining porcelain interior. Prudie sat on the sink, her legs swinging back and forth in sync with the rock beat. She was using a plastic cup to dump water onto the drenched dog's back.

Effectively pinned behind Razor's massive rump was one Haley Jo Simpson, her petite frame scrunched up against the back wall of tile. Her shorts and tank top were soaked, lying plastered, in the most interesting and provocative way, to her wet, smooth skin.

Both she and Razor were covered head to toe in perfumed bubbles. The sweet smell of vanilla hit Sam full force. He inhaled deeply. So this was where that delightful smell came from whenever he got close to Haley Jo. Vanilla bubble bath.

Prudie glanced up and squealed in delight. She leaped off her perch. "Daddy! You're home."

Haley Jo grinned weakly and gave him a small wave. "Howdy, Chief. We didn't think you'd be back so soon."

"Obviously," he said, leaning down for a quick kiss from Prudie. He reached up with one hand to turn down the radio. "Do we have to listen to that so loud?"

Prudie rolled her eyes. "Everyone knows you have to listen to Lighthouse loud, Daddy."

"Where's Sarah?"

"Uh—she had to leave a little early. Something about her boyfriend locking his keys in his car..." Haley Jo's voice trailed off, and she scrubbed nervously at Razor Beak's sudsy rump. The dog lifted his head in ecstasy and glanced at Sam out of one eye. If he could have talked, Sam was sure the dog would have told him to *get lost* and to quit interrupting the best damn doggie massage he'd ever received.

"Razor rolled in cow doodie again. Haley Jo and I decided to get him cleaned up before dinner."

"Speaking of dinner, why don't you run down to The China Palace and have Danny make us up a big take-out order." Sam reached into his back pocket, pulled out his money clip and peeled off two twenties.

Prudie's smile grew bigger. "Woo-hooo! Chinese. Can I get an order of spareribs?"

"Yes. And tell Danny to throw in a quart of wonton soup."

Prudie spun around toward Haley Jo. "And what do you like, Haley Jo?"

Sam bit back the comment that said that Ms. Simpson wouldn't be joining them. Especially since she was entirely too wet, too sudsy and too sexy to sit at his dining room table. The fact that her appearance was wreaking havoc with his insides had nothing to do with his not wanting her there. Nope, nothing at all.

Haley Jo seemed to have picked up on what he was thinking. "That's okay, Prudie. I'm just going to finish up here with Razor and then head back over to the office."

"You can't eat over at the office. You have to eat Chinese with Daddy and me." Prudie scowled hard and shot one of her I-don't-like-this-one-bit glances in his direction. "Right, Daddy?"

Sam shoved the money in his daughter's hand. "Sure, Prudie. Just go get the food. I'm famished."

Prudie grinned triumphantly and skipped out the door. As she disappeared, Razor Beak made a lunge to get out of the tub to follow, and Sam reached down and shoved the beast back over the lip of the tub.

The big dog's back legs skidded out from under him and he slid backward, bumping up against Haley Jo. She squealed and her feet squeaked on the bottom of the tub. Before Sam could catch her, she slid down, ending up with the dog on top of her and a cascade of bubbles up around her ears.

Concerned, Sam jumped forward to grab one of her outstretched arms, but she was giggling so hard that when he pulled she was dead weight.

Razor Beak, seeing an opening, scrambled to his feet, jumped the side of the tub and disappeared out the door. Vanilla-scented bubbles floated behind him on the air. They mixed nicely with the few choice words that escaped Sam's mouth.

"Sorry," Haley Jo said weakly. She didn't look sorry. She could barely keep from crying she was laughing so hard.

"Are you okay?" he asked, hauling her up.

She nodded, apparently no longer able to even speak.

He got her on her feet and let go, and she almost went over backward again. He caught her under the arms and lifted her out, surprised at how light she was. Giggling, she grabbed on to him, oblivious to the fact that she was soaking him.

"Don't let go," she said. "I think I bruised parts of me that I never even knew existed."

He set her on the bath mat and stepped back, suddenly very conscious of how wet they both were. His own clothing was now plastered to his frame.

She stopped laughing and stared up at him. "Sorry. I didn't mean to get you all wet."

He swallowed against the sudden dryness invading his throat. "Not a problem. It just seems a bit warm in here."

She reached across and loosened his tie and unbuttoned the top button of his shirt. His hand moved to stop her, but something shy and terribly vulnerable seemed to enter her eyes. A fear of refusal perhaps. He dropped his hand back down as the air between them turned hot and heavy.

She stepped closer, and he felt the featherlightness of her feet touch his. He glanced down to see her bare toes covering the smooth leather of his shoes.

"Haley—"

She ignored him and slid a hand up along his chest, the warmth of her touch seeping down through the wet cloth of his shirt. Sam was sure that at any moment steam would start to rise up off him. His heart rate ticked up a few beats, moving to a quick salsa beat beneath her hand, and her warm gaze held him captive, seeming to beg his indulgence.

Her other hand grabbed his belt and pulled him closer. She stood on tiptoes and pressed her lips to his bare skin, directly above the button she had so skillfully opened. He bent his head, and air hissed between his lips as he felt her tongue slide, smooth, wet and hot, up along the side of his neck to his ear.

"You rescued me. You're my hero," she whispered in his ear before moving her mouth over to settle on his.

Her lips were soft and tentative at first, and then, when he leaned closer, she seemed to gain courage, and her kiss hardened, her lips sliding over his with an urgency that surprised him. This wasn't the slow, easy kiss from the other night. The one he had controlled and ended when he was ready to end it. This was something hotter. Wilder. Deeper. More uncontrollable.

Sam pulled her up against him, his hand cupping her behind and lifting her up to press her against him. She gave a little jump and wrapped her legs around him, but her lips never left his. He felt the smooth glide of her tongue over his lips as he opened to her advance. She was making soft little sounds in the back of her throat, something urgent and pleading. Her fingers were tunneling through his hair at the back of his neck and one of her feet had wedged between his buttocks, urging him forward.

Sam's vision clouded and his head felt as though someone had started to toast the edges of his brain. Damn but she tasted fine. The scent of vanilla seemed to surround him, sucking him up into a whirlwind of free-flowing emotions.

Haley Jo hitched herself higher on him, and her mouth became more demanding, her tongue touching the side of his, twisting and darting, then coming back for soft, tender caresses.

The downstairs door slammed and Prudie's voice floated up the stairwell. "Hey, you guys, I'm back. Hurry up and come down for dinner! Danny threw in extra fried wonton and hot sauce."

They sprung apart as if someone had hooked them up to the wrong end of a car battery. Her expression stricken and her hand pressed to her lips, Haley Jo backed up until her legs hit the commode and she sat down with a jolt.

Unable to tear his gaze from hers, Sam leaned back against the doorway and tried to catch his breath. He sucked hot, moist air in short, choppy gulps and stuck a hand out to brace himself against the opposite side of the door frame. He was so hard and ready that it hurt to even think about stopping.

"I guess we're back to repeating that little mistake we made the other night," Haley Jo said quietly, her own breath jagged and uneven.

"So it would appear," Sam said shortly.

She flinched at his tone and folded her arms across her chest, covering the wet, paper-thin condition of her shirt.

Sam immediately regretted his tone. It wasn't her fault. She had simply responded to his own intense attraction to her. Hell, they were both responding to it like two jackrabbits in heat.

Sam knew that he could have and should have stopped her as soon as she touched him. Instead he had reveled in her touch and encouraged her sweet overtures of seduction.

"I'm really sorry, Sam," she whispered, the green of her eyes so intense in the steamy room that he felt as though he might drown in them.

"Hey, not your fault. I could have stopped you at any point, and I didn't." He reached up and brushed his hair back off his forehead. "Look, I'll get you a dry shirt and a pair of my old running shorts—you can put them on for dinner." He forced a grin. "A safety pin on the shorts might keep them up and at least you'll be dry...not to mention a little less desirable."

"You think I'm desirable, Sam?"

"Hell, Haley Jo, I almost performed a tonsillectomy on you. If that isn't a clue to just how desirable I find you, I don't know what is."

He glanced toward the stairs, but all was quiet. Apparently Prudie had gone out to the kitchen to set the table and open the containers of takeout.

He shrugged. "I'm being honest with you. I'm just not in a position right now to get involved with anyone."

She cocked her head. "*Not in a position* as in right this minute because Prudie is downstairs and might walk in on us at any moment? Or *not in a position* at this point in your life?"

Sam grabbed ahold of his tie and slid it out from beneath his collar, wrapping it around the palm of his hand as he tried to form an answer that didn't hurt her too much. Damn. Things were already too complicated. He was worrying about how she was going to take his rejection as if her feelings mattered to him.

He gazed into her eyes and realized with a sharp jolt that he really did care how she felt. That her reaction to him truly did matter. And for one brief moment, he considered not saying anything. Or saying something sweet and laughable. A few words that would make her laugh and throw her arms around him again.

But another part of him, the sane, rational part of his brain, spoke up and warned him of the dangers of such thinking, and he realized he needed to get things back on track. And quickly.

Haley Jo seemed to sense his hesitation, and she leaned forward, her lush lips moist and kissable even now when he intended to push her away. He didn't want to hurt her. Hell, he just wanted to gather her up in his arms and press himself against her until she became a part of him.

"As in—this isn't an option at this point in my life."

Disappointment flickered across her face. "At least you're honest."

"You deserve honesty."

"May I ask why not?"

"Because you live in New York, and I live here. I have a daughter to worry about, and you have a training program to get back to."

"But there are dental hygienist programs in small towns," she said matter-of-factly. "And even if there wasn't one right around here, we could date and see each other on weekends. We could see what happens. Test the waters so to speak."

Sam could feel his old anxieties about getting trapped into something that meant pain in the long run close in on him. He bent over the tub and used the sprayer to wash the remaining bubbles down the drain. He could feel Haley Jo's gaze burning into his back. She was waiting for his answer.

He straightened up. "Long-distance relationships don't work."

He opened the medicine cabinet and grabbed the hairbrush, handing it to her.

Haley Jo took it and tried to ignore the crushing numbness that settled into her limbs at his statement. "Sure. I understand. No problem." She fished a barrette out of her pocket and twisted the mass of red curls up into a ponytail and clipped it into place.

She glanced up at him and smiled wanly. Funny. Her smile felt as phony and frozen as his looked.

"Look, I promise not to make a pest of myself for the rest of my stay here. I'm not usually so forward. I'm glad you let me know where we stand with all this."

She stood up and stepped around him, needing to get out of the enclosed space. Needing to cool off. If she stared at his long, lean frame another minute she was afraid she'd ignite into a roaring flame of wanton fire. His clothes were so wet they seemed to outline every muscle and groove of his hard body.

"Wait. I'll get you the clothes and we can have dinner," he said.

Haley Jo shook her head. "No, that's okay. You go enjoy dinner with Prudie. I need to take a shower and get some of this perfume off me. Thanks for the invitation, though."

She escaped down the stairs before he could say anything else. The thing she was most afraid of was hearing him say something pitying—as if he had to throw a bone her way because he'd just rejected her. Hell, if he could resist the obvious sexual pull they both felt for each other, then she was just as strong as he was. He wasn't going to outstay the staying power of this sexual camel.

HER BARE FEET hit the wooden floor of the living room and Prudie popped her head out of the kitchen. She held a sparerib in her hand and red sauce was smeared across her lips. "Hurry up, Haley Jo! It's getting cold. Where's Daddy?"

"Oh, he'll be down in a minute. He's just getting changed—he got a little splashed when Razor took off for parts unknown."

Prudie giggled. "Razor's out back, rolling in mud. I don't think he appreciated the smell of your bubble bath as much as I did."

"Well you keep it, sweetie," Haley Jo said, as she padded her way into the kitchen and headed for the door.

"Where are you going?"

Haley Jo grabbed the doorknob. "Oh, I'm feeling a bit tired after wrestling with Razor. I'm going to skip dinner and go right to bed." She shot a quick reassuring smile in Prudie's direction. "But thanks for inviting me anyway."

Prudie launched herself across the kitchen and wedged herself between Haley Jo and the door. "No way! You promised you'd eat Chinese with us. And you can't leave. I won't let you."

"Let Haley Jo leave, Prudie."

His voice sent shivers of regret down Haley Jo's spine. Regrets that made her never want to turn around and see his face again. How could he just deny what they were both feeling for each other? It was like instant attraction. Something rare and wonderful and he wanted to simply tuck it away somewhere and forget about it. Well, phooey on him. He wasn't going to make her run away. He might want to run from the feeling, but Haley Jo Simpson didn't run from things like that. She faced them head-on.

Anger stiffened her spine and she turned back around and almost crumpled into a trembling heap of flesh on the linoleum floor.

He stood in the doorway leading to the living room, all six feet two inches of him. He'd changed quickly—a pair of well-worn jeans with a very interesting little frayed hole in the middle of his right thigh. Who would have expected him to be the kind of guy who wore jeans with a hole in them?

He'd thrown on a short-sleeved, royal-blue crewneck shirt, and his hair, although still damp, was neatly combed back into place. She had to make two fists because her fingers itched to go over and mess those dark strands until they fell into his darkly lashed eyes.

"I'm not moving," Prudie said. Her lower lip, the one that looked so much like her father's, stuck out a good mile and half. She threw the sparerib in the sink and folded her arms. "You guys promised, and I ran all the way down to The China Palace and back. The least you could do is eat with me. Like you said you would."

"Prudie—" Sam began, his tone deeper, harder. It didn't even faze Prudie. She shook her head and leaned back against the door, bracing herself for a good fight.

"It's okay, Sam. I'll stay and have some dinner." She glanced at Prudie. "Get me a sweatshirt so I don't drip all over everything."

A grin as wide as the Hudson River broke out across Prudie's face, and she ran from the room, returning a few seconds later with a slate-gray sweatshirt with New York State Police Academy stamped across the front.

She handed it to Haley Jo. "Here. It's Daddy's and it will be a little big, but it will keep you warm."

Haley Jo nodded her thanks and slipped the heavy shirt over her head, thankful for its warmth in view of the icy stare coming to her from the opposite side of the kitchen.

As she thrashed around inside the sweatshirt, trying to find the neck and armholes, his scent engulfed her. He must have worn the shirt recently, perhaps during one of the cool evenings while walking Razor. It reminded her of their kiss a few short minutes ago.

"Here, let me help you." His deep voice surrounded her from outside the warmth of the shirt.

Haley Jo poked her head out of the neck hole and found him standing right next to her, his hands adjusting and pulling the shirt over her. The tips of his fingers brushed the back of her neck as he helped her into the shirt.

"Thank you." She placed her hand on his forearm, and she saw him blink and step back. She dropped her hand immediately. "I'm sorry. I was a little disorientated there for a minute."

Concern immediately crossed his face. "Are you okay? Do you think you hit your head when you fell in the tub?"

"You fell in the tub, Haley Jo?" Prudie asked, her own concern evident in the high-pitched tone of her voice.

Haley Jo glanced up and smiled, determined to get through the meal without once revealing that the dizziness she was feeling had nothing to do with falling and everything to do with the close proximity of one Chief Samuel Matthews.

"I'm fine. Both of you sit down and eat. I don't know about you all, but I'm starved."

Which, of course, was an outright lie. Because from the moment Sam had said he wasn't interested, a huge lump had taken up residence in the back of her throat. And Haley Jo figured she'd be lucky if she could get one skinny, Chinese pea pod past it.

Sam watched her for a moment. His eyes told her he knew what was going on inside her, but Haley Jo could tell from the determined glint lingering in the depths of his baby blues that he wasn't going to relent.

She smiled and moved past him to sit down. It was a relief when Prudie took up the seat across from her, the concern melting from her eyes as she shoved a container of wonton soup across the table at her. "Here," she said. "Try some of this. It's Daddy's favorite." She glanced up at Sam. "Right, Daddy?"

Sam joined them at the table, one large hand reaching over to lightly ruffle the hair on top of Prudie's head. "That's right, gremlin."

Prudie ducked and shot him a glare. "Watch the hair!"

For the first time, Sam realized that his daughter's hair wasn't caught up in its usual scraggly pigtails. Someone had braided it into some type of intricate weave. The warmer, lighter shades of brown, bleached by the July sun, lay brightly against the darker shades, and the side pieces, the ones usually determined to fly about her face, were held back by two delicate silver barrettes.

Sam found himself considering his daughter's face, taking in the oval shape emerging from childhood roundness. She was growing up. When had that happened? How had he missed it?

"Sorry, Prudie. It looks very nice."

Prudie beamed. "Haley Jo did it. She took a lot of time getting it just right." She lifted her hand to touch one of the barrettes. "And she's letting me use her barrettes. Her mom gave them to her when she was twelve, but Haley Jo said I'm mature enough to wear them and be careful with them. They're real silver."

Sam glanced over at Haley Jo, but she was avoiding eye contact and pushing two spareribs and some vegetable fried rice around on her plate.

"I appreciate your taking the time, Haley Jo."

She nodded her head and took a quick bite, her gaze never leaving her plate.

Sam took a deep breath. He needed to set things right. He didn't want her feeling as though he didn't want her around. That she was some type of Typhoid Mary or something equally as contagious. He genuinely liked the woman. Hell, truth be known, he liked her way too much, and something told him that she knew it, too. Not much chance she could have missed that fact when she was so close to him in the bathroom a few minutes ago.

But now was definitely not the time for him to get involved with anyone. No matter how well she fit. Sam paused. She did fit. In fact, she more than fit. It was as if she had been made specifically to sit at his kitchen table on his right and across from Prudie.

No, he refused to get pulled into this. He picked up his fork and stabbed a mushroom, bringing it up to his mouth and defiantly shoving it in, effectively cutting off the apology on the tip of his tongue.

He had been assigned to shelter and protect her, not start a torrid love affair. No matter how much he wanted her in his arms and in his bed, Sam knew that it was best to simply finish the meal and then allow Haley Jo to go back over to his office. There was no future in a relationship with a woman who lived in the city, wore three-inch heels and was registered to start dental hygienist classes in less than two weeks. He had learned nine years ago that his future was right here.

9

SAM HADN'T DARED to come home for lunch since the day he'd kissed Haley Jo in the bathroom, choosing instead to catch a bite on the road whenever he felt hungry. Deep down inside, he knew why. Plain and simple, he was chicken. He couldn't face Haley Jo and her sweet questioning looks whenever he entered the room.

But Sam also knew that not coming home for lunch wasn't fair to Prudie. She was used to his stopping by for a sandwich in the middle of the day, especially on those rare occasions when things slowed down.

He decided that today was the day he'd get back into his old routine. He parked his car in front of the office so Eleanor would know he was close by and turned off the engine. He sat for a moment contemplating the light rain hitting the windshield. It wasn't heavy enough to keep the tourists cooped up inside, but it had been pretty steady all morning.

A few tourists were out in front of The Pear Tree Gift Shop, browsing through the bins Libby, the owner, had set out under the awnings. Several more visitors were walking along the street, brightly colored umbrellas sheltering them from sporadic downpours.

Sam climbed out and walked across the front lawn to his porch. He hadn't dared to go into the office to check in for fear of seeing Haley Jo forlornly playing solitaire on his computer.

Somehow the thought of that small face propped up on the heel of her hand or those brilliant green eyes rising up to eagerly greet whoever walked through the door was more than Sam could bear.

Angry with himself, he grabbed a stack of mail out of the mailbox and opened the front door. Wild disarray hit him head-on. It was if a tornado had hit while he was out. An assortment of board games lay all over the floor.

Someone—no doubt Prudie—had started a game of Twister, but when she finished or tired of the game, she had simply left the plastic mat lying on the floor. It wasn't like Sarah to let Prudie get so disorganized. He wondered if Prudie had invited a friend over, and the two had given Sarah a run for her money.

The crowning glory was finding Razor Beak on the couch, stretched out on his back, his huge head hanging off one end and his tongue lolling out. He blinked and glanced up at Sam with sleepy hound dog eyes. As soon as the beast realized who was coming into the room, he jumped down and trotted off upstairs, his bony tail between his legs. He knew better than to be found on the furniture.

The TV was fixed on the comedy channel, but was playing to an empty room. Canned laughter filled the air. Striding over to the set, Sam flicked it off and paused to listen. A cupboard in the kitchen slammed, and he heard the dishes in the dish rack rattle as someone dug around for something. Probably Sarah making lunch.

From upstairs, he could hear Prudie's radio blaring away, and he figured she was up there. Perhaps it was time to have a little chat with Sarah about keeping Prudie on track during the summer months. He didn't mind Prudie enjoying herself with her friends, but she was also the type of child who needed a lot of structure. Too much freedom and she was bound to start drifting into mischief.

As he neared the kitchen, Sam realized he'd been mistaken. Prudie wasn't upstairs, he could hear her talking away to Sarah. When he reached the doorway, he also realized he'd been wrong about the other person in the kitchen being Prudie's sitter.

Haley Jo stood in front of his stove, brandishing a spatula

and wearing one of his chef-type aprons wrapped around her tiny waist. It reached well below her shorts. She wore a halter top, just two thin strings tied across her slender back. The sight of her smooth skin with a spray of soft brown freckles speckling her shoulders almost sent him to his knees.

Lucky for him, the sight of Prudie sitting cross-legged on the counter, a chef's hat pulled down over her sparrow-brown pigtails put his lust on semi hold. He contemplated the distance to the refrigerator and the freezer compartment. Maybe if he held a handful of ice cubes to the back of his neck, he'd cool down enough to speak coherently.

But he didn't need to worry. Both Haley Jo and Prudie were so absorbed in whatever it was they were doing that they hadn't even realized he'd entered the house.

Of course, that said a lot about the lack of security on Jake's part. But as soon as he had the thought, Sam knew he was being unfair. No doubt Jake and Eleanor knew exactly where Haley Jo was, and his concern was likely blown way out of proportion.

"So how do we make them green?" Prudie asked.

"With food coloring of course." Haley Jo opened one of the cupboards and rummaged through his neatly organized condiments. "Your dad sure is orderly about his spices."

Prudie giggled and reached over to pull down the package of food coloring. "He is a bit of a stick-in-the-mud sometimes. I'm always telling him to loosen up." She glanced up at Haley Jo, her hand poised over the fry pan with the green food coloring. "How much should I put in?"

Haley Jo shrugged. "You've got me. I've never made green eggs and ham before. Just squirt in a few drops and we'll go from there."

Prudie squeezed the bottle, and Sam watched in fascination as the two leaned their heads together over the pan, brown strands mingling with red.

Prudie sat up and wrinkled her nose in disgust. "Eeeuuuwww! That is gross-looking."

"Don't you dare say that. We're going to eat this stuff no matter what. It's good luck to eat green eggs and ham."

"Whoever told you a big whopper like that?"

Sam grinned as Haley Jo shot his daughter a wounded look. "What do you mean whopper? It's true." She reached up and playfully yanked one of Prudie's pigtails. "Besides, it's our first creation together, and that means we have to eat it—it's a friendship meal." She used a fork to flip one of the ham slices. "Quick, more green dye."

Prudie complied, but her face took on a pensive look. It was a look Sam had seen many times before. An expression she wore right before she hit him with some deep, soul-searching question.

"Haley Jo?"

"Yes, sweetie?"

"I have a question."

"Ask away."

"When a mom leaves her kid, does it mean that her kid did something bad...like something that would make her never want to come back?"

The tips of Sam's fingers went numb, and the muscles in his jaw tightened beyond endurance. What was he supposed to do now? There was no way Haley Jo was going to know how to handle this. Hell, he didn't even know how to handle it, and he was the seasoned parent.

He watched as Haley Jo set the spatula down and leaned over. She gently cupped Prudie's chin. "Look at me."

Prudie shifted her gaze.

"Moms leave for a lot of different reasons, sweetie. But not one of those reasons has anything to do with you being bad or saying the wrong thing. Some moms just have a hard time learning how to be moms, and they run because they're scared." She stepped in closer, her slender body seeming to somehow shelter Prudie's. "But what is really neat about life is that you only need one person in this world to love you to make it special."

Prudie's lower lip trembled, and Sam knew she was fighting tears. "Are you sure?" she asked, her voice hoarse.

"I'm absolutely positive, sweetheart," Haley Jo said.

Tears spilled down Prudie's cheeks, and she leaned forward, wrapping her skinny arms around Haley Jo's neck and burying her face against her shoulder. From where he stood, Sam could see Haley Jo's own arms tighten around Prudie.

"Haley Jo?" Prudie asked, her voice muffled.

"Yes, sweetie?"

"Do you have a special someone to love you?"

Sam watched as Haley Jo's hand paused in midstroke. He held his breath, watching her seemingly swallow hard before answering, "Not yet, sweetie. But I haven't given up hope."

Sam turned and left the way he'd come in. He tried to tell himself it was because the two of them needed to eat their friendship meal in peace. But the real reason was his uncertainty that he could face Haley Jo without doing what he had sworn he'd never do again—kiss her with all the passion and fire he denied existed.

10

"Now, Dearie, I brought you my award-winning Wilted Dandelion Salad and a pot of my Buzzard's Breath Chili."

Eighty-year-old Ludi Mills Bradford shoved a plastic-covered bowl into Haley Jo's hands and motioned for her companion, Alma Mae Quincy, to hand over the other dish.

Haley Jo knew from Eleanor's whispered comment right before the two women had walked through the front door that they lived in Reflection Lake's Retirement high-rise. A high-rise that encompassed four floors. Eleanor had warned her that Ludi was the town matriarch. No one messed with Ludi.

Haley Jo smiled and accepted their offerings with a gracious smile. Ludi wasn't the first visitor to stop by bearing gifts. In fact, if Haley Jo's numbers were correct, Ludi and Alma Mae were numbers twenty and twenty-one respectively. Too many more covered dishes and the chief was going to have to purchase a new freezer to put them all in.

Of course, Haley Jo wasn't stupid. She knew that everyone in town was stopping by because they were dying of curiosity. None of them could wait to get a gander of the city girl sleeping in Chief Matthews's jail cell. Word travels fast in a small town.

"I really appreciate this," Haley Jo said, setting the dishes on the counter. "I'm sure the chief will enjoy a taste for lunch."

"Just keep your eye on that one over there." Ludi squinted her eyes and pointed a shaky finger in Chester's direction. "That's Arnold's boy and I know he can eat a cow right down to its hoofs before it even has a chance to moo for help."

Chester hung his head. "Shucks, Miz Ludi, I just appreciate your good cookin'."

Ludi waved a hand as if to dismiss him, but there was no missing her pleased grin. "Oh, go on with you, Chester. You're such a chow hound that you'd say the same thing if Eleanor offered you one of her hard-as-a-rock oatmeal raisin cookies. Why, I bit down on one of those things at the last church social and cracked my dentures. Doc Reynolds had to make me up a whole new upper plate."

Haley Jo shot a covert glance in Eleanor's direction. Oh, things were not going well. Eleanor looked about ready to blow. Her face had turned a lovely shade of purple, and her grip on her cane had turned her knuckles paper white.

Unfortunately, Ludi seemed oblivious. She turned a sharp gaze on Haley Jo. "Well, I see that everyone was right. You're just a little bit of a thing."

"Everyone?" Haley Jo asked weakly.

"Everyone I've sent over to visit naturally." She narrowed her eyes again. "What? You didn't think I'd check you out?"

Haley Jo shrugged helplessly. How was she supposed to answer that? Apparently Ludi Mills Bradford figured everyone knew she had her finger on the pulse of the town.

Before she had a chance to respond, Ludi reached out and poked Haley Jo in the ribs. She glanced accusingly in Eleanor's direction. "What are you feeding the poor girl? She's all skin and bones. I thought Samuel's mama taught him better than this."

Eleanor sniffed. "The chief is doing a fine job of running this town without you sticking your nose in, Ludi Bradford."

Off to the side, Chester sucked in a loud but noticeably panicked gulp of air. He looked about ready to bolt. Haley Jo figured if she grabbed his shirttail as he ran past, she too could get out safely. Even shy Alma Mae appeared ready to run for the hills.

"Young people should learn to speak better to their elders," Ludi said.

"Senile old women should know when to quit poking their noses into things," Eleanor shot back.

Haley Jo opened her mouth, ready to apologize for something. Anything. But then, before all hell could break loose, the front door swung open and a tall, rawboned woman with short, bleach blond hair breezed in. "Hello, everyone." She shifted her broad shoulders to adjust the baby carrier on her back.

"Good morning, Tina," Ludi said stiffly.

Haley Jo breathed a sigh of relief. This had to be Ollie's wife, Tina Sykes, the mayor. She held out a hand. "I'm Haley Jo. Pleased to meet you."

Tina pumped her hand, almost lifting Haley Jo off the floor with the force of her strength. She was more than a match for her giant of a husband.

"Pleased to meet you, Haley Jo." Tina glanced around. "So, what's everyone up to?"

"Ludi and I are seeing who caves first in the insult department," Eleanor said bluntly.

"You're an amateur, Eleanor," Ludi said, laughing softly. "But I have to admit you're getting better. When I pass on I know the town will be in good hands."

The entire group seemed to take a collective sigh of relief. A disaster had been diverted. The two women had apparently called a quick truce.

Tina took that moment to swing the baby carrier off her back and set it on the counter. She pulled her infant out of it. "I came over to brag."

"What? He's lifting his head?" Eleanor asked as they all gathered around her.

"Better than that. He's cutting his first tooth," Tina said.

"Pfff. You'll change that tune when he starts gnawing on you with that thing," Ludi said matter-of-factly.

The group's attention was quickly diverted again by the new task of cooing over baby Ozzie. In spite of Ludi's claim that the tooth wasn't a big deal, they all seemed pretty impressed. Although she was completely ignorant of the mysteries of babyhood, Haley Jo happily joined the women in their chorus of ooohs and ahhhs. It wasn't hard. Ozzie was an adorable little fireplug—all chubby cheeks, dimpled knees and drool on pink rosebud lips.

For the first time in her life, Haley Jo wondered what it might be like to cradle a tiny—okay, maybe not so tiny—bundle like Ozzie in the crook of her arm. But strangely enough, in Haley Jo's case, her bundle of joy had a pair of killer blue eyes and a head of thick black hair.

As soon as the daydream took form, Haley Jo decided she'd better invite the women into the office for coffee. Anything to get her mind off the thought of having babies. She was a career woman. She couldn't be thinking thoughts like that. Especially thoughts that included a miniature version of one Sam Matthews. That particular daydream was downright dangerous.

THE VISITS from the townspeople didn't stop after Ludi's drop-in. People just kept streaming through the front door, and Haley Jo found herself the new unofficial welcoming committee and impromptu hostess of Reflection Lake's Police Department.

Sam continued to keep a close eye on her, catching her a few times when she tried to make plans to visit some of her new friends. Even the big lingerie party at Tina Sykes's house Wednesday night was speedily nixed. Chester volunteered to take her, but Sam simply glared at him until he slunk off.

On Friday morning, Haley Jo woke up early and dressed quickly, very conscious of the fact that there was no privacy even though none of the guys in the office came to the back without first calling down the hallway for permission. Chester even joked about wiring up a little doorbell at the end of the hall for them to ring.

She walked out to the front office and glanced around. Chester was in his usual spot. He grinned and quit the program he was running. "Mornin', Haley Jo. Sleep well?"

She nodded.

"The chief isn't around. He seems to be running a little late this morning."

Haley Jo moved over to the counter and poured herself a cup of coffee as Chester pulled himself upright with a soft grunt. "I'm going to pop over to Petra's Bakery to grab a paper." He grinned sheepishly. "And maybe a few of her custard-filled torpedoes. You want something?"

"No, thanks. No torpedoes for me. With all this sitting around and waiting, I think I've put on at least five pounds."

He grinned. "Not in any places I can see."

"You're good for my ego, Chester."

"You mind answering the phone while I'm gone?"

"Sure."

Chester ducked out the door and ran across the street.

Haley Jo stirred in some powdered creamer. Sure she'd answer the phone. And she'd make the coffee and do some filing. She'd do anything they asked as long as she could hang around forever. How pitiful could a person get? A lot worse, she figured.

She sipped her coffee and allowed her gaze to travel over to the side door. A familiar little hitch settled into her chest, pressing up against her breastbone. She had labeled it her Chief Matthews hitch, an annoying ailment, that as far as she had been able to determine, was incurable. And after the passionate kiss they'd shared in his bathroom two days ago, the hitch appeared whenever she knew he was about to step back into her life.

She took another swallow of coffee and contemplated the doorknob. It still hadn't moved, and she found herself quietly counting off the minutes in her head. How much more pathetic could a person get?

As if on cue, the door opened and Sam stepped through. He did a quick survey of the office and settled his gaze on her. There was no missing the wary look in his eyes.

"Good morning. Chester around?"

"He ran over to get the paper. He said he'd be right back."

Sam nodded and then moved toward the coffeepot. Haley Jo set her own cup down and fumbled to pour him one.

"Thanks. But there isn't any need to wait on me."

"Oh, I know. I'm just trying to make myself useful around here."

He nodded vaguely and accepted the mug from her, careful to keep his fingers from coming into contact with hers. He looked as if he were going to say something else, but then he turned and walked over to his desk.

Haley Jo watched him walk away and struggled not to say something. Anything. What she didn't need to do right now was to start babbling. But these polite conversations and heavy silences were beginning to take a toll on her.

He seemed oblivious to her dilemma, calmly sitting down at his desk and pulling a file off the top of the pile in his In box. He sipped his coffee as he read.

Grabbing a stack of files off of Eleanor's desk, Haley Jo sat down and tried to copy Sam's calm demeanor. If this was how he wanted to play out her time here, then there wasn't much she could do about it.

She arranged the first three folders and reached for a fourth. The stack slid off the edge of the desk and spilled onto the floor.

"Oh for pity's sake."

Sam glanced up. "Need a hand?"

"No. I can get it." She bent down and scooped the mess into a pile. It was going to take her hours to sort everything into their proper folders. Busywork. Mind-blowing, heart-numbing work. Standing up, she dropped the stack onto the desk. They hit the hard wood with a loud clap.

Sam glanced up again, his eyebrow lifting.

"I'm sorry, but I can safely say that I'm going slowly insane." She yanked the kerchief off her head and twisted it, wringing it so tight it became a twisted band of color in her hands. "Wait! I take that back. I'm not *going* insane. I'm already there!"

She walked over to pace the floor in front of his desk. "In fact, I'm certifiably nuts. Crazy. Bonkers."

"No need to convince me," he said dryly. "But if you feel this need to emote, go right ahead. Just do it a little quieter, please. I have a lot of paperwork to get caught up on."

Haley Jo gritted her teeth and whipped the scarf against the side of her leg.

Ouch. That hurt.

She stuffed the kerchief in her pocket. "Thanks ever so much for your support. You'd think a law enforcement person would have the ability to recognize emotional stress when he saw it. That he'd have a little sympathy for a person going stir-crazy."

Sam sighed and set the file aside. "Okay. What's the problem?"

"I just told you, I'm going over the edge."

He nodded and then lifted the stack of papers he'd been working on and shuffled them, getting the edges to align before slipping them into a file.

She watched in frustration as he paused to carefully place the file on a neat stack sitting in the exact center of his In basket. She gritted her teeth. The man got even neater and more controlled the more emotional she got. They'd never make it as a couple.

Make it as a couple?

Where had that little gem come from? They're weren't a couple. They weren't anywhere close to being a couple. Oh sure, they had kissed a few times—hot passionate kisses that nearly fried her insides. But Haley Jo didn't know what made her think they had actual couple potential.

Sam sat back and folded his hands across his flat stomach. His expression was resigned. "I knew you'd find life here in Reflection Lake too boring for your tastes."

Haley Jo's heart thumped. Yikes! He was taking her comments as a condemnation of the town. She loved the town. She'd never felt more like she belonged anywhere.

"That's not how I feel at all."

"You just got done telling me how bored you are."

"About being cooped up in here. That has nothing to do with the town. I love the town. I'd give anything to be able to walk out that door, go down to the high-rise and have morning coffee with Ludi and Alma Mae."

Sam rolled his eyes. "What? You have a death wish? Those two ladies would pick you clean of every piece of information you have inside of two minutes."

Haley Jo laughed. "Well, I like them. And everyone else who has come to visit. I feel as though I belong."

"So if you're feeling like that why exactly are you complaining of boredom? And how exactly do you propose I help you deal with it?"

"Loosen up a bit. Quit insisting that I stay locked up in here like some kind of prisoner."

Sam shook his head, his facial features reverting to his familiar *lawman* look. In other words, the expression that told her he was going to say no to anything she asked for.

"Obviously you're having a hard time grasping this protective custody thing. Bottom line—it's too dangerous for you to be wandering around town unprotected."

She let out a cry of exasperation. "Will you get real. It's dangerous to get behind the wheel of a car, but I do it every day."

He picked up a letter and tore it open. "The answer is no."

"That's it? No explanation. No discussion. Just no?"

"Just no."

"I'm not a little kid, Sam."

He leaned back in his chair again and lifted his arms, clasping them behind his head. Haley Jo struggled to keep her eyes up off his chest and away from the sight of his shirt stretching tightly across his muscular chest.

"I know that."

"It feels as though I've spent a lifetime in that cell."

"I can see that this discussion is going to continue to go in circles." He sat forward again. "What are we talking about here? A short walk? A stop at the local Wal-Mart? What exactly are you negotiating for?"

Haley Jo grinned. This might be her one and only chance. She needed to word things carefully. "I don't know...I was thinking a hockey game maybe. And then fish fry at Kellum's afterward."

The apologetic look she was sure she'd seen creeping across his face a moment ago disappeared in a flash. *"Absolutely not."*

Haley Jo scrambled around the corner of his desk and perched on the edge, an inch away from him. He didn't meet her gaze but instead, yanked several sheets of paper out from beneath her left cheek.

"Come on, Sam. I'm not asking for all that much."

"No."

"Why?"

"Because everyone in town is going to be there. And I can't protect you."

"Please."

"Not a chance."

She stared at him hard, putting all her effort into the wounded, trapped-animal look. She hid her glee when the tiniest hint of compassion twitched at the corner of his firm lips. Oh baby, she was getting to him

"Okay, I'll compromise. How about I buzz you through the McDonald's drive-through."

Damn. She didn't have him. "As nice as that sounds—and please know I appreciate your offer, especially since I'd give up the entire contents of my cosmetic case for a Big Mac right now—I'm going to decline that offer. What I really want to do is watch you play hockey and then eat fish at Kellum's."

"How'd you know I was playing hockey tonight?"

She grinned. "I couldn't sleep last night and I shared a pizza with Chester."

"Chester has a big mouth." He shook his head. "This isn't a negotiable item, Haley Jo. I can't watch you and play hockey, too."

"But I'll sit off to the side." She leaned forward, willing him to relent. "I promise to be totally inconspicuous. No one will even know I'm there."

Sam's eyes widened and he laughed. "Yeah, right. You, Haley Jo Simpson, goddess and princess of showiness, hereby agree to be totally inconspicuous. Why do you think I'm having a hard time buying this?"

Haley Jo folded her hands in her lap and carefully pressed her knees together. Sister Mary Josephine, her third-grade teacher, would have been proud.

"I can do it. I really can. You just have to trust me."

"I know you. And as much as I'd like to say I trust you, I know you couldn't be inconspicuous at your own funeral."

Haley Jo jumped down off the desk. "Oh, now that was a low blow. How nice was that—threatening me with my own funeral?"

He sighed. "Sorry. But you have to admit that keeping a low profile is not your best feature."

"The only thing I'm in danger of dying from in this godforsaken town is complete and utter boredom."

"That means I've done my job. If you're bored, you're safe."

"Fine! But I know when I'm being bullied, and I don't like it."

He ignored her and opened a file.

She plopped down in the chair next to his desk and crossed her legs. She suppressed a grin as his gaze skimmed the length of her calf up to the hem of her dress. His fingers tightened on the file, bending the papers tucked inside.

"Do you mind? I'm trying to work."

"I don't mind at all. Work away." She lifted a hand and calmly examined her fingernails. "I don't have anything to do at the moment. Of course, if I knew I was going to go out for the evening, I might be inclined to go and pick out an appropriate outfit. But since I'll be sitting in all evening...well, there just isn't any reason to leave."

"I'm not changing my mind," he said, continuing to peruse a stack of papers.

Haley Jo smiled sweetly. "Okay, if you say so." She started to swing her foot, her shoe slipping off and teetering on the tips of her toes. She started to hum softly.

A muscle in Sam's jaw began to jump in time to her humming. "I'm not changing my mind."

Haley Jo shrugged. "Not a problem." She used her thumb to tap on the edge of the desk.

He slapped the papers down on the desk and stood up. "Fine. You can go."

"I can?" she said. "How absolutely wonderful."

He held up a finger. "You can go—as long as you agree to sit in the back and tone down the usual fashion show."

Haley Jo nodded and leaned across to plant a quick kiss on his cheek. She paused, her lips pressed against the warmth of his skin. The soft scent of laundry detergent clung to his collar and mingled with the faint smell of shaving cream lingering on his smooth cheek.

His closeness and his scent made her light-headed, and a small voice inside her head whispered for her to put her arms around his neck and hang on tight. To hold on for dear life and never let go. But instead, she stood up and stepped back.

"Sorry, I got a little carried away."

Sam nodded, his gaze troubled.

"Well, I guess I'll go find something suitably drab and uninteresting to wear tonight."

At the head of the hallway, she glanced back. "I think my see-through blouse, black lace bra, miniskirt and goldfish purse will be just the thing to wear."

He stood up, the chair whipping backward and hitting the wall. "I thought you understo—" He stopped when he caught her wink.

She whirled back around and laughed. "I swear! I was just kidding."

"Haley Jo—" His tone had a deep note of warning to it.

But she simply waved airily and left, leaving him to finish up whatever it was that he needed to do.

After all, Haley Jo figured she had tortured him enough for one afternoon, and if she ever felt the need to indulge some more, there was always this evening. Something told her that Sam had no idea what he was in for.

THAT EVENING, Sam dropped Prudie off at her best friend's house for a planned overnight. He checked with Shannon's mother to make sure they were all in agreement about the rules—no sleeping in the backyard tent unless Mrs. Bradley decided she was willing to risk possible back injury by sleeping out there with them. Preferably with her body draped across the exit to keep the two girls in the tent.

The last time Prudie and Shannon had slept in the tent, they had slipped out around midnight to ride down Main Street on their bikes. If that's all they'd done, no one would have been upset. But the two rascals had decided to conduct their own personal toilet papering spree of some of the homes of Reflection Lake's more prominent citizens.

Teresa Bradley had thought it was pretty funny, but Sam and Ken Bradley hadn't seemed quite as ready to see the humor in the incident. Of course, Sam figured that was because the two men ended up being the ones to climb up some of the really tall maple trees to get the wet, clingy stuff down.

Sam had been all for making the girls do it, but the reality of how high some of the trees were settled in and he relented. Prudie knew, however, that she was currently on probation regarding overnights, and Sam was pretty sure she'd carry this one off without any major incidents. At least he could delude himself with that thought for now.

As he pulled out of the Bradley driveway, headed back for the office, he saw Andy driving toward him. He pulled up alongside Sam's truck.

"What brings you out this way?" Sam asked.

"I stopped by the office—Eleanor told me you were

here. I thought I'd swing by and tell you in person rather than call."

"Tell me what? Good news?"

Andy grinned. "Excellent news. The dentist's wife confessed less than an hour ago to two homicide detectives in the city. Apparently, the fact that we were able to trace the candy purchase back to her convinced her that she needed to come clean."

"That was pretty quick."

Andy laughed. "They sent down one of our best interrogators to talk to her along with two of New York's finest. Mrs. Rocca folded pretty quickly according to the lieutenant who called me."

Sam slid his truck into Park and glanced in the mirror. They were on a dead-end street so the chance of anyone needing to get by was pretty slim. "Did she explain why she choked him?"

"Well there's a bit of a problem with that. According to this Lieutenant Connors, Mrs. Rocca outright denies ever trying to choke the guy. And it doesn't seem as if she could have been in the room and down on Long Island at their summer home—which reliable witnesses say she was during the time Dr. Rocca was chowing down on chocolate-covered cherries."

"You're not thinking that Haley Jo did the choking, are you?"

Andy shrugged. "We know from the coroner that the choking occurred after the guy died from the poison. Maybe Haley Jo got a little carried away when she found him half-naked in her room and took it out on his neck."

Sam shook his head. "No way, Andy. It didn't happen that way."

"Hey, relax. I'm just suggesting one possibility." He stretched his arm out along the open window, obviously pacing himself. "It isn't as if she killed the guy. He was already dead. She might have just been a little angry."

Sam gritted his teeth. "You're not getting this. There is no way in hell that Haley Jo Simpson grabbed a scarf out of her suitcase, wrapped it around the guy's neck and proceeded to choke him. She bathed my Great Dane in vanilla bubble bath and feng shui-ed my office. That's not the kind of person who goes around choking people with scarves."

"Well, normally I'd agree, Sam, but I'm stumped. Who else could have done it?"

"There had to be someone else in that room."

"You suggesting a threesome?"

"Get your mind out of the gutter, Andy," Sam warned. "Someone who came into the room when Haley Jo was in the bathroom. Another person who had a grudge against Dr. Rocca."

"Well that could be half of Manhattan from what we've been able to determine. The guy was trash with a capital *T*."

"So we need to look harder." Sam shifted in his seat. "Anything on the guy Haley Jo saw in the hall when she arrived at her room?"

"Nothing."

Sam put his car into Drive. "Keep on it. I think there's more to this than we're seeing."

"I think you'd like to keep Haley Jo in protective custody forever," Andy said softly.

Sam turned to stare at his friend. "What exactly does that mean?"

"Just what I said. I think you'd like to keep Haley Jo hidden away in your jail cell indefinitely. That way you never have to admit how much you like her or face the fact that she's going to leave."

"This case has gotten to you, Andy," Sam said, taking his foot off the brake and easing his car forward.

"Maybe," Andy said, "but you should think about what I said."

"Yeah, right. I'll do that." Sam pulled away. No one was going to tell him that he'd thought this whole Haley Jo thing out wrong. Both of them had already come to the conclusion that they weren't suited for each other. Attraction and plain lust didn't a relationship make.

He stopped at the end of the road and glanced in the rearview mirror. Andy was using one of the driveways to turn his vehicle around. He might be Sam's best friend, but Sam knew he was wrong. Nothing Andy said could convince him otherwise. Besides, he didn't have time to examine this now. A quick check of his watch told him he had just enough time to get over to the hockey arena.

As he switched on the indicator, Sam met his own eyes in the mirror. "Chicken," he said quietly and then pulled out onto the main road.

THE DRAKE MEMORIAL ARENA was an oversize, warehouse type structure. It housed Reflection Lake's single most important recreational and social outlet—the ice rink.

Sam pulled into the parking lot, and was lucky to find a spot. He grabbed his hockey bag off the seat and climbed out of the car. The lot was already full. The men's early summer hockey league had gained quite a following over the years. Most nights, the stands were packed.

Of course, a handful of the townspeople who came did so to get out of the heat. But the majority of the people came because they were die-hard hockey fans. People who liked their hockey rough and year-round, and Reflection Lake Men's League delivered both.

Sam yanked open the arena's side door and stepped inside, taking a deep breath as he entered the locker room. A smile immediately broke across his face. He loved the smell of the place—dampness, burned coffee and sweat.

The simple act of being in the locker room never failed to bring back strong, sweet memories of childhood. Memories of stumbling out of his dad's truck half-asleep at 5:30 a.m., his duffel bag dragging along the ground as he fumbled through the door leading to the locker room.

He dropped his gear bag onto the bench in front of his locker and sat down. He kicked off his sneakers, shucked his clothes and pulled on his equipment. Reaching into his bag, he pulled out a roll of tape—a hockey player's single most important accessory. He used the tape to secure his knee and elbow pads.

He shoved his bare feet into his skates and laced them up, careful to wrap the laces around the upper part of the boot three times. Not two. Not four. But three times. He grabbed the tape again and wrapped his ankles.

Pausing a minute, he glanced around. The benches were covered with half-empty sports bags, some of them spilling discarded shoulder pads or knee pads over the sides and onto the cement floor.

He grinned and stood up. He was late but knew that the other players wouldn't start the game until he got there. The sounds of their voices, calling to each other—laughter and rough teasing—filtered back through the doors leading to the ice surface. From the sounds of things, his buddies were already warming up.

Sam grabbed his gloves, helmet and stick and headed for the rink. With his gloves tucked under one arm, he shoved his helmet on and snapped the chin strap. As he opened the gate leading to the ice, he glanced up at the stands, scanning the crowd for Haley Jo.

She was nowhere in sight. Just row upon row of cheerful but unimaginatively dressed Reflection Lake citizens. Not a single colorful, overdressed peacock among them. He pulled on his gloves and let his stick hit the ice with a slap.

Perhaps she had reconsidered, decided not to come. Probably a good thing. He hadn't been all that encouraging, but in spite of his saying he didn't want her there, a small jolt of disappointment shot through him.

He checked the opposite side of the stands. Still no sign of her. He shook his head. Leave it to Haley Jo to make a fuss and then not show up. She was like a firefly on a hot summer's evening. Free-spirited and unpredictable. An entity barely human. Pinning her down was like trying to keep that firefly inside a jar—a next-to-impossible feat.

Sam pushed the silly romantic thoughts aside. He needed to concentrate on the game or he'd get his clock royally cleaned. The guys who played in this league didn't have time for people who had their heads stuck up in the clouds or anywhere else for that matter.

A few players from both sides skated the length of the rink, while the others hovered around their assigned positions. Sam realized he was later than he'd originally thought. There'd be no time for strategizing.

Rudy Allenson, one of the best blue liners in the league, swept past, headed for his position as defenseman. "You're center stage, Sammy," he called over one shoulder. "Don't let us down. This team thinks they're hot stuff."

Sam nodded and skated up to the line, nodding to the two men flanking him on either side. Across from him, his counterpart watched him stone-faced.

"Evenin', Stagniki," Sam said, resting his arm on top of his stick.

"Matthews," Stagniki, the Blue Panthers's team captain, said around his mouth guard.

"We going to have a nice clean game tonight?"

"Anything's possible." Stagniki glanced back toward his own prize defenseman, Billy Maddock, and then back at Sam. His grin widened and it could only be described as menacing. "But then Mad Dog isn't looking like he's in one of his *nice* moods."

Within seconds, they were involved in the heat of the game, and Sam forgot about Billy Maddock and just skated. Every few minutes, he'd get distracted enough to look into the stands to check for a certain redhead, but none were visible.

In the second period, Sam felt the tempo of the game change. Even though the ice was a little soft and it felt as though they were playing on slick glass, Sam knew his team had settled into a groove.

It felt particularly sweet when Rudy hit the puck with a smooth sweep and it floated across the ice to nestle against Sam's stick. He cradled the puck lovingly in the curve of his blade and took off with a powerful push. The ice beneath his skates sang, and he knew no one could stop him. Not that they wouldn't try.

The Panthers's goalie watched him through the holes of his mask, his stick poised to stop any attempts to trespass into his territory.

"Get ready for it, buddy," Sam whispered under his breath. "Because it's coming right down your throat if you don't move." He hit his stride midrink and stretching out, moved fast and sleek.

He could sense the guard right on his heels, but he didn't bother glancing around. No need. Concentrate on the goal. From a distance he could hear the crowd screaming, but he shut them out.

He swept to the left, faking out his shadow, who whizzed past on the right. He heard the man swear just before he headed down the opposite side.

The goalie hunkered down low, waiting for the shot. Sam grinned and cut across in front of the net. He drew back and smacked the biscuit with a satisfying crack. It hung, suspended in midair for a fraction of a second and then sailed across the ice, slipping between the goalie's feet and into the net. The roar of the crowd filled his ears, and he lifted his stick in answer.

Sam slid to a smooth stop next to the boards, shooting up a spray of shaved ice, and he heard a familiar voice rise up above the crowd, "Wooo-hooo! Way to go, Matthews, you sexy thing!"

A ripple of laughter rolled over the crowd, and a few females whooped in agreement.

Sam didn't need to look up into the stands to know who had made the catcall. It was Haley Jo. He was surprised at the sense of relief that rocketed through him at the sound of her voice. Surprisingly, it didn't even matter that she was shouting at him from the stands in front of the entire town. He was simply glad she was there.

He glanced up to see her sitting smack-dab in the middle of the crowd, directly behind the team's box. So much for her keeping to the sidelines. She was flanked on either side by Andy and Eleanor. When she noticed him looking in her direction, she bounced up and waved. Apparently, she didn't think he could see her.

Sam closed his eyes for a brief second and prayed for strength. When he opened his eyes, Haley Jo was still waving. Covering one arm was a brilliant red foam hand, the kind with We're #1 printed on the front and one finger waggling breezily in the air. Only the most secure and overly zealous of fans would dare to show up at a game with it on. It was so big she could have slipped it over her head and worn the thing as a dress.

And perhaps that might have been a good idea, since she was wearing less than nothing to begin with. Sam couldn't have missed her now if he tried. She stuck out like a ballerina at a lumberjacks' convention, her slender legs encased in skintight, neon-green capri pants, a skimpy yellow halter top was her so-called shirt, and a sheer lime-green long-sleeved thing completed her outfit.

Sam couldn't help but wonder if she was under the silly misconception that the gauze shirt would keep her warm in the cool arena. But then, he forgot about that and found himself studying the creamy white column of her neck. Oh, to be sitting next to her at that moment nibbling on that line of perfection. The thought sent a jolt of need so intense—so sharp and clean—through him that Sam was forced to lean on his stick to get his wind back.

Oblivious to her effect on him, she grinned and continued to wave, a collection of silver bracelets on her arm jangling wildly up and down. So much for her promise to stay inconspicuous.

As he watched, her face changed. The wide smile crumbled and reformed into a perfect O. But that's all he remembered before being hit from behind. A heart-stopping, throat-closing slam from the rear that sent him crashing headfirst into the boards.

11

ICE STUNG Sam's cheek, and the entire left side of his face hurt so bad he thought he might have lost it against the boards when he'd gone down. Sucking moist air, he rolled over onto his back and stared up at the ceiling. At least he hadn't lost consciousness, and he could breathe and move.

"You okay?"

He glanced to the right to see Rudy leaning over him. Good. His eyes still functioned. "I think so. What hit me?"

"I believe that would be Mr. Mad Dog Maddock. Apparently, he didn't like the fact that you scored against him. So he took your skinny ass out."

From a distance, Sam heard Haley Jo arguing with someone. He turned his head some more and groaned aloud. From ice level, he spied two familiar feet in three-inch heels standing toe-to-toe with the referee. Lifting his head just a bit, he saw Haley Jo poking her finger in the middle of the poor guy's chest.

"Don't tell me what I can and can't do," she said. "He's hurt, and I'm going over there."

"Ma'am, please. Spectators are *not* permitted on the ice during a game," the ref tried to explain with infinite politeness.

Of course, true to form, Haley Jo was having none of it. She jammed her hands on her hips and gave the poor guy a glare that would have slain a lesser man. "In case you missed it, the game isn't going on right now. That big lug over there hit Chief Matthews from behind."

The ref sighed heavily. "I realize that, ma'am. And I promise you I'll deal with it."

Haley Jo folded her arms, and the toe of her shoe tapped out an impatient pattern on the ice. "I'm waiting."

"For what, ma'am?"

"For you to take care of that—that beast over there. The one who hit Chief Matthews." She shot a special no-nonsense glare in Mad Dog's direction. "You oughta be ashamed of yourself. Hitting a man when he isn't looking."

Sam glanced at Rudy. "Please tell me Mad Dog didn't hear that."

Rudy laughed. "To tell you the truth, the big brute is looking pretty ashamed of himself."

As they spoke, Haley Jo turned in Sam's direction, her delicate features etched with concern.

She waved. "Hang on, Sam. I'm coming." Sure enough, she struck out across the ice on high heels. She used a tentative, gliding step, balancing on tippy toes, her arms pinwheeling out from her sides in an effort to maintain her precarious balance.

Groaning again, Sam dropped his head and then winced when it met the ice. "This is not good. Not good at all."

Rudy laughed. "I beg to disagree, buddy. That's some feisty little filly you got there. Wouldn't mind her rescuing me."

Sam squeezed his eyes shut and prayed for strength. "She's not my filly, and she's *not* rescuing anyone, least of all me."

"Well, whatever she's doing, she's definitely on her way over here."

"Help me up."

"You sure you don't want to rest there for a minute? Doc Edwards is on his way."

Sam sat up. "Get me up now! If I'm laid out like a slab of beef on ice, Doc will bench me for sure."

Rudy hauled him up, and Sam tried to ignore the squeal of protest coming from every bone of his body. He was definitely nuts. What sane, thirty-three-year-old man thought he could play on a men's hockey league with a bunch of twenty-year-olds?

HALEY JO SCRAMBLED across the ice, slid into Sam and grabbed a handful of his shirt to keep from falling. Unfortunately, he wasn't too stable either, and they started to go over. But at the last minute, his friend grabbed the both of them and yanked them upright.

She tipped her head back to get a better look at Sam. He didn't appear happy to see her. The huge bruise swelling up under his left eye wasn't a pretty sight, and the split over the same eye was bleeding.

"Nice goal, handsome. Too bad Godzilla knocked you on your butt in front of everyone."

He frowned. "What are you doing down here? I thought you and I agreed that you'd stay inconspicuous."

She shrugged. "I was inconspicuous for about half the game, but I couldn't see anything. I begged Andy to let me sit in a better seat."

"Andy should know better."

"Andy likes me. He thinks you're overprotective. Besides, I got a little concerned when you did that flying face plant against the boards. I should have remembered that your head is filled with cement and that you probably didn't feel a thing." She reached up and touched the swelling under his left eye. "You're going to have a doozy of a shiner."

He flinched and then gently pushed her hand away. "I'm fine. Just do me a favor and go back and sit down."

"You're not planning on playing any more, are you?"

"No, he's not," a voice interrupted.

They turned to see a rumpled old gentleman shuffling his way across the ice.

"I'm okay, Doc. I can finish the game," Sam protested.

"I'll be the judge of that, Chief." The doctor held up three fingers. "How many fingers am I holding up?"

"Three," Sam said with confidence.

"Wrong. Five. Get off the ice."

Haley Jo cocked her head. She was pretty sure the doctor had held up three fingers. But a quick wink from the doctor clued her in to his plan of benching Sam for the rest of the game. Even the town physician wasn't above pulling a fast one to keep the chief from getting himself killed. She grinned and winked back.

"I saw that wink. You cheated," Sam said as the doctor and his teammate escorted him off the ice.

"I didn't wink," Haley Jo said. "I got something in my eye."

Sam scowled. "Don't pull that sweet innocent look with me." He glanced down at her. "And what are you doing showing up at a hockey game dressed like you're going to the disco?"

"The disco? No one goes to the disco anymore. What are you, in a time warp or something?"

The crowd around them seemed to hush, everyone leaning forward to listen.

"No one in Reflection Lake wears those—those—" he motioned toward her pants "—cutoff pants you're wearing. In case you haven't noticed, you've got goose bumps on your goose bumps. And you're wearing high heels while walking on bleachers and ice."

"And your point is...?"

"My point is—you look ridiculous."

A collective hiss issued from the crowd.

"Well, color me silly. Here I thought I'd done pretty good choosing something to wear from a single suitcase filled with conference clothes. I should have realized when I packed that I might just possibly end up locked up in some smelly old jail cell in the middle of nowhere with the chief of the fashion police in attendance."

The *middle of nowhere*. The comment hit Sam hard. Maybe because he'd been expecting it. Waiting for it actually. And now she'd said it, and from the angry expression on her face, Sam was pretty sure she meant it. Her talk earlier about liking the small town flavor and the easy pace had all been a crock. She couldn't wait to get back to the fast-paced life of the city. He should have known. Hell, he had known. It's why he'd been pushing her away as fast as she had been pushing her way in.

"In case you haven't noticed, you haven't been locked up for one solitary second that you've been here." He spoke through clenched teeth. "Of course, if that's your preference I can always arrange for that to happen."

"Oh, so now we're into bondage, are we? Or perhaps you're just having a hard time deciding how to really show your appreciation for your guests."

Out of the corner of his eye, Sam could see the crowd's heads pinging back and forth between the two of them, and if their expressions were any indication, they weren't happy with him.

"If I'm not mistaken," he said, "you were the one who begged me to take you out on the town. Now you're calling it Nowheresville? Perhaps you're the one who needs to make up your mind, sweetheart."

She reached out and jabbed him in the chest. "Don't you dare call me sweetheart when you don't mean it."

"You tell him, girlfriend!" a woman in the crowd yelled out. A few accompanying shouts of agreement followed.

Haley Jo smiled and lifted her chin. "I've loved every minute of being here in this town...with the minor exception of having to deal with you and your bullying."

"I do not bully you."

Chester, who was sitting in the penalty box, lifted a hand and said, "Uh...Chief? Technically, you do kinda bully her."

"Who asked you?"

Chester slunk back down.

Haley Jo stabbed his chest with her finger again. "Don't you speak to Chester like that."

"Okay, break it up you two," Rudy said. He glanced at Doc. "Is he really out of the game?"

Doc nodded. "Sorry, Chief, but you're benched for the remainder of the game. In fact, let's get you over to my office and we'll stitch up that eye. That way you can be over to Kellum's eating fried fish in no time."

Sam didn't give up exactly, but the two men hustled him off the ice and into the dressing room before he had a chance to say or do anything else. Haley Jo stayed behind, the crowd gathering around her in sympathy.

AN HOUR OR SO LATER, with the cut over his eye properly stitched and a warning from Doc to stay off the ice for at least two weeks, Sam and Andy drove into the parking lot of Kellum's.

Kellum's Restaurant and Bar was located on the outskirts of town, on the north side of the lake. It was an old fishing shanty that one of the local citizens, Sinker Kellum, had built forty-five years ago.

Sinker had told anyone who was willing to listen, especially his wife, Estelle, that he'd taken up ice fishing, and that ice fishing was good for his stress level. Of course at the time, Sinker hadn't fooled anyone, with the exception of Estelle. They all knew the place was actually Sinker's designated drinking hut. The reason they weren't fooled is that a person has to put his ice shanty out *on* the actual ice in order to ice fish. Sinker's hut never left the shore.

Over the years, Sinker's hut got to be a pretty popular place. Guys would wander on down to *see how the fish were biting,* and several hours later, they'd stumble home blinder than two moles huddled in a game sack.

The eating part started when some of the visitors would bring along their day's catch and Sinker would fry up their perch as sweet and tender and flaky as a mouth could ask for. Not long after, a line out the door started to develop and Sinker had to build on several additions to his ice shanty. Over the years, he added one amenity after another until one day he applied for a liquor license—according to Sinker, he was tired of giving the stuff away for free. Shortly thereafter, he opened the place as Kellum's Restaurant and Bar.

No one ever called dining at Kellum's classy, but the place was a favored local hangout, and on occasion, seventy-five-year-old Sinker Kellum still strapped on the apron and took his place at the stove, frying up a batch of perch for his more distinguished customers.

"You sure you're feeling okay? Doc said he had to put in four stitches." Andy asked this as he pulled into what looked to be the only open parking spot.

"Stings a little. But the old coot wouldn't give me a shot of novocaine. You'd think from the way he hoarded that stuff that he had it shipped over the mountains by mule train." Sam undid his seat belt and climbed out.

He could see that some nice soul had driven his truck over from the arena, leaving it next to the entrance to the restaurant. He hoped the driver hadn't been Haley Jo. It wouldn't look good if the person he was supposed to have in protective custody was joyriding around town in his own vehicle.

Andy shut off the engine and stuffed the keys in his pocket. "So are you up to this?"

"Relax. I'm just going in to see if Haley Jo is done eating, and then we're heading home. I'm beat."

"Did you just hear yourself?"

Sam had a feeling he was going to regret asking. "Hear what?"

"You said we're heading *home*—and the *we* you were referring to included Haley Jo."

"And that's significant how?"

Andy laughed. "You're talking about taking Haley Jo *home?* As in your home. Your castle. Your humble abode."

"I know what my house is," Sam grumbled.

"I don't know about you. But that sounds darn right domesticated to me."

Sam picked up his pace. "You know what? You're making my headache worse. Will you just leave the high school matchmaking to the teenagers?"

Andy shrugged. "Deny it all you want. But I still say you've got it bad."

Sam groaned in frustration. It wasn't even worth arguing about. Perhaps simply ignoring the situation would work. He pushed open the front door of the restaurant, and a wall of noise hit him like a shock wave. It was as if every person jammed into the place was talking at once, and no one was listening.

He loved Kellum's. In fact, he had worked behind the counter the summer when he was nineteen. The place smelled of fried fish, coleslaw and candle wax. A jukebox in the corner played a mixture of country-and-western, soft rock and dance. And the selections that got played varied on what kind of crowd held the majority of seats for that particular night.

Tonight, it was a nice mix of old folks and young professionals—the hockey crowd. They were standing three deep at the bar and all the tables were taken. No one bothered waiting for a table to empty, they simply shoved their way through and joined whomever had the least number of diners sitting at their table. It was a loose, festive atmosphere.

He stopped short and surveyed the room, unable to shake the feeling that something was different. Not quite right. And then it hit him. In a restaurant where the typical dress code was T-shirts, jeans and sneakers, more than half the women present were dressed in high heels and the silly, but undeniably sexy short pants that Haley Jo seemed to favor.

Sam clenched his teeth. Apparently, the female residents of Reflection Lake had decided to teach him a little lesson in humility by wearing exactly what he'd told Haley Jo no one would wear to a hometown hockey game and fish fry.

He turned and glared at Andy. "What the hell is going on around here?"

Andy shrugged. "How should I know? In case you've forgotten, I've been with you all evening." He pointed toward the back of the room. "There's Gail. She's waving to us. She must have saved us seats."

He pushed his way past Sam and headed in that direction. Everywhere Sam looked there was a woman in capri pants and high heels. Of course the ultimate was when Hank Reynolds, Kellum's bartender and former Reflection Lake all state fullback stepped out from behind the bar in a pair of glitter-encrusted football pants covering his hairy legs.

"This is all your fault. I don't know what you did, but you sure ticked some ladies off, Chief. I'd watch my step tonight," Hank gestured toward his clothing. "They made me squeeze into these—these things. They tried to make me wear a pair of Cynthia Higgins's heels, but I drew the line at that."

Sam nodded numbly. Somehow the thought of Hank in a pair of heels owned by Cynthia Higgins, their tallest female resident, was more than he could wrap his brain around. He headed in the direction that Andy had taken a few minutes earlier. Several women glanced at him and then away again. A few sniffed as if they smelled something bad. There was no mistaking the disdain in their eyes as they sashayed off in their heels and capri pants. Obviously, his comment to Haley Jo about her manner of dress had made quite an impression on some of the fans.

He did a quick survey of the place and finally spied Haley Jo. She was in the center of Kellum's tiny dance floor, surrounded by at least three or four local guys, all frantically vying for her attention. She seemed completely oblivious to their efforts.

She danced up a storm, her arms extended up over her head, her eyes closed, and her body swaying to some retro disco beat. Her silver bracelets glittered in the overhead lights, and her hips moved slowly, hypnotically. Sensuously. Sam gripped the back of the chair in front of him, digging his nails into the hard wood.

As much as he would have liked to deny it, the hot heat of jealousy shot through him like white lightning. Damn, the woman got under his skin with the simple movement of her hips. He didn't want to feel this way. To need her so much that the simple act of seeing her dance with other men was enough to send him into a green haze of envy.

"She looks like she's having a good time," Andy said as he reached the table against the back wall.

"Too good of a time if you ask me," he mumbled, dropping down into an empty seat.

"We've been wondering when you'd get here," Gail

said. She reached for the pitcher of beer and poured Andy a cold one. She then glanced at Sam. "I assume Doc told you to abstain from the hard stuff." She shoved a tall iced tea over to him. "Haley Jo ordered this for you." She grinned. "She had them put a bit of mint in it. She thought it might make it more palatable for you."

Sam frowned. Great. He was late to the party. The woman he loved was out on the dance floor boogying her heart out with three or four hunky looking locals, who looked hungry enough to eat her whole, and he was forced to sit on the sidelines nursing a lousy iced tea while everyone else savored a cold brew. Not to mention the fact that his head throbbed so bad it seemed to have picked up the pulse of the disco beat. Life definitely couldn't get much worse.

"Are you going to spend the whole evening pouting?" Andy settled into the chair across from him, his arm reaching out to drape along the back of Gail's chair.

"Probably." Sam took a gulp of the tea and grimaced. "Have you all finished eating?"

Gail shook her head. "Sinker has taken a real liking to Haley Jo. He got out his apron and wandered into the kitchen to create."

"Sinker's cooking for her?" Now that was a first. A stranger appears and even old Sinker goes off the deep end. Good old reliable, stubborn Sinker.

"At this point, I think he'd make her a full partner in the place," Eleanor said. "Personally, I think he's seriously in love. I'd watch out and not eat anything he prepares. He might just get it in his thieving heart to poison you and run off with your woman."

Sam sighed. "For the hundredth time, she's not my woman."

The couple exchanged knowing glances and smug smiles. Sam gave up and glanced toward the dance floor again.

One of the men had Haley Jo's hand and he twirled her around. She laughed up at him, her eyes shining and her hair swinging out behind her in a spiraling cascade of red. Sam shoved the iced tea out of his way and climbed to his feet.

"Don't kill the guy when you ask her to dance," Andy warned as Sam headed off in the direction of the gyrating mass of bodies a few feet away.

When Haley Jo saw him coming, her face lit up and she jumped up and down waving—as if he hadn't seen her from the moment he had entered the joint.

"Sam! Over here, Sam."

The five men, a new one having entered the pack surrounding her, all glared in his direction. She was oblivious, pushing them aside as she moved to greet him. He was surprised when she threw her arms around his neck and stretched up on tippy toes to gently kiss his cheek.

"You okay?" she asked, her concern evident.

"I'm fine," he said, gruffly, eyeing the five guys who had stopped dancing and were now standing in a line, hands on hips and mouths grim. "Your friends look a bit put out."

She laughed and linked arms with him. "Oh, ignore them. They're babies, all of them. I think the oldest is about twenty with hormones of a randy fourteen-year-old. I'm glad you saved me." She rubbed his forearm, getting him to focus back on her. "Does your head hurt? You've got a frown line the size of a pepperoni stick between your eyes. Do you need to go sit down?"

Did he need to go sit down? What did she think he was—an old man? An invalid? "Hell, no. I want to dance."

"I don't think that would be a good idea. I think you should relax."

"I think I should dance." He pulled her back onto the dance floor.

She made a face and was about to argue when the music changed and something slow and sweet started to play. Her frown disappeared, and she melted into his arms, her arms sliding up around his neck and her fingers threading into his hair, as if they belonged there. She snuggled in.

"Can we go home after this?" she asked.

Home? She was calling the jail cell home? What was that all about? "You seemed to be having a great time charming all the youngsters hanging around the dance floor."

She laughed and tilted her head back. "I was stalling for time."

"Huh?"

"Gail and Eleanor." She nodded her head toward the table. "They kept pumping me for information about us. I know how much you hate anyone knowing anything. So I decided to just dance until you got here and rescued me."

"What about dinner?"

"Tell Sinker we want it as takeout."

"He won't be pleased. He likes to see his customers' expressions of ecstasy as they bite into his perch."

"Tough. I'm ready to go. And you're looking past ready to go."

He smiled and moved her toward the edge of the dance floor. She was so light she seemed to float, her small feet following his with ease. As he let her go and started to push a path through the crowd, she reached out and snatched up his hand, lacing her fingers through his and holding tight. It was as if she were a tiny star latching on to him, a cosmic spray of brilliance and loveliness spreading out behind him.

She waved to a surprised-looking Gail, Andy and Eleanor. But then they just went back to looking all happy and smug. Sam figured they'd all claim they knew he was going to leave with her and then they'd pump him for information. But at that moment, Sam hardly cared. Haley Jo was going *home* with him.

12

HALEY JO WAS STILL smiling to herself when they arrived at Sam's place and he parked the truck next to the side door. The motion sensor light clicked on automatically, bathing them in its soft, yellow light. He reached down and turned off the engine, and for a moment they both sat motionless.

She listened to the engine tick, reveling in the warm breeze drifting in the window and fanning her face. "I had a good time. Thanks for putting up with me."

He nodded, shoved the keys into his pocket and climbed out. Then he paused, his hand on the door. He glanced back at her, a small smile on his lean face. "I had a good time, too."

"Even though I made you dance?"

"Yeah, even though you made me dance." He walked around to her side of the truck and opened the door. "Come on, I'll walk you over to your cell." She couldn't miss the twinkle of amusement dancing in his eyes.

"Don't make fun of my private cell. A lot of people in the city would give up a month's paycheck to have that much space. Besides, I've developed quite an attachment to it." What she didn't say—or couldn't say—was that the attachment was really to him. To his daughter, Prudie. And to his quaint little town of Reflection Lake.

But Haley Jo was smart enough to know that if she even hinted that she felt that way, she'd scare him off, and that would hurt more than keeping her feelings safely bottled up inside.

Sam smiled and then winced. "Ouch. Don't make me laugh."

"Poor thing." She scooted to the edge of the seat and reached out to gently touch his left cheek. The bruise, an interesting combination of rich purple and blue, was spreading out across the sharp blade of his cheekbone. "Does it hurt?"

He gazed down at her, the blue of his eyes pulling her toward him. "Only when I laugh."

He stood still and allowed her to explore the bruise with the tips of her fingers. "Unfortunately or fortunately—depending on how you look at it—I seem to laugh an awful lot when I'm around you."

She leaned forward and bestowed a soft kiss on his cheek, her fingers sliding down the side of his neck to his chest. "Be careful. You wouldn't want to be around me if I was nagging and ragging on you all the time like a wife."

She felt him stiffen, and she immediately wanted to take the wife comment back. She was rushing things again, forgetting how phobic he was around the issues of marriage and commitment.

He took a step back, and Haley Jo could see the wariness in his eyes. It made her want to scream at him to relax. To let things happen without needing to be in total control every second. She wanted to remind him that she wasn't Peggy, and that just because she was a *city girl*, she wasn't some kind of monster who would jump the first train out of town with the express purpose of breaking his heart. Or Prudie's heart for that matter.

Why couldn't he realize that she was just as much a lost cause as he was? That he made her blood simmer like caramel candy cooking on a full burn?

Pulling her gaze away, she kicked off her heels, determined to get him to relax. "Come on. I'll accept your offer of a walk home, but only if you let me do it barefoot." She wiggled her toes, curling them in the soft, dewy grass.

Sam bent down and scooped up her shoes, allowing them to dangle on the end of one finger. "You're the only woman I've ever met who is sexy in heels, out of heels or in an ugly ass pair of hiking boots."

"But you've never seen me in hiking boots."

He wiggled his eyebrows up and down and something light and playful sparked again in his eyes. "Oh, but I have. In fact, I've pictured you in quite a few different outfits."

"Ooo, now that's intriguing," she said, stepping closer. "Tell me, did black lace and satin play a role in any of those daydreams of yours?"

"Oh, they most assuredly did." He reached across and reeled her in closer. "I can be very inventive when it comes to fantasizing."

She stumbled slightly when her belly brushed up against his upper thigh, but she steadied herself by laying her palm flat on his chest and absorbing the feel of his heart beating beneath her hand. Their gazes locked, and it felt as though he were looking right through to her soul, reading her mind and knowing what she wanted.

A relentless heat swept through her, turning up the temperature of her blood to a slow, roiling boil. And at that moment, Haley Jo knew she wanted him so badly that she was willing to strip naked right there on the front lawn and throw herself into his arms begging for him to make love to her.

She grinned. Who cared what the neighbors thought? Heck, half the town, including Gail, Eleanor, Tina and Ludi, were already rooting for her. They probably had the brass band ready to hit the streets as soon as they realized the deed had been done.

She reached up and slid her hand down the front of his shirt, her fingers hooking into the waistband of his jeans; her fingers dangling directly below, taunting and teasing just a tad. There wasn't going to be any confusion about what she wanted. Haley Jo figured she deserved at least one night of unbelievable loving before he made her pack her bags and vacate his jail cell.

"Too bad my suitcase is so far away. I could probably

dig around and find something black and decidedly lacy to make your fantasy seem even a bit more real."

He lowered his head and laid a kiss at the corner of her mouth. "As promising as that sounds, I don't think I'm going to need any lace or satin to make this all a reality. I'm thinking I just need you."

She wanted him to move over and kiss her on the lips, but he seemed to sense her eagerness and moved instead to the line of her neck. The sensation of his lips on her skin was exquisite. Like liquid fire spreading unchecked.

She tilted her head back, and he accommodated her by skimming along her neck down to the V of her halter top. Her breathing was ragged. But then, so was his.

"If we're not careful, this is going to jump right past fantasy and directly into reality right here on the front lawn of your house," she whispered.

He laughed softly, never lifting his lips off her, and she shivered at the feel of his hot breath on her breasts. "Well then I guess we better move this party inside."

Before she could comment, he scooped her up and carried her inside. It was like being whisked away upon a warm summer wind—his body heat, the smell of pine and fresh air clinging to his skin and surrounding her.

He kicked the door shut, crossed the living room in three strides and started up the stairs. Haley Jo giggled and laid her head back against his shoulder.

"Hope you don't keel over on me. Doc Edwards will have my hide for using and abusing an invalid."

"Nah, you're as light as a feather."

She peeked over his shoulder. "Razor Beak is following us. I think he's worried you're going to drop me."

"I think he's more worried that you're going to take up his side of the bed."

"I thought he slept with Prudie."

"Razor is like a four-hundred-pound gorilla. He sleeps where he wants to sleep."

Sam stumbled a bit on the landing and she squealed, "Don't let go!"

He juggled her weight, teasing her with the possibility of dropping her. Behind them Razor growled, not too pleased with their horseplay.

"Giddy up, you lazy slug," Haley Jo ordered, reaching behind him to swat his butt.

"Keep that up and I'll drop you right here and have my way with you on this landing."

"Promises. Promises."

She wrapped her arms around his neck and nibbled delicately. He fell back against the wall and pulled her closer to him, his head dipping down to cover her lips. She tasted the tiny cut in the corner of his mouth, lapping at it gently, and then eased herself into the warmth of his mouth. It was like entering a furnace.

"Oh, jeez. I'm not going to make it." He sighed and slid down the length of the wall until he was sitting on the floor of the landing, with her on his lap. She rose up and straddled him.

Razor took one look at the direction things were going and galloped away, his tail swinging wildly behind him.

"I think we embarrassed Razor." Haley Jo frantically worked the buttons of Sam's shirt.

"Good, I wasn't interested in ravishing you here on the landing with him in attendance."

His own fingers were busy untying the strings of her halter top. He had it off in a matter of seconds, and his lips went to her breast, gently working the tip of her nipple as his hands slid down to work the button of her pants. She moaned softly and quickly moved to get his shirt off his shoulders. Her forearm brushed up against the bandage over his left eye.

"Ouch!"

"Sorry." She leaned forward and kissed the spot.

"Forget it." His breathing was ragged, and he slid her pants down off her hips. She did the same for him.

Somehow they managed to wiggle out of their clothing, and when it all lay in a heap beside them, Haley Jo moved up and over him, covering him with her warmth and devotion. And as she settled onto him, accepting him into her, she shivered and reveled in their closeness.

Gazing down into his eyes, she could see her past. Her future. Her commitment. And as he rolled, taking her gently in his hands and settling her beneath him, she smiled. This was what she'd been searching for—this intense pleasure, total acceptance and sweet giving. Above her, Sam called her name and urged her with him over the edge. And Haley Jo went with him willingly.

HALEY JO ROLLED OVER onto her back and stretched. The sheets whispered against her naked skin, and with a smile, she reached out for Sam. The spot next to her was empty.

She sat up. He was sitting in the chair near the window, pulling on his boots. She grinned. "You're dressed."

He didn't look up. "I promised Andy I'd meet him for coffee." He stood up and walked over to his dresser, stuffing his wallet into his back pocket and buckling on his leather belt.

Something was wrong. His expression was tight and as uniformly blank as his pressed khakis.

"What's going on?" Haley Jo pulled the sheet around her.

"Nothing. Everything is fine. I just have to get moving."

"You're regretting last night, aren't you?"

He smiled stiffly. "Not at all. It was wonderful." He grabbed a handful of change and jammed it in his pocket. The coins clinked going in, the only sound in the bedroom.

"Then why do I feel as though you'd rather stick rusty nails through the soles of your feet than look at me right now?"

He walked over to the bed and pecked the top of her head with a quick kiss. "Look, Haley Jo, I'd love to stay and analyze all this. But I have a meeting. I'll talk to you later." He headed for the door.

"Don't you run out on me, Sam Matthews." She scrambled to her feet, standing in the middle of the bed clutching the sheet to her. "You're just scared because you let your guard down for a minute and let me in. Don't sneak off."

"I'm not sneaking off. I'm going to work."

"I promise I won't hurt you."

He paused, his back to her. She could tell he was debating with himself whether or not to get into this now. She prayed he'd turn around. That he'd give her a chance.

He did turn around. "I know I'm going to regret this, but what are you talking about?"

"You're scared because you let me in."

"I'm not scared. I'm late."

"You're afraid. Frightened I'll hurt you like Peggy hurt you."

He shook his head. "Give me some credit. I know you're not Peggy. But I also know that you're twenty-four years old and just starting your life. I'm not foolish enough to believe that you're ready to bury yourself alive in a tiny dead-end town like Reflection Lake, tied to a husband and his kid from a previous marriage."

Haley Jo sucked in hot air between clenched teeth. Would this guy ever get a clue? "Who the hell are you to decide how and where I should live my life?"

She jammed her hands on her hips but quickly reconsidered when the sheet fell to her waist. Somehow arguing while your nipples stuck out like two headlights on a cloudy night didn't carry the same level of dignity she was going for in this situation. She yanked the sheet back into place.

He looked weary. "I'm sorry, Haley Jo, but I really have a better handle on this than you do. We were hot for each other. We made love. We woke up. End of story."

"*Hot* for each other?" Heat infused her cheeks. "So that's what happened last night. I was *hot* for you." She smacked a palm against her forehead. "Thanks ever so much for clearing that little mystery up for me. I would have never figured it out."

He didn't answer, simply stood in the doorway and watched her with sad but unflinching eyes.

"You don't get this, do you?"

"Get what?" he asked.

"That I love you. That I'm not giving anything up by saying that and agreeing to stay here in this so-called dead-end town. I happen to like it here."

He shook his head. "You say that now but when the newness wears off—when the day-to-day drudgery sets in—you'll regret that decision. Better to go and finish what you started and if you still feel the same way in two years or so, we'll talk."

"You've got this all planned out, don't you?"

She could tell he thought that was the way it was supposed to be. Everything planned out. Everything neat and tidy. No loose ends. No spontaneous joy. It was like last night on the landing had never happened.

She sat down on the edge of the bed with a soft sigh. "Okay, Sam. Whatever you say. Just hurry up and get things wrapped up. I need to get home."

She gave up. With those few words, she let go of it all. She cried uncle. Sam nodded and left without saying another word, and Haley Jo felt as though he took her heart with him.

13

"HE DOESN'T love me, Mel," Haley Jo wailed into her cell phone. She pressed a hand over her lips and tried to hold back the tears.

"Oh, Jo-Jo, I'm sorry, sweetie." Melanie's voice came over the wires soft and reassuring.

Haley Jo found herself wishing she were back in the city, lying on Melanie's bed, crying her eyes out while her friend stroked her back and offered up sugared tea with tiny triangles of cinnamon toast. It was their favorite breakup meal, one that each had prepared for the other a million times during their friendship.

"Would it make you feel better if I sent Cy up there to put a big hurt on the stupid lug?"

Haley Jo thought of the purple bruise on Sam's cheek and cringed. "No, I don't want to hurt him. He doesn't mean to hurt me—he thinks he's *saving* me from myself." She sniffed noisily and grabbed a tissue out of the bottom of her purse. "He just doesn't feel the same way about me that I feel about him."

"Well, then he's stupid," Melanie said matter-of-factly. "How can he not love you? You're sweet. Sensitive. Smart. Fun to be with—"

"Uh, as much as I appreciate this support, Mel, it's not necessary to go overboard with the character validation." She used the tissue to swipe at the end of her nose. "Just let me whine a little, and then I'll be okay."

"Gotcha. Whine away."

Haley Jo started to open her mouth to wail when from

over the phone came the sound of someone yelling in the background.

"Oh! Cy's home," Melanie said. "I'll call you back. I'm going to see if he'll drive me up there so I can bring you home. You need to be here with me."

"No! Wait—" The phone clicked in Haley Jo's ear. "Oh, shoot." Haley Jo retracted the antenna with a snap and shoved the phone back in her purse.

Here she had thought she'd have time for a good cry and a sympathetic chat with her best friend. Instead, she'd gotten hung up on and ditched in favor of the lovely and no doubt engaging Cy. Talk about humiliation.

All she could hope for was that the creep didn't offer to actually drive up to Reflection Lake with Melanie in tow. Haley Jo could just imagine Sam's reaction when the sullen, tattooed and multiple-body-pierced Cy, as described by Melanie, showed up with her equally fluffy and ditzy friend. She almost laughed. Sam thought *she* dressed outrageously. Wait until he got a load of Melanie's outfits.

But her smile died fairly quickly. The thought of leaving Sam and Prudie and riding back to the city without them wasn't a cheerful prospect.

"You okay?"

She looked up to see Eleanor standing in the doorway of the cell. "Oh, sure. I'm fine." She stuffed the tissue in the pocket of her jeans and smiled. "See! I'm fine."

"Your eyes are all red. It looks like you've been crying. Did that idiot Sam hurt you? Because if he did, he'll have to answer to me."

"No, Sam didn't do anything, Eleanor. I just get weepy like this sometimes." She stood up and smoothed her shirt, determined not to make things any worse than they already were.

"Well, if you say so. Prudie has an orthodontist's appointment this afternoon. You mind going with her? It's right before Sarah's supposed to go home and I have a feeling Sam's going to be tied up the rest of the afternoon."

Haley Jo liked the idea of having something to do. It

would keep her mind off stuff she couldn't change no matter how much she wanted to. "Sure thing. Does Prudie know?"

"I've already called over to her friend's house. Mrs. Bradley is going to feed the two of them lunch, let them take a dip in the pool and then she'll drop Prudie off around four. That will give you both plenty of time to get over to Dr. Reynolds's office. Jake will drive you over."

"He doesn't need to do that. It's just down the street."

Eleanor frowned. "Don't be contradicting me. When Sam Matthews says you're not to go anywhere unescorted, you don't go anywhere unescorted."

Haley Jo laughed. "Okay. Okay. Sorry I suggested otherwise."

"Fine. Now you come out around noon and have lunch with me. Mrs. Benson brought over a lovely rice-and-tuna casserole. We'll warm that up and have us a nice chat."

"That sounds nice, Eleanor. I think I'll just tidy things up a bit until then." *So I don't have to sniff and snuffle and have you ask me all kinds of embarrassing questions,* she thought.

She glanced around the cell, noting the number of personal items scattered about. It was a comfortable clutter. One Sam Matthews probably wouldn't like very much, but one that felt good to her. She hadn't realized until that moment how entrenched she'd gotten over the past week and a half. The place was actually beginning to look homey. Welcoming.

"I guess it'll be a good time for me to get some things packed. I can't imagine being here that much longer. Andy said things were moving along concerning the case."

Eleanor nodded in agreement and turned to head back down the hall. "If Sam wasn't such a turkey, he'd get his act together, and you wouldn't be worrying about when and if you were leaving." She sniffed dismissively. "Some men just don't have the good sense they were born with—and that boy is a prime example of what I'm talking about."

Haley Jo smiled and bent to pull her suitcase out from

under the cot. She heard Eleanor shuffle back down the hall, her cane hitting the linoleum with a telltale thump with each step. Haley Jo figured that Sam was in for a talking-to when he got back to the office. She hoped she was already at the orthodontist's office when that happened.

SAM SHIFTED restlessly in the chair in front of Andy's desk and glanced at his watch. It was already 3:00 p.m. and the message from Eleanor said that Prudie had a 4:30 appointment with Doc Reynolds. He needed to finish up here and get back over to Reflection Lake. With the tourist traffic the way it was, he knew it would take him at least thirty-five minutes.

He leaned back, tipping his chair up on its back legs and shot a glance out the door and down the hall. Andy was nowhere in sight. He'd left ten minutes ago, promising to get them both coffee before filling him in on the latest information on the Rocca case. Now it was as if the guy had dropped off the face of the earth.

Sam allowed the front legs of his chair to hit the floor with a thump. Too much longer and he'd just have to leave without an update. He needed to make this appointment with Dr. Reynolds. Prudie was having a fit with the whole idea of braces, and he knew it would go easier if he was there to soothe her jangled nerves. Otherwise, Doc Reynolds might end up losing a finger.

At that moment, Andy breezed in, balancing two mugs of coffee in one hand and a handful of fax sheets in the other. "Good news!" he said, plunking one of the mugs down in front of Sam.

"They weren't out of creamer?"

"No, as usual there was only that powdered stuff you hate. I figured you want black." Andy dropped down into his seat and grinned across the desk. "It looks like the city boys might have come up with something."

Sam sat forward. "What?"

Andy tapped the stack of fax pages. "It seems that one

of the employees of Dr. Rocca—" he leaned forward and checked the sheet "—A Ms. Melanie Gerrard—"

"That's Haley Jo's good friend. She's talked about her a few times."

Andy raised an eyebrow. "You don't say. Well it seems that Ms. Gerrard was the young woman who was supposed to go on the trip with Dr. Rocca, but canceled out at the last minute."

Sam waved a hand. "I know all that. Haley Jo told us that."

"Well what she didn't mention is that Ms. Gerrard has a very jealous boyfriend by the name of Gregory Allen Scott."

"And...?"

Andy grinned. He was obviously holding out and enjoying every minute of it. "Mr. Scott's nickname is Cyclone or Cy and he has a small cyclone—"

"—tattooed on his right hand between the thumb and index finger," Sam finished for him.

Damn! They had the guy. There was no reason for Gregory "Cyclone" Scott to have been in the hotel the same time as Haley Jo and Dr. Rocca. Cy Scott had let himself into Haley Jo's room to kill the wife-cheating, girlfriend-stealing dentist. Unfortunately, he hadn't talked to Mrs. Rocca ahead of time. If he had it might have saved him a little jail time, seeing as she had already acted on her plans to off the good doctor with a box of deadly chocolates.

"Have they picked him up yet?" Sam asked.

Andy frowned. "That's the only crummy part of this whole thing. According to the guy in charge of things down there, they sent a team over to pick Scott up for questioning, but no one was home." He took a sip of coffee and shrugged. "But they've got someone keeping an eye on the place, and when Scott shows up, they'll bring him in."

Sam shook his head. "That's not good enough. I want this guy in custody now. They need to be a little more proactive. Where do they think he's gone?"

"Relax, Sam. No one knows where we've got Haley Jo stashed. She's safe."

"I'll relax when he's locked up." Sam stood up. "I need to get back. Prudie has an appointment, and I don't feel good about leaving Haley Jo alone until this guy is behind bars. Give me a call as soon as you hear anything."

"Sure, Sam. But have you considered how—"

Sam ignored him and walked out, intent on reaching the two people he cared most about in this world.

PRUDIE CHEWED her bottom lip and glanced up at the clock over Dr. Reynolds's receptionist's desk for the tenth time in the past twenty minutes.

"He's late," she said. "He promised this morning that he'd get here in time for the appointment."

Haley Jo looked up from the Chinese checkers board sitting on the coffee table and nodded. "Yep, he's definitely late."

Prudie frowned. Obviously, she felt Haley Jo wasn't exhibiting the proper degree of concern and sympathy. "He's never late."

Haley Jo's fingers hovered over one of her red marbles, but at the last minute she pulled them back and reconsidered her position. Prudie, with a minimum of effort, had effectively hemmed her in, preventing her from getting her men to the other side of the board.

She frowned. "You know your dad will get here if he can."

Prudie jumped up and ran to the window, checking the tiny parking lot out front. She pressed her nose against the glass and gripped the windowsill so tight her knuckles turned white.

Haley Jo sighed and stood up. "You and your father are the two most time-enslaved souls I've ever met."

Prudie whirled around and shot her a questioning look.

"That means you get so wrapped up in whether or not you're going to be somewhere on time that you don't enjoy the journey getting there."

"I don't consider a *journey* to the orthodontist enjoyable," Prudie said acidly. She turned back around, her narrow shoulders tense.

Haley Jo came up behind her and gently placed her hands on her shoulders, marveling to herself at the tiny feel of the child's bones beneath her fingers. "Relax, sweetie. Your dad isn't the type to forget a promise. If he can get away, he'll get here."

Prudie sighed and leaned back against her, her head settling just below Haley Jo's breasts. "I know. I just hate having anyone poke around in my mouth without him here to hold my hand."

Haley Jo reached down and hugged her, allowing her hand to slip into the little girl's. "I know it's not the same, but will you settle for me as a substitute?"

"We're ready for you, Prudie," Dr. Reynolds's assistant called out from the doorway leading to the examining rooms.

Prudie glanced up at her, her brown eyes solemn and a little bit frightened. Her small hand tightened around Haley Jo's, and she nodded silently.

Haley Jo smiled and led her down the hall. For the first time in her life, she felt truly needed, and she marveled at the gentle curl of contentment that unfolded inside her belly at the trust Prudie had placed in her.

SAM DOWNSHIFTED through the gears and swore softly under his breath. This was the fourth line of cars he'd gotten stuck behind in the last fifteen minutes. Everyone seemed to be moving in slow motion.

It was as if there was a conspiracy to keep him from checking up on Haley Jo and getting to Prudie's appointment. For some reason, he had a tiny niggle of anxiety itching away at the back of his neck, and although he wasn't the type to buy into that psychic crap, Sam was also not the type to ignore his instincts. A good cop listened to his instincts. And right now, his instincts were telling him that something wasn't right.

He considered putting on his lights and flicking on the siren, but he kept his hands on the steering wheel. This was a personal matter. He wasn't the type to abuse his authority simply because he was feeling a little anxious.

More than likely the anxiety he was feeling was a direct result of his guilt. A well-deserved guilt trip related to the way he'd hurt Haley Jo earlier. How could he have been so damn stupid? It wasn't as if she had forced herself on him. He had carried her up those stairs to his bedroom last night with his eyes open and his heart near to bursting.

He shoved a hand restlessly through his hair. In fact, the more he thought about it, the more he realized what a jerk he'd made of himself. He laughed, something short and seriously lacking in humor. No big surprises there. Haley Jo had as much as told him that this morning when he'd slunk off like a coward.

Time to face up to facts. The woman had gotten under his skin fair and square. She hadn't played any games. She'd nibbled away at his heart until he couldn't think of anything but her and how to make her fit into their lives.

But Sam knew he was being realistic. Haley Jo was young, and she needed the opportunity to make of her life what she really wanted it to be. She didn't need to bury herself alive in a dead-end town, married to a cop with a ready-made family. Maybe after she had a taste of life. Perhaps then she'd settle.

He reached down and keyed his radio open.

"Matthews to base. Come in, base."

"Go ahead, Chief." Eleanor's voice came over the radio.

"I'm running a little late—"

"No kidding, Sherlock," Eleanor cut in. "Relax. I sent Prudie over to Dr. Reynolds for her appointment. Our guest went with her."

Sam grinned at Eleanor's clever shielding of Haley Jo's name over the radio. But he wasn't ignorant of the fact that every scanner in town knew exactly who his guest referred to. And seeing as almost every house in town had a police scanner sitting in their living room, next to the TV, Sam figured the majority of Reflection Lake's citizens now knew that he was late for his daughter's dental appointment and the woman he was supposed to be protecting was accompanying his daughter to Doc Reynolds's office.

"Relax, Sam. Jake took them both over to the appointment, and he'll pick them up when they're done—if you're not back in time, that is."

"Thanks, Eleanor." Sam sat back and forced himself to relax. Jake would watch over the two of them until he arrived.

"Now that wasn't too bad, was it?" Haley Jo said, climbing out of the squad car.

"I guess not," Prudie grumbled. "But I'm still mad at Daddy for not getting there on time." She glanced up quickly at Haley Jo. "Not that you weren't a good substitute."

Haley Jo laughed. "Don't worry, sweetie. I understand." She pointed to the Chinese checkers board sitting on the seat. "Don't forget the game."

Prudie nodded and grabbed it off the seat, the marbles rattling around inside.

Haley Jo leaned down and poked her head in the front window. "Thanks for the ride, Jake. Prudie and I will be over at the house if anyone is looking for us."

Jake nodded and climbed out, then walked toward the front steps of the police station. "Okay, but call if you two need anything."

Haley Jo and Prudie cut across the lawn, heading for the house. Razor rounded a corner and trotted over. He smelled suspiciously of cow manure.

"Guess you'll be getting another bath, old boy. Only this time I think we'll just hose you down." Haley Jo patted the beast's head and as she straightened up, she noticed for the first time that a green sedan sat in the driveway. But still no sign of Sam.

"Looks like we've got company." She started for the

front porch and then stumbled when one of her heels sank into the soft lawn.

"Darn heels," she mumbled, bending down to slip off her shoes. She tucked them under one arm. "You and I need to go shopping for a good solid pair of hiking boots for me."

Prudie whirled around, a frown wrinkling her pert nose. "Don't do that, Haley Jo. Everyone around here wears hiking boots. You're different." She grinned and reached out to stroke the shiny bright leather of the pumps. "And that's what I like about you."

"Thanks, Prudie." Haley Jo said. "Maybe your dad will let you come down and visit me in the city."

She reached out and wrapped an arm around the ten-year-old's narrow shoulders, pulling her in close. Prudie's small hands grasped her around the waist, and she stared up at Haley Jo. "I don't want you to leave."

"I have to start school in two weeks," she said. "But I promise that I'll come up for a visit. Heck, wild horses and crazy cabdrivers couldn't keep me away." Neither could disbelieving, overly suspicious police chief fathers. Even if Sam told her he wanted her to walk away and never look back, Haley Jo knew that was impossible to do. He might be able to do it, but she knew it wasn't in her to do the same.

Prudie held her anchored in place for another minute, her warm brown eyes searching hers, delving deep. "I believe you," she whispered finally.

Haley Jo held tight. "Good thing. Because I'm not in the habit of lying."

Locked together, they climbed the front porch. As they opened the front door, Haley Jo blocked Razor from bounding in. "Not a chance, Beakster. You need to wait outside until I can hose you off."

It wasn't until the front door closed that the man stepped out of the kitchen, a brownie in one hand and a wide grin cutting across his craggy face.

"I thought you were never going to get here," he said, his tone friendly and upbeat.

Haley Jo glanced at Prudie, confused. Perhaps the man was a friend of the family who had free rein to enter the house anytime he wanted. But when Prudie looked at her, her expression was puzzled.

"Who are you?" Haley Jo asked.

"A good friend of Melanie's."

"Mel? Mel's here!" Relief washed over Haley Jo. "You must be Cy. Melanie had some crazy idea that she needed to come up and rescue me." She laughed and glanced around. "Where is she?"

"Mel didn't come." Cy used the back of his hand to swipe the crumbs off his upper lip, and Haley Jo stiffened. The tiny tattoo of the cyclone stood out clearly on his white skin. Her grip on Prudie's shoulder tightened as Cy smiled.

"What are you doing here?" she demanded.

"Why, I've come to pick you up, of course. Melanie sent me." His smile made Haley Jo's stomach churn.

Haley Jo nudged an unsuspecting Prudie backward toward the front door. "Uh...that's okay. I've decided not to leave."

Prudie shot her a confused look but something in Haley Jo's expression must have warned her not to say anything. Instead, she shifted the Chinese checkers box in front of her and stared at Cy suspiciously.

Cy popped the last bit of brownie into his mouth and chewed. "Oh, but you have to leave with me. Melanie insists."

"I'll come with you, just let Prudie go. She doesn't know anything." Haley Jo stepped in front of the little girl.

Cy shook his head. "Sorry, sweet stuff, but the little girl comes. Guilt by association, you know."

Haley Jo allowed one shoe to drop to the floor and got a better grip on the other one. Kicking deadbeat boyfriends out of her apartment when they got too frisky had given her enough experience to feel her aim just might hit home.

As Cy started toward them, Haley Jo drew back her arm

and let the high heel fly. The three-inch heel boinked Cy right in the middle of his forehead with a resounding clunk.

"Run, Prudie!" Haley Jo yelled.

"In a minute!" Prudie screamed, wiggling around Haley Jo and darting forward to throw open the box of Chinese checkers. A stream of marbles rolled and bounced on the hardwood floor. Cy stumbled, his arms flailing as his legs slipped out from beneath him. He hit the floor with a grunt.

Frantically, Haley Jo fumbled with the front door. She finally got it open and a waiting Razor charged through. He leaped on top of Cy, all four paws pinning the guy to the floor. He growled something low and deep, and Cy froze.

Haley Jo grabbed Prudie and shoved her out the door, following closely on her heels. They ran into Sam's arms as he was coming up the steps at a full run. He scooped them up and around, depositing them on the front lawn. Haley Jo was never so glad to see a man. He was her knight in shining armor, even though he was dressed in freshly pressed khaki.

"Get over to the office. And get Chester," he ordered, before taking off up the steps and into the house.

14

SAM WATCHED the tiny prop plane land and roll down the runway toward the small, Plattsburgh airport terminal. He turned away from the chain-link fence and glanced back at the parking lot.

Haley Jo sat in the front seat of his truck, her expression pretty much unreadable. But Sam knew what she was feeling. She was still ticked off that he was going to actually do it. That he'd really put her on a plane and send her home.

Their farewell meal last night had been tense. Sam had been too chicken to face her alone. So he'd called in reinforcements, inviting Andy and Gail, Eleanor and her husband and Jake over. Chester had even darted over from the office for a quick goodbye. And Prudie had presided over the whole affair like some kind of regal princess. Of course, she had snubbed him a few times, angry that he was *letting Haley Jo leave*. Like he had much of a choice. No one seemed to understand that Haley Jo had a life outside Reflection Lake, and it didn't include them.

He shook his head and walked inside the terminal, headed for the ticket counter. He already had Haley Jo's ticket stuck in the front pocket of his shirt, but he wanted to check with the agent once more to make sure the plane was going to be on time. He hoped that Haley Jo had called her friend Melanie for a ride home when she landed at J.F.K. He hated to think of her having to take a taxi into the city. A person should be met by a friend when arriving home.

He stood in front of the tiny board listing the four flights in and out of the airport that day. His entire body felt numb. Out of touch.

"Were you hoping that the plane would be taking off earlier than expected?"

He turned to see Haley Jo standing next to him, her whole face solemn, serious.

"You know that isn't how I feel about you leaving."

She sighed. "Actually, I have no idea how you feel. Once Cy was put into custody and things quieted down yesterday, I thought you and I would have a chance to talk. But then you invited all those people to eat dinner with us."

"They all wanted to say goodbye."

She nodded and walked over to the soda machine, digging down into the pocket of her miniskirt for change. He wondered how a person could even keep a penny in the skimpy thing, let alone the required dollar.

He pulled a bill out of his pocket. "Here, let me get it." He reached around her and his forearm brushed the outer edge of her right breast.

She jumped.

"Sorry," he mumbled, feeding the crumpled bill into the slot.

"No problem," she said. "It was an accident."

An accident that he wanted to happen every day of his life and now it wouldn't. Couldn't, actually, because he was sending her away. How could he let her walk out of his life as if nothing had happened?

He hit the Sprite button with the side of his hand and bent down to grab the can as it rolled into the bin at the bottom of the machine. He knew her so well that he didn't have to ask what kind of soda she wanted.

He pulled the tab and handed the already sweating can to her. She nodded her thanks and took a long gulp. He watched her throat work to swallow the cold liquid, and he forced himself to look away. The simple sight of the clean line of neck, leading down to the smooth rounded sheen of her breasts above the low cut of her skimpy knit shirt made him ache.

"I left my bathrobe for Prudie. She likes wearing it." She traced one finger along the wet edge of the can.

He nodded.

"I bought a book on feng shui for Eleanor. I left it in your desk to give to her when she retires." She glanced up at him and smiled. It was a sweet, forlorn smile. "She's thinking of opening her own decorating business. Don't you dare tease her about it if she actually does."

He held up a hand. "Hey, far be it from me to rib a woman about what she wants to do with the rest of her life."

"And there's an autographed poster of The Rock coming for Chester. Make sure he gets it when it comes in."

"The Rock? What or who is that?"

She sighed again, letting him know that she was disappointed in his obvious lack of knowledge in whatever it was that Chester was into. She acted like the guy was their child or something.

"It's the wrestler he likes."

"Oh, right."

She took another sip of her soda. "Make sure you give Jake this Friday off."

"Why?"

"Because he has a date with Kathy Hunter—that new clerk in the Mountain Run Drugstore."

"Okay. Friday it is."

"And I left a bottle of my vanilla bubble bath on the kitchen counter. Razor's gotten quite used to the smell. I think he actually likes it."

The hell with Razor. He was stealing that bottle of bubble bath for himself. He didn't care what anyone thought—when he got lonely he just might retire to the bathroom for a nice long soak and allow the smell of vanilla and the memory of Haley Jo to surround him. He ran a hand through his hair. Damn. That was just too pathetic.

Haley Jo seemed oblivious to his dilemma. "Make sure

you cut up those scraps of meat for Razor. Last time you fed the poor sweetie he hacked up a big hunk of steak you had given him."

"He's simply eating too fast."

"Doesn't matter the reason. Make sure you cut it up into smaller pieces."

He nodded and waited. She snapped her fingers and dug around in her purse, pulling out a small white card. "This is Prudie's next orthodontist appointment. Be sure that you're there for this one. She's still very nervous about Dr. Reynolds introducing anything shiny into her mouth. She'll need to hang on to your hand."

"How do you keep track of all this stuff?"

She reached up and pulled her ticket out of his pocket, pausing to tuck it in the side of her little bag. "Because I listen when people tell me about their lives."

He put a hand over his heart. "Ouch. You didn't need to stab me so hard."

She reached up and patted his cheek. "You're a good man, Sam Matthews. You're just a little clueless when it comes to people."

"No presents for me?"

She pressed her lips together and looked up at him with the most exquisite sadness he'd ever seen in a person's eyes. "I gave you everything I had. You either didn't want it or didn't need it. I'm not sure which."

He reached out and almost touched her, but stopped himself at the last minute. He couldn't complicate things now. "That's not true. We just have different things going on in our lives right now."

"Flight 134, to Albany and on to New York now boarding."

They stared at each other, a heavy silence descending over them. Suddenly it was as if the world around them had disappeared.

"I'll miss you," she said softly.

"Same here."

"I don't have to go. I can stay."

"No, you can't. You have a world waiting for you out there."

"I have a world waiting for me back in Reflection Lake."

He smiled. "Go taste the world a bit and then come back and tell me that."

"You're not going to change your mind, are you?"

He shook his head.

She stepped in close and threw her arms around his neck, pulling him tight to her. "I love you, Sam Matthews. I just wish you weren't so bullheaded that you could see that."

"Have a good life, Haley Jo Simpson."

She kissed him hard, her lips tight and dry but her cheeks wet with tears. He set her back down and gently wiped the wetness from her face. She smiled and then walked away, her shoulders straight. She never looked back. Not even once.

15

Two weeks later

"WHAT DO YOU MEAN you're not going?" Melanie demanded, smacking the stack of mail she held in the palm of her hand. "Today's the first day of classes. You know...the day you become the dental hygienist you've always dreamed of becoming."

Haley Jo drew her legs up and snuggled her shoulder deeper into the couch cushion. "I'm not going so stop bugging me."

Melanie moved to stand over her. "I'm worried about you, Jo-Jo. Ever since you came back from Reflection Lake you've moped around here like the world was coming to an end. What's going on?"

"Nothing." She picked up the remote.

"Don't give me that nothing excuse. You've got the man mopes bad. It's that Sam Matthews, isn't it?"

Haley Jo didn't bother looking up, she just used the remote to surf the channels, looking for a talk show. Any talk show. One with yammering, arguing people who would make her feel less like a lazy, useless slug. There was something about watching *You Burned my House, Stole my Car, Framed me for Dealing, and Kidnapped my Dog. Marry me Today, or Get Out!* that uplifted a person with a serious case of the man mopes.

Of course, the fact that she had lost her apartment while stuck up in Reflection Lake and was now being forced to mooch off Melanie didn't do much for her self-esteem either. Could things get much worse? More than likely someone would think up some type of tragedy to lay on her doorstep, or in this case Melanie's doorstep, if she gave it enough time.

"Are you listening to me?" Melanie asked.

"Of course I'm listening," she lied.

"Then what did I say?"

"I forget."

Melanie snorted. "A likely story. I *said*—you have a letter from someone in Reflection Lake."

Haley Jo sat bolt upright. "Where? Give it to me."

Melanie tapped the corner of the letter against her bottom lip. "I'm not sure you deserve this. You've been pretty miserable to me this past week."

"Give me the letter or die," Haley Jo said, snatching it out of her hands. She glanced at the return address, and her heart stopped racing. It wasn't the name she'd been hoping to see. She tried not to be disappointed. "Oh, it's from Eleanor."

Melanie plopped down in the chair opposite her. "Not from Mr. Tall, Dark and Legally Stupid, Chief Sam Matthews, huh?"

"He's not stupid, Mel."

"He is if he let you go."

"He wasn't ready for a commitment. Besides, we both decided it would make more sense for me to come back here, finish school and then if we still felt the same way about each other, we could see if a relationship made sense."

"Oh, yeah, now there's a plan. Stay apart for two

years and if you don't die of a broken heart in the interim, maybe you'll get back together. Sign me up for that plan!"

Haley Jo slipped her finger under the flap of the envelope and ripped it open. "Sam's got Prudie to think about. And his job. And I have school to finish."

"Oh yeah, that makes loads of sense, especially since you're sitting here in front of my TV instead of getting ready for class."

Haley Jo ignored her.

"I think you're both being pretty shortsighted about all this." Melanie didn't have a reputation for giving up easily.

She looked up. "Oh right, I forgot. You're the resident expert on building solid and lasting relationships. You and ole Cy planning to pick up where you left off when he gets out of the slammer?"

As soon as the words were out of her mouth, Haley Jo regretted them. "Oh, shoot, Mel, I'm sorry. I didn't mean to say that."

Her friend waved a hand. "Don't worry. You can't say anything that I haven't already said to myself about that whole crazy scene. Believe me, I've learned my lesson." Melanie walked toward her bedroom. "I'm going to go take a shower. You need to get yourself together if you expect to make your first class."

Haley Jo nodded and proceeded to open the envelope. There wasn't a letter inside, but when she tipped the envelope upside down, a tiny newspaper clipping and a white business card fluttered out. The article was a help wanted ad:

Experienced Receptionist/Typist Needed
Mature applicants only. Computer literate,

good people skills.
Full-time, excellent benefit package.

The small white card had today's date scrawled across it with the time 5:30 p.m. Beneath it was a short message in Eleanor's handwriting saying, "Don't you dare be late!"

"Oh, my gosh," Haley Jo said.

Melanie turned back around. "What?"

"Eleanor is retiring. They're hiring a new receptionist and she sent me an interview date."

"When?"

"Today." Haley Jo shook her head. "There's no way I can get there in time."

Melanie grabbed the phone and dumped it in her lap. "Hurry up and call the airport. You have just enough time to get dressed, get down to the airport and fly out of here."

"I can't afford a plane ticket." Even as she said it, Haley Jo was clutching the phone to her chest. "I can't do this."

"Hell, yes you can! We'll use my credit card, and you'll pay me back with your first check from the new job," Melanie said, as she flipped through the pages of the phone book, trying to find the right number. "If you don't at least try to convince him there's enough room in his life for you, then you'll regret it for the rest of your life."

"You're absolutely right." Haley Jo punched in the number Melanie pointed to and grinned. She'd wear her metallic miniskirt with the fringed halter top she'd picked up the other day at a little shop in the Village. And the faux alligator heels and bag would be the perfect finishing touches. Sam would be so bowled over he wouldn't be able to refuse her the job, or anything else.

Sam stretched and glanced at the clock on the wall. One more interview and he was free for the rest of the day. He fingered the white appointment card Eleanor had left for him.

> Woman coming in at 5:30 p.m. today for interview.
> Can't remember her name, but I scheduled her because she has all the right qualifications.
> Don't screw it up!

It was probably a good thing Eleanor had decided to fold up her tent and retire. The fact that she'd forgotten the name of the applicant coming in for an interview irritated the heck out of him. How was he supposed to know what to call the woman?

He leaned back in his chair and laced his fingers behind his head. No matter. He'd manage. Besides, he was pretty sure he already knew who was going to get the job. The tight-lipped, efficient woman who had dressed in a boxy business suit and had no discernible sense of humor. She'd be the perfect addition to the office—not overly talkative and infinitely more serious than any secretary he had ever had the pleasure to work with. They'd get all kinds of work done with someone like that running the office.

As he made a note to himself to call the woman later on tonight to tell her she had the job, Sam tried to ignore the little voice inside him that shouted that he was a total fool. He knew what the voice was all about, so he did his best to push it away.

Haley Jo was gone. She'd been back in her beloved city for two weeks already, and they hadn't heard a peep out of her. Not that he had expected to. It just showed him that she really hadn't wanted to stay. She was too much of a city girl to enjoy things up here in the boondocks.

The tiny bell over the door rang and he glanced up and swallowed hard.

Of course she hadn't changed one iota in that two weeks' time. Burnished red curls and a radiant smile greeted him. He couldn't help but grin. Damn, but she was beautiful.

"Afternoon, Chief. I believe I'm your 5:30 appointment."

"You're late," he said gruffly.

Haley Jo shook her head. "I think your clock is fast. I'll have to correct that once I'm hired."

"Pretty darn sure of yourself, aren't you?"

The smile widened. "Oh, yeah, I'm very sure of myself."

She walked behind the counter and boosted herself up on the corner of his desk. He watched with hungry eyes as she crossed her legs, her silky skin whispering softly to him. He wet his dry lips. "You're going to have to dress a lot more conservatively, if you plan to work here, ma'am."

"Oh, I don't think so, Chief." She leaned forward and grabbed his tie, yanking on it gently until he sat up. "I have a very strong feeling that you're going to adore the way I dress around here. And you're going to love how I dress when I'm in your bedroom, too."

"Now I know you're getting too cocky. My bedroom indeed. All I'm hiring today is a receptionist."

She inched herself forward and trapped him between her legs, her hands reaching out to gently cup the sides of his face. "Oh, but you misunderstand. I'm applying for the position of Mrs. Matthews." She kicked off her heels and shifted forward to sit directly on his lap.

"I'm feeling a little apprehensive here."

She laughed, something low and throaty. "I think you're feeling something all right. But it isn't apprehension."

He laughed and pulled her to him, his heart swelling to bursting as she giggled and slanted her mouth over his, kissing him hard and possessively.

When he finally came up for air, he managed to gasp, "You're hired."

"I accept. Of course, you'll have to work my schedule around my classes. I still intend to get my license as a dental hygienist."

He touched the side of her face, his gaze telling her that he'd give her anything she asked for. "I wouldn't have it any other way."

Haley Jo leaned forward and gently planted a kiss on his lips, marveling at how easy it all was when they stopped angsting about how it would all work out. "After I left, I thought I'd never feel whole again."

"You and me both. I love you, Ms. Haley Jo Simpson."

"I love you, too, Chief Matthews."

As they bent their heads to explore that feeling of wholeness a little bit more, the door swung open.

"Haley Jo!"

Leaving her arms around his neck, Haley Jo looked up to see Prudie standing framed in the doorway. Tears gathered in the corners of the child's eyes and threatened to spill over.

"You came back," she whispered.

Haley Jo held out a hand, motioning for the youngster to join them. "You bet I did, Prudie. I needed to come back and beat you at Chinese checkers. You didn't think I was a quitter, did you?"

Prudie ran to them and wrapped her arms around the two of them, holding tight. Soft sobs wracked her slight frame. "I thought I'd never see you again."

Haley Jo hugged her tight, reveling in the feel of holding her man and her soon-to-be daughter in her arms, their warmth and love pressed up against her safe and secure. Somehow, in the deepest part of her heart, Haley Jo knew that things didn't get much better than this.

HARLEQUIN® Duets™

"EXCELLENT! Carol Finch has the ability to combine thrilling adventure and passionate romance into her long line of masterful romances that entice readers into turning the pages."

"A winning combination of humor, romance...."
–*Romantic Times*

Enjoy a DOUBLE DUETS from bestselling author Carol Finch

Meet the Ryder cousins of Hoot's Roost, Oklahoma, where love comes sweepin' down the plain! These cowboy bachelors don't give a hoot about settlin' down, but when a bevy of strong-willed women breezes into town, they might just change their minds. Read Wade's and Quint's story in:

Lonesome Ryder? and Restaurant Romeo

#81, August 2002

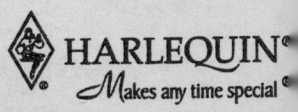

HARLEQUIN®
Makes any time special®

Visit us at www.eHarlequin.com

HDCF

Three masters of the romantic suspense genre come together in this special Collector's Edition!

Unveiled

NEW YORK TIMES BESTSELLING AUTHORS
TESS GERRITSEN
STELLA CAMERON

And Harlequin Intrigue® author

AMANDA STEVENS

Nail-biting mystery...heart-pounding sensuality...and the temptation of the unknown come together in one magnificent trade-size volume. These three talented authors bring stories that will give you thrills *and* chills like never before!

Coming to your favorite retail outlet in August 2002.

HARLEQUIN®
Makes any time special®

Visit us at www.eHarlequin.com

PHU

eHARLEQUIN.com

community | membership
buy books | authors | online reads | magazine | learn to write

Visit eHarlequin.com to discover your one-stop shop for romance:

buy books

- Choose from an extensive selection of Harlequin, Silhouette, MIRA and Steeple Hill books.
- Enjoy top Harlequin authors and *New York Times* bestselling authors in Other Romances: Nora Roberts, Jayne Ann Krentz, Danielle Steel and more!
- Check out our deal-of-the-week specially discounted books at up to 30% off!
- Save in our Bargain Outlet: hard-to-find books at great prices! Get 35% off your favorite books!
- Take advantage of our low-cost flat-rate shipping on all the books you want.
- Learn how to get FREE Internet-exclusive books.
- In our Authors area find the currently available titles of all the best writers.
- Get a sneak peek at the great reads for the next three months.
- Post your personal book recommendation online!
- Keep up with all your favorite miniseries.

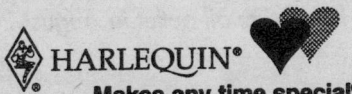

HARLEQUIN®
Makes any time special®—online...

Visit us at
www.eHarlequin.com

HINTBB

If you enjoyed what you just read,
then we've got an offer you can't resist!

Take 2 bestselling love stories FREE!

Plus get a FREE surprise gift!

Clip this page and mail it to Harlequin Reader Service®

IN U.S.A.	IN CANADA
3010 Walden Ave.	P.O. Box 609
P.O. Box 1867	Fort Erie, Ontario
Buffalo, N.Y. 14240-1867	L2A 5X3

YES! Please send me 2 free Harlequin Duets™ novels and my free surprise gift. After receiving them, if I don't wish to receive anymore, I can return the shipping statement marked cancel. If I don't cancel, I will receive 2 brand-new novels every month, before they're available in stores! In the U.S.A., bill me at the bargain price of $5.14 plus 50¢ shipping & handling per book and applicable sales tax, if any*. In Canada, bill me at the bargain price of $6.14 plus 50¢ shipping & handling per book and applicable taxes**. That's the complete price—what a great deal! I understand that accepting the 2 free books and gift places me under no obligation ever to buy any books. I can always return a shipment and cancel at any time. Even if I never buy another book from Harlequin, the 2 free books and gift are mine to keep forever.

111 HEN DC7P
311 HEN DC7Q

Name	(PLEASE PRINT)	
Address	Apt.#	
City	State/Prov.	Zip/Postal Code

* Terms and prices subject to change without notice. Sales tax applicable in N.Y.
** Canadian residents will be charged applicable provincial taxes and GST.
All orders subject to approval. Offer limited to one per household and not valid to current Harlequin Duets™ subscribers.
® and ™ are registered trademarks of Harlequin Enterprises Limited.

DUETS01

Princes...Princesses...
London Castles...New York Mansions...
To live the life of a royal!

In 2002, Harlequin Books lets you escape to a world of royalty with these royally themed titles:

Temptation:
January 2002—*A Prince of a Guy* (#861)
February 2002—*A Noble Pursuit* (#865)

American Romance:
The Carradignes: American Royalty (Editorially linked series)
March 2002—*The Improperly Pregnant Princess* (#913)
April 2002—*The Unlawfully Wedded Princess* (#917)
May 2002—*The Simply Scandalous Princess* (#921)
November 2002—*The Inconveniently Engaged Prince* (#945)

Intrigue:
The Carradignes: A Royal Mystery (Editorially linked series)
June 2002—*The Duke's Covert Mission* (#666)

Chicago Confidential
September 2002—*Prince Under Cover* (#678)

The Crown Affair
October 2002—*Royal Target* (#682)
November 2002—*Royal Ransom* (#686)
December 2002—*Royal Pursuit* (#690)

Harlequin Romance:
June 2002—*His Majesty's Marriage* (#3703)
July 2002—*The Prince's Proposal* (#3709)

Harlequin Presents:
August 2002—*Society Weddings* (#2268)
September 2002—*The Prince's Pleasure* (#2274)

Duets:
September 2002—*Once Upon a Tiara/Henry Ever After* (#83)
October 2002—*Natalia's Story/Andrea's Story* (#85)

Celebrate a year of royalty with Harlequin Books!

Available at your favorite retail outlet.

HARLEQUIN®
Makes any time special ®

Visit us at www.eHarlequin.com

HSROY02